Reginald Cruden

by

Talbot Baines Reed

Double 9
BOOKS

Reginald Cruden
by Talbot Baines Reed

ISBN: 978-93-63052-84-0

Published by

DOUBLE 9 BOOKS

2/13-B, Ansari Road
Daryaganj, New Delhi – 110002
info@double9books.com
www.double9books.com
Tel. 011-40042856

ABOUT THE AUTHOR

Talbot Baines Reed was an English author of boys' fiction who lived from April 3, 1852, to November 28, 1893. He created a type of school stories that lasted until the middle of the 20th century. The Fifth Form at St. Dominic's is one of his most well-known works. He often and regularly wrote for The Boy's Own Paper (B.O.P.). Most of his writing was first published there. Reed became a well-known typefounder through his family's business. He also wrote the standard work on the subject, History of the Old English Letter Foundries. John Reed was a colonel in Oliver Cromwell's army during the English Civil War. The Reed family came from him. Their home was in Maiden Newton, which is in the county of Dorset. They moved to London at the end of the 18th century. Andrew Reed (1787–1862), Talbot Reed's grandpa, was a minister in the Congregational Church and the founder of many charitable organizations, such as the London Orphan Asylum and a hospital for people who could not get better. He was also a well-known hymn writer. His "Spirit Divine, attend our prayers" can still be found in many hymnals today. Talbot Baines Reed grew up in a happy family where Charles Reed was very religious and thought that tough outdoor games were the best way to raise boys.

CONTENTS

Chapter One
An interrupted Bathe

It was a desperately hot day. There had been no day like it all the summer. Indeed, Squires, the head gardener at Garden Vale, positively asserted that there had been none like it since he had been employed on the place, which was fourteen years last March. Squires, by the way, never lost an opportunity of reminding himself and the world generally of the length of his services to the family at Garden Vale; and on the strength of those fourteen years he gave himself airs as if the place belonged not to Mr Cruden at all, but to himself. He was the terror of his mistress, who scarcely dared to peep into a greenhouse without his leave, and although he could never exactly obtain from the two young gentlemen the respect to which he considered himself entitled, he still flattered himself in secret "they couldn't do exactly what they liked with his garden!"

To-day, however, it was so hot that even Squires, after having expressed the opinion on the weather above mentioned, withdrew himself into the coolest recess of his snug lodge and slept sweetly, leaving the young gentlemen, had they been so minded, to take any liberty they liked with "his" garden.

The young gentlemen, however, were not so minded.

They had been doing their best to play lawn tennis in the blazing sun with two of their friends, but it was too hot to run, too hot to hit, and far too hot to score, so the attempt had died away, and three of them now reclined on the sloping bank under the laurel hedge, dividing their time between lazily gazing up at the dark-blue sky and watching the proceedings of the fourth of their party, who still remained in the courts.

This last-mentioned youth, who, to judge by his countenance, was brother to one of those who lolled on the bank, presented a curious contrast to the general languor of the afternoon. Deserted by his companions in the sport, he was relieving himself of some of his superfluous energy by the novel diversion of playing tennis with himself. This he accomplished by serving the ball high up in the air and then jumping the net, so as to take it on the other side, following up his return by another leap over the net, and so on till either he or the ball came to grief. On an ordinary day the exertion involved in this pastime would be quite enough for any ordinary individual, but on a day like the present, with the thermometer at ninety in the shade, it was a trifle too much even to watch.

"For goodness' sake shut up, Horrors," said the elder brother. "We might as well be playing ourselves as watch you at that sort of thing."

The young gentleman addressed as Horrors was at that moment in the midst of one of his aerial flights, and had neither leisure nor breath to answer.

"Do you hear?" repeated the other. "If you want to keep warm, go indoors and put on a great-coat, but don't fag us to death with that foolery."

"Eight!" exclaimed the young athlete, scoring the number of times the ball had crossed the net, and starting for another jump. "Shut up, Reg, till I've done."

He soon was done. Even Horace Cruden could not keep it up for ever, and at his tenth bound his foot caught in the net, and he came all fours on to the court.

"There, now you're happy!" said his brother. "Now you may as well come and sit here out of the cold."

Horace picked himself up, laughing.

"All very well," said he. "I'm certain I should have done it twelve times if you hadn't put me off my jump. Never mind, I'll do it yet."

"Oh, Horace," interposed one of the others, beseechingly, "if you love us, lie down now. I'm quite ill watching you, I assure you. We'll all vow we saw you do it twelve times; we'll put it in the *Times* if you like, and say the net was five feet ten; anything, as long as you don't start at it again."

This appeal had the effect of reducing the volatile Horace to a state of quiescence, and inducing him to come and share the shade with his companions.

"Never saw such a lazy lot," said he, lying flat on his back and balancing his racquet on his finger; "you won't do anything yourselves and you won't let any one else do anything. Regular dogs in the manger."

"My dear fellow," said the fourth of the party in a half drawl, "we've been doing nothing but invite you in to the manger for the last hour, and you wouldn't come. Can't you take a holiday while we've got one?"

"Bad luck to it," said Reginald; "there's only a week more."

"I don't see why you need growl, old man," said the visitor who had spoken first; "you'll get into the sixth and have a study to yourself, and no mathematics unless you like."

"Poor Harker," said Horace, "he's always down on mathematics. Anyhow, I shan't be sorry to show up at Wilderham again, shall you, Bland?"

"Depends on the set we get," drawled Bland (whose full name was Blandford). "I hear there's a crowd of new fellows coming, and I hate new fellows."

"A fellow must be new some time or other," said Horace. "Harker and I were new boys once, weren't we, Harker?"

Harker, who had shared the distinction of being tossed with Horace in the same blanket every night for the first week of his sojourn at Wilderham, had not forgotten the fact, and ejaculated,—

"Rather!"

"The mischief is," continued Blandford, "they get such a shady lot of fellows there now. The school's not half as respectable as it was—there are far too many shopkeepers' sons and that sort of—"

"Sort of animal, he'd like to say," laughed Horace. "Bland can't get over being beaten for the French prize by Barber, the tailor's son."

Blandford flushed up, and was going to answer when Reginald interposed.

"Well, and suppose he can't, it's no wonder. I don't see why those fellows shouldn't have a school for themselves. It's not pleasant to have the fellow who cuts your waistcoat crowing over you in class."

Horace began to whistle, as he generally did when the conversation took a turn that did not please him.

"Best way to remedy that," said he, presently, "is not to get beaten by your tailor's son."

"Shut up, Horace," said the elder brother; "what's the use of making yourself disagreeable? Bland's quite right, and you know you think so yourself."

"Oh, all serene," said Horace, cheerfully; "shouldn't have known I thought so unless you had told me. What do you think, Harker?"

"Well," said Harker, laughing, "as I am disreputable enough to be the only son of a widow who has barely enough to live on, and who depends on the charity of a cousin or some one of the sort for my education, I'm afraid Bland and I would have to go to different schools."

Every one laughed at this confession, and Reginald said,—

"Oh, but you're different, Harker—besides, it isn't money makes the difference—"

"The thing is," interposed Horace, "was your father in the wholesale or retail trade?—that's the difference!"

"I wish you'd shut up, Horace," said Reginald tartly; "you always spoil any argument with your foolery."

"Now that's hard lines," said Horace, "when I thought I was putting the case beautifully for you. Never mind. What do you say to a bathe in the river, you fellows?"

"Too much fag to get towels," said Reginald; "but if you like to go for them, and don't ask us to look at our watches and see in how many seconds you run up to the house and back, we'll think about it."

"Thanks," said Horace, and started up to the house whistling cheerily.

"Awfully hot that brother of yours make? a fellow," said Blandford, watching him disappear.

"Yes," said Reginald, yawning, "he is rather flighty, but he'll turn out all right, I hope."

"Turn out!" said Harker; "why he's all right already, from the crown of his head to the sole of his boot."

"Except," said Blandford, "for a slight crack in the crown of his head. It's just as well, perhaps, he's not the eldest son, Reg."

"Well," said Reginald laughing, "I can hardly fancy Horace the head of the family."

"Must be a rum sensation," said Harker, "to be an heir and not have to bother your head about how you'll get your bread and butter some day. How many hundred millions of pounds is it you'll come in for, Reg? I forget."

"What a humbug you are!" said Reginald; "my father's no better off than a lot of other people."

"That's a mild way of putting it, anyhow," said Blandford.

And here the conversation ended.

The boys lay basking in the sun waiting for Horace's return. He was unusually long in coming.

"Seems to me," said Blandford, "he's trying how long he can be instead of how quick—for a variety."

"Just like him," said Reginald.

Five minutes passed away, and ten, and fifteen, and then, just as the boys were thinking of stirring themselves to inquire what had become of him, they heard his steps returning rapidly down the gravel walk.

"Well," cried Reginald, without sitting up, "have you got them at last?"

Horace's voice startled them all as he cried,—

"Reg! Reg! come quick, quick!"

There was no mistaking either the tones or the white face of the boy who uttered them.

Reginald was on his feet in an instant, rushing in the direction of the house, towards which his brother had already started.

"What is it, Horace?" he said as he overtook him.

"Something about father—a telegram," gasped the other.

Not another word was spoken as they ran on and reached the hall door.

The hall door stood open. Just outside on the hot stone steps lay the towels where Horace had dropped them five minutes ago. Carlo, the dog, lay across the mat, and lazily lifted his head as his master approached. Within stood Mrs Cruden, pale and trembling, with a telegram in her hand, and in the back-ground hovered three or four servants, with mingled curiosity and anxiety on their faces.

Despite the heat, Reginald shivered as he stood a moment at the door, and then sprang towards the telegram, which his mother gave into his hand. It was from Mr Cruden's coachman, dated from Saint Nathaniel's Hospital.

"Master was took ill driving from City—brought here, where he is very bad indeed. Doctor says no hope."

One needs to have received such a message oneself to understand the emotions with which the two brothers read and re-read the pitiless words. Nothing but their own hard breathing broke the stillness of those few minutes, and who knows in that brief space what a lifetime seemed crowded?

Horace was the first to recover his self-possession.

"Mother," said he, and his voice sounded strange and startling in the silence, "there's a train to the City in five minutes. I'll go by that."

And he was off. It was three-quarters of a mile to the station, and there was no time to parley. Even on an errand like this, many would have abandoned the endeavour as an impossibility, especially in such a heat. But Horace was a good runner, and the feat was nothing uncommon for him.

As he flung himself into the train he gave one quick glance round, to see if Reginald had possibly followed him; but no, he was alone; and as the whistle shrieked and the train steamed out of the station, Horace for the first time had a moment to reflect.

Not half an hour ago he had been lying with his brother and companions on the tennis lawn, utterly unconscious of any impending calamity. What ages ago that seemed! For a few minutes all appeared so confused and unreal that his mind was a blank, and he seemed even to forget on what errand he was bound.

But Horace was a practical youth, and before that half-hour's journey to the City was accomplished he was at least collected in mind, and prepared to face the trial that awaited him.

There was something about the telegram that convinced him it meant more than it said. Still, a boy's hopefulness will grasp at a straw, and he battled with his despair. His father was not dead—he would recover—at the hospital he would have the best medical assistance possible. The coachman who sent the telegram would be sure to make things out at the worst. Yes, when he got to Saint Nathaniel's he would find it was a false alarm, that there was nothing much the matter at all, and when his mother and Reginald arrived by the next train, he would be able to meet them with reassuring news. It was not more than a ten-minutes' cab-drive from the terminus—the train was just in now; in twelve minutes this awful suspense would be at an end.

Such was the hurried rush of thoughts through the poor boy's brain during that dismal journey. He had sprung from the carriage to a hansom cab almost before the train had pulled up, and in another moment was clattering over the stones towards the hospital.

The hopes of a few minutes before oozed away as every street corner brought him nearer his destination, and when at last the stately front of Saint Nathaniel's loomed before him, he wished his journey could never end. He gazed with faltering heart up at the ward windows, as if he could read his fate there. The place seemed deserted. A few street boys were playing on the pavement, and at the door of the in-patients' ward a little cluster of visitors were collected round a flower stall buying sweet mementoes of the country to brighten the bedsides of their friends within. No one heeded the pale scared boy as he alighted and went up the steps.

A porter opened the door.

"My father, Mr Cruden, is here; how is he?"

"Is it the gentleman that was brought in in a fit?"

"Yes, in his carriage—is he better?"

"Will you step in and see the doctor?"

The doctor was not in his room when the boy was ushered in, and it seemed an age before he entered.

"You are Mr Cruden's son?" said he gravely.

"Yes—is he better?"

"He was brought here about half-past three, insensible, with apoplexy."

"Is he better now?" asked Horace again, knowing perfectly well what the dreaded answer would be.

"He is not, my boy," said the doctor gravely. "We telegraphed to your mother at once, as you know—but before that telegram could have reached her your poor father—"

It was enough. Poor Horace closed his ears convulsively against the fatal word, and dropped back on his chair with a gasp.

The doctor put his hand kindly on the boy's shoulder.

"Are you here alone?" said he, presently.

"My mother and brother will be here directly."

"Your father lies in a private ward. Will you wait till they come, or will you go up now?"

A struggle passed through the boy's mind. An instinctive horror of a sight hitherto unknown struggled hard with the impulse to rush at once to his father's bedside. At length he said, falteringly,—

"I will go now, please."

When Mrs Cruden and Reginald arrived half an hour later, they found Horace where the doctor had left him, on his knees at his father's bedside.

Chapter Two
A Come-down in the World

Mr Cruden had the reputation of being one of the most respectable as well as one of the richest men in his part of the county. And it is fair to say he took far more pride in the former quality than the latter. Indeed, he made no secret of the fact that he had not always been the rich man he was when our story opens. But he was touchy on the subject of his good family and his title to the name of gentleman, which he had taught his sons to value far more than the wealth which accompanied it, and which they might some day expect to inherit.

His choice of a school for them was quite consistent with his views on this point. Wilderham was not exactly an aristocratic school, but it was a school where money was thought less of than "good style," as the boys called it, and where poverty was far less of a disgrace than even a remote connection with a "shop." The Crudens had always been great heroes in the eyes of their schoolfellows, for their family was unimpeachable, and even with others who had greater claims to be considered as aristocratic, their ample pocket-money commended them as most desirable companions.

Mr Cruden, however, with all his virtues and respectability, was not a good man of business. People said he let himself be imposed upon by others who knew the value of money far better than he did. His own beautiful estate at Garden Vale, Rumour said, was managed at double the expense it should be; and of his money transactions and speculations in the City— well, he had need to be the wealthy man he was, said his friends, to be able to stand all the fleecing he came in for there!

Nevertheless, no one ever questioned the wealth of the Crudens, least of all did the Crudens themselves, who took it as much for granted as the atmosphere they breathed in.

On the day on which our story opens Mr Cruden had driven down into the City on business. No one knew exactly what the business was, for he kept such matters to himself. It was an ordinary expedition, which consisted usually of half a dozen calls on half a dozen stockbrokers or secretaries of companies, with perhaps an occasional visit to the family lawyer or the family bank.

To-day, however, it had consisted of but one visit, and that was to the bank. And it was whilst returning thence that Mr Cruden was suddenly seized with the stroke which ended in his death. Had immediate assistance been at hand the calamity might have been averted, but neither the coachman nor footman was aware of what had happened till the carriage was some distance on its homeward journey, and a passer-by caught sight of the senseless figure within. They promptly drove him to the nearest hospital, and telegraphed the news to Garden Vale; but Mr Cruden never recovered consciousness, and, as the doctor told Horace, before even the message could have reached its destination he was dead.

We may draw a veil over the sad scenes of the few days which followed—of the meeting of the widow and her sons at the bedside of the dead, of the removal of the loved remains home, of the dismal preparations for the funeral, and all the dreary details which occupy mourners in the house of death. For some time Mrs Cruden, prostrated by the shock of her bereavement, was unable to leave her room, and the burden of the care fell on the two inexperienced boys, who had to face it almost single-handed.

For the Crudens had no near relatives in England, and those of their friends who might have been of service at such a time feared to intrude, and so stayed away. Blandford and Harker, the boys' two friends who had been visiting at Garden Vale at the time of Mr Cruden's death, had left as quietly and considerately as possible; and so great was the distraction of those few sad days that no one even noticed their absence till letters of condolence arrived from each.

It was a dreary week, and Reginald, on whom, as the elder son and the heir to the property, the chief responsibility rested, was of the two least equal to the emergency.

"I don't know what I should have done without you, old man," said he to Horace on the evening before the funeral, when, all the preparations being ended, the two boys strolled dismally down towards the river. "You ought to have been the eldest son. I should never have thought of half the things there were to be done if you hadn't been here."

"Of course, mother would have known what was to be done," said Horace, "if she hadn't been laid up. She's to get up this evening."

"Well, I shall be glad when to-morrow's over," said Reginald; "it's awful to have it all hanging over one like this. I can't believe father was alive a week ago, you know."

"No more can I," said the other; "and I'm certain we shall not realise how we miss him for long enough yet."

They walked on for some distance in silence, each full of his own reflections.

Then Horace said, "Mother is sure to want to stay on here, she's so fond of the place."

"Yes, it's a comfort she won't have to move. By the way, I wonder if she will want us to leave Wilderham and stay at home now."

"I fancy not. Father wanted you to go to Oxford in a couple of years, and she is sure not to change his plan."

"Well, I must say," said Reginald, "if I am to settle down as a country gentleman some day, I shall be glad to have gone through college and all that sort of thing before. If I go up in two years, I shall have finished before I'm twenty-three. Hullo, here's mother!"

The boys ran forward to greet Mrs Cruden, who, pale but smiling, came quietly down the garden towards them, and after a fond embrace laid her hands on the arm of each and walked slowly on between them.

"You two brave boys," said she, and there was a cheery ring in her voice that sent comfort into the hearts of both her sons, "how sorry I am to think of all you have had to go through, while I, like a silly weak woman, have been lying in bed."

"Oh, mother," said Horace, with a face that reflected already the sunshine of hers, "how absurd to talk like that! I don't believe you ought to be out here now."

"Oh yes, I ought. I've done with that, and I am strong enough now to stand beside the boys who have stood so bravely by their mother."

"We'd be a nice pair of boys if we didn't, eh, Reg?" said Horace.

Reginald's reply was a pressure of his mother's hand, and with a rainbow of smiles over their sorrowful hearts the three walked on lovingly together; the mother with many a brave, cheery word striving to lift her sons above their trouble, not only to hope of earthly comfort, but to trust in that great Father of the fatherless, beside whom all the love of this world is poor and fleeting.

At length they turned to go in, and Mrs Cruden said,—

"There is a letter from Mr Richmond, the lawyer, saying he will call this evening to talk over some business matters. I suppose he will be here by now."

"Couldn't he have waited till after to-morrow?" said Horace.

"He particularly asked to come to-night," said the mother. "At any rate, I would like you both to be with me while he is here. We must not have any secrets from one another now."

"I suppose it's about the will or the estate," said Reginald.

"I suppose so. I don't know," said Mrs Cruden. "Mr Richmond always managed your father's business affairs, you know, so he will be able to tell us how matters stand."

They reached the house, and found Mr Richmond had already arrived and was awaiting them in the library.

Mr Richmond was a solemn, grave personage, whose profession was written on his countenance. His lips were so closely set that it seemed as if speaking must be a positive pain to him, his eyes had the knack of looking past you, as though he was addressing not you but your shadow on the wall, and he ended every sentence, no matter what its import, with a mechanical smile, as though he were at that instant having his photograph taken. Why Mr Cruden should have selected Mr Richmond as his man of business was a matter only known to Mr Cruden himself, for those who knew the lawyer best did not care for him, and, without being able to deny that he was an honest man and a well-meaning man, were at least glad that their affairs were in the hands of some one else.

He rose and solemnly greeted the widow and her two sons as they entered.

"I am sorry to intrude at such a time," said he, "but as your late husband's adviser, I considered it right to call and make you acquainted with his affairs."

Here Mr Richmond smiled, greatly to Reginald's indignation.

"Thank you," said Mrs Cruden; "sit down, please, Mr Richmond."

Mr Richmond obeyed, dubiously eyeing the two boys as he did so.

"These are your sons, I presume?" said he to Mrs Cruden.

"They are," said she.

Mr Richmond rose and solemnly shook hands with each of the lads, informing each with a smile as he did so that he was pleased to make his acquaintance.

"You wish the young gentlemen to remain, perhaps?" he inquired, as he resumed his seat.

"To be sure," said Mrs Cruden, somewhat nettled at the question; "go on, please, Mr Richmond."

"Certainly, madam," said the lawyer. "May I ask if you are acquainted with the late Mr Cruden's state of affairs?"

"I wish to hear that from you," said the widow, "and with as little delay as possible, Mr Richmond."

"Certainly, madam. Mr Cruden honoured me with his confidence on these matters, and I believe, next to himself, I knew more about them than any one else."

Here Mr Richmond paused and smiled.

"In fact," continued he, "I may almost say I knew more about them than he did himself, for your excellent husband, Mrs Cruden, was not a good man of business."

Reginald could not stand the smile which accompanied this observation, and said, somewhat hotly,—

"Look here, Mr Richmond, if you will say what you've got to say without laughing and speaking disrespectfully of my father, we shall be glad."

"Certainly, Master Cruden," said the lawyer, a trifle disconcerted by this unexpected interruption. Then turning to the widow he continued,—

"The fact is, madam, the late Mr Cruden was, I fear, under the impression that he was considerably better off than he was."

Mr Richmond paused as if for a reply, but as no one spoke he continued,—

"I am sorry to say this appears to have been the case to a much larger extent than even I imagined. Your late husband, Mrs Cruden, I believe spent largely on his estate here, and unfortunately kept no accounts. I have frequently entreated him to reckon over his expenditure, but he always replied that it was considerably under his income, and that there was no need, as long as that was the case, to trouble himself about it."

A nervous movement among his listeners was the only reply the lawyer received to this last announcement, or to the smile which accompanied it.

"Mr Cruden *may* have been correct in his conjecture, madam, although I fear the contrary."

"If my father said a thing," blurted out Reginald at this point, "I see no reason for doubting his word."

"None in the least, my dear Master Cruden; but unfortunately your father did not know either what his income was or what his expenditure was."

"Do *you* know what they were?" said Reginald, not heeding the deprecating touch of his mother's hand on his.

"As far as I understand the state of your father's affairs," said Mr Richmond, undisturbed by the rude tone of his inquisitor, "his income was entirely derived from interest in the stock of two American railways, in which he placed implicit confidence, and in one or the other of which he insisted on investing all capital which came to his hand. The total income from these two sources would in my opinion just about cover Mr Cruden's various expenses of all kinds."

There was something like a sigh of relief from the listeners as Mr Richmond reached this point. But it died away as he proceeded.

"In his choice of an investment for his capital Mr Cruden consulted no one, I believe, beyond himself. For some time it seemed a fortunate investment, and the shares rose in value, but latterly they took a turn for the worse, and early this year I am sorry to say one of the railways suspended payment altogether, and Mr Cruden lost a considerable portion of his fortune thereby."

"I heard my husband say some months ago that he had made some slight loss in the City," said Mrs Cruden, "but I imagined from the light manner in which he treated it that it was quite trifling, and would be quickly repaired."

"He did hope that would be the case. Although all his friends urged him to sell out at once, he insisted on holding on, in the hope of the railway recovering itself."

"And has it recovered?" asked Mrs Cruden, with a tremble in her voice.

"I regret to say it has not, Mrs Cruden. On the contrary, it was declared bankrupt a few days ago, and what is still more deplorable, it has involved in its own ruin the other railway in which the remainder of your husband's property was invested, so that all the shares which stand in his name in both concerns are now worth no more than the paper they are printed on."

Mr Richmond came to the point at last with startling abruptness, so much so that for a moment or two his listeners sat almost petrified by the bad news, and unable to say a word. The lawyer finished what he had to say without waiting.

"Your husband heard this lamentable news, Mrs Cruden, on the occasion of his last visit to the City. The only call he made that day was at his banker's, where he was told all, and there is no reason to doubt that the shock produced the stroke from which he died."

"Mr Richmond," said Mrs Cruden, after a while, like one in a dream, "can this be true? What *does* it all mean?"

"Alas! madam," said the lawyer, "it would be no kindness on my part to deny the truth of what I have told you. It means that unless you or your late husband are possessed of some means of income of which I know nothing, your circumstances are reduced to a very low point."

"But there must be some mistake," said Horace. "*Both* railways can't have gone wrong; we shall surely save something?"

"I wish I could hold out any hope. I have all the documents at my office, and shall be only too glad, Mrs Cruden, to accompany you to the bank for your own satisfaction."

Mrs Cruden shuddered and struggled bravely to keep down the rising tears. A long pause ensued, every moment of which made the terrible truth clearer to all three of the hearers, and closed every loophole of hope.

"What can be done?" said Horace at last.

"Happily there is Garden Vale," said Reginald, and there was a choking in the throat of the heir as he spoke; "we shall have to sell it."

"The contents of it, you will, Master Cruden," said the lawyer; "the estate itself is held on lease."

"Well, the contents of it," said Reginald, bitterly; "you are not going to make out they don't belong to us?"

"Certainly not," said Mr Richmond, on whom the taunt was quite lost; "unless, as I trust is not the case, your father died in debt."

"Do you mean to say," said Horace, slowly, like one waking from a dream, "do you mean to say we are ruined, Mr Richmond?"

"I fear it is so," said the lawyer, "unless Mr Cruden was possessed of some means of income with which I was not acquainted. I regret very much, Mrs Cruden, having to be the bearer of such bad news, and I can only say the respect I had for your late husband will make any assistance I can offer you, by way of advice or otherwise, a pleasure." And Mr Richmond bowed himself out of the room with a smile.

It was a relief to be left alone, and Mrs Cruden, despite her weakness and misery, struggled hard for the sake of her boys to put a brave face on their trouble.

"Reg, dear," said she to her eldest son, who had fairly broken down, and with his head on his hand was giving vent to his misery, "try to bear it. After all, we are left to one another, and—"

The poor mother could not finish her sentence, but bent down and kissed the wet cheek of the boy.

"Of course it means," said Horace, after a pause, "we shall have to give up Garden Vale, and leave Wilderham too. And Reg was sure of a scholarship next term. I say, mother, what *are* we to do?"

"We are all strong enough to do something, dear boy," said Mrs Cruden.

"I'll take care *you* don't have to do anything, mother," said Reginald, looking up. "I'll work my fingers to the bones before you have to come down to that." He spoke with clenched teeth, half savagely.

"Even if we can sell all the furniture," continued Horace, taking a practical view of the situation, "it wouldn't give us much to live on."

"Shut up, Horace!" said Reginald. "What's the use of making the worst of everything? Hasn't mother had quite enough to bear already?"

Horace subsided, and the three sat there in silence until the daylight faded and the footman brought in the lights and announced that coffee was ready in the drawing-room.

There was something like a shock about this interruption. What had they to do with men-servants and coffee in the drawing-room, they who an hour or two ago had supposed themselves wealthy, but now knew that they were little better than beggars?

"We shall not want coffee," said Mrs Cruden, answering for all three. Then when the footman had withdrawn, she said,—

"Boys, I must go to bed. God bless you, and give us all brave hearts, for we shall need them!"

The funeral took place next day. Happily it was of a simple character, and only a few friends were invited, so that it was not thought necessary to alter the arrangements in consequence of Mr Richmond's announcement of the evening before. But even the slight expense involved in this melancholy ceremony grated painfully on the minds of the boys, who forgot even their dead father in the sense that they were riding in carriages for which they could not pay, and offering their guests refreshments which were not theirs to give. The little cemetery was crowded with friends and acquaintances of the dead—country gentry most of them, who sought to show their respect for their late neighbour by falling into the long funeral procession and joining the throng at the graveside.

It was a severe ordeal for the two boys to find themselves the centres of observation, and to feel that more than half the interest exhibited in them was on account of their supposed inheritance.

One bluff squire came up after the funeral and patted Reginald on the back.

"Never mind, my boy," said he; "I was left without a father at your age. You'll soon get over it, and your mother will have plenty of friends. Glad to see you up at the Hall any day, and your brother too. You must join our hunt next winter, and keep up the family name. God bless you!"

Reginald shrank from this greeting like a guilty being, and the two desolate boys were glad to escape further encounters by retreating to their carriage and ordering the coachman to drive home at once.

A few days disclosed all that was wanting to make their position quite clear. Mr Cruden's will confirmed Mr Richmond's statement as to the source of his income. All his money was invested in shares of the two ruined railways, and all he had to leave besides these was the furniture and contents of Garden Vale. Even this, when realised, would do little more than cover the debts which the next week or two brought to light. It was pitiful the way in which that unrelenting tide of bills flowed in, swamping gradually the last hope of a competency, or even means of bare existence, for the survivors.

Neither Mrs Cruden nor her sons had been able to endure a day's delay at Garden Vale after the funeral, but had hurried for shelter to quiet lodgings at the seaside, kept by an old servant, where in an agony of suspense they awaited the final result of Mr Richmond's investigations.

It came at last, and, bad as it was, it was a comfort to know the worst. The furniture, carriages, and other contents of Garden Vale had sufficed to pay all debts of every description, with a balance of about £350 remaining over and above, to represent the entire worldly possessions of the Cruden family, which only a month ago had ranked with the wealthiest in the county.

"So," said Mrs Cruden, with a shadow of her old smile, as she folded up the lawyer's letter and put it back in her pocket, "we know the worst at last, boys."

"Which is," said Reginald, bitterly, "we are worth among us the magnificent sum of sixteen pounds per annum. Quite princely!"

"Reg, dear," said his mother, "let us be thankful that we have anything, and still more that we may start life owing nothing to any one."

"Start life!" exclaimed Reginald; "I wish we could end it with—"

"Oh, hush, hush, my precious boy!" exclaimed the widow; "you will break my heart if you talk like that! Think how many there are to whom this little sum would seem a fortune. Why, it may keep a roof over our heads, at any rate, or help you into situations."

"Or bury us!" groaned Reginald.

The mother looked at her eldest son, half in pity, half in reproach, and then burst into tears.

Reginald sprang to her side in an instant.

"What a beast I am!" he exclaimed. "Oh, mother, do forgive me! I really didn't think what I was saying."

"No, dear Reggie, I know you didn't," said Mrs Cruden, recovering herself with a desperate effort. "You mustn't mind me, I—I scarcely—know—I—"

It was no use trying. The poor mother broke down completely, and on that evening it was impossible to talk more about the future.

Next morning, however, all three were in a calmer mood, and Horace said at breakfast, "We can't do any good here, mother. Hadn't we better go to London?"

"I think so; and Parker here knows of a small furnished lodging in Dull Street, which she says is cheap. We might try there to begin with. Eh, Reg?"

Reginald winced, and then replied, "Oh, certainly; the sooner we get down to our right level the better."

That evening the three Crudens arrived in London.

Chapter Three
Number Six, Dull Street

Probably no London street ever rejoiced in a more expressive name than Dull Street. It was not a specially dirty street, or a specially disreputable street, or a specially dark street. The neighbourhood might a hundred years ago have been considered "genteel," and the houses even fashionable, and some audacious antiquarians went so far as to assert that the street took its name not from its general appearance at all, but from a worthy London alderman, who in the reign of George the First had owned most of the neighbouring property.

Be that as it may, Dull Street was—and for all I know may still be—one of the dullest streets in London. A universal seediness pervaded its houses from roof to cellar; nothing was as it should be anywhere. The window sashes had to be made air-tight by wedges of wood or paper stuck into the frames; a bell in Dull Street rarely sounded after less than six pulls; there was scarcely a sitting-room but had a crack in its grimy ceiling, or a handle off its ill-hung door, or a strip of wall-paper peeling off its walls. There were more chairs in the furnished apartments of Dull Street with three legs than there were with four, and there was scarcely horsehair enough in the twenty-four sofas of its twenty-four parlours to suffice for an equal quantity of bolsters.

In short, Dull Street was the shabbiest genteel street in the metropolis, and nothing could make it otherwise.

A well-built, tastefully-furnished house in the middle of it would have been as incongruous as a new patch in an old garment, and no one dreamt of disturbing the traditional aspect of the place by any attempt to repair or beautify it.

Indeed, the people who lived in Dull Street were as much a part of its dulness as the houses they inhabited. They were for the most part retired tradesmen, or decayed milliners, or broken-down Government clerks, most of whom tried to eke out their little pensions by letting part of their lodgings to others as decayed and broken-down as themselves.

These interesting colonists, whose one bond of sympathy was a mutual seediness, amused themselves, for the most part, by doing nothing all day long, except perhaps staring out of the window, in the remote hope of catching sight of a distant cab passing the street corner, or watching to see how much milk their opposite neighbour took in, or reading the news of the week before last in a borrowed newspaper, or talking scandal of one neighbour to another.

"Jemima, my dear," said a middle-aged lady, who, with her son and daughter, was the proud occupant of Number 4, Dull Street—"Jemima, my dear, I see to-day the bill is hout of the winder of number six."

"Never!" replied Jemima, a sharp-looking young woman of twenty, who had once in her life spent a month at a ladies' boarding-school, and was therefore decidedly genteel. "I wonder who's coming."

"A party of three, so I hear from Miss Moulden's maid, which is niece to Mrs Grimley: a widow,"—here the speaker snuffled slightly—"and two childer—like me."

"Go on!" said Jemima. "Any more about them, ma?"

"Well, my dear, I do hear as they 'ave come down a bit."

"Oh, ah! lag!" put in the speaker's son, a lawyer's clerk in the receipt of two pounds a week, to whom this intelligence appeared particularly amusing; "we know all about that—never heard that sort of tale before, have we, ma? Oh no!" and the speaker emphasised the question by giving his widowed mother a smart dig in the ribs.

"For shame, Sam! don't be vulgar!" cried the worthy lady; "how many times have I told you?"

"All right, ma," replied the legal young gentleman; "but it is rather a wonner, you know. What were they before they came down?"

"Gentlefolk, so I'm told," replied the lady, drawing herself up at the very mention of the name; "and I hintend, and I 'ope my children will do the same, to treat them as fellow-creatures with hevery consideration."

"And how old is the babies, ma?" inquired Miss Jemima, whose gentility sometimes had the advantage of her grammar.

"The babies!" said the mother; "why, they're young gentlemen, both of 'em—old enough to be your sweethearts!"

Sam laughed profusely.

"Then what did you say they was babies for?" demanded Jemima, pettishly.

"I never!"

"You did, ma, I heard you! Didn't she, Sam?"

"So you did, ma. Come now, no crackers!" said Sam.

"I never; I said 'childer,'" pleaded the mother.

"And ain't babies childer?" thundered Miss Jemima.

"'Ad 'er there, Jim!" chuckled the dutiful Samuel, this time favouring his sister with a sympathetic nudge. "Better give in, and own you told a cracker, ma!"

"Shan't!" said the lady, beginning to whimper. "Oh, I wish my poor 'Oward was here to protect me! He was a gentleman, and I'm glad he didn't live to see what a pair of vulgar brats he'd left behind him, that I am!"

"There you go!" said Sam; "taking on at nothing, as per usual! No one was saying anything to hurt you, old girl. Simmer down, and you'll be all the better for it. There now, dry your eyes; it's all that Jim, she's got such a tongue! Next time I catch you using language to ma, Jim, I'll turn you out of the house! Come, cheer up, ma."

"Yes, cheer up, ma," chimed in Jemima; "no one supposes you meant to tell fibs; you couldn't help it."

Amid consolations such as these the poor flurried lady subsided, and regained her former tranquillity of spirit.

The Shucklefords—such was the name of this amiable family—were comparatively recent sojourners in Dull Street. They had come there six years previously, on the death of Mr Shuckleford, a respectable wharfinger, who had saved up money enough to leave his wife a small annuity. Shortly before his death he had been promoted to the command of one of the Thames steamboats plying between Chelsea and London Bridge, in virtue of which office he had taken to himself—or rather his wife had claimed for him—the title of "captain," and with this patent of gentility had held up her head ever since. Her children, following her good example, were not slow to hold up their heads too, and were fully convinced of their own gentility. Samuel Shuckleford had, as his mother termed it, been "entered for the law" shortly after his father's death, and Miss Jemima Shuckleford, after the month's sojourn at a ladies' boarding-school already referred to, had settled down to assist her mother in the housework and maintain the dignity of the family by living on her income.

Such were the new next-door neighbours of the Crudens when at last they arrived, sadly, and with the new world before them, at Number 6, Dull Street.

Mr Richmond, who, with all his unfortunate manner, had acted a friend's part all along, had undertaken the task of clearing up affairs at Garden Vale, superintending the payment of Mr Cruden's debts, the sale of his furniture, and the removal to Dull Street of what little remained to the family to remind them of their former comforts.

It might have been better if in this last respect the boys and their mother had acted for themselves, for Mr Richmond appeared to have hazy notions as to what the family would most value. The first sight which met the boys' eyes as they arrived was their tennis-racquets in a corner of the room. A very small case of trinkets was on Mrs Cruden's dressing-table, and not one of the twenty or thirty books arranged on the top of the sideboard was one which any member of the small household cared anything about.

But Mr Richmond had done his best, and being left entirely to his own devices, was not to be blamed for the few mistakes he had made. He was there to receive Mrs Cruden when she arrived, and after conducting the little party hurriedly through the three rooms destined for their accommodation, considerately retired.

Until the moment when they were left to themselves in the shabby little Dull Street parlour, not one of the Crudens had understood the change which had come over their lot. All had been so sudden, so exciting, so unlooked-for during the last few weeks, that all three of them had seemed to go through it as through a dream. But the awakening came now, and a rude and cruel one it was.

The little room, dignified by the name of a parlour, was a dingy, stuffy apartment of the true Dull Street type. The paper was faded and torn, the ceiling was discoloured, the furniture was decrepit, the carpet was threadbare, and the cheap engraving on the wall, with its title, "As Happy as a King," seemed to brood over the scene like some mocking spirit.

They passed into Mrs Cruden's bedroom, and the thought of the delightful snug little boudoir at Garden Vale sent a shiver through them as they glanced at the bare walls, the dilapidated half-tester, the chipped and oddly assorted crockery.

The boys' room was equally cheerless. One narrow bed, a chair, and a small washstand, was all the furniture it boasted of, and a few old cuttings of an antiquated illustrated paper pinned on to the wall afforded its sole decoration.

A low, dreary whistle escaped from Horace's lips as he surveyed his new quarters, followed almost immediately by an equally dreary laugh.

"Why," gasped he, "there's no looking-glass! However is Reg to shave?"

It was an heroic effort, and it succeeded. Mrs Cruden's face lit up at the sound of her son's voice with its old sunshine, and even Reginald smiled grimly.

"I must let my beard grow," said he. "But, mother, I say," and his voice quavered as he spoke, "what a miserable room yours is! I can't bear to think of your being cooped up there."

"Oh, it's not so bad," said Mrs Cruden, cheerily. "The pink in the chintz doesn't go well with the scarlet in the wall-paper, certainly, but I dare say I shall sleep soundly in the bed all the same."

"But such a wretched look-out from the window, mother, and such a *vile* jug and basin!"

Mrs Cruden laughed.

"Never mind about the jug and basin," said she, "as long as they hold water; and as for the look-out—well, as long as I can see my two boys' faces happy, that's the best view I covet."

"You never think about yourself," said Reginald, sadly.

"I say, mother," said Horace, "suppose we call up the spirits from the vasty deep and ask them to get tea ready."

This practical suggestion met with general approbation, and the little party returned more cheerily to the parlour, where Horace performed marvellous exploits with the bell-handle, and succeeded, in the incredible time of seven minutes, in bringing up a small slipshod girl, who, after a good deal of staring about her, and a critical survey of the pattern of Mrs Cruden's dress, contrived to gather a general idea of what was required of her.

It was a queer meal, half ludicrous, half despairing, that first little tea-party in Dull Street. They tried to be gay. Reginald declared that the tea his mother poured out was far better than any the footman at Garden Vale used to dispense. Horace tried to make fun of the heterogeneous cups and saucers. Mrs Cruden tried hard to appear as though she was taking a hearty meal, while she tasted nothing. But it was a relief when the girl reappeared and cleared the table.

Then they unpacked their few belongings, and tried to enliven their dreary lodgings with a few precious mementoes of happier days. Finally, worn out in mind and body, they took shelter in bed, and for a blessed season forgot all their misery and forebodings in sleep.

There is no magic equal to that which a night's sleep will sometimes work. The little party assembled cheerfully at the breakfast-table next morning, prepared to face the day bravely.

A large letter, in Mr Richmond's handwriting, lay on Mrs Cruden's plate. It contained three letters—one from the lawyer himself, and one for each of the boys from Wilderham. Mr Richmond's letter was brief and business-like.

"Dear Madam,—Enclosed please find two letters, which I found lying at Garden Vale yesterday. With regard to balance of your late husband's assets in your favour, I have an opportunity of investing same at an unusually good rate of interest in sound security. Shall be pleased to wait on you with particulars. Am also in a position to introduce the young gentlemen to a business opening, which, if not at first important, may seem to you a favourable opportunity. On these points I shall have the honour of waiting on you during to-morrow afternoon, and meanwhile beg to remain,—

"Your obedient servant,—

"R. Richmond."

"We ought to make sure what the investment is," said Reginald, after hearing the letter read, "before we hand over all our money to him."

"To be sure, dear," said Mrs Cruden, who hated the sound of the word investment.

"I wonder what he proposes for us?" said Horace. "Some clerkship, I suppose."

"Perhaps in his own office," said Reginald. "*What* an opening that would be!"

"Never you mind. The law's very respectable; but I know I'd be no good for that. I might manage to serve tea and raisins behind a grocer's counter, or run errands, or—"

"Or black boots," suggested Reginald.

"Black boots! I bet you neither you nor I could black a pair of boots properly to save our lives."

"It seems to me we shall have to try it this very morning," said Reginald, "for no one has touched mine since last night."

"But who are your letters from?" said Mrs Cruden. "Are they very private?"

"Not mine," said Horace. "It's from old Harker. You may read it if you like, mother."

Mrs Cruden took the letter and read aloud,—

"Dear Horrors—"

("That's what he calls me, you know," explained Horace, in a parenthesis.)

"I am so awfully sorry to hear of your new trouble about money matters, and that you will have to leave Garden Vale. I wish I could come over to see you and help you. All the fellows here are awfully cut up about it, and lots of them want me to send you messages. I don't know what I shall do without you this term, old man, you were always a brick to me. Be sure and write to me and tell me everything. As soon as I can get away for a day I'll come and see you, and I'll write as often as I can.

"Your affectionate,—

"T. Harker.

"P.S.—Wilkins, I expect, will be the new monitor in our house. He is sure now to get the scholarship Reg was certain of. I wish to goodness you were both back here."

"He might just as well have left out that about the scholarship," said Reginald; "it's not very cheering news to hear of another fellow stepping into your place like that."

"I suppose he thought we'd be curious to know," said Horace.

"Precious curious!" growled Reginald.

"But who's your letter from, Reg?" asked Mrs Cruden.

"Oh, just a line from Bland," replied he, hastily putting it into his pocket; "he gives no news."

If truth must be told, Blandford's letter was not a very nice one, and Reginald felt it. He did not care to hear it read aloud in contrast with Harker's warm-hearted letter. Blandford had written,—

"Dear Cruden,—I hope it's not true about your father's money going all wrong. It is a great sell, and fellows here, I know, will be very sorry. Never mind, I suppose there's enough left to make a decent show; and between you and me it would go down awfully well with the fellows here if you could send your usual subscription to the football club. Harker says you'll have to leave Garden Vale. I'm awfully sorry, as I always enjoyed my visits there so much. What are you going to do? Why don't you try for the army? The exams are not very hard, my brother told me, and of course it's awfully respectable, if one must work for one's living. I must stop now, or I shall miss tennis. Excuse more.

"Yours truly,—

"G. Blandford."

Reginald knew the letter was a cold and selfish one, but it left two things sticking in his mind which rankled there for a long time. One was that, come what would, he would send a guinea to the school football club. The other was—was it *quite* out of the question that he should go into the army?

"Awfully rough on Reg," said Horace, "being so near that scholarship. It'll be no use to Wilkins, not a bit, and fifty pounds a year would be something to—"

Horace was going to say "us," but he pulled up in time and said "Reg."

"Well," said Reg, "as things have turned out it might have come in useful. I wonder if it wouldn't have been wiser, mother, for me to have stayed up this term and made sure of it?"

"I wish you could, Reg; but we have no right to think of it. Besides, you could only have held it if you had gone to college."

"Oh, of course," said Reg; "but then it would have paid a good bit of my expenses there; and I might have gone on from there to the army, you know, and got my commission."

Mrs Cruden sighed. What an awakening the boy had still to pass through!

"We must think of something less grand than that, my poor Reg," said she; "and something we can share all together. I hope Mr Richmond will be able to hear of some business opening for me, as well as you, for we shall need to put our resources together to get on."

"Mother," exclaimed Reginald, overwhelmed with sudden contrition, "what a selfish brute you must think me! You don't think I'd let you work while I had a nerve left. I'll do anything—so will Horace, but you *shall not*, mother, you *shall not*."

Mrs Cruden did not argue the point just then, and in due time Mr Richmond arrived to give a new direction to their thoughts.

The investment he proposed seemed a good one. But, in fact, the little family knew so little about business generally, and money matters in particular, that had it been the worst security possible they would have hardly been the wiser.

This point settled, Mr Richmond turned to his proposals for the boys.

"As I said in my letter, Mrs Cruden," said he, "the opening is only a modest one. A company has lately been formed to print and publish an evening paper in the city, and as solicitor to the company I had an opportunity of mentioning your sons to the manager. He is willing to take them, provided they are willing to work. The pay will begin at eighteen shillings a week, but I hope they will soon make their value felt, and command a better position. They are young yet."

"What shall we have to do?" asked Horace.

"That I cannot exactly say," said the lawyer; "but I believe the manager would expect you to learn the printer's business from the beginning."

"What would the hours be?" asked Mrs Cruden.

"Well, as it is an evening paper, there will fortunately be no late night work. I believe seven in the morning to eight at night were the hours the manager mentioned."

"And—and," faltered the poor mother, who was beginning to realise the boys' lot better than they did themselves—"and what sort of companions are they likely to have, Mr Richmond?"

"I believe the manager is succeeding in getting respectable men as workmen. I hope so."

"Workmen!" exclaimed Reginald, suddenly. "Do you mean we are to be workmen, Mr Richmond? Just like any fellows in the street. Couldn't you find anything better than that for us?"

"My dear Master Cruden, I am very sorry for you, and would gladly see you in a better position. But it is not a case where we can choose. This opening has offered itself. Of course, you are not bound to accept it, but my advice is, take what you can get in these hard times."

"Oh, of course, we're paupers, I—forgot," said Reg, bitterly, "and beggars mayn't be choosers. Anything you like, mother," added he, meeting Mrs Cruden's sorrowful look with forced gaiety. "I'll sweep a crossing if you like, Mr Richmond, or black your office-boy's boots,—anything to get a living."

Poor boy! He broke down before he could finish the sentence, and his flourish ended in something very like a sob.

Horace was hardly less miserable, but he said less. Evidently, as Reg himself had said, beggars could not be choosers, and when presently Mr Richmond left, and the little family talked the matter over late into the afternoon, it was finally decided that the offer of the manager of the *Rocket* Newspaper Company, Limited, should be accepted, and that the boys should make their new start in life on the Monday morning following.

Chapter Four
The "Rocket" Newspaper Company, Limited

The reader may imagine that the walk our two heroes took Citywards that Monday morning was not a very cheerful one. It seemed like walking out of one life into another. Behind, like a dream, were the joyous, merry days spent at Garden Vale and Wilderham, with no care for the future, and no want for the present. Before them, still more like a dream, lay the prospect of their new work, with all its anxiety, and drudgery, and weariness, and the miserable eighteen shillings a week it promised them; and, equally wretched at the present moment, there was the vision of their desolate mother, alone in the Dull Street lodgings, where they had just left her, unable at the last to hide the misery with which she saw her two boys start out into the pitiless world.

The boys walked for some time in silence; then Horace said,—

"Old man, I hope, whatever they do, they'll let us be together at this place."

"We needn't expect any such luck," said Reginald. "It wouldn't be half so bad if they would."

"You know," said Horace, "I can't help hoping they'll take us as clerks, at least. They must know we're educated, and more fit for that sort of work than—"

"Than doing common labourer's work," said Reg. "Rather! If they'd put us to some of the literary work, you know, Horace—editing, or correcting, or reporting, or that sort of thing, I could stand that. There are plenty of swells who began like that. I'm pretty well up in classics, you know, and— well, they might be rather glad to have some one who was."

Horace sighed.

"Richmond spoke as if we were to be taken on as ordinary workmen."

"Oh, Richmond's an ass," said Reg, full of his new idea; "he knows nothing about it. I tell you, Horace, they wouldn't be such idiots as to waste our education when they could make use of it. Richmond only knows the manager, but the editor is the chief man, after all."

By this time they had reached Fleet Street, and their attention was absorbed in finding the by-street in which was situated the scene of their coming labours. They found it at last, and with beating hearts saw before them a building surmounted by a board, bearing in characters of gold the legend, *Rocket* Newspaper Company, Limited.

The boys stood a moment outside, and the courage which had been slowly rising during the walk evaporated in an instant. Ugly and grimy as the building was, it seemed to them like some fairy castle before which they shrank into insignificance. A board inscribed, "Work-people's Entrance," with a hand on it pointing to a narrow side court, confronted them, and mechanically they turned that way. Reginald did for a moment hesitate as he passed the editor's door, but it was no use. The two boys turned slowly into the court, where, amid the din of machinery, and a stifling smell of ink and rollers, they found the narrow passage which conducted them to their destination.

A man at a desk half way down the passage intercepted their progress.

"Now, then, young fellows, what is it?"

"We want to see the manager, please," said Horace.

"No use to-day, my lad. No boys wanted; we're full up."

"We want to see the manager," said Reginald, offended at the man's tone, and not disposed to humour it.

"Tell you we want no boys; can't you see the notice up outside?"

"Look here!" said Reginald, firing up, and heedless of his brother's deprecating look; "we don't want any of your cheek. Tell the manager we're here, will you, and look sharp?"

The timekeeper stared at the boy in amazement for a moment, and then broke out with, —

"Take your hook, do you hear, you — or I'll warm you."

"It's a mistake," put in Horace, hurriedly. "Mr Richmond said we were to come here to see the manager at nine o'clock."

"And couldn't you have said so at first?" growled the man, with his hand still on his ruler, and glaring at Reginald, "without giving yourselves airs as if you were gentry? Go on in, and don't stand gaping there."

"For goodness' sake, Reg," whispered Horace, as they knocked at the manager's door, "don't flare up like that, you'll spoil all our chance."

Reg said nothing, but he breathed hard, and his face was angry still.

"Come in!" cried a sharp voice, in answer to their knock.

They obeyed, and found a man standing with a pen in his mouth at a desk, searching through a file of papers. He went on with his work till he found what he wanted, apparently quite unconscious of the boys' presence. Then he rang a bell for an overseer, whistled down a tube for a clerk, and shouted out of the door for a messenger, and gave orders to each. Then he sent for some one else, and gave him a scolding that made the unlucky recipient's hair stand on end; then he received a visit from a friend, with whom he chatted and joked for a pleasant quarter of an hour; then he took up the morning paper and skimmed through it, whistling to himself as he did so; then he rang another bell and told the errand-boy who answered it to bring him in at one o'clock sharp a large boiled beef underdone, with carrots and turnips, and a pint of "s. and b." (whatever that might mean). Then he suddenly became aware of the fact that he had visitors, and turned inquiringly to the two boys.

"Mr Richmond—" began Horace, in answer to his look.

But the manager cut him short.

"Oh, ah! yes," he said. "Nuisance! Go to the composing-room and ask for Mr Durfy."

Saying which he sat down again at his desk, and became absorbed in his papers.

It was hardly a flattering reception, and gave our heroes very little chance of showing off their classical proficiency. They had at least expected, as Mr Richmond's nominees, rather more than a half glance from the manager; and to be thus summarily turned over to a Mr Durfy before they had as much as opened their mouths was decidedly unpromising.

Reginald did make one feeble effort to prolong the interview, and to impress the manager at the same time.

"Excuse me," said he, in his politest tones, "would you mind directing us to the composing-room? My brother and I don't know the geography of the place yet."

"Eh? Composing-room? Get a boy to show you. Plenty outside."

It was no go, evidently; and they turned dismally from the room.

The errand-boy was coming up the passage as they emerged—the same errand-boy they had seen half an hour ago in the manager's room; but, as their classical friends would say—

"Quantum mutatus ab illo Hectore!"

Reginald Cruden | 35

His two arms were strung with the handles of frothing tin cans from the elbow to the wrist. He carried two tin cans in his mouth. His apron was loaded to bursting with bread, fish, cheese, potatoes, and other edibles; the necks of bottles protruded from all his pocket's,—from the bosom of his jacket and from the fob of his breeches,—and round his neck hung a ponderous chain of onions. In short, the errand-boy was busy; and our heroes, even with their short experience of business life, saw that there was little hope of extracting information from him under present circumstances.

So they let him pass, and waited for another. They had not to wait long, for the passage appeared to be a regular highway for the junior members of the staff of the *Rocket* Newspaper Company, Limited. But though several boys came, it was some time before one appeared whose convenience it suited to conduct our heroes to the presence of Mr Durfy. Just, however, as their patience was getting exhausted, and Reginald was making up his mind to shake the dust of the place from his feet, a boy appeared and offered to escort them to the composing-room.

They followed him up several flights of a rickety staircase, and down some labyrinthine passages to a large room where some forty or fifty men were busy setting up type. At the far end of this room, at a small table, crowded with "proofs," sat a red-faced individual whom the boy pointed out as "Duffy."

"Well, now, what do *you* want?" asked he, as the brothers approached.

"The manager said we were to ask for Mr Durfy," said Reginald.

"I wish to goodness he'd keep you down there; he knows I'm crowded out with boys. He always serves me that way, and I'll tell him so one of these days."

This last speech, though apparently addressed to the boys, was really a soliloquy on Mr Durfy's part; but for all that it failed to enchant his audience. They had not, in their most sanguine moments, expected much, but this was even rather less than they had counted on.

Mr Durfy mused for some time, then, turning to Reginald, he said,—

"Do you know your letters?"

Here was a question to put to the captain of the fifth at Wilderham!

"I believe I do," said Reginald, with a touch of scorn in his voice which was quite lost on the practical Mr Durfy.

"What do you mean by believe? Do you, or do you not?"

"Of course I do."

"Then why couldn't you say so at once? Take this bit of copy and set it up at that case there. And you, young fellow, take these proofs to the sub-editor's room, and say I've not had the last sheet of the copy of the railway accident yet, and I'm standing for it. Cut away."

Horace went off.

"After all," thought he to himself, "what's the use of being particular? I suppose I'm what they call a 'printer's devil'; nothing like starting modestly! Here goes for my lords the sub-editors, and the last page of the railway accident."

And he spent a festive ten-minutes hunting out the sub-editor's domains, and possessing himself of the missing copy.

With Reginald, however, it fared otherwise. A fellow may be head of the fifth at a public school, and yet not know his letters in a printing-office, and after five or ten-minutes' hopeless endeavour to comprehend the geography of a typecase, he was obliged to acknowledge himself beaten and apprise Mr Durfy of the fact.

"I'm sorry I misunderstood you," said he, putting the copy down on the table. "I'm not used to printing."

"No," said Mr Durfy, scornfully, "I guessed not. You're too stuck-up for us, I can tell you. Here, Barber."

An unhealthy-looking young man answered to the name.

"Take this chap here to the back case-room, and see he sweeps it out and dusts the cases. See if that'll suit your abilities, my dandy"; and without waiting to hear Reginald's explanations or remonstrances, Mr Durfy walked off, leaving the unlucky boy in the hands of Mr Barber.

"Now, then, stir your stumps, Mr Dandy," said the latter. "It'll take you all your time to get that shop straight, I can tell you, so you'd better pull up your boots. Got a broom?"

"No," muttered Reg, through his teeth, "I've not got a broom."

"Go and get that one, then, out of the corner there."

Reginald flushed crimson, and hesitated a moment.

"Do you 'ear? Are you deaf? Get that one there."

Reginald got it, and trailing it behind him dismally, followed his guide to the back case-room. It was a small room, which apparently had known neither broom nor water for years. The floor was thick with dirt, and the cases ranged in the racks against the walls were coated with dust.

"There you are," said Mr Barber. "Open the window, do you 'ear? and don't let none of the dust get out into the composing-room, or there'll be a row. Come and tell me when you've done the floor, and I'll show you 'ow to do them cases. Rattle along, do you 'ear? or you won't get it done to-day;" and Mr Barber, who had had his day of sweeping out the shops, departed, slamming the door behind him.

Things had come to a crisis with Reginald Cruden early in his business career.

He had *come* into the City that morning prepared to face a good deal. He had not counted on much sympathy or consideration from his new employers; he had even vaguely made up his mind he would have to rough it at first; but to be shut up in a dirty room with a broom in his hand by a cad who could not even talk grammar was a humiliation on which he had never once calculated.

Tossing the broom unceremoniously into a corner, he opened the door and walked out of the room. Barber was already out of sight, chuckling inwardly over the delicious task he had been privileged to set to his dandy subordinate, and none of the men working near knew or cared what this pale, handsome new boy did either in or out of the back case-room.

Reginald walked through them to the passage outside, not much caring where he went or whom he met. If he were to meet Mr Barber, or Mr Durfy, or the manager himself, so much the better. As it happened, he met Horace, looking comparatively cheerful, with some papers in his hand.

"Hullo, Reg," said he; "have they promoted you to a 'printer's devil' too? Fancy what Bland would say if he saw us! Never mind, there's four hours gone, and in about another six we shall be home with mother again."

"I shall be home before then," said Reg. "I'm going now. I can't stand it, Horace."

Horace stared at his brother in consternation.

"Oh, Reg, old man, you mustn't; really you mustn't. Do let's stick together, however miserable it is. It's sure to seem worse at first."

"It's all very well for you, Horace, doing messenger work. You haven't been set to sweep out a room."

Horace whistled.

"Whew! that *is* a drop too much! But," he added, taking his brother's arm, "don't cut it yet, old man, for mother's sake, don't. I'll come and help you do it if I can. Why couldn't they have given it me to do, and let you go the messages!"

Reginald said nothing, but let his brother lead him back slowly to the big room presided over by Mr Durfy.

"Where is it?" Horace inquired of him at the door.

"That little room in the corner."

"All right. I'll come if I possibly can. Do try it, old man, won't you?"

"I'll try it," said Reginald, with something very like a groan as he opened the door and walked grimly back to the back case-room.

Horace, full of fear and trembling on his brother's account, hurried with his copy to Mr Durfy, and waited impatiently till that grandee condescended to relieve him of it.

"Is there anything else?" he inquired, as he gave it up.

"Anything else? Yes, plenty; but don't come bothering me now."

Horace waited for no more elaborate statement of Mr Durfy's wishes, but thankfully withdrew, and made straight for Reginald.

He found him half hidden, half choked by the dust of his own raising, as he drew his broom in a spiritless way across the black dry floor.

He paused in his occupation as Horace entered, and for a moment, as the two stood face to face coughing and sneezing, a sense of the ludicrous overcame them, and they finished up their duet with a laugh.

"I say," said Horace, as soon as he could get words, "I fancy a little water would be an improvement here."

"Where are we to get it from?" said Reg.

"I suppose there must be some about. Shall I go and see?"

"We might tip one of those fellows outside a sixpence to go and get us some."

"Hold hard, old man!" said Horace, laughing again. "We're not so flush of sixpences as all that. I guess if we want any water we shall have to get it ourselves. I'll be back directly."

Poor Reg, spirited up for a while by his brother's courage, proceeded more gingerly with his sweeping, much amazed in the midst of his misery to discover how many walks in life there are beyond the capacity even of the captain of the fifth of a public school.

He was not, however, destined on the present occasion to perfect himself in the one that was then engaging his attention. Horace had scarcely disappeared in quest of water when the door opened, and no less a personage than the manager himself entered the room.

He was evidently prepared neither for the dust nor the duster, and started back for a moment, as though he were under the impression that the clouds filling the apartment were clouds of smoke, and Reginald was another Guy Fawkes caught in the act. He recovered himself shortly, however, and demanded sharply,—

"What are you doing here, making all this mess?"

"I'm trying to carry out Mr Durfy's instructions," replied Reginald, leaning on his broom, and not at all displeased at the interruption.

"Durfy's instructions? What do you mean, sir?"

"Mr Durfy's—"

"That will do. Here you," said the manager, opening the door, and speaking to the nearest workman, "tell Mr Durfy to step here."

Mr Durfy appeared in a very brief space.

"Durfy," said the manager, wrathfully, "what do you mean by having this room in such a filthy mess? Aren't your instructions to have it swept out once a week? When was it swept last?"

"Some little time ago. We've been so busy in our department, sir, that—"

"Yes, I know; you always say that. I'm sick of hearing it. Don't let me find this sort of thing again. Send some one at once to sweep it out; this lad doesn't know how to hold a broom. Take care it's done by four o'clock, and ready for use. Pheugh! it's enough to choke one."

And the manager went off in a rage, coughing.

Satisfactory as this was, in a certain sense, for Reginald, it was not a flattering way of ending his difficulties, nor did the spirit in which Mr Durfy accepted his chief's reprimand at all tend to restore him to cheerfulness.

"Bah, you miserable idiot, you! Give up that broom, and get out of this, or I'll chuck you out."

"I don't think you will," said Reginald, coolly dropping the broom and facing his enemy.

He was happier at that moment than he had been for a long time. He could imagine himself back at Wilderham, with the school bully shouting at him, and his spirits rose within him accordingly.

"What do you say? you hugger-mugger puppy you—you—"

Mr Durfy's adjectives frequently had the merit of being more forcible than appropriate, and on the present occasion, what with the dust and his own rage, the one he wanted stuck in his throat altogether.

"I said I don't think you will," repeated Reginald.

Mr Durfy looked at his man and hesitated. Reginald stood five foot nine, and his shoulders were square and broad, besides, he was as cool as a cucumber, and didn't even trouble to take his hands out of his pockets. All this Mr Durfy took in, and did not relish; but he must not cave in too precipitately, so he replied, with a sneer,—

"Think! A lot you know about thinking! Can't even hold a broom. Clear out of here, I tell you, double quick; do you hear?"

Reginald's spirits fell. It was clear from Mr Durfy's tone he was not going to attempt to "chuck him out," and nothing therefore could be gained by remaining.

He turned scornfully on his heel, knowing that he had made one enemy, at any rate, during his short connection with his new business.

And if he had known all, he could have counted two; for Mr Durfy, finding himself in a mood to wreak his wrath on some one, summoned the ill-favoured Barber to sweep out the back case-room, and gave his orders so viciously that Barber felt distinctly aggrieved, and jumping to the conclusion that Reginald had somehow contrived to turn the tables on him, he registered a secret vow, there and then, that he would on the first opportunity, and on all subsequent opportunities, be square with that luckless youth.

Caring very little about who hated him or who liked him, Reginald wandered forth, to intercept the faithful Horace with the now unnecessary water; and the two boys, finding very little to occupy them during the rest of the day, remained in comparative seclusion until the seven o'clock bell rang, when they walked home, possibly wiser, and certainly sadder, for their first day with the *Rocket* Newspaper Company, Limited.

Chapter Five
The Crudens at Home

If anything could have made up to the two boys for the hardships and miseries of the day, it was the sight of their mother's bright face as she awaited them that evening at the door of Number 6, Dull Street. If the day had been a sad and lonely one for Mrs Cruden, she was not the woman to betray the secret to her sons; and, indeed, the happiness of seeing them back was enough to drive away all other care for the time being.

Shabby as the lodgings were, and lacking in all the comforts and luxuries of former days, the little family felt that evening, as they gathered round the tea-table and unburdened their hearts to one another, more of the true meaning of the word "home" than they had ever done before.

"Now, dear boys," said Mrs Cruden, when the meal was over, and they drew their chairs to the open window, "I'm longing to hear your day's adventures. How did you get on? Was it as bad as you expected?"

"It wasn't particularly jolly," said Reginald, shrugging his shoulders— "nothing like Wilderham, was it, Horrors?"

"Well, it was a different sort of fun, certainly," said Horace. "You see, mother, our education has been rather neglected in some things, so we didn't get on as well as we might have done."

"Do you mean in the literary work?" said Mrs Cruden. "I'm quite sure you'll get into it with a little practice."

"But it's not the literary work, unluckily," said Reginald.

"Ah! you mean clerk's work. You aren't as quick at figures, perhaps, as you might be?"

"That's not exactly it," said Horace. "The fact is, mother, we're neither in the literary not the clerical department. I'm a 'printer's devil'!"

"Oh, Horace! what *do* you mean?" said the horrified mother.

"Oh, I'm most innocently employed. I run messages; I fetch and carry for a gentleman called Durfy. He gives me some parliamentary news to carry to one place, and some police news to carry to another place—and, by-the-way, they read very much alike—and when I'm not running backwards or forwards I have to sit on a stool and watch him, and be ready to jump up and wag my tail the moment he whistles. It's a fact, mother! Think of getting eighteen shillings a week for that! It's a fraud!"

Mrs Cruden could hardly tell whether to laugh or cry.

"My poor boy!" she murmured; then, turning to Reginald, she said, "And what do you do, Reg?"

"Oh, I sweep rooms," said Reg, solemnly; "but they've got such a shocking bad broom there that I can't make it act. If you could give me a new broom-head, mother, and put me up to a dodge or two about working out corners, I might rise in my profession!"

There was a tell-tale quaver in the speaker's voice which made this jaunty speech a very sad one to the mother's ears. It was all she could do to conceal her misery, and when Horace came to the rescue with a racy account of the day's proceedings, told in his liveliest manner, she was glad to turn her head and hide from her boys the trouble in her face.

However, she soon recovered herself, and by the time Horace's story was done she was ready to join her smiles with those which the history had drawn even from Reginald's serious countenance.

"After all," said she, presently, "we must be thankful for what we have. Some one was saying the other day there never was a time when so many young fellows were out of work and thankful to get anything to do. And it's very likely too, Reg, that just now, when they seem rather in confusion at the office, they really haven't time to see about what your regular work is to be. Wait a little, and they're sure to find out your value."

"They seem to have done that already as far as sweeping is concerned. The manager said I didn't know how to hold a broom. I was quite offended," said Reginald.

"You are a dear brave pair of boys!" said the mother, warmly; "and I am prouder of you in your humble work than if you were kings!"

"Hullo," said Horace, "there's some one coming up our stairs!"

Sure enough there was, and more than one person, as it happened. There was a knock at the door, followed straightway by the entrance of an elderly lady, accompanied by a young lady and a young gentleman, who sailed into the room, much to the amazement and consternation of its occupants.

"Mrs Cruden, I believe?" said the elderly lady, in her politest tones.

"Yes," replied the owner of that name.

"Let me hintroduce myself—Mrs Captain Shuckleford, my son and daughter—neighbours of yours, Mrs Cruden, and wishing to be friendly. We're sorry to hear of your trouble; very trying it is. My 'usband, Mrs Cruden, has gone too."

"Pray take a seat," said Mrs Cruden. "Reg, will you put chairs?"

Reg obeyed, with a groan.

"These are your boys, are they?" said the visitor, eyeing the youths. "Will you come and shake 'ands with me, Reggie? What a dear, good-looking boy he is, Mrs Cruden! And 'ow do you do, too, my man?" said she, addressing Horace. "Pretty well? And what do they call you?"

"My name is Horace," said "my man," blushing very decidedly, and retreating precipitately to a far corner of the room.

"Ah, dear me! And my 'usband's name, Mrs Cruden, was 'Oward. I never 'ear the name without affliction."

This was very awkward, for as the unfortunate widow could not fail to hear her own voice, it was necessary for consistency's sake that she should show some emotion, which she proceeded to do, when her daughter hurriedly interposed in an audible whisper, "Ma, don't make a goose of yourself! Behave yourself, do!"

"So I am be'aving myself, Jemima," replied the outraged parent, "and I don't need lessons from you."

"It's very kind of you to call in," said Mrs Cruden, feeling it time to say something; "do you live near here?"

"We live next door, at number four," said Miss Jemima; "put that handkerchief away, ma."

"What next, I wonder! if my 'andkerchief's not my hown, I'd like to know what is? Yes, Mrs Cruden. We heard you were coming, and we wish to treat you with consideration, knowing your circumstances. It's all one gentlefolk can do to another. Yes, and I 'ope the boys will be good friends. Sam, talk to the boys."

Sam needed no such maternal encouragement, as it happened, and had already swaggered up to Horace with a familiar air.

"Jolly weather, ain't it?"

"Yes," said Horace, looking round wildly for any avenue of escape, but finding none.

"Pretty hot in your shop, ain't it?" said the lawyer's clerk.

"Yes," again said Horace, with a peculiar tingling sensation in his toes which his visitor little dreamed of.

Horace was not naturally a short-tempered youth, but there was something in the tone of this self-satisfied lawyer's clerk which raised his dander.

"Not much of a berth, is it?" pursued the catechist.

"No," said Horace.

"Not a very chirrupy screw, so I'm told—eh?"

This was rather too much. Either Horace must escape by flight, which would be ignominious, or he must knock his visitor down, which would be rude, or he must grin and bear it. The middle course was what he most inclined to, but failing that, he decided on the latter.

So he shook his head and waited patiently for the next question.

"What do you do, eh? dirty work, ain't it?"

"Yes, isn't yours?" said Horace, in a tone that rather surprised the limb of the law.

"Mine? No. What makes you ask that?" he inquired.

"Only because I thought I'd like to know," said Horace artlessly.

Mr Shuckleford looked perplexed. He didn't understand exactly what Horace meant, and yet, whatever it was, it put him off the thread of his discourse for a time. So he changed the subject.

"I once thought of going into business myself," he said; "but they seemed to think I'd do better at the law. Same time, don't think I'm a nailer on business chaps. I know one or two very respectable chaps in business."

"Do you?" replied Horace, with a touch of satire in his voice which was quite lost on the complacent Sam.

"Yes. Why, in our club—do you know our club?"

"No," said Horace.

"Oh—I must take you one evening—yes, in our club we've a good many business chaps—well-behaved chaps, too."

Horace hardly looked as overwhelmed by this announcement as his visitor expected.

"Would you like to join?"

"No, thank you."

"Eh? you're afraid of being black-balled, I suppose? No fear, I can work it with them. I can walk round any of them, I let you know; they wouldn't do it, especially when they knew I'd a fancy for you, my boy."

If Horace was grateful for this expression of favour, he managed to conceal his feelings wonderfully well. At the same time he had sense enough to see that, vulgar and conceited as Samuel Shuckleford was, he meant to be friendly, and inwardly gave him credit accordingly.

He did his best to be civil, and to listen to all the bumptious talk of his visitor patiently, and Sam rattled away greatly to his own satisfaction, fully believing he was impressing his hearer with a sense of his importance, and cheering his heart by the promise of his favours and protection.

With the unlucky Reginald, meanwhile, it fared far less comfortably.

"Jemima, my dear," said Mrs Shuckleford, who in all her domestic confidences to Mrs Cruden kept a sharp eye on her family—"Jemima, my dear, I think Reggie would like to show you his album!"

An electric shock could not have startled and confused our hero more. It was bad enough to hear himself called "Reggie," but that was nothing to the assumption that he was pining to make himself agreeable to Miss Jemima— he to whom any lady except his mother was a cause of trepidation, and to whom a female like Miss Jemima was nothing short of an ogress!

"I've not got an album," he gasped, with an appealing look towards his mother.

But before Mrs Cruden could interpose to rescue him, the ladylike Miss Jemima, who had already regarded the good-looking shy youth with approval, entered the lists on her own account, and moving her chair a trifle in his direction, said, in a confidential whisper,—

"Ma thinks we're not a very sociable couple, that's what it is."

A couple! He and Jemima a couple! Reginald was ready to faint, and looked towards the open window as if he meditated a headlong escape that way. As to any other way of escape, that was impossible, for he was fairly cornered between the enemy and the wall, and unless he were to cut his way through the one or the other, he must sit where he was.

"I hope you don't mind talking to me, Mr Reggie," continued the young lady, when Reginald gave no symptom of having heard the last observation. "We shall have to be friends, you know, now we are neighbours. So you haven't got an album?"

This abrupt question drove poor Reginald still further into the corner. What business was it of hers whether he had got an album or not? What right had she to pester him with questions like that in his own house? In fact, what right had she and her mother and her brother to come there at all? Those were the thoughts that passed through his mind, and as they did so indignation got the better of good manners and everything else.

"Find out," he said.

He could have bitten his tongue off the moment he had spoken. For Reginald was a gentleman, and the sound of these rude words in his own voice startled him into a sense of shame and confusion tenfold worse than any Miss Shuckleford had succeeded in producing.

"I beg your pardon," he gasped hurriedly. "I—I didn't mean to be rude."

Now was the hour of Miss Jemima's triumph. She had the unhappy youth at her mercy, and she took full advantage of her power. She forgave him, and made him sit and listen to her and answer her questions for as long as she chose; and if ever he showed signs of mutiny, the slightest hint, such as "You'll be telling me to mind my own business again," was enough to reduce him to instant subjection.

It was a bad quarter of an hour for Reginald, and the climax arrived when presently Mrs Shuckleford looked towards them and said across the room,—

"Now I wonder what you two young people are talking about in that snug corner. Oh, never mind, if it's secrets! Nice it is, Mrs Cruden, to see young people such good friends so soon. We must be going now, children," she added. "We shall soon see our friends in our own 'ouse, I 'ope."

A tender leave-taking ensued. For a while, as the retreating footsteps of the visitors gradually died away on the stairs, the little family stood motionless, as though the slightest sound might recall them. But when at last the street-door slammed below, Reginald flung himself into a chair and groaned.

"Mother, we can't stay here. We must leave to-morrow!"

Horace could not help laughing.

"Why, Reg," he said, "you seemed to be enjoying yourself no end."

"Shut up, Horace, it's nothing to laugh about."

"My dear boy," said Mrs Cruden, "you think far more about it than you need. After all, they seem kindly disposed persons, and I don't think we should be unfriendly."

"That's all very well," said Reg, "if there was no Jemima in the question."

"I should say it's all very well," said Horace, "if there was no Sam in the question; though I dare say he means to be friendly. But didn't you and Jemima hit it, then, Reg? I quite thought you did."

"Didn't I tell you to shut up?" repeated Reg, this time half angrily. "I don't see, mother," he added, "however poor we are, we are called on to associate with a lot like that."

"They have not polished manners, certainly," said Mrs Cruden; "but I do think they are good-natured, and that's a great thing."

"I should think so," said Horace. "What do you think? Samuel wants to propose me for his club, which seems to be a very select affair."

"All I know is," said Reginald, "nothing will induce me to go into their house. It may be rude, but I'm certain I'd be still more rude if I did go."

"Well," said Horace, "I vote we take a walk, as it's a fine evening. I feel a trifle warm after it all. What do you say?"

They said Yes, and in the empty streets that evening the mother and her two sons walked happy in one another's company, and trying each in his or her own way to gain courage for the days of trial that were to follow.

The brothers had a short consultation that night as they went to bed, *not* on the subject of their next door neighbours.

"Horrors," said Reg, "what's to be done about the *Rocket*? I can't stop there."

"It's awful," said Horace; "but what else can we do? If we cut it, there's mother left a beggar."

"Couldn't we get into something else?"

"What? Who'd take us? There are thousands of fellows wanting work as it is."

"But surely we're better than most of them. We're gentlemen and well educated."

"So much the worse, it seems," said Horace. "What good is it to us when we're put to sweep rooms and carry messages?"

"Do you mean to say you intend to stick to that sort of thing all your life?" asked Reg.

"Till I can find something better," said Horace. "After all, old man, it's honest work, and not very fagging, and it's eighteen shillings a week."

"Anyhow, I think we might let Richmond know what a nice berth he's let us in for. Why, his office-boy's better off."

"Yes, and if we knew as much about book-keeping and agreement stamps and copying presses as his office-boy does, we might be as well off. What's the good of knowing how many ships fought at Salamis, when we don't even know how many ounces you can send by post for twopence? At least, I don't. Good-night, old man."

And Horace, really scarcely less miserable at heart than his brother, buried his nose in the Dull Street pillow and tried to go to sleep.

Chapter Six
Reginald's Prospects develop

It was in anything but exuberant spirits that the two Crudens presented themselves on the following morning at the workman's entrance of the *Rocket* Newspaper Company, Limited. The bell was beginning to sound as they did so, and their enemy the timekeeper looked as though he would fain discover a pretext for pouncing on them and giving them a specimen of his importance. But even his ingenuity failed in this respect, and as Horace passed him with a good-humoured nod, he had, much against his will, to nod back, and forego his amiable intentions.

The brothers naturally turned their steps to the room presided over by Mr Durfy. That magnate had not yet arrived, much to their relief, and they consoled themselves in his absence by standing at the table watching their fellow-workmen as they crowded in and proceeded with more or less alacrity to settle down to their day's work.

Among those who displayed no unseemly haste in applying themselves to their tasks was Barber, who, with the dust of the back case-room still in his mind, and equally on his countenance, considered the present opportunity of squaring up accounts with Reginald too good to be neglected. For reasons best known to himself, Mr Barber determined that his victim's flagellation should be moral rather than physical. He would have liked to punch Reginald's head, or, better still, to have knocked Reginald's and Horace's heads together. But he saw reasons for denying himself that pleasure, and fell back on the more ethereal weapons of his own wit.

"Hullo, puddin' 'ead," he began, "'ow's your pa and your ma to-day? Find the Old Bailey a 'ealthy place, don't they?"

Reginald favoured the speaker by way of answer with a stare of mingled scorn and wrath, which greatly elevated that gentleman's spirits.

"'Ow long is it they've got? Seven years, ain't it? My eye, they won't know you when they come out, you'll be so growed."

The wrath slowly faded from Reginald's face, as the speaker proceeded, leaving only the scorn to testify to the interest he took in this intellectual display.

Horace, delighted to see there was no prospect of a "flare-up," smiled, and began almost to enjoy himself.

"I say," continued Barber, just a little disappointed to find that his exquisite humour was not as electrical in its effect as it would have been on any one less dense than the Crudens, "'ow is it you ain't got a clean collar on to-day, and no scent on your 'andkerchers—eh?"

This was getting feeble. Even Mr Barber felt it, for he continued, in a more lively tone,—

"Glad we ain't got many of your sickening sort 'ere; snivelling school-boy brats, that's what you are, tired of pickin' pockets, and think you're goin' to show us your manners. Yah! if you wasn't such a dirty ugly pair of puppy dogs I'd stick you under the pump—so I would."

Reginald yawned, and walked off to watch a compositor picking up type out of a case. Horace, on the other hand, appeared to be deeply interested in Mr Barber's eloquent observations, and inquired quite artlessly, but with a twinkle in his eye,—"Is the pump near here? I was looking for it everywhere yesterday."

It was Mr Barber's turn to stare. He had not expected this, and he did not like it, especially when one or two of the men and boys near, who had failed to be convulsed by his wit, laughed at Horace's question.

After all, moral flagellation does not always answer, and when one of the victims yawns and the other asks a matter-of-fact questions it is disconcerting even to an accomplished operator. However, Barber gallantly determined on one more effort.

"Ugh—trying to be funny, are you, Mr Snubnose? Best try and be honest if you can, you and your mealy-mug brother. It'll be 'ard work, I know, to keep your 'ands in your own pockets, but you'd best do it, do you 'ear—pair of psalm-singin' twopenny-ha'penny puppy dogs!"

This picturesque peroration certainly deserved some recognition, and might possibly have received it, had not Mr Durfy's entrance at that particular moment sent the idlers back suddenly to their cases.

Reginald, either heedless of or unconcerned at the new arrival, remained listlessly watching the operations of the compositor near him, an act of audacity which highly exasperated the overseer, and furnished the key-note for the day's entertainment.

For Mr Durfy, to use an expressive term, had "got out of bed the wrong side" this morning. For the matter of that, after the blowing-up about the back case-room, he had got into it the wrong side last night, so that he was doubly perturbed in spirit, and a short conversation he had just had with the manager below had not tended to compose him.

"Durfy," said that brusque official, as the overseer passed his open door, "come in. What about those two lads I sent up to you yesterday? Are they any good?"

"Not a bit," growled Mr Durfy; "fools both of them."

"Which is the bigger fool?"

"The old one."

"Then keep him for yourself—put him to composing, and send the other one down here. Send him at once, Durfy, do you hear?"

With this considerately worded injunction in his ears it is hardly to be wondered at that Mr Durfy was not all smiles as he entered the domain which owned his sway.

His eye naturally lit on Reginald as the most suitable object on which to relieve his feelings.

"Now, then, there," he called out. "What do you mean by interfering with the men in their work?"

"I'm not interfering with anybody," said Reginald, looking up with glowing cheeks, "I'm watching this man."

"Come out of it, do you hear me? Why don't you go about your own work?"

"I've been waiting here ten-minutes for you."

"Look here," said Mr Durfy, his tones getting lower as his passion rose; "if you think we're going to keep you here to give us any of your impudence you're mistaken; so I can tell you. It's bad enough to have a big fool put into the place for charity, without any of your nonsense. If I had my way I'd give you your beggarly eighteen shillings a week to keep you away. Go to your work."

Reginald's eyes blazed out for a moment on the speaker in a way which made Horace, who heard and saw all, tremble. But he overcame himself with a mighty effort, and said,—

"Where?"

Mr Durfy glanced round the room.

"Young Gedge!" he called out.

A boy answered the summons.

"Clear that rack between you and Barber, and put up a pair of cases for this fool here, and look after him. Off you go! and off *you* go," added he, rounding on Reginald, "and if we don't make it hot for you among us I'm precious mistaken."

It was a proud moment certainly for the cock of the fifth at Wilderham to find himself following meekly at the heels of a youngster like Gedge, who had been commissioned to put him to work and look after him. But Reginald was too sick at heart and disgusted to care what became of himself, as long as Mr Durfy's odious voice ceased to torment his ears. The only thing he did care about was what was to become of Horace. Was he to be put in charge of some one too, or was he to remain a printer's devil?

Mr Durfy soon answered that question.

"What are you standing there for?" demanded he, turning round on the younger brother as soon as he had disposed of the elder. "Go down to the manager's room at once; you're not wanted here."

So they were to be separated! There was only time to exchange one glance of mutual commiseration and then Horace slowly left the room with sad forebodings, more on his brother's account than his own, and feeling that as far as helping one another was concerned they might as well be doomed to serve their time at opposite ends of London.

Gedge, under whose imposing auspices Reginald was to begin his typographical career, was a diminutive youth who, to all outward appearances, was somewhere about the tender age of fourteen, instead of, as was really the case, being almost as old as Reginald himself. He was facetiously styled "Magog" by his shopmates, in allusion to his small stature, which required the assistance of a good-sized box under his feet to enable him to reach his "upper case." His face was not an unpleasant one, and his voice, which still retained its boyish treble, was an agreeable contrast to that of most of the "gentlemen of the case" in Mr Durfy's department.

For all that, Reginald considered himself much outraged by being put in charge of this chit of a child, and glowered down on him much as a mastiff might glower on a terrier who presumed to do the honour of his back yard for his benefit.

However, the terrier in this case was not at all disheartened by his reception, and said cheerily as he began to clear the frame, —

"You don't seem to fancy it, I say. I don't wonder. Never mind, I shan't lick you unless you make me."

"Thanks," said Reginald, drily, but scarcely able to conceal a smile at this magnanimous declaration.

"Magog" worked busily away, putting away cases in the rack, dusting the frame down with his apron, and whistling softly to himself.

"Thanks for helping me," said he, after a time, as Reginald still stood by doing nothing. "I could never have done it all by myself."

Reginald blushed a little at this broad hint, and proceeded to lift down a case. But he nearly upset it in doing so, greatly to his companion's horror.

"You'd better rest," he said, "you'll be fagged out. Here, let me do it. There you are. Now we're ready to start you. I've a good mind to go and get old Tacker to ring up the big bell and let them know you're just going to begin."

Reginald could hardly be offended at this good-natured banter, and, as Gedge was after all a decent-looking boy, and aspirated his "h's," and did not smell of onions, he began to think that if he were doomed to drudge in this place he might have been saddled with a more offensive companion.

"It's a pity to put Tacker to the trouble, young 'un," said he; "he'll probably ring when I'm going to leave off, and that'll do as well."

"That's not bad for you," said Gedge, approvingly; "not half bad. Go on like that, and you'll make a joke in about a fortnight."

"Look here," said Reginald, smiling at last. "I shall either have to punch your head or begin work. You'd better decide which you'd like best."

"Well, as Durfy is looking this way," said Gedge, "I suppose you'd better begin work. Stick that pair of empty cases up there—the one with the big holes below and the other one above. You needn't stick them upside down, though, unless you particularly want to; they look quite as well the right way. Now, then, you'd better watch me fill them, and see what boxes the sorts go in. No larks, now. Here goes for the 'm's.'"

So saying, Mr "Magog" proceeded to fill up one box with types of the letter "m," and another box some distance off with "a's," and another with "b's," and so on, till presently the lower of the two cases was nearly full. Reginald watched him with something like admiration, inwardly wondering if he would ever be able to find his way about this labyrinth of boxes, and strongly of opinion that only muffs like printers would think of arranging the alphabet in such an absurdly haphazard manner. The lower case being full up, Gedge meekly suggested that as he was yet several feet from his full size, they might as well lift the upper case down while it was being filled. Which done, the same process was repeated, only with more apparent regularity, and the case having been finally tilted up on the frame above the lower case, the operator turned round with a pleased expression, and said,—

"What do you think of that?"

"Why, I think it's very ridiculous not to put the 'capital J' next to the 'capital I,'" said Reginald.

Gedge laughed.

"Go and tell Durfy that; he'd like to hear it."

Reginald, however, denied himself the pleasure of entertaining Mr Durfy on this occasion, and occupied himself with picking up the types and inspecting them, and trying to learn the geography of his cases.

"Now," said "Magog," mounting his box, and taking his composing-stick in his hand, "keep your eye on me, young fellow, and you'll know all about it."

And he proceeded to "set-up" a paragraph for the newspaper from a manuscript in front of him at a speed which bewildered Reginald and baffled any attempt on his part to follow the movements of the operator's hand among the boxes. He watched for several minutes in silence until Gedge, considering he had exhibited his agility sufficiently, halted in his work, and with a passing shade across his face turned to his companion and said,—

"I say, isn't this a beastly place?"

There was something in his voice and manner which struck Reginald. It was unlike a common workman, and still more unlike a boy of Gedge's size and age.

"It is beastly," he said.

"I'm awfully sorry for you, you know," continued Gedge, in a half-whisper, and going on with his work at the same time, "because I guess it's not what you're used to."

"I'm not used to it," said Reginald.

"Nor was I when I came. My old screw of an uncle took it into his head to apprentice me here because he'd been an apprentice once, and didn't see why I should start higher up the ladder than he did. Are you an apprentice?"

"No, not that I know of," said Reginald, not knowing exactly what he was.

"Lucky beggar! I'm booked here for nobody knows how much longer. I'd have cut it long ago if I could. I say, what's your name?"

"Cruden."

"Well, Cruden, I'm precious glad you've turned up. It'll make all the difference to me. I was getting as big a cad as any of those fellows there, for you're bound to be sociable. But you're a nicer sort, and it's a good job for me, I can tell you."

Apart from the flattery of these words, there was a touch of earnestness in the boy's voice which struck a sympathetic chord in Reginald's nature, and drew him mysteriously to this new hour-old acquaintance. He told him of his own hard fortunes, and by what means he had come down to his present position. Gedge listened to it all eagerly.

"Were you really captain of the fifth at your school?" said he, almost reverentially. "I say! what an awful drop this must be! You must feel as if you'd sooner be dead."

"I do sometimes," said Reginald.

"I know I would," replied Gedge, solemnly, "if I was you. Was that other fellow your brother, then?"

"Yes."

Gedge mused a bit, and then laughed quietly.

"How beautifully you two shut up Barber between you just now," he said; "it's the first snub he's had since I've been here, and all the fellows swear by him. I say, Cruden, it's a merciful thing for me you've come. I was bound to go to the dogs if I'd gone on as I was much longer."

Reginald brightened. It pleased him just now to think any one was glad to see him, and the spontaneous way in which this boy had come under his wing won him over completely.

"We must manage to stick together," he said. "Horace, you know, is working in another part of the office. It's awfully hard lines, for we set our minds on being together. But it can't be helped; and I'm glad, any way, you're here, young 'un."

The young 'un beamed gratefully by way of response.

The paragraph by this time was nearly set-up, and the conversation was interrupted by the critical operation of lifting the "matter" from the stick and transferring it to a "galley," a feat which the experienced "Magog" accomplished very deftly, and greatly to the amazement of his companion. Just as it was over, and Reginald was laughingly hoping he would not soon be expected to arrive at such a pitch of dexterity, Mr Durfy walked up.

"So that's what you call doing your work, is it? playing the fool, and getting in another man's way. Is that all you've done?"

Reginald glared at him, and answered,—

"I'm not playing the fool."

"Hold your tongue and don't answer me, you miserable puppy! Let me see what you have done."

"I've been learning the boxes in the case," said Reginald.

Mr Durfy sneered.

"You have, have you? That's what you've been doing the last hour, I suppose. Since you've been so industrious, pick me out a lower-case 'x,' do you hear?"

Reginald made a vague dive at one of the boxes, but not the right one, for he produced a 'z.'

"Ah, I thought so," said Mr Durfy, with a sneer that made Reginald long to cram the type into his mouth. "Now let's try a capital 'J.'"

As it happened, Reginald knew where the capital "J" was, but he made no attempt to reach it, and answered,—

"If you want a capital 'J,' Mr Durfy, you can help yourself."

"Magog" nearly jumped out of his skin as he heard this audacious reply, and scarcely ventured to look round to notice the effect of it on Mr Durfy. The effect was on the whole not bad. For a moment the overseer was dumbfounded and could not speak. But a glance at the resolute pale boy in front of him checked him in his impulse to use some other retort but the tongue. As soon as words came he snarled,—

"Ho! is it that you mean, my beauty? All right, we'll see who's master here; and if I am, I'm sorry for you."

And he turned on his heel and went.

"You've done it now," said "Magog," in an agitated whisper—"done it clean."

"Done what?" asked Reginald.

"Done it with Durfy. He will make it hot for you, and no mistake. Never mind, if the worst comes to the worst you can cut. But hold on as long as you can. He'll make you go some time or another."

"He won't make me go till I choose," replied Reginald. "I'll stick here to disappoint him, if I do nothing else."

The reader may have made up his mind already that Reginald was a fool. I'm afraid he was. But do not judge him harshly yet, for his troubles are only beginning.

Chapter Seven
An Exciting End to a Dull Day

Horace meanwhile had wended his way with some trepidation and curiosity to the manager's sanctum. He felt uncomfortable in being separated from Reginald at all, especially when the latter was left single-handed in such an uncongenial atmosphere as that breathed by Mr Durfy and Barber. He could only hope for the best, and, meanwhile, what fate was in store for himself?

He knocked at the manager's door doubtfully and obeyed the summons to enter.

Brusque man as the manager was, there was nothing disagreeable about his face as he looked up and said, "Oh—you're the youngster Mr Richmond put in here?"

"Yes, sir, my brother and I are."

"Yes, and I hear you're both fools. Is that the case?"

"Reginald isn't, whatever I am," said Horace, boldly.

"Isn't he? I'm told he's the bigger fool of the two. Never mind that, though—"

"I assure you," began Horace, but the manager stopped him.

"Yes, yes. I know all about that. Now, listen to me. I dare say you're both well-meaning boys, and Mr Richmond is interested in you. So I've promised to make room for you here, though it's not convenient, and the wages you are to get are out of all proportion to your value—so far."

Horace was glad at least that the manager dropped in those last two words.

"If your brother is clever and picks up his work soon and doesn't give himself airs he'll get on faster than you. I can't put you at case, but they want a lad in the sub-editor's room. Do you know where that is?"

"Yes, sir," said Horace, "I took some proofs there yesterday. But, sir—"

"Well, what?" said the manager, sharply.

"Is there no possibility of Reginald and me being together?" faltered the boy.

"Yes—outside if you're discontented," said the manager.

It was evidently no use, and Horace walked dismally to the door.

The manager looked after him.

"Take my advice," said he, rather more kindly than he had hitherto spoken; "make the best of what you've got, young fellow, and it'll be better still in time. Shut the door after you."

The sub-editor's room—or rooms, for there was an inner and an outer sanctum—was in a remote dark corner of the building, so dark that gas was generally burning in it all day long, giving its occupants generally the washed-out pallid appearance of men who do not know when day ends or night begins. The chief sub-editor was a young, bald-headed, spectacled man of meek appearance, who received Horace in a resigned way, and referred him to the clerks in the outer room, who would show him how he could make himself useful.

Feeling that, so far as he was concerned, he had fallen on his feet, and secretly wishing poor Reginald was in his shoes, Horace obeyed and retired to the outer room.

The occupants of that apartment were two young gentlemen of from eighteen to twenty years of age, who, it was evident at a glance, were not brothers. One was short and fair and chubby, the other was lank and lean and cadaverous; one was sorrowful and lugubrious in countenance; the other seemed to be spending his time in trying hard not to smile, and not succeeding. The only thing they did appear to share in common was hard work, and in this they were so fully engrossed that Horace had to stand a full minute at the table before they had leisure to look up and notice him.

"The gentleman in there," said Horace, addressing the lugubrious youth as being the more imposing of the two, "said if I came to you you could set me to work."

The sad one gave a sort of groan and said,—

"Ah, he was right there. It *is* work."

"I say," said the other youth, looking up, "don't frighten the kid, Booms; you'll make him run away."

"I wish *I* could run away," said Booms, in an audible soliloquy.

"So you can if you like, you old crocodile. I say, young 'un, have you got a chair?"

Horace had to confess he had not a chair about him.

"That's a go; we've only two here. We shall have to take turns on them. Booms will stand first, won't you, Booms?"

"Oh, of course," said Booms, rising and pushing his chair towards Horace.

"Thanks," said Horace, "but I'd sooner stand, really."

"No, no," said Booms, resignedly; "I'm to stand, Waterford says so."

"Sit down, young 'un," said Waterford, "and don't mind him. He won't say so, but he's awfully glad to stand up for a bit and stretch his legs. Now, do you see this lot of morning papers—you'll see a lot of paragraphs marked at the side with a blue pencil. You've got to cut them out. Mind you don't miss any. Sure you understand?"

Horace expressed himself equal to this enormous task, and set to work busily with his scissors.

If he had had no one but himself to consider he would have felt comparatively happy. He found himself in a department of work which he liked, and which, though at first not very exciting, promised some day to become interesting. His chief was a gentleman not likely to interfere with him as long as he did his work steadily, and his companions were not only friendly but entertaining. If only Reginald could have a seat at this table too, Horace felt he could face the future cheerily. How, he wondered, was the poor fellow getting on that moment in his distant uncongenial work?

"You're not obliged to read all the paragraphs, you know," said Waterford, as Horace's hand slackened amid these musings. "It's a close shave to get done as it is, and he's marked a frightful lot this morning."

He was right. All the cuttings had to be taken out and pasted on sheets before twelve o'clock, and it took the three of them, hard at work with scissors and paste, to get the task accomplished. They talked very little, and joked still less; but when it was all done, like three honest men, they felt pleased with themselves, and decidedly amiable towards one another.

"Now Booms is going out for the grub, aren't you, Booms? He'll get some for you too, young 'un, if you like."

"No, thanks; I'd be very glad, but I promised to have dinner with my brother—he's a compositor here."

"Lucky man!" groaned Booms. "Think of having nothing to do but pick up types instead of slaving like this every day!"

"See the sausages are hot this time, won't you, Booms? And look alive, there's a dear fellow."

Booms retired sadly.

"Good-natured chap, Booms," said Waterford; "rather a risk of imposing on him if one isn't careful. He's an awfully decent fellow, but it's a sad pity he's such a masher."

"A what?" asked Horace.

"A masher. He mayn't look it, but he goes it rather strong in that line after hours. He doesn't mean it, poor soul; but he's mixed up with some of our reporters, and tries to go the pace with them. I don't care for that sort of thing myself, but if you do, he's just your man. You wouldn't think it to look at him, would you?"

"Certainly not," replied Horace, much impressed by this confidence and the revelation it afforded.

As Booms re-entered shortly afterwards, looking very gloomy, burdened with two plates, two mugs, and a sheaf of knives and forks under his arm, he certainly did not give one the impression of a very rakish character, and Horace could scarcely refrain from smiling as he tried to picture him in his after-hours character.

He left the couple to their sausages, and went out, in the vain hope of finding Reginald somewhere. But there was no sign of workmen anywhere, and, to his disgust, he ascertained from a passing boy that the compositors' dinner-hour did not begin till he was due back at his work. Everything seemed to conspire to sever the two brothers, and Horace dejectedly took a solitary and frugal repast. He determined, at all hazards, to wait a minute after the bell summoning him back to work had ceased pealing, and was rewarded by a hasty glimpse of his brother, and the exchange of a few hurried sentences. It was better than nothing, and he rushed back to his room just in time to save his reputation for punctuality.

The afternoon passed scarcely less busily than the morning. They sat— and Booms had contrived to raise a third chair somewhere—with a pile of work in front of them which at first seemed hopeless to expect to overtake.

There were effusions to "decline with thanks," and others to enter in a book and send up to the composing-room; there were some letters to write and others to answer; there were reporters' notes to string together and telegrams to transcribe. And all the while a dropping fire of proofs and revises and messages was kept up at them from without, which they had to carry to their chief and deal with according to his orders.

Horace, being inexperienced, was only able to take up the simpler portions of this miscellaneous work, but these kept him busy, "hammer and tongs," with scarcely time to sneeze till well on in the afternoon.

The *Rocket*, unlike most evening papers, waited till the evening before it appeared, and did not go to press till five o'clock. After that it issued later editions once an hour till eight o'clock, and on special occasions even as late as ten.

The great rush of the day, therefore, as Horace soon discovered, was over at five o'clock, but between that hour and seven there was always plenty to do in connection with the late editions and the following day's work. At seven o'clock every one left except a sub-editor and one of the clerks, and one or two compositors, to see after the eight o'clock and any possible later edition.

"As soon as you get your hand in, young 'un, you'll have to take your turn at late work. Booms and I take every other night now."

Horace could say nothing against this arrangement, though it meant more separation from Reginald. At present, however, his hand not being in, he had nothing to keep him after the seven o'clock bell, and he eagerly escaped at its first sound to look for Reginald.

Not, however, till he had witnessed a strange sight.

About a quarter to seven Booms, whose early evening it was, showed signs of uneasiness. He glanced sorrowfully once or twice at the clock, then at Horace, then at Waterford. Then he got up and put his papers away. Finally he mused on a washhand basin in a corner of the room, and said dolefully,—

"I must dress, I think, Waterford."

"All serene," said Waterford, briskly, "the young 'un and I will finish up here." Then nudging Horace, he added in a whisper, "He's going to rig up now. Don't pretend to notice him, that's all."

Booms proceeded to divest himself of his office coat and waistcoat and collar, and to roll up the sleeves of his flannel shirt, preparatory to an energetic wash. He then opened a small box in a corner of the room, from which he produced, first a clothes-brush, with which he carefully removed all traces of dust from his nether garments; after that came a pair of light-coloured "pats," which he fitted on to his boots; then came a bottle of hair-oil, and afterwards a highly-starched "dicky," or shirt-front, with a stud in it, which by a complicated series of strings the owner contrived to fasten round his neck so as to conceal effectually the flannel shirt-front underneath.

Once more he dived, and this time the magic box yielded up what seemed to Horace's uninitiated eyes to be a broad strip of stiff cardboard, but which turned out to be a collar of fearful and wonderful proportions, which, when once adjusted, fully explained the wisdom displayed by the wearer in not deferring the brushing of his trousers and the donning of his "pats" to a later stage of the proceedings. For nothing, not even a pickpocket at his gilt watch-chain with its pendant "charms," could lower his chin a quarter of an inch till bed-time. But more was yet to come. There were cuffs to put on, which left one to guess what had become of Mr Booms's knuckles, and a light jaunty necktie to embellish the "dicky." Then, with a plaintive sigh, he produced a blue figured waistcoat, and after it a coat shaped like the coat of a robin to cover all. Finally there appeared a hat, broad-brimmed, low-crowned, and dazzling in its glossiness, a pair of gay dogskin gloves, a crutch walking-stick, a pink silk handkerchief, and then this joint work of art and nature was complete!

"All right?" said he, in melancholy tones, as he set his hat a little on one side of his head, and, with his stick under his arm, began with his gloves.

Waterford got up and walked slowly and critically round him, giving a few touches here and there, and brushing a little stray dust from his collar.

"All right, dear boy. Mind how you go, and—"

"Oh!" groaned Booms, in tones of dire distress, "I knew I should forget something. Would you mind, Waterford?"

"What is it?"

"My glass—it's in the box, and—and I should have got it out before I put the collar on. Thanks; I should have been lost without it. Oh! if I *had* forgotten it!"

With this awful reflection in his mind he bade a sorrowful good-night and walked off, with his head very erect, his elbows high up, and one hand fondling the nearly-neglected eyeglass.

"Pretty, isn't it?" said Waterford, as he disappeared.

"It is—rot," said Horace, emphatically. "Why ever don't you laugh him out of it?"

"My dear boy, you might as well try to laugh the hair off his head. I've tried it a dozen times. After all, the poor dear fellow means no harm."

"But what does he do now?"

"Oh, don't ask me. According to his own account he's the fastest man about town—goes to all the shows, hobnobs with all the swells, smokes furious cigars, and generally 'mashes.' But my private notion is he moons about the streets with the handle of his stick in his mouth and looks in a few shop windows, and gets half a dozen oysters for supper, and then goes home to bed. You see he couldn't well get into much mischief with that collar on. If he went in for turn-downs I'd be afraid of him."

The bell cut further conversation short, and in another minute Horace and Reginald were walking arm-in-arm in the street outside.

There was much to talk about, much to lament over, and a little to rejoice over. Horace felt half guilty as he told his brother of his good fortune, and the easy quarters into which he had fallen. But Reginald was in too defiant a mood to share these regrets as much as he would have done at any other time. As long as Durfy wanted to get rid of him, so long was he determined to stay where he was, and meanwhile in young Gedge he had some one to look after, which would make the drudgery of his daily work tolerable.

Horace did not altogether like it, but he knew it was no use arguing then on the subject. They mutually agreed to put the best face on everything before their mother. She was there to meet them at the door, and it rejoiced her heart to hear their brave talk and the cheery story of their day's adventures. All day long her heart had gone out to them in yearnings of prayer and hope and love, and it repaid her a hundred-fold, this hour of happy meeting, with the sunlight of their faces and the music of their voices filling her soul.

As soon as supper was over Reginald suggested a precipitate retreat into the streets, for fear of another neighbourly incursion. Mrs Cruden laughingly yielded, and the trio had a long walk, heedless where they went, so long as they were together. They wandered as far as Oxford Street, looking into what shops were open, and interested still more in the ever-changing stream of people who even at ten o'clock at night crowded the pavements. They met no one they knew, not even Booms. But it mattered little to them that no one noticed them. They had one another, and there was a sense of security and comfort in that which before these last few weeks they had never dreamed of.

They were about to turn out of Oxford Street on their homeward journey when a loud shout close by arrested their attention. Looking round, they saw a boy with disordered dress and unsteady gait attempting to cross the road just as a hansom cab was bearing down at full speed on the place where he stood. They only saw his back, but it was evident he was either ill or dazed, for he stood stupidly where he was, with the peril in full-view, but somehow helpless to avoid it. The cabman shouted and pulled at his horse's head. But to the horrified onlookers it was only too clear that nothing could stop his career in time. He was already within a yard or two of the luckless boy when Reginald made a sudden dash into the road, charging at him with a violence that sent him staggering forward two paces and then brought him to the earth. Reginald fell too, on the top of him, and as the cab dashed past it just grazed the sole of his boot where he lay.

It was all the work of a moment—the shout, the vision of the boy, and the rescue—so sudden, indeed, that Mrs Cruden had barely time to clutch Horace by the arm before Reginald lay prone in the middle of the road. In another moment Horace was beside his brother, helping him up out of the mud.

"Are you hurt, old man?"

"Not a bit," said Reginald, very pale and breathless, but rising to his feet without help. "Look out—there's a crowd—take mother home, and I'll come on as soon as I've seen this fellow safe. I'm not damaged a bit."

With this assurance Horace darted back to his mother in time to extricate her from the crowd which, whatever happens, is sure to collect in the streets of London at a minute's warning.

"He's all right," said Horace—"not hurt a bit. Come on, mother, out of this; he'll probably catch us up before we're home. I say," said he, and his voice trembled with excitement and brotherly pride as he spoke, "wasn't it splendid?"

Mrs Cruden would fain have stayed near, but the crowd made it impossible to be of any use. So she let Horace lead her home, trembling, but with a heart full of thankfulness and pride and love for her young hero.

Reginald, meanwhile, with the coolness of an old football captain, proceeded to pick up his man, and appealed to the crowd to stand back and give the fellow room.

The boy lay half-stunned with his fall, his face covered with mud, but to Reginald's delight he was able to move and with a little help stand on his feet. As he did so the light from the lamp of the cab fell on his face, and caused Reginald to utter an exclamation of surprise and horror.

"Young Gedge!"

The boy looked at him for a moment in a stupid bewildered way, and then gave a short startled cry.

"Are you hurt?" said Reginald, putting his arm round him.

"No—I—I don't think—let's get away."

Reginald called to the crowd to stand back and let them out, an order which the crowd obeyed surlily and with a disappointed grunt. Not even a broken leg! not even the cabman's number taken down! One or two who had seen the accident patted Reginald on the back as he went by, but he hurried past them as quickly as he could, and presently stood in the seclusion of a by-street, still supporting his companion on his arm.

"Are you hurt?" he inquired again.

"No," said Gedge; "I can walk."

The two stood facing one another for a moment in silence, breathless still, and trembling with the excitement of the last few minutes.

"Oh, Cruden!" cried the boy at last, seizing Reginald's arm, "what will you think of me? I was—I—I'd been drinking—I'm sober now, but—"

Reginald cut him short gently but firmly.

"I know," said he. "You'd better go home now, young 'un."

Gedge made no answer, but walked on, with his arm still in that of his protector.

Reginald saw him into an omnibus, and then returned sadly and thoughtfully homeward.

"Humph!" said he to himself, as he reached Dull Street, "I suppose I shall have to stick on at the *Rocket* after all."

Chapter Eight
Mr Durfy gives Reginald a Testimonial

Reginald Cruden was a young man who took life hard and seriously. He was not brilliant—indeed, he was not clever. He lacked both the good sense and the good-humour which would have enabled him, like Horace, to accept and make the best of his present lot. He felt aggrieved by the family calamity, and just enough ashamed of his poverty to make him touchy and intractable to a degree which, as we have seen already, amounted sometimes almost to stupidity.

Still Reginald was honest. He made no pretence of enjoying life when he did not enjoy it. He disliked Mr Durfy, and therefore he flared up if Mr Durfy so much as looked at him. He liked young Gedge, and therefore it was impossible to leave the youngster to his fate and let him ruin himself without an effort at rescue.

It is one thing to snatch a heedless one from under the hoofs of a cab-horse and another to pick him up from the slippery path of vice and set him firmly on his feet. Reginald had thought nothing of the one, but he looked forward with considerable trepidation to meeting the boy next morning and attempting the other.

Gedge was there when he arrived, working very busily, and looking rather troubled. He flushed up as Reginald approached, and put down his composing-stick to shake hands with him. Reginald looked and felt by a long way the more uncomfortable and guilty of the two, and he was at least thankful that Gedge spared him the trouble of beginning.

"Oh! Cruden," said the boy, "I know exactly what you're going to say. You're going to tell me you're deceived in me, and that I'm a young fool and going to the dogs as hard as I can. I don't wonder you think so."

"I wasn't going to say that," said Reginald. "I was going to ask you how you were."

"Oh, I'm all right; but I know you're going to lecture me, Cruden, and I'm sure you may. There's nothing you can say I don't deserve. I only wish I could make you believe I'll never be such a fool again. I've been making resolutions all night, and now you've come here I'm sure I shall be able to break it off. If you will only stand by me, Cruden! I owe you such a lot. If you only knew how grateful I was!"

"Perhaps we'd better not talk about it now," said Reginald, feeling very uncomfortable and rather disconcerted at this glib flow of penitence.

But young Gedge was full of it yet, and went on,—

"I'm going to turn over a new leaf this very day, Cruden. I've told the errand-boy he's not to get me any beer, and I'm determined next time that beast Durfy asks me to go—"

"What!" exclaimed Reginald; "was it with him you used to go?"

"Yes. I know you'll think all the worse of me for it, after the blackguard way he's got on to you. You see, before you came I didn't like—that is, I couldn't well refuse him; he'd have made it so hot for me here. I fancy he found out I had some pocket-money of my own, for he generally picked on me to come and have drinks with him, and of course I had to pay. Why, only last night—look out, here he comes!"

Sure enough he was, and in his usual amiable frame of mind.

"Oh, there you are, are you?" he said to Reginald, with a sneer. "Do you know where the lower-case 'x' is now, eh?"

Reginald, swelling with the indignation Gedge's story had roused in him, turned his back and made no answer.

Nothing, as he might have known by this time, could have irritated Mr Durfy more.

"Look here, young gentleman," said the latter, coming close up to Reginald's side and hissing the words very disagreeably in his ear, "when I ask a question in this shop I expect to get an answer; mind that. And what's more, I'll have one, or you leave this place in five minutes. Come, now, give me a lower-case 'x.'"

Reginald hesitated a moment. Suppose Mr Durfy had it in him to be as good as his word. What then about young Gedge?

He picked up an "x" sullenly, and tossed it at the overseer's feet.

"That's not giving it to me," said the latter, with a sneer of triumph already on his face. "Pick it up directly, do you hear? and give it to me."

Reginald stood and glared first at Mr Durfy, then at the type.

Yesterday he would have defiantly told him to pick it up himself, caring little what the cost might be. But things had changed since then. Humiliating as it was to own it, he could not afford to be turned off. His pride could not afford it, his care for young Gedge could not afford it, the slender family purse could not afford it. Why ever did he not think of it all before, and spare himself this double indignity?

With a groan which represented as much inward misery and humiliation as could well be compressed into a single action, he stooped down and picked up the type and handed it to Mr Durfy.

It was well for him he did not raise his eyes to see the smile with which that gentleman received it.

"Next time it'll save you trouble to do what you're told at once, Mr Puppy," he said. "Get on with your work, and don't let me catch you idling your time any more."

And he walked off crowned with victory and as happy in his mind as if he had just heard of the decease of his enemy the manager.

It was a bad beginning to the day for Reginald. He had come to work that morning in a virtuous frame of mind, determined, if possible, to do his duty peaceably and to hold out a helping hand to young Gedge. It was hard enough now to think of anything but his own indignities and the wretch to whom he owed them.

He turned to his work almost viciously, and for an hour buried himself in it, without saying a word or lifting his eyes from his case. Then young Gedge, stealing a nervous glance at his face, ventured to say,—

"I say, Cruden, I wish I could stand things like you. I don't know what I should have done if that blackguard had treated me like that."

"What's the use?" said Reginald. "He wants to get rid of me, and I'm not going to let him."

"I'm jolly glad of it for my sake. I wish I could pay him out for you."

"So you can."

"How?"

"Next time he wants you to go and drink, say No," said Reginald.

"Upon my word I will," said Gedge; "and I don't care how hot he makes it for me, if you stick by me, Cruden."

"You know I'll stick by you, young 'un," said Reginald; "but that won't do you much good, unless you stick by yourself. Suppose Durfy managed to get rid of me after all—"

"Then I should go to—to the dogs," said Gedge, emphatically.

"You're a greater fool than I took you for, then," said Reginald. "If you only knew," he added more gently, "what a job it is to do what's right myself, and how often I don't do it, you'd see it's no use expecting me to be good for you and myself both."

"What on earth am I to do, then? I'm certain I can't keep square myself; I never could. Who's to look after me if you don't?"

Like a brave man, Reginald, shy and reserved as he was, told him.

I need not repeat what was said that morning over the type cases. It was not a sermon, nor a catechism; only a few stammering laboured words spoken by a boy who felt himself half a hypocrite as he said them, and who yet, for the affection he bore his friend, had the courage to go through with a task which cost him twenty times the effort of rescuing the boy yesterday from his bodily peril.

Little good, you will say, such a sermon from such a perverse, bad-humoured preacher as Reginald Cruden, could do! Very likely, reader; but, after all, who are you or I to say so? Had any one told Reginald a week ago what would be taking place to-day, he would have coloured up indignantly and hoped he was not quite such a prig as all that. As it was, when it was all over, it was with no self-satisfied smile or inward gratulation that he returned to his work, but rather with the nervous uncomfortable misgivings of one who says to himself, —

"After all I may have done more harm than good."

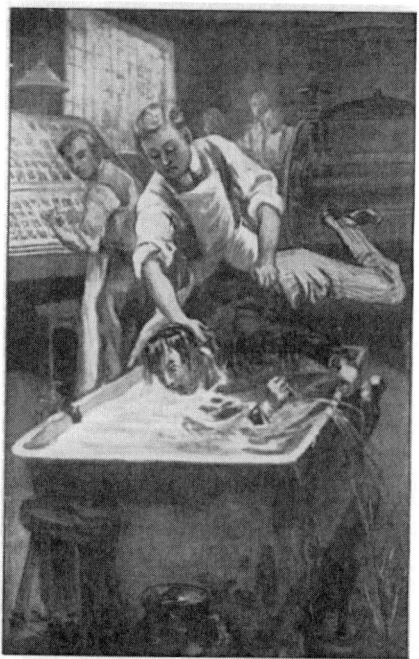

Carried him to the water tank and dipped his head therein three times.

By the end of a fortnight Reginald, greatly to Mr Durfy's dissatisfaction, was an accomplished compositor. He could set-up almost as quickly as Gedge, and his "proofs" showed far fewer corrections. Moreover, as he was punctual in his hours, and diligent at his work, it was extremely difficult for the overseer or any one else to find any pretext for abusing him.

It is true, Mr Barber, who had not yet given up the idea of asserting his moral and intellectual superiority, continued by the ingenious device of "squabbling" his case, and tampering with the screw of his composing-stick, and other such pleasing jokes not unknown to printers, to disconcert the new beginner on one or two occasions. But ever since Reginald one morning, catching him in the act of mixing up his e's with his a's, had carried him by the collar of his coat and the belt of his breeches to the water tank and dipped his head therein three times with no interval for refreshment between, Mr Barber had moderated his attentions and become less exuberant in his humour.

With the exception of Gedge, now his fast ally, Reginald's other fellow-workmen concerned themselves very little with his proceedings. One or two, indeed, noticing his proficiency, hinted to him that he was a fool to work for the wages he was getting, and some went so far as to say he had no right to do so, and had better join the "chapel" to save trouble.

What the "chapel" was Reginald did not trouble even to inquire, and replied curtly that it was no business of any one else what his wages were.

"Wasn't it?" said the deputation. "What was to become of them if fellows did their work for half wages, they should like to know?"

"Are you going off, or must I make you?" demanded Reginald, feeling he had had enough of it.

And the deputation, remembering Barber's head and the water tank, withdrew, very much perplexed what to do to uphold the dignity of the "chapel."

They decided to keep their "eye" on him, and as they were able to do this at a distance, Reginald had no objection at all to their decision.

He meanwhile was keeping his eye on Gedge and Mr Durfy, and about a fortnight after his arrival at the *Rocket*, a passage of arms occurred which, slight as it was, had a serious influence on the future of all three parties concerned.

The seven o'clock bell had rung, and this being one of Horace's late evenings, Reginald proposed to Gedge to stroll home with him and call and see Mrs Cruden.

The boy accepted readily, and the two were starting off arm in arm when Mr Durfy confronted them. Reginald, who had never met his adversary beyond the precincts of the *Rocket* before, did not for a moment recognise the vulgar, loudly dressed little man, sucking his big cigar and wearing his pot hat ostentatiously on one side; but when he did he turned contemptuously aside and said,—

"Come on, young 'un."

"Come on, young 'un!" echoed Mr Durfy, taking his cigar from his mouth and flicking the ashes in Reginald's direction, "that's just what I was going to say. Young Gedge, you're coming with me to-night. I've got orders for the Alhambra, my boy, and supper afterwards."

"Thank you," said Gedge, rather uncomfortably, "it's very kind of you, Mr Durfy, but I've promised Cruden to go with him."

"Promised Cruden! What do you mean? Cruden'll keep till to-morrow; the orders won't."

"I'm afraid I can't," said Gedge.

"Afraid! I tell you I don't mean to stand here all night begging you. Just come along and no more nonsense. We'll have a night of it."

"You must excuse me," said the boy, torn between Reginald on the one hand and the fear of offending Durfy on the other.

The latter began to take in the position of affairs, and his temper evaporated accordingly.

"I won't excuse you; that's all about it," he said; "let go that snivelling lout's arm and do what you're told. Let the boy alone, do you hear?" added he, addressing Reginald, "and take yourself off. Come along, Gedge."

"Gedge is not going with you," said Reginald, keeping the boy's arm in his; "he's coming with me, aren't you, young 'un?"

The boy pressed his arm gratefully, but made no reply.

This was all Mr Durfy wanted to fill up the vials of his wrath.

"You miserable young hound you," said he, with an oath; "let go the boy this moment, or I'll turn you out of the place—and him too."

Reginald made no reply. His face was pale, but he kept the boy's arm still fast in his own.

"Going with you, indeed?" shouted Mr Durfy; "going with you, is he? to learn how to cant and sing psalms! Not if I know it—or if he does, you and he and your brother and your old fool of a mother—"

Reginald Cruden | 73

Mr Durfy never got to the end of that sentence. A blow straight from the shoulder of the Wilderham captain sent him sprawling on the pavement before the word was well out of his mouth.

It had come now. It had been bound to come sooner or later, and Reginald, as he drew the boy's arm once more under his own, felt almost a sense of relief as he stood and watched Mr Durfy slowly pick himself up and collect his scattered wardrobe.

It was some time before the operation was complete, and even then Mr Durfy's powers of speech had not returned. With a malignant scowl he stepped up to his enemy and hissed the one menace, —

"All right!" and then walked away.

Reginald waited till he had disappeared round the corner, and then, turning to his companion, took a long breath and said, —

"Come along, young 'un; it can't be helped."

The reader must forgive me if I ask him to leave the two lads to walk to Dull Street by themselves, while he accompanies me in the wake of the outraged and mud-stained Mr Durfy.

That gentleman was far more wounded in his mind than in his person. He may have been knocked down before in his life, but he had never, as far as he could recollect, been quite so summarily routed by a boy half his age earning only eighteen shillings a week! And the conviction that some people would think he had only got his deserts in what he had suffered, pained him very much indeed.

He did not go to the Alhambra. His clothes were too dirty, and his spirits were far too low. He did, in the thriftiness of his soul, attempt to sell his orders in the crowd at the theatre door. But no one rose to the bait, so he had to put them back in his pocket on the chance of being able to "doctor up" the date and crush in with them some other day. Then he mooned listlessly up and down the streets for an hour till his clothes were dry, and then turned into a public-house to get a brush down and while away another hour.

Still the vision of Reginald standing where he had last seen him with young Gedge at his side haunted him and spoiled his pleasure. He wandered forth again, feeling quite lonely, and wishing some one or something would turn up to comfort him. Nor was he disappointed.

"The very chap," said a voice suddenly at his side when he was beginning to despair of any diversion.

"So it is. How are you, my man? We were talking of you not two minutes ago."

Durfy pulled up and found himself confronted by two gentlemen, one about forty and the other a fashionable young man of twenty-five.

"How are you, Mr Medlock?" said he to the elder in as familiar a tone as he could assume; "glad to see you, sir. How are you, too, Mr Shanklin, pretty well?"

"Pretty fair," said Mr Shanklin. "Come and have a drink, Durfy. You look all in the blues. Gone in love, I suppose, eh? or been speculating on the Stock Exchange? You shouldn't, you know, a respectable man like you."

"He looks as if he'd been speculating in mud," said Mr Medlock, pointing to the unfortunate overseer's collar and hat, which still bore traces of his recent calamity. "Never mind; we'll wash it off in the Bodega. Come along."

Durfy felt rather shy at first in his grand company, especially with the consciousness of his muddy collar. But after about half an hour in the Bodega he recovered his self-possession, and felt himself at home.

"By the way," said Mr Medlock, filling up his visitor's glass, "last time we saw you you did us nicely over that tip for the Park Races, my boy! If Alf and I hadn't been hedged close up, we should have lost a pot of money."

"I'm very sorry," said Durfy. "You see, another telegram came after the one I showed you, that I never saw; that's how it happened. I really did my best for you."

"But it's a bad job, if we pay you to get hold of the *Rocket's* telegrams and then lose our money over it," said Mr Medlock. "Never mind this time, but you'd better look a little sharper, my boy. There's the Brummagem Cup next week, you know, and we shall want to know the latest scratches on the night before. It'll be worth a fiver to you if you work it well, Durfy. Fill up your glass."

Mr Durfy obeyed, glad enough to turn the conversation from the miscarriage of his last attempt to filch his employers' telegrams for the benefit of his betting friends' and his own pocket.

"By the way," said Mr Shanklin, presently, "Moses and I have got a little Company on hand just now, Durfy. What do you think of that?"

"A company?" said Mr Durfy; "I'll wager it's not a limited one, if you're at the bottom of it! What's your little game now?"

"It's a little idea of Alf's," said Mr Medlock, whose Christian name was Moses, "and it ought to come off too. This is something the way of it. Suppose you were a young greenhorn, Durfy—which I'm afraid you aren't—and saw an advertisement in the *Rocket* saying you could make two hundred and fifty pounds a year easy without interfering with your business, eh? what would you do?"

"If I was a greenhorn," said Durfy, "I'd answer the advertisement and enclose a stamped envelope for a reply."

"To be sure you would! And the reply would be, we'd like to have a look at you, and if you looked as green as we took you for, we'd ask for a deposit, and then allow you to sell wines and cigars and that sort of fancy goods to your friends. You'd sell a dozen of port at sixty shillings, do you see? half the cash down and half on delivery. We'd send your friend a dozen at twelve and six, and if he didn't shell out the other thirty bob on delivery, we'd still have the thirty bob he paid down to cover our loss. Do you twig?"

Durfy laughed. "Do you dream all these things," he said, "or how do you ever think of them?"

"Genius, my boy; genius," said Mr Medlock. "Of course," he added, "it couldn't run for long, but we might give it a turn for a month or two."

"The worst of it is," put in Mr Shanklin, "it's a ticklish sort of business that some people are uncommon sharp at smelling out; one has to be very careful. There's the advertisement, for instance. You'll have to smuggle it into the *Rocket*, my boy. It wouldn't do for the governors to see it; they'd be up to it. But they'd never see it after it was in, and the *Rocket's* just the paper for us."

"I'll try and manage that," said Durfy. "You give it me, and I'll stick it in with a batch of others somehow."

"Alf thinks we'd better do the thing from Liverpool," continued Mr Medlock, "and all we want is a good secretary—a nice, green, innocent, stupid, honest young fellow—that's what we want. If we could pick up one of that sort, there's no doubt of the thing working."

Mr Durfy started and coloured up, and then looked first at Mr Medlock and then at Mr Shanklin.

"What's the matter? Do you think *you'd* suit the place?" asked the former, with a laugh.

"No; but I know who will!"

"You do! Who?"

"A young puppy under me at the *Rocket*?" said Durfy, excitedly; "the very man to a T!" And he thereupon launched into a description of Reginald's character in a way which showed that not only was he a shrewd observer of human nature in his way, but, when it served his purpose, could see the good even in a man he hated.

"I tell you," said he, "he's born for you, if you can only get him! And if you don't think so after what I've said, perhaps you'll believe me when I tell you, on the quiet, he knocked me down in the gutter this very evening because I wanted to carry off a young convert of his to make a night of it at the Alhambra. There, what do you think of that? I wouldn't tell tales of myself like that for fun, I can tell you!"

"There's no mistake about that being the sort of chap we want," said Mr Medlock.

"If only we can get hold of him," said Mr Shanklin.

"Leave that to me," said Mr Durfy; "only if he comes to you never say a word about me, or he'll shy off."

Whereupon these three guileless friends finished their glasses and separated in great good spirits and mutual admiration.

Chapter Nine
Samuel Shuckleford comes of Age

Reginald, meanwhile, blissfully unconscious of the arrangements which were being made for him, spent as comfortable an evening as he could in the conviction that to-morrow would witness his dismissal from the *Rocket*, and see him a waif on the great ocean of London life. To his mother, and even to young Gedge, he said nothing of his misgivings, but to Horace, as the two lay awake that night, he made a clean breast of all.

"You'll call me a fool, I suppose," he said; "but how could I help it?"

"A fool! Why, Reg, I know I should have done the same. But for all that, it *is* unlucky."

"It is. Even eighteen shillings a week is better than nothing," said Reginald, with a groan. "Poor mother was saying only yesterday we were just paying for our keep, and nothing more. What will she do now?"

"Oh, you'll get into something, I'm certain," said Horace; "and meanwhile—"

"Meanwhile I'll do anything rather than live on you and mother, Horrors; I've made up my mind to that. Why," continued he, "you wouldn't believe what a sneak I've been already. You know what Bland said about the football club in his letter? No, I didn't show it to you. He said it would go down awfully well if I sent the fellows my usual subscription. I couldn't bear not to do it after that, and I—I sold my tennis-bat for five shillings, and took another five shillings out of my last two weeks' wages, and sent them half a sov. the other day."

Horace gave an involuntary whistle of dismay, but added, quickly,—

"I hope the fellows will be grateful for it, old man; they ought to be. Never mind, I'm certain we shall pull through it some day. We must hope for the best, anyhow."

And with a brotherly grip of the hand they turned over and went to sleep.

Reginald presented himself at the *Rocket* next morning in an unusual state of trepidation. He had half made up his mind to march straight to the manager's room and tell him boldly what had happened, and take his discharge from him. But Horace dissuaded him.

"After all," he said, "Durfy may think better of it."

"Upon my word I hardly know whether I want him to," said Reginald, "except for young Gedge's sake and mother's. Anyhow, I'll wait and see, if you like."

Mr Durfy was there when he arrived, bearing no traces of last night's *fracas*, except a scowl and a sneer, which deepened as he caught sight of his adversary. Reginald passed close to his table, in order to give him an opportunity of coming to the point at once; but to his surprise the overseer took no apparent notice of him, and allowed him to go to his place and begin work as usual.

"I'd sooner see him tearing his hair than grinning like that," said young Gedge, in a whisper. "You may be sure there's something in the wind."

Whatever it was, Mr Durfy kept his own counsel, and though Reginald looked up now and then and caught him scowling viciously in his direction, he made no attempt at hostilities, and rather appeared to ignore him altogether.

Even when he was giving out the "copy" he sent Reginald his by a boy, instead of, as was usually his practice, calling him up to the table to receive it. Reginald's copy on this occasion consisted of a number of advertisements, a class of work not nearly as easy and far less interesting than the paragraphs of news which generally fell to his share. However, he attacked them boldly, and, unattractive as they were, contrived to get some occupation from them for his mind as well as his hand.

Here, for instance, was some one who wanted "a groom, young, good-looking, and used to horses." How would that suit him? And why need he be good-looking? And what was the use of saying he must be used to horses? Who ever heard of a groom that wasn't? The man who put in that advertisement was a muff. Here was another of a different sort:

"J.S. Come back to your afflicted mother and all shall be forgiven."

Heigho! suppose "J.S." had got a mother like Mrs Cruden, what a brute he must be to cut away. What had he been doing to her? robbing her? or bullying her? or what? Reginald worked himself into a state of wrath over the prodigal, and very nearly persuaded himself to leave out the promise of forgiveness altogether.

"If the young gentleman who dropped an envelope in the Putney omnibus on the evening of the 6th instant will apply to B, at 16, Grip Street, he may hear of something to his advantage."

How some people were born to luck! Think of making your fortune by dropping an envelope in a Putney omnibus. How gladly he would pave the floor of every omnibus he rode in with envelopes if only he could thereby hear anything to his advantage! He had a great mind to stroll round by Number 16, Grip Street that evening to see who this mysterious "B" could be.

"To intelligent young men in business.—Add £50 a year to your income without any risk or hindrance whatever to ordinary work.—Apply confidentially to Omega, 13, Shy Street, Liverpool, with stamp for reply. None but respectable intelligent young men need apply."

Hullo! Reginald laid down his composing-stick and read the advertisement over again: and after that he read it again, word by word, most carefully. £50 a year! Why, that was as much again as his present income, and without risk or interfering with his present work too! Well, his present work might be his past work to-morrow; but even so, with £50 a year he would be no worse off, and of course he could get something else to do as well by way of ordinary work. If only he could bring in £100 a year to the meagre family store! What little luxuries might it not procure for his mother! What a difference it might make in that dreary, poky Dull Street parlour, where she sat all day! Or if they decided not to spend it, but save it up, think of a pound a week ready against a rainy day! Reginald used to have loose enough ideas of the value of money; but the last few weeks had taught him lessons, and one of them was that a pound a week could work wonders.

"Apply confidentially." Yes, of course, or else any duffer might snatch at the prize. It was considerate, too, to put it that way, for of course it would be awkward for any one in a situation to apply unless he could do it confidentially—and quite right too to enclose a stamp for a reply. No one who wasn't in earnest would do so, and thus it would keep out fellows who applied out of mere idle curiosity. "None but respectable intelligent young men need apply." Humph! Reginald's conscience told him he was respectable, and he hoped he was also moderately intelligent, though opinions might differ on that point. "Omega"—that sounded well! The man knew Greek—possibly he was a classical scholar, and therefore sure to be a gentleman. Oh, what a contrast to the cad Durfy! "Liverpool." Ah, there was the one drawback; and yet of course it did not follow the £50 a year was to be earned in Liverpool, otherwise how could it fail to interfere with ordinary business? Besides, why should he advertise in the *Rocket* unless he meant to get applications from Londoners?

Altogether Reginald was pleased with the advertisement. He liked the way it was put, and the conditions it imposed, and, indeed, was so much taken up with the study of it that he almost forgot to set it up in type.

"Whatever are you dreaming about?" said young Gedge. "You've stood like that for a quarter of an hour at least. You'll have Durfy after you if you don't mind."

The name startled Reginald into industry, and he set the advertisement up very clearly and carefully, and re-read it once or twice in the type before he could make up his mind to go on to the next.

The thought of it haunted him all day. Should he tell Horace, or Gedge, or his mother of it? Should he go and give Durfy notice then and there? No, he would reply to it before he told any one; and then, if the answer *was* unsatisfactory—which he could not think possible—then no one would be the wiser or the worse for it.

The day flew on leaden wings. Gedge put his friend's silence down to anxiety as to the consequences of yesterday's adventure and did and said what he could to express his sympathy. Mr Durfy alone, sitting at his table, and directing sharp glances every now and then in his direction, could guess the real meaning of his pre-occupation, and chuckled to himself as he saw it.

Reginald spent threepence on his way home that evening—one in procuring a copy of the *Rocket*, and two on a couple of postage-stamps. Armed with these he walked rapidly home with Horace, giving him in an absent sort of way a chronicle of the day's doings, but breathing not a word to him or his mother subsequently about the advertisement.

After supper he excused himself from joining in the usual walk by saying he had a letter to write, and for the first time in his life felt relieved to see his mother and brother go and leave him behind them.

Then he pulled out the newspaper and eagerly read the advertisement once more in print. There it was, not a bit changed! Lots of fellows had seen it by this time, and some of them very likely were at this moment answering it. They shouldn't get the start of him, though!

He sat down and wrote—

"Sir,—Having seen your advertisement in the *Rocket*, I beg to apply for particulars. I am respectable and fairly intelligent, and am at present employed as compositor in the *Rocket* newspaper-office. I shall be glad to increase my income. I am 18 years of age, and beg to enclose stamp for a reply to this address.

"Yours truly,—

"Reginald Cruden."

He was not altogether pleased with this letter, but it would have to do. If he had had any idea what the advertiser wanted intelligent young men for, he might have been able to state his qualifications better. But what was the use of saying "I think I shall suit you," when possibly he might not suit after all?

He addressed the letter carefully, and wrote "private and confidential" on the envelope; and then walked out to post it, just in time, after doing so, to meet his mother and Horace returning from their excursion.

"Well, Reg, have you written your letter?" said his mother, cheerily. "Was it to some old schoolfellow?"

"No, mother," said Reginald, in a tone which meant, "I would rather you did not ask me." And Mrs Cruden did not ask.

"I think," said she, as they stopped at their door—"I almost think, boys, we ought to return the Shucklefords' call. It's only nine o'clock. We might go in for a few minutes. I know you don't care about it; but we must not be rude, you know. What do you think, Reg?"

Reg sighed and groaned and said, "If we must we must"; and so, instead of going in at their own door, they knocked at the next.

The tinkle of a piano upstairs, and the sound of Sam's voice, audible even in the street, announced only too unmistakably that the family was at home, and a collection of pot hats and shawls in the hall betrayed the appalling fact, when it was *too* late to retreat, that the Shucklefords had visitors! Mrs Shuckleford came out and received them with open arms.

"'Ow 'appy I am to see you and the boys," said she. "I suppose you saw the extra lights and came in. Very neighbourly it was. We thought about sending you an invite, but didn't like while you was in black for your 'usband. But it's all the same now you're here. Very 'appy to see you. Jemima, my dear, come and tell Mrs Cruden and the boys you're 'appy to see them; Sam too—it's Sam's majority, Mrs Cruden; twenty-one he is to-day, and his pa all over—oh, 'ow 'appy I am you've come."

"We had no idea you had friends," said Mrs Cruden, nervously. "We'll call again, please."

"No you don't, Mrs Cruden," said the effusive Mrs Shuckleford; "'ere you are, and 'ere you stays—I am so 'appy to see you. You and I can 'ave a cosy chat in the corner while the young folk enjoy theirselves. Jemima, put a chair for Mrs C. alongside o' mine; and, Sam, take the boys and see they have some one to talk to 'em."

The dutiful Sam, who appeared entirely to share his mother's jubilation at the arrival of these new visitors, obeyed the order with alacrity.

"Come on, young fellows," said he; "just in time for shouting proverbs. You go and sit down by Miss Tomkins, Horace, her in the green frock; and you had better go next Jemima, Cruden. When I say 'three and away' you've got to shout. Anything'll do, so long as you make a noise."

"No, they must shout their right word," said Miss Tomkins, a vivacious-looking young person of thirty.

"Come close," said she to Horace, "and I'll whisper what you've got to shout. Whisper, 'Dog,' that's your word."

Horace seated himself dreamily where he was told, and received the confidential communication of his partner with pathetic resignation. He only wished the signal to shout might soon arrive. As for Reginald, when he felt himself once more in the clutches of the captivating Jemima, and heard her whisper in his ear the mysterious monosyllable "love," his heart became as ice within him, and he sat like a statue in his chair, looking straight before him. Oh, how he hoped "Omega" would give him some occupation for his evenings that would save him from this sort of thing!

"Now call them in," said Sam.

A signal was accordingly given at the door, and in marched a young lady, really a pleasant, sensible-looking young person, accompanied by a magnificently-attired young gentleman, who, to Horace's amazement, proved to be no other than the melancholy Booms.

There was, however, no time just now for an exchange of greetings.

Mr Booms and his partner were placed standing in the middle of the floor, and the rest of the company were seated in a crescent round them. There was a pause, and you might have heard a pin drop as Samuel slowly lifted his hand and said in a stage whisper,—

"Now then, mind what you're at. When I say 'away.' One, two, three, and a—"

At the last syllable there arose a sudden and terrific shout which sent Mrs Cruden nearly into a fit, and made the loosely-hung windows rattle as if an infernal machine had just exploded on the premises.

The shout was immediately followed by a loud chorus of laughter, and cries of, —

"Well, have you guessed it?"

"Yes, I know what it is," said the pleasant young lady. "Do you know, Mr Booms?"

"No," he said, sadly; "how could I guess? What is it, Miss Crisp?"

"Why, 'Love me, *love* my dog,' isn't it?"

"Right. Well guessed!" cried every one; and amid the general felicitation that ensued the successful proverb-guessers were made room for in the magic circle, and Horace had a chance of exchanging "How d'ye do?" with Mr Booms.

"Who'd have thought of meeting you here?" said he, in a whisper.

"I didn't expect to meet you," said the melancholy one. "I say, Cruden, please don't mention — *her*."

"Her? Whom?" said Horace, bewildered.

Booms's reply was a mournful inclination of the head in the direction of Miss Crisp.

"Oh, I see. All right, old man. You're a lucky fellow, I think. She looks a jolly sort of girl."

"Lucky! Jolly! Oh, Cruden," ejaculated his depressed friend.

"Why, what's wrong?" said Horace. "Don't you think she's nice?"

"She is; but Shuckleford, Cruden, is not."

"Hullo, you two," said the voice of the gentleman in question at this moment; "you seem jolly thick. Oh, of course, shopmates; I forgot; both in the news line. Eh? Now, who's for musical chairs? Don't all speak at once."

"I shall have to play the piano now, Mr Reginald," said Miss Jemima, making a last effort to get a word out of her silent companion. "I'm afraid you're not enjoying yourself a bit."

Reginald rose instinctively as she did, and offered her his arm. He was half dreaming as he did so, and fancying himself back at Garden Vale. It was to his credit that when he discovered what he was doing he did not withdraw his arm, but conducted his partner gallantly to the piano, and said, —

"I'm afraid I'm a bad hand at games."

"Musical chairs is great fun," said Miss Jemima. "I wish I could play it and the piano both. You have to run round and round, and then, when the music stops, you flop down on the nearest chair, and there's always one left out, and the last one wins the game. Do try it."

Reginald gave a scared glance at the chairs being arranged back to back in a long line down the room, and said,—

"May I play the piano instead? and then you can join in the game."

"What! do *you* play the piano?" exclaimed the young lady, forgetting her dignity and clapping her hands. "Oh, my eye, what a novelty! Ma, Mr Reginald's going to play for musical chairs! Sam, do you hear? Mr Cruden plays the piano! Isn't it fun?"

Reginald flung himself with a sigh down on the cracked music-stool. Music was his one passion, and the last few months had been bitter to him for want of it. He would go out of his way even to hear a street piano, and the brightest moments of his Sundays were often those spent within sound of the roll of the organ.

It was like a snatch of the old life to find his fingers once more laid caressingly on the notes of a piano; and as he touched them and began to play, the Shucklefords, the *Rocket*, "Omega," all faded from his thoughts, and he was lost in his music.

What a piano it was! Tinny and cracked and out of tune. The music was in the boy's soul, and it mattered comparatively little. He began with Weber's "last waltz," and dreamed off from it into a gavotte of Corelli's, and from that into something else, calling up favourite after favourite to suit the passing moods of his spirit, and feeling happier than he had felt for months.

But Weber's "last waltz" and Corelli's gavottes are not the music one would naturally select for musical chairs; and when the strains continue uninterrupted for five or ten-minutes, during the whole of which time the company is perambulating round and round an array of empty chairs, the effect is somewhat monotonous. Mrs Shuckleford's guests trotted round good-humouredly for some time, then they got a little tired, then a little impatient, and finally Samuel, as he passed close behind the music-stool, gave the performer a dig in the back, which had the desired effect of stopping the music suddenly. Whereupon everybody flopped down on the seat nearest within reach. Some found vacancies at once, others had to scamper frantically round in search of them, and finally, as the chairs were one fewer in number than the company, one luckless player was left out to enjoy the fun of those who remained in.

"All right," said Samuel, when the first round was decided, and a chair withdrawn in anticipation of the next; "I only nudged you to stop a bit sooner, Cruden. The game will last till midnight if you give us such long doses."

Doses! Reginald turned again to the piano and tried once more to lose himself in its comforting music. He played a short German air of only four lines, which ended in a plaintive, wailing cadence. Again the moment the music ceased he heard the scuffling and scampering and laughter behind him, and shouts of,—

"Polly's out! Polly's out!"

"I say," said Shuckleford, as they stood ready for the next round, "give us a jingle, Cruden; 'Pop goes the Weasel,' or something of that sort. That last was like the tune the cow died of. And stop short in the middle of a line, anyhow."

Reginald rose from the piano with flushed cheeks, and said,—"I'm afraid I'm not used to this sort of music. Perhaps Miss Shuckleford—"

"Yes, Jim, you play. You know the way. You change places with Jim, Cruden, and come and run round."

But Reginald declined the invitation with thanks, and took up a comic paper, in which he attempted to bury himself, while Miss Shuckleford hammered out the latest polka on the piano, stopping abruptly and frequently enough to finish half a dozen rounds in the time it had taken him to dispose of two.

Fresh games followed, and to all except the Crudens the evening passed merrily and happily. Even Horace felt the infection of the prevalent good-humour, and threw off the reserve he had at first been tempted to wear in an effort to make himself generally agreeable. Mrs Cruden, cooped up in a corner with her loquacious hostess, did her best too not to be a damper on the general festivity. But Reginald made no effort to be other than he felt himself. He could not have done it if he had tried. But as scarcely any one seemed afflicted on his account, even his unsociability failed to make Samuel Shuckleford's majority party anything but a brilliant success.

In due time supper appeared to crown the evening's delights. And after supper a gentleman got up and proposed a toast, which of course was the health of the hero of the occasion.

Samuel replied in a facetious County Court address, in which he expressed himself "jolly pleased to see so many friends around him, and hoping they'd all enjoyed their evening, and that if there were any of them still to come of age—(laughter)—they'd have as high an old time of it as he had had to-night. He was sure ma and Jim said ditto to all he said. And before he sat down he was very glad to see their new next-door neighbours. (Hear, hear.) They'd had their troubles, but they could reckon on friends in that room. The young fellows were bound to get on if they stuck to their shop, and he'd like to drink the health of them and their ma." (Cheers.)

The health was drunk. Mrs Cruden looked at Reginald, Horace looked at Reginald, but Reginald looked straight before him and bit his lips and breathed hard. Whereupon Horace rose and said,—

"We think it very kind of you to drink our healths; and I am sure we are much obliged to you all for doing so."

Which said, the Shucklefords' party broke up, and the Crudens went home.

Chapter Ten
"Will you walk into my Parlour?"
said the Spider to the Fly

The two days which followed the despatch of the letter to "Omega" were long and anxious ones for Reginald Cruden. It would have been a great relief to him had he felt free to talk the matter over with Horace; but somehow that word "confidential" in the advertisement deterred him. For all that, he made a point of leaving the paper containing it in his brother's way, if by any chance the invitation to an additional £50 a year might meet his eye. Had it done so, it is doubtful whether Reginald would have been pleased, for he knew that if it came to selecting one of the two, Horace would probably pass for quite as respectable and considerably more intelligent a young man than himself. Still, he had no right to stand in his brother's way if fate ordained that he too should be attracted by the advertisement. He therefore left the paper lying conspicuously about with the advertisement sheet turned toward the beholder.

Horace, however, had too much of the *Rocket* in his business hours to crave for a further perusal of it during his leisure. He kicked it unceremoniously out of his way the first time he encountered it; and when Reginald saw it next it was in a mangled condition under the stairs in the suspicious company of the servant-girl's cinder-shovel.

On the second morning, when he arrived at his work, a letter lay on his case with the Liverpool postmark, addressed R. Cruden, Esquire, *Rocket* Office, London. In his excitement and haste to learn its contents it never occurred to him to notice the unexpected compliment conveyed in the word "Esquire"; and he might have remained for ever in blissful ignorance of the fact, had not his left-hand neighbour, the satirical Mr Barber, considered the occasion a good one for a few flashes of wit.

"'Ullo, Esquire, 'ow are you, Esquire? There is somebody knows you, then. Liverpool, too! That's where all the chaps who rob the till go to. R. Cruden, Esquire—my eye! What's the use of putting any more than 'London' on the envelope—such a well-known character as you? Stuck-up idiot!"

To this address Reginald attended sufficiently to discover that it was not worth listening to; after which he did not even hear the concluding passages of his neighbour's declamation, being absorbed in far more interesting inquiries. He tore the envelope open and hurriedly read—

"Sir,—Your favour is to hand, and in reply we beg to say we shall be glad to arrange an interview. One of our directors will be in town on Monday next, and can see you between one and two o'clock at Weaver's Hotel. Be good enough to treat this and all further communications as strictly confidential.—We are, Sir, yours faithfully,—

"The Select Agency Corporation.

"P.S.—Ask at Weaver's Hotel for Mr Medlock.

"Liverpool."

The welcome contents of this short note fairly staggered him. If the tone of the advertisement had been encouraging, that of this letter was positively convincing. It was concise, business-like, grammatical and courteous. Since his trouble Reginald had never been addressed by any one in the terms of respect conveyed in this communication. Furthermore, the appointment being between one and two—the dinner-hour—he would be able to keep it without difficulty or observation, particularly as Weaver's Hotel was not a stone's throw from the *Rocket* office. Then again, the fact of his letter being from a "corporation" gratified and encouraged him. A Select Agency Corporation was not the sort of company to do things meanly or inconsiderately. They were doubtless a select body of men themselves, and they required the services of select servants; and it was perfectly reasonable that in an affair like this, which *might* lead to nothing, strict mutual confidence should be observed. Supposing in the end he should see reason to decline to connect himself with the Corporation (Reginald liked to think this possible, though he felt sure it was not probable), why, if he had said much about it previously, it *might* be to the prejudice of the Corporation! Finally, he thought the name "Medlock" agreeable, and was generally highly gratified with the letter, and wished devoutly Monday would come round quickly.

The one drawback to his satisfaction was that he was still as far as ever from knowing in what direction his respectable and intelligent services were likely to be required. Monday came at last. When he went up on the Saturday to receive his wages he had fully expected to learn Mr Durfy's intentions with regard to him, and was duly surprised when that gentleman actually handed him his money without a word, and with the faintest suspicion of a smile.

"He's got a nailer on you, old man, and no mistake," said Gedge, dolefully. "I'd advise you to keep your eye open for a new berth, if you get the chance; and, I say, if you can only hear of one for two!"

This last appeal went to Reginald's heart, and he inwardly resolved, if Mr Medlock turned out to be as amiable a man as he took him for, to put in a word on Gedge's behalf as well as his own at the coming interview.

The dinner-bell that Monday tolled solemnly in Reginald's ears as he put on a clean collar and brushed his hair previously to embarking on his journey to Weaver's Hotel. What change might not have taken place in his lot before that same bell summoned him once more to work? He left the *Rocket* a needy youth of £47 10 shillings a year. Was he to return to it passing rich of £97 10 shillings?

Weaver's Hotel was a respectable quiet resort for country visitors in London, and Reginald, as he stood in its homely entrance hall, felt secretly glad that the Corporation selected a place like this for its London headquarters rather than one of the more showy but less respectable hotels or restaurants with which the neighbourhood abounded.

Mr Medlock was in his room, the waiter said, and Mr Cruden was to step up. He did step up, and was ushered into a little sitting-room, where a middle-aged gentleman stood before the fire-place reading the paper and softly humming to himself as he did so.

"Mr Cruden, sir," said the waiter.

"Ah! Mr Cruden, good morning. Take a seat. John, I shall be ready for lunch in about ten-minutes."

Reginald, with the agitating conviction that his fate would be sealed one way or another in ten-minutes, obeyed, and darted a nervous glance at his new acquaintance.

He rather liked the looks of him. He looked a comfortable, well-to-do gentleman, with rather a handsome face, and a manner by no means disheartening. Mr Medlock in turn indulged in a careful survey of the boy as he sat shyly before him trying to look self-possessed, but not man of the world enough to conceal his anxiety or excitement.

"Let me see," said Mr Medlock, putting his hands in his pocket and leaning against the mantel-piece, "you replied to the advertisement, didn't you?"

"Yes, sir," said Reginald.

"And what made you think you would suit us?"

"Well, sir," stammered Reginald, "you wanted respectable intelligent young men—and—and I thought I—that is, I hoped I might answer that description."

Mr Medlock took one hand out of his pocket and stroked his chin.

"Have you been in the printing trade long?"

"Only a few weeks, sir."

"What were you doing before that?"

Reginald flushed.

"I was at school, sir—at Wilderham."

"Wilderham? Why, that's a school for gentlemen's sons."

"My father was a gentleman, sir," said the boy, proudly.

"He's dead then?" said Mr Medlock. "That is sad. But did he leave nothing behind him?"

"He died suddenly, sir," said Reginald, speaking with an effort, "and left scarcely anything."

"Did he die in debt? You must excuse these questions, Mr Cruden," added the gentleman, with an amiable smile; "it is necessary to ask them or I would spare you the trouble."

"He did die in debt," said Reginald, "but we were able to pay off every penny he owed."

"And left nothing for yourself when it was done? Very honourable, my lad; it will always be a satisfaction to you."

"It is, sir," said Reginald, cheering up.

"You naturally would be glad to improve your income. How much do you get where you are?"

"Eighteen shillings a week."

Mr Medlock whistled softly.

"Eighteen shillings; that's very little, very poor pay," said he. "I should have thought, with your education, you could have got more than that."

It pleased Reginald to have his education recognised in this delicate way.

"We had to be thankful for what we could get," said he; "there are so many fellows out of work."

"Very true, very true," said Mr Medlock, shaking his head impressively, "we had no less than 450 replies to our advertisement."

Reginald gave a gasp. What chance had he among 450 competitors?

Mr Medlock took a turn or two up and down the room, meditating with himself and keeping his eye all the time on the boy.

"Yes," said he, "450—a lot, isn't it? Very sad to think of it."

"Very sad," said Reginald, feeling called upon to say something.

"Now," said Mr Medlock, coming to a halt in his walk in front of the boy, "I suppose you guess I wouldn't have asked you to call here if I and my fellow-directors hadn't been pleased with your letter."

Reginald looked pleased and said nothing.

"And now I've seen you and heard what you've got to say, I think you're not a bad young fellow; but—"

Mr Medlock paused, and Reginald's face changed to one of keen anxiety.

"I'm afraid, Mr Cruden, you're not altogether the sort we want."

The boy's face fell sadly.

"I would do my best," he said, as bravely as he could, "if you'd try me. I don't know what the work is yet, but I'm ready to do anything I can."

"Humph!" said Mr Medlock. "What we advertise for is sharp agents, to sell goods on commission among their friends. Now, do you think you could sell £500 worth of wine and cigars and that sort of thing every year among your friends? You'd need to do that to make £50 a year, you know. You understand? Could you go round to your old neighbours and crack up our goods, and book their orders and that sort of thing? I don't think you could, myself. It strikes me you are too much of a gentleman."

Reginald sat silent for a moment, with the colour coming and going in his cheeks; then he looked up and said, slowly—

"I'm afraid I could not do that, sir—I didn't know you wanted that."

So saying he took up his hat and rose to go.

Mr Medlock watched him with a smile, if not of sympathy, at any rate of approval, and when he rose motioned him back to his seat.

"Not so fast, my man; I like your spirit, and we may hit it yet."

Reginald resumed his seat with a new interest in his anxious face.

"You wouldn't suit us as a drummer—that is," said Mr Medlock, hastily correcting himself, "as a tout—an agent; but you might suit us in another way. We're looking out for a gentlemanly young fellow for secretary—to superintend the concern for the directors, and be the medium of communication between them and the agents. We want an educated young man, and one we can depend upon. As to the work, that's picked up in a week easily. Now, suppose—suppose when I go back to Liverpool I were to recommend you for a post like that, what would you say?"

Reginald was almost too overwhelmed for words; he could only stammer,—

"Oh, sir, how kind of you!"

"The directors would appoint any one I recommended," continued Mr Medlock, looking down with satisfaction on the boy's eagerness; "you're young, of course, but you seem to be honest, that's the great thing."

"I think I can promise that," said Reginald, proudly.

"The salary would begin at £150 a year, but we should improve it if you turned out well. And you would, of course, occupy the Company's house at Liverpool. We should not ask for a premium in your case, but you would have to put £50 into the shares of the Corporation to qualify you, and of course you would get interest on that. Now," said he, as Reginald began to speak, "don't be in a hurry. Take your time and think it well over. If you say 'Yes,' you may consider the thing settled, and if you say 'No'—well, we shall be able to find some one else. Ah, here comes lunch—stop and have some with me—bring another plate, waiter."

Reginald felt too bewildered to know what to think or say. He a secretary of a company with £150 a year! It was nearly intoxicating. And for the post spontaneously offered to him in the almost flattering way it had been—this was more gratifying still. In his wildest dreams just now he never pictured himself sitting down as secretary to the Select Agency Corporation to lunch with one of its leading directors!

Mr Medlock said no more about "business", but made himself generally agreeable, asking Reginald about his father and the old days, inquiring as to his mother and brother, and all about his friends and acquaintances in London.

Reginald felt he could talk freely to this friend, and he did so. He confided to him all about Mr Durfy's tyranny, about his brother's work at the *Rocket*, and even went so far as to drop out a hint in young Gedge's favour. He told him all about Wilderham and his schoolfellows there, about the books he liked, about the way he spent his evenings, about Dull Street— in fact, he felt as if he had known Mr Medlock for years and could talk to him accordingly.

"I declare," said that gentleman, pulling out his watch, after this pleasant talk had been going on a long time, "it's five minutes past two. I'm afraid you'll be late."

Reginald started up.

"So I shall, I'd no idea it was so late. I'm afraid I had better go, sir."

"Well, write me a letter to Liverpool to-morrow, or Wednesday at the latest, as we must fill up the place soon. Think it well over. Good-bye, my man. I hope I shall see you again before long. By the way, of course, you won't talk about all this out of doors."

"Oh, no," said Reginald, "I haven't even mentioned it yet at home."

Mr Medlock laughed.

"Well, if you come to Liverpool you'll have to tell them something about it. See, here's a list of our directors, your mother may recognise some of the names. But beyond your mother and brother don't talk about it yet, as the Corporation is only just starting."

Reginald heartily concurred in this caution, and promised to act on it, and then after a friendly farewell hastened back to the *Rocket* office. The clock pointed nearly a quarter past two when he entered.

He was not the sort of fellow to slink in when no one was looking. In fact, he had such a detestation of that sort of thing that he went to the other extreme, and marched ostentatiously past Mr Durfy's table, as though to challenge his observation.

If that was his intention he was not disappointed.

"Oh," said the overseer, with a return of the old sneer, which had been dormant ever since the night Reginald had knocked him down. "You *have* come, have you? And you know the hour, do you?"

"Yes, it's a quarter past two," said Reginald.

"Is it?" sneered Mr Durfy, in his most offensive way.

"Yes, it is," replied the boy, hotly.

What did he care for Durfy now? To-morrow in all probability he would have the satisfaction of walking up to that table and saying, "Mr Durfy, I leave here on Saturday," meanwhile he was not disposed to stand any of his insolence.

But he hardly expected what was coming next.

"Very well, then you can just put your hat on your head and go back the way you came, sir."

"What do you mean?" said Reginald, in startled tones.

"Mean? what I say!" shouted Durfy. "You're dismissed, kicked out, and the sooner you go the better."

So this was the dignified leave-taking to which he had secretly looked forward! Kicked out! and kicked out by Durfy! Reginald's toes tingled at the very thought.

"You've no right to dismiss me for being a few minutes late," said he.

It was Durfy's turn now to be dignified. He went on writing, and did his best to affect oblivion of his enemy's presence.

Reginald, too indignant to know the folly of such an outburst, broke out,—

"I shall not take my dismissal from you. I shall stay here as long as I choose, and when I go I'll go of my own accord, you cad, you—"

Mr Durfy still went on writing with a cheerful smile on his countenance.

"Do you hear?" said Reginald, almost shouting the words. "I'm not going to please you. I shall go to please myself. I give *you* notice, and thank Heaven I've done with you."

Durfy looked up with a laugh.

"Go and make that noise outside," he said. "We can do without you here. Gedge, my man, put those cases beside you back into the rack, and go and tell the porter he's wanted."

The mention of Gedge's name cowed Reginald in an instant, and in the sudden revulsion of feeling which ensued he was glad enough to escape from the room before fairly breaking down under a crushing sense of injury, mortification, and helplessness. Gedge was at the door as he went out.

"Oh, Cruden," he whispered, "what will become of me now? Wait for me outside at seven o'clock; please do."

That afternoon Reginald paced the streets more like a hunted beast than a human being. All the bad side of his nature—his pride, his conceit, his selfishness—was stirred within him under a bitter sense of shame and indignity. He forgot how much his own intractable temper and stupid self-importance had contributed to his fall, and could think of nothing but Durfy's triumph and the evil fate which at the very moment, when he was able to snap his fingers in the tyrant's face, had driven him forth in disgrace with the tyrant's fingers snapped in his face. He had not spirit or resolution enough to wait to see Gedge or any one that evening, but slunk away, hating the sight of everybody, and wishing only he could lose himself and forget that such a wretch as Reginald Cruden existed.

Ah! Reginald. It's a long race to escape from oneself. Men have tried it before now with better reason than you, and failed. Wait till you have something worse to run from, my honest, foolish friend. Face round like a man, and stand up to your pursuer. You have hit out straight from the shoulder before to-day. Do it again now. One smart round will finish the business, for this false Reginald is a poor creature after all, and you can knock him out of time and over the ropes with one hand if you like. Try it, and save your running powers for an uglier foeman some other day!

Reginald did fight it out with himself as he walked mile after mile that afternoon through the London streets, and by the time he reached home in the evening he was himself again.

He met his mother's tears and Horace's dismal looks with a smile of triumph.

"So you've heard all about it, have you?" said he.

"Oh, Reginald," said his mother, in deep distress, "how grieved I am for you!"

"You needn't be, mother," said Reginald, "for I've got another situation far better and worth three times as much."

And then he told them, as far as he felt justified in doing so, of the advertisement and what it had led to, finishing up with a glowing description of Mr Medlock, whom he only regretted he had not had the courage to ask up to tea that very evening.

But there was a cloud on the bright horizon which his mother and Horace were quicker to observe than he.

"But, Reg," said the latter, "surely it means you'd have to go to Liverpool?"

"Yes; I'm afraid it does. That's the one drawback."

"But surely you won't accept it, then?" said the younger brother.

Reginald looked up. Horace's tone, if not imperious, had not been sympathetic, and it jarred on him in the fulness of his projects to encounter an obstacle.

"Why not?" he replied. "It's all very well for you, in your snug berth, but I must get a living, mustn't I?"

"I should have thought something might turn up in London," persisted Horace.

"Things don't turn up as we want them," said Reginald, tartly. "Look here, Horace, you surely don't suppose I prefer to go to Liverpool to staying here?"

"Of course not," said Horace, beginning to whistle softly to himself. It was a bad omen, and Mrs Cruden knew it.

"Come," said she, cheerily, "we must make the best of it. These names, Reg, in the list of directors Mr Medlock gave you, seem all very respectable."

"Do you know any of them?" asked Reginald. "Mr Medlock thought you might."

"I know one or two by name," replied she. "There's the Bishop of S—, I see, and Major Wakeman, who I suppose is the officer who has been doing so well in India. There's a Member of Parliament, too, I see. It seems a good set of directors."

"Of course they aren't likely all to turn up at board meetings," said Reginald, with an explanatory air.

"I don't see myself what business a bishop has with a Select Agency Corporation," said Horace, determined not to see matters in a favourable light.

"My dear fellow," said Reginald, trying hard to keep his temper, "I can't help whether you see it or not. By the way, mother, about the £50 to invest. I think Mr Richmond—"

Mrs Cruden started.

"This exciting news," said she, "drove it out of my head for the moment. Boys, I am very sorry to say I had a note to-day stating that Mr Richmond was taken ill while in France, and is dead. He was one of our few old friends, and it is a very sad blow."

She was right. The Crudens never stood in greater need of a wise friend than they did now.

Chapter Eleven
Reginald takes his Fate into his own Hands

The next day Reginald wrote and accepted the invitation of the directors of the Select Agency Corporation. He flattered himself he was acting deliberately, and after fully weighing the pros and cons of the question. True, he still knew very little about his new duties, and had yet to make the acquaintance of the Bishop of S— and the other directors. But, on the other hand, he had seen Mr Medlock, and heard what he had to say, and was quite satisfied in his own mind that everything was all right. And, greatest argument of all, he had no other place to go to, and £150 a year was a salary not to be thrown away when put into one's hands.

Still, he felt a trifle uncomfortable about the necessity of going to Liverpool and breaking up the old home. Of course, he could not help himself, and Horace had no right to insinuate otherwise. All the same, it was a pity, and if there had not been the compensating certainty of being able to send up regular contributions to the family purse, which would help his mother to not a few comforts hitherto denied, he would have been more troubled still about it.

"What will you do about the £50?" said Horace next day, forcing himself to appear interested in what he inwardly disapproved.

"Oh," said Reginald, "I'd intended to ask Richmond to lend it me. It's not exactly a loan either; it would be the same as his investing in the company in my name. The money would be safe, and he'd get his interest into the bargain. But of course I can't go to him now."

"No; and I don't know whom else you could ask," said Horace.

"They might let me put in a pound a week out of my salary," said Reginald. "That would still leave me two pounds a week, and of that I could send home at least twenty-five shillings."

Horace mused.

"It seems to me rather queer to expect you to put the money in," said he.

"It may be queer, but it's their rule, Mr Medlock says."

"And whatever does the Corporation do? It's precious hazy to my mind."

"I can't tell you anything about it now," said Reginald; "the concern is only just started, and I have promised to treat all Mr Medlock told me as confidential. But I'm quite satisfied in my mind, and you may be too, Horace."

Horace did not feel encouraged to pursue the discussion after this, and went off alone to work in low spirits, and feeling unusually dismal.

"By the way," said Reginald, as he started, "bring young Gedge home with you. I meant to see him last night, but forgot."

Reginald spent the day uneasily for himself and his mother in trying to feel absolutely satisfied with the decision he had come to, and in speculating on his future work. Towards afternoon, weary of being all day in the house, he went out for a stroll. It was a beautiful day, and the prospect of a walk in the park by daylight was a tempting one.

As he was passing down Piccadilly, he became aware of some one approaching him whom he knew, and whom, in another moment, he recognised as Blandford.

There was some excuse certainly for not taking in his old schoolfellow's identity all at once, for the boy he had known at Wilderham only a few months ago had suddenly blossomed forth into a man, and had exchanged the airy bearing of a school-boy for the half-languid swagger of a man about town.

"Hullo, Bland, old man!" exclaimed Reginald, lighting up jubilantly at the sight of an old familiar face, "how are you? Who would have thought of seeing you?"

Blandford was surprised too, and for a moment critically surveyed the boy in front of him before he replied.

"Ah, Cruden, that you? I shouldn't have known you."

Reginald's face fell. He became suddenly aware, and for the first time in his life, that his clothes were shabby, and that his boots were in holes.

"I shouldn't have known you," he replied; "you look so much older than when I saw you last."

"So I am; but, I say," added Bland, reddening as an acquaintance passed and nodded to him, "I'm rather in a hurry, Cruden, just now. If you're not engaged this evening, come and dine with me at seven at the Shades, and we can have a talk. Good-bye."

And he went on hurriedly, leaving Reginald with an uncomfortable suspicion that if he—Reginald—had been more smartly dressed, and had worn gloves and a tall hat, the interview would have been more cordial and less hasty.

However, the longing he felt for the old happy days that were past decided him to appear at the Shades at the hour appointed, although it meant absence from home on one of his few remaining evenings, and, still more, a further desertion of young Gedge.

He repented of his resolution almost as soon as he had made it. What was to be gained by assuming a false position for an evening, and trying to delude himself into the notion that he was the equal of his old comrade? Did not his clothes, his empty pockets, the smart of Durfy's tongue, and even the letter now on its way to Mr Medlock, all disprove it? And yet, three months ago, he was a better man all round than Blandford, who had been glad to claim his friendship and accept his father's hospitality. Reginald rebelled against the idea that they two could still be anything to one another than the friends they had once been; but all the while the old school saw came back into his mind—that imposition sentence he had in his day written out hundreds of times without once thinking of its meaning: *Tempora mutantur et nos mutamur in illis.*

He reached the Shades a few minutes before seven, and waited outside till his friend arrived. He had not to wait long, for Blandford and a couple of companions drove up punctually in a hansom—all of them, to Reginald's horror, being arrayed in full evening dress.

"Hullo, Cruden, you've turned up then," said Blandford. "What, not in regimentals? You usen't to be backward in that way. Never mind; they say dress after seven o'clock here, but they're not strict. We can smuggle you in."

Oh, how Reginald wished he was safe back in Dull Street!

"By the way," continued Blandford, "these are two friends of mine, Cruden—Mr Shanklin and Mr Pillans. Cruden's an old Wilderham fellow, you know," he added, in an explanatory aside.

The gentleman introduced as Mr Shanklin stared curiously at Reginald for a few seconds, and then shook hands. Had the boy known as much of that gentleman as the reader does, he would probably have displayed considerably more interest in his new acquaintance than he did. As it was, he would have been glad of an excuse to avoid shaking hands with either him or his empty-headed companion, Mr Pillans. He went through the ceremony as stiffly as possible, and then followed the party within.

"Now, then," said Blandford, as they sat down at one of the tables, "what do you say? It'll save trouble to take the table d'hôte, eh? are you game, you fellows? Table d'hôte for four, waiter. What shall we have to drink? I say hock to start with."

"I wont take any wine," said Reginald, with an effort.

"Why not? You're not a teetotaler, are you?"

"I won't take any wine," repeated Reginald decisively; and, to his satisfaction, he was allowed to do as he pleased.

The dinner passed as such entertainments usually do, diminishing in interest as it went on. In his happiest days, Reginald always hated what the boys used to call "feeds," and he found that three months' altered circumstances had by no means reconciled him to the infliction. He shirked the last two or three courses, and grew heartily tired of the sight of a plate.

"You wondered how I came to be in town?" said Blandford. "The fact is, my uncle went off the hooks a few weeks ago, and as I'm his heir, you know, I came up, and haven't gone back yet. I don't think I shall either."

"No; what's the use, with the pot of money you've come in for?" said Mr Shanklin. "You're far more comfortable up in town."

"Yes, and *you're* a nice boy to show a fellow about town," said Blandford, laughing, "Wilderham's all very well, you know, Cruden," continued he, "but it's a grind being cooped up there when you've got your chance of a fling."

"Well, you've not wasted your chances, my boy," said Mr Pillans, who, besides being empty-headed, was unhealthy in complexion, and red about the eyes.

Blandford appeared rather flattered than otherwise by this observation, and told Mr Pillans to shut up and not tell tales out of school.

"I suppose Wilderham hasn't changed much since last term?" asked Reginald wistfully.

"Oh no; plenty of fellows left and new ones come—rather a better lot, take them all round, than we had last term."

"Has the football club been doing well again?" asked the old boy.

"Oh, middling. By the way, the fellows growled rather when you only sent them half-a-sov. instead of a sov."

Reginald coloured up. Little his comrade knew what that half-sovereign had cost him!

He relapsed into silence, and had to derive what compensation he could from the fast talk in which the other three engaged, apparently heedless of his presence.

In due time the meal ended, and Blandford called for the bills.

Until that moment Reginald had never imagined for a moment but that he had been dining as his old schoolfellow's guest. He had understood Blandford's request of his company as an invitation, and as an invitation he had accepted it, and as an invitation he had repented of it. What, then, was his embarrassment to find a bill for six shillings and sixpence laid down before him as his share of the entertainment!

For a moment a flush of relief passed across his face. He was glad not to find himself under obligations to Blandford after all. But in another moment relief was changed to horror as he remembered that three shillings was all the money he had about him. Oh, the humiliation, the anguish of this discovery! He would have had anything happen rather than this.

He sat staring at the bill like a being petrified.

"Come along," said Blandford, "let's go to the smoking-room. I suppose you fellows will have coffee there. Coffee for four, waiter. Are you ready?"

But Reginald did not move, nor did the waiter.

"What's the row?" said Blandford to the latter.

The waiter pointed to Reginald's bill.

"Oh, he's waiting for your bill, Cruden. Look sharp, old man!"

The colour came and went in Reginald's face, as though he had been charged with some hideous crime. And it seemed like a deliberate mockery of his trouble that his three companions and the waiter stood silent at the table, eyeing him, and waiting for his answer.

"I'm sorry," he said at length, bringing up the words with a tremendous effort, "I find I've not money enough to pay it. I made a mistake in coming here."

All four listeners stood with faces of mingled amazement and amusement at the boy's agitation and the tragic manner in which he accounted for it. Any one else would have carried it off with a jest; but to Reginald it was like passing through the fire.

"Would you mind—may I trouble you—that is, will you lend me three-and-sixpence, Blandford?" he said at last.

Blandford burst out laughing.

"I thought at least you'd swallowed a silver spoon!" said he. "Here, waiter, I'll settle that bill. How much is it?"

"No," said Reginald, laying down his three shillings; "if you can lend me three-and-sixpence, that's all I want."

"Bosh!" said Blandford, pitching half a sovereign to the waiter; "take it out of that, and this coffee too, and come along into the smoking-room, you fellows."

Reginald would fain have escaped; but the horrid dread of being suspected of caring more about his dinner than his company deterred him, and he followed dejectedly to the luxurious smoking-room of the Shades.

He positively refused to touch the coffee or the cigar, even though Blandford took care to remind him they had been paid for. Nor, except when spoken to, could he bring himself to open his lips or take part in the general talk.

Blandford, however, who, ever since the incident of the bill, seemed to consider himself entitled to play a patronising part towards his schoolfellow, continued to keep him from lapsing into obscurity.

"Where's your brother living?" he asked presently.

"He's in town, too," said Reginald. "My mother and he and I live together."

"Where? I'd like to call on your mother."

"We live in Dull Street," said Reginald, beginning in sheer desperation to pluck up heart and hang out no more false colours.

"Dull Street? That's rather a shady locality, isn't it?" said Mr Pillans.

Reginald rounded on him. Blandford might have a right to catechise him; but what business was it of this numbskull's where he lived?

"You're not obliged to go there," he said, with a curl of his lip, "unless you like."

Mr Shanklin smiled at this sally, a demonstration which considerably incensed the not too amiable Mr Pillans.

"I'll take precious care I don't," said the latter.

Reginald said "Thanks!" drily, and in a way so cutting that Mr Shanklin and Blandford both laughed this time.

"Look here," said the unwholesome Pillans, looking very warm, "what do you say that for? Do you want to cheek me?"

Reginald Cruden | 103

"Don't be a fool, Pillans. It doesn't matter to you where he lives," said Blandford.

"Thank goodness it don't—or whether he pays his rent either."

"It's a pity you had to leave Garden Vale," said Blandford, apparently anxious to turn the conversation into a more pacific channel; "such a jolly place it was. What do you do with yourself all day long in town?"

Reginald smiled.

"I work for my living," said he, keeping his eye steadily fixed on Mr Pillans, as if waiting to catch the first sign of an insult on his part.

"That's what we all do, more or less," said Mr Shanklin. "Blandford here works like a nigger to spend his money, don't you, old man?"

"I do so," said Blandford, "with your valuable assistance."

"And with somebody else's assistance too," said Mr Pillans, with a shrug in the direction of Reginald.

Reginald understood the taunt, and rose to his feet.

"You're not going?" said Blandford.

"I am. I don't forget I owe you for my dinner, Blandford; and I shan't forget that I owe you also for introducing me to a blackguard. Good-night."

And without allowing his hearers time to recover from the astonishment into which these words had thrown them, he marched out of the Shades with his head in the air.

It was a minute before any of the three disconcerted companions could recover the gift of speech. At last Mr Shanklin burst out into a laugh.

"Capital, that was," he said; "there's something in the fellow. And," he added internally, and not in the hearing of either of his companions, "if he's the same fellow Medlock has hooked, our fortune's made."

"All very well," said Pillans; "but he called me a blackguard."

This simple discovery caused still greater merriment at the expense of the outraged owner of the appellation.

"I've a good mind to go after him, and pull his nose," growled he.

"Nothing would please him better," said Blandford. "But you'd better leave your own nose behind, my boy, before you start, or there won't be much of it left. I know Cruden of old."

"You won't see much more of him now," sneered Pillans, "now he owes you for his dinner."

"It strikes me, Bland was never safer of a six-and-six in his life than he is of the one he lent to-night," said Mr Shanklin. "Unless I'm mistaken, the fellow would walk across England on his bare feet to pay it back."

Mr Shanklin, it was evident, could appreciate honesty in any one else. He was highly delighted with what he had seen of the new secretary. If anything could float the Select Agency Corporation, the lad's unsuspicious honesty would do it. In fact, things were looking up all round for the precious confederates. With Reginald to supply them with honesty, with easy-going spendthrifts, like Blandford and Pillans, to supply them with money, and with a cad like Durfy to do their dirty work for them, they were in as comfortable and hopeful a way as the promoters of such an enterprise could reasonably hope to be.

The trio at the Shades soon forgot Reginald in the delights of one another's sweet society. They played billiards, at which Mr Shanklin won. They also played cards, at which, by a singular coincidence, Mr Shanklin won too. They then went to call on a friend who knew the "straight tip" for the Saint Leger, and under his advice they laid out a good deal of money, which (such are the freaks of fortune) also found its way somehow into Mr Shanklin's pocket-book. Finally, they supped together, and then went home to bed, each one under the delusion that he had spent a very pleasant evening.

Reginald was far from sharing the same opinion as he paced home that evening. How glad he should be to be out of this hateful London, where everything went wrong, and reminded him that he was a pauper, dependent on others for his living, for his clothes, for his—faugh! for his dinner! Happily he had not to endure it much longer. At Liverpool, he would be independent. He would hold a position not degrading to a gentleman; he would associate with men of intellect and breeding; he would even have the joy of helping his mother to many a little luxury which, as long as he remained in London, he could never have given her. He quickened his pace, and reached home. Gedge had been there, spiritless and forlorn, and had left as soon as he could excuse himself.

"Out of sight, out of mind," he had said, with a forced laugh, to Horace when the latter expressed his regret at Reginald's absence.

Mrs Cruden and Horace both tried to look cheerful; but the cloud on the horizon was too large now to be covered with a hand.

When Reginald announced that he had written and accepted the invitation to Liverpool, there was no jubilation, no eager congratulation.

"What shall we do without you?" said Mrs Cruden.

"It is horrid having to go, mother," said the boy; "but we must make the best of it. If you look so unhappy, I shall be sorry I ever thought of it."

His mother tried to smile, and said,—

"Yes, we must try and make the best of it, dear boys; and if we cannot seem as glad as we should like to be, it's not to be wondered at at first, is it?"

"I hope you'll get holidays enough now and then to run up," said Horace.

"Oh yes; I don't fancy there'll be much difficulty about that," replied Reg. "In fact, it's possible I may have to come up now and then on business."

There was a silence for a few seconds, and then he added rather nervously,—

"By the way, mother, about the £50. I had intended to ask Mr Richmond to advance it, although I should have hated to do so. But now, I was wondering—do you think there would be any objection to taking it out of our money, and letting it be invested in my name in the Corporation? It really wouldn't make any difference, for you'd get exactly the same interest for it as you got through Mr Richmond; and, of course, the principal would belong to you too."

"I see no objection," said Mrs Cruden. "It's our common stock, and if we can use it for the common good, so much the better."

"Thanks," said Reginald. "If you wouldn't mind sending a line to Mr Richmond's clerk to-morrow, he could let me have the cheque to take down or Monday with me."

The three days that followed were dismal ones for the three Crudens. There are few miseries like that of an impending separation. We wish the fatal moment to arrive and end our suspense. We know of a thousand things we want to say, but the time slips by wasted, and hangs drearily on our hands. We have not the spirit to look forward, or the heart to look back. We long to have it all over, and yet every stroke of the clock falls like a cruel knell on our ears. We long that we could fall asleep, and wake to find ourselves on the other side of the crisis we dread.

So it was with the Crudens; and when at last the little trio stood on the Monday on the platform of Euston Station, all three felt that they would give anything to have the last few days back again.

"I'll write, mother, as often as ever I can," said Reginald, trying to speak as if the words did not stick in his throat.

"Tell us all about your quarters, and what you have to do, and all that," said Horace.

Mrs Cruden had no words. She stood with her eyes fixed on her boy, and felt she needed all her courage to do that steadily.

"Horrors," said Reg, as the guard locked the carriage door, and the usual silence which precedes the blowing of the whistle ensued, "keep your eye on young Gedge, will you? there's a good fellow."

"I will, and I'll—"

But here the whistle sounded, and amid the farewells that followed, Reginald went out into his new world, leaving them behind, straining their eyes for a last look, but little dreaming how and when that little family should meet again.

Chapter Twelve
Horace learns an Art, pays a Bill, and lends a Helping Hand

"I say, Cruden," said Waterford to Horace one morning, shortly after Reginald's departure from London, "I shall get jealous if you don't pull up."

"Jealous of me?" said Horace. "Whatever for?"

"Why, before you came I flattered myself I was a bit of a dab at the scissors-and-paste business, but you've gone and cut me out completely."

"What rot!" said Horace, laughing. "There's more than enough cutting out to do with the morning papers to leave any time for operating on you. Besides, any duffer can do work like that."

"That's all very well," said Waterford. "There's only one duffer here that can do as much as me and Booms put together, and that's you. Now, if you weren't such a racehorse, I'd propose to you to join our shorthand class. You'll have to learn it some time or other, you know."

"The very thing I'd like," said Horace. "That is," he added, "if it won't take up all a fellow's evenings. How often are the classes?"

"Well, as often as we like. Generally once a week. Booms's washerwoman—"

"Whatever has she to do with shorthand?" asked Horace.

"More than you think, my boy. She always takes eight days to wash his collars and cuffs. He sends them to her on Wednesdays, and gets them back on the next day week, so that we always practise shorthand on the Wednesday evening. Don't we, Booms?" he inquired, as the proud owner of that name entered the office at that moment.

"There you are," sighed he. "How do I know what you are talking about?"

"I was saying we always worked up our shorthand on Wednesday evenings."

"If you say so," said the melancholy one, "it must be so."

"I was telling Cruden he might join us this winter."

"Very well," said the other, resignedly; "but where are you going to meet? Mrs Megson has gone away, and we've no reader."

"Bother you, Booms, for always spotting difficulties in a thing. You see," added he, to Horace, "we used to meet at a good lady's house who kept a day school. She let us go there one evening a week, and read aloud to us, for us to take it down in shorthand. She's gone now, bad luck to her, and the worst of it is we're bound to get a lady to take us in, as we've got ladies in our class, you see."

At the mention of ladies Booms groaned deeply.

"Why, I tell you what," said Horace, struck by a brilliant idea. "What should you say to my mother? I think she would be delighted; and if you want a good reader aloud, she's the very woman for you."

Waterford clapped his friend enthusiastically on the back.

"You're a trump, Cruden, to lend us your mother; isn't he, Booms?"

"Oh yes," said Booms. "I've seen her, and—" here he appeared to undergo a mental struggle—"I like her."

"At any rate, I'll sound her on the matter. By the way, she'll want to know who the ladies are."

"It'll only be one this winter, I'm afraid," said Waterford, "as the Megsons have gone. It's a Miss Crisp, Cruden, a friend of Booms's, who—"

"Whom I met the other night at the Shucklefords'?" said Horace.

Booms answered the question with such an agonised sigh that both his companions burst out laughing.

"Dear old Booms can tell you more about her than I can," said Waterford. "All I know is she's a very nice girl indeed."

"I agree with you," said Horace; "I'm sure she is. You think so too, don't you, Booms?"

"You don't know what I think," said Booms; which was very true.

One difficulty still remained, and this appeared to trouble Horace considerably.

He did not like to refer to it as long as the melancholy masher was present, but as soon as he had gone in to fetch the papers, Horace inquired of his friend,—

"I say, Waterford, do you mean to say he chooses the very night he hasn't got a high collar to—"

"Hush!" cried Waterford, mysteriously, "it's a sore question with him; but *he couldn't write if he had one.* We never mention it, though."

It is needless to say Mrs Cruden fell in most cordially with the new proposal. She needed little persuasion to induce her to agree to a plan which meant the bright presence of her son and his friends in her house, and it gave her special satisfaction to find her services on such occasions not only invited, but indispensable; and it is doubtful whether any of the party looked forward more eagerly to the cheery Wednesday evenings than she did.

It was up-hill work, of course, for Horace, at first; in fact, during the first evening he could do nothing but sit and admire the pace at which Miss Crisp, followed more haltingly by Booms and Waterford, took down the words of *Ivanhoe* as fast as Mrs Cruden read them. But, by dint of hard, unsparing practice, he was able, a week later, to make some sort of a show, and as the lessons went on he even had the delight of finding himself, as Waterford said, 'in the running' with his fellow-scholars. This success was not achieved without considerable determination on the boy's part; but Horace, when he did take a thing up, went through with it. He gave himself no relaxation for the first week or two. Every evening after supper he produced his pencil and paper, and his mother produced her book, and for two steady hours the work went on. Even at the office, in the intervals of work, he reported everything his ears could catch, not excepting the melancholy utterances of Booms and the vulgar conversation of the errand-boy.

One day the sub-editor summoned him to the inner room to give him some instructions as to a letter to be written, when the boy much astonished his chief by taking a note of every word, and producing the letter in a few moments in the identical language in which it had been dictated.

"You know shorthand, then?" inquired the mild sub-editor.

"Yes, sir, a little."

"I did not know of this before."

"No, sir; I only began lately. Booms and Waterford and I are all working it up."

The sub-editor said nothing just then, but in future availed himself freely of the new talent of his juniors. And what was still more satisfactory, it was intimated not many days later to Horace from headquarters, that as he appeared to be making himself generally useful, the nominal wages at which he had been admitted would be increased henceforth to twenty-four shillings a week.

This piece of good fortune was most opportune; for now that Reginald's weekly contribution was withdrawn, and pending the payment of his first quarter's salary at Christmas, the family means had been sorely reduced, and Horace and his mother had been hard put to it to make both ends meet. Even with this augmented pay it might still have been beyond accomplishment had not their income been still further improved in a manner which Horace little suspected, and which, had he known, would have sorely distressed him.

Mrs Cruden, between whom and the bright Miss Crisp a pleasant friendship had sprung up, had, almost the first time the two ladies found themselves together, inquired of her new acquaintance as to the possibility of finding any light employment for herself during the hours when she was alone. Miss Crisp, as it happened, did know of some work, though hardly to be called light work, which she herself, having just at present other duties on hand, had been obliged to decline. This was the transcribing of the manuscript of a novel, written by a lady, in a handwriting so enigmatical that the publishers would not look at it unless presented in a legible form. The lady was, therefore, anxious to get it copied out, and had offered Miss Crisp a small sum for the service. Mrs Cruden clutched eagerly at the opportunity thus presented. The work was laborious and dreary in the extreme, for the story was long and insipid, and the wretched handwriting danced under her eyes till they ached and grew weak. But she persevered boldly, and for three hours a day pored over her self-imposed task. When Horace returned at evening no trace of it was to be seen, only the pale face and weary eyes of his mother, who yet was ready with a smile to read aloud as long as the boy wished, and pretend that she only enjoyed a labour which was really taxing her both in health and eyesight.

Reginald had written home once or twice since his departure, but none of his letters had contained much news. He said very little either about his work or his employers, but from the dismal tone in which he drew comparisons between London and Liverpool, and between his present loneliness and days before their separation, it was evident enough he was homesick. In a letter to Horace he said, —

"I get precious little time just now for anything but work, and what I do get I don't know a soul here to spend it with. There's a football club here, but of course I can't join it. I go walks occasionally, though I can't get far, as I cannot be away from here for long at a time, and never of an evening. You might send me a *Rocket* now and then, or something to read. What about young Gedge? See Durfy doesn't get hold of him. Could you ever scrape up six-and-six, and pay it for me to Blandford, whose address I give below? It's something he lent me for a particular purpose when I last saw him. Do try. I would enclose it, but till Christmas I have scarcely enough to keep myself. I wish they would pay weekly instead of quarterly. I would be awfully obliged if you would manage to pay the six-and-six somehow or other. If you do, see he gets it, and knows it comes from me, and send me a line to say he has got it. Don't forget, there's a brick. Love to mother and young Gedge. I wish I could see you all this minute."

Horace felt decidedly blue after receiving this letter, and purposely withheld it from his mother. Had he been sure Reginald was prosperous and happy in his new work, this separation would not have mattered so much, but all along he had had his doubts on both these points, and the letter only confirmed them.

At any rate he determined to lose no time in easing his brother's mind of the two chief causes of his anxiety. The very next Saturday he appropriated six-and-six of his slender wages, and devoted the evening to finding out Blandford's rooms, and paying him the money.

Fortunately his man was at home, an unusual circumstance at that hour of the night, and due solely to the fact that he and Pillans, his fellow-lodger, were expecting company; indeed, the page-boy (for our two gay sparks maintained a "tiger" between them) showed Horace up the moment he arrived, under the delusion that he was one of the guests. Blandford and his friend, sitting in state to receive their distinguished visitors, among whom were to be the real owner of a racehorse, a real jockey, a real actor, and a real wine-merchant, these open-hearted and knowing young men were considerably taken aback to find a boy of Horace's age and toilet ushered into their august presence. Blandford would have preferred to appear ignorant of the identity of the intruder, but Horace left him no room for that amiable fraud.

"Hullo, Bland!" said he, just as if he had seen him only yesterday at Wilderham, "what a jolly lot of stairs you keep in this place. I thought I should never smoke you out. How are you, old man?"

And before the horrified dandy could recover from his surprise, he found his hand being warmly shaken by his old schoolfellow.

Horace, sublimely unconscious of the impression he was creating, indulged in a critical survey of the apartment, and said,—

"Snug little crib you've got—not quite so jolly, though, as the old study you and Reg had at Wilderham. How's Harker, by the way?"

And he proceeded to stroll across the room to look at a picture.

Blandford and Pillans exchanged glances. Wrath was in the face of the one, bewilderment in the face of the other.

"Who's your friend?" whispered the latter.

"An old schoolfellow who—"

"Nice lot of fellows you seem to have been brought up with, upon my word," said Mr Pillans.

"I suppose he'll be up for Christmas," pursued Horace. "Jolly glad I shall be to see him, too. I say, why don't you come and look us up? The *mater* would be awfully glad, though we've not very showy quarters to ask you to. Ah! that's one of the prints you had in the study at school. Do you remember Reg chipping that corner of the frame with a singlestick?"

"Excuse me, Cruden," began Blandford, in a severe tone; "my friend and I are just expecting company."

"Are you? Well, I couldn't have stayed if you'd asked me. Are any of the old school lot coming?"

"The fact is, we can do without you, young fellow," said Mr Pillans.

Horace stared. It had not occurred to him till that moment that his old schoolfellow could be anything but glad to see him, and he didn't believe it now.

"Will Harker be coming?" he inquired, ignoring Mr Pillans' presence.

"No, no one you know is coming," said Blandford, half angrily, half nervously.

"That's a pity. I'd have liked to see some of the old lot. Ever since we came to grief none of them has been near us except Harker. He called one day, like a brick, but he won't be up again till Christmas."

"Good-night," said Blandford.

His tone was quite lost on Horace.

"Good-night, old man. By the way, Reg—you know he's up in the North now—asked me to pay you six-and-six he owed you. He said you'd know about it. Is it all right?"

Blandford coloured up violently.

"I'm not going to take it. I told him so," said he. "Oh yes, you are, you old humbug," said Horace, "so catch hold. A debt's a debt, you know."

"It's not a debt," said Blandford. "I gave it to him, so good-night."

"No, that won't do," said Horace. "He doesn't think so—"

"The fact is, the beggar couldn't pay for his own dinner, and Blandford had to pay it for him. He managed it very neatly," said Mr Pillans.

Horace fired up fiercely.

"What do you mean? Who's this cad you keep about the place, Blandford?"

"If you don't go I'll kick you down the stairs!" cried Mr Pillans, by this time in a rage.

Horace laughed. Mr Pillans was his senior in years and his superior in inches, but there was nothing in his unhealthy face to dismay the sturdy school-boy.

"Do you want me to try?" shouted Mr Pillans.

"Not unless you like," replied Horace, putting the money down on the table and holding out his hand to Blandford.

The latter took it mechanically, too glad to see his visitor departing to offer any obstacle.

"I'll look you up again some day," said Horace, "when your bulldog here is chained up. When Reg and Harker are up this Christmas, we must all get a day together. Good-night."

And he made for the door, brushing up against the outraged Mr Pillans on his way.

"Take that for an impudent young beggar!" said the latter as he passed, suiting the action to the word with a smart cuff directed at the visitor's head.

Horace, however, was quick enough to ward it off.

"I thought you'd try that on," he said, with a laugh; "you're—"

But Mr Pillans, who had by this time worked himself into a fury by a method known only to himself, cut short further parley by making a desperate rush at him just as he reached the door.

The wary Horace had not played football for three seasons for nothing. He quietly ducked, allowing his unscientific assailant to overbalance himself, and topple head first on the lobby outside, at the particular moment when the real owner of the racehorse and the real wine-merchant, who had just arrived, reached the top of the stairs.

"Hullo, young fellow!" said the sporting gentleman; "practising croppers, are you? or getting up an appetite? or what? High old times you're having up here among you! Who's the kid?"

"Stop him!" gasped Pillans, picking himself up; "don't let him go! hold him fast!"

The wine-merchant obligingly took possession of Horace by the collar, and the company returned in solemn procession to the room.

"Now, then," said Horace's captor, "what's the row? Let's hear all about it. Has he been collaring any of your spoons? or setting the house on fire? or what? Who is he?"

"He's cheeked me!" said Pillans, brushing the dust off his coat. "Hold him fast, will you? till I take it out of him."

But the horse-racer was far too much of a sportsman for that.

"No, no," said he, laughing; "make a mill of it and I'm your man. I'll bet two to one on the young 'un to start with."

The wine-merchant said he would go double that on Pillans, whereupon the sporting man offered a five-pound note against a half-sovereign on his man, and called out to have the room cleared and a sponge brought in.

How far his scientific enthusiasm would have been rewarded it is hard to say, for Blandford at this juncture most inconsiderately interposed.

"No, no," said he, "I'm not going to have the place made a cock-pit. Shut up, Pillans, and don't make an ass of yourself; and you, Cruden, cut off. What did you ever come here for? See what a row you've made."

"It wasn't I made the row," said Horace. "I'm awfully sorry, Bland. I'd advise you to cut that friend of yours, I say. He's an idiot. Good-bye."

And while the horse-racer and the wine-merchant were still discussing preliminaries, and Mr Pillans was privately ascertaining whether his nose was bleeding, Horace departed in peace, partly amused, partly vexed, and decidedly of opinion that Blandford had taken to keeping very queer company since he last saw him.

The great thing was that Horace could now write and report to Reg that the debt had been paid.

His way home led him past the *Rocket* office. It was half-past ten, and the place looked dark and deserted. Even the lights in the editor's windows were out, and the late hands had gone home. Just at the corner Horace encountered Gedge, one of the late hands in question.

"Hullo, young 'un!" he said. "Going home?"

"Yes, I'm going home," said young Gedge.

"I heard from my brother yesterday. He was asking after you."

"Was he?" said the boy half-sarcastically. "He does remember my name, then?"

"Whatever do you mean? Of course he does," said Horace. "You know that well enough."

"I shouldn't have known it unless you'd told me," said Gedge, with a cloud on his face; "he's never sent me a word since he left."

"He's been awfully busy—he's scarcely had time to write home. I say, young 'un, what's the row with you? What makes you so queer?"

"Oh, I don't know," said the boy wearily; "I used to fancy somebody cared for me, but I was mistaken. I was going to the dogs fast enough when Cruden came here; I pulled up then, because I thought he'd stand by me; but now he's gone and forgotten all about me. I'll—well, there's nothing to prevent me going to the bad; and I may as well make up my mind to it."

"No, no," said Horace, taking his arm kindly; "you mustn't say that, young 'un. The last words Reg said to me when he went off were, 'Keep your eye on young Gedge, don't forget'; the very last words, and he's reminded me of my promise in every letter since. I've been a cad, I know, not to see more of you; but you mustn't go thinking that you've no friends. If it were only for Reg's sake I'd stick to you. Don't blame him, though, for I know he thinks a lot about you, and it would break his heart if you went to the bad. Of course you can help going to the bad, old man; we can all help it."

The boy looked up with the clouds half brushed away from his face.

"I don't want to go to the bad," said he; "but I sort of feel I'm bound to go, unless some one sticks up for me. I'm so awfully weak-minded, I'm not fit to be trusted alone."

"Hullo, I say," whispered Horace, suddenly stopping short in his walk, "who's that fellow sneaking about there by the editor's door?"

"He looks precious like Durfy," said Gedge; "I believe it is he."

"What does he want there, I wonder—he wasn't on the late shift to-night, was he?"

"No; he went at seven."

"I don't see what he wants hanging about when everybody's gone," said Horace.

"Unless he's screwed and can't get home—I've known him like that. That fellow's not screwed, though," he added; "see, he's heard some one coming, and he's off steady enough on his legs."

"Rum," said Horace. "It looked like Durfy, too. Never mind, whoever it is, we've routed him out this time. Good-night, old man; don't go down on your luck, mind, and don't go abusing Reg behind his back, and don't forget you're booked to come home to supper with me on Monday, and see my mother. Ta-ta."

Chapter Thirteen
The new Secretary takes the Reins

It is high time to return to Reginald, whom we left in a somewhat dismal fashion, straining his eyes for a last sight of his mother and brother as they waved farewell to him on the Euston platform.

If the reader expects me to tell him that on finding himself alone our hero burst into tears, or broke out into repentant lamentations, or wished himself under the wheels of the carriage, I'm afraid he will be disappointed.

Reginald spent the first half-hour of his solitary journey in speculating how the oil in the lamp got round at the wick. He considered the matter most attentively, and kept his eyes fixed on the dim light until London was miles behind him, and the hedges and grey autumn fields on either hand proclaimed the country. Then his mind abandoned its problems, and for another half-hour he tried with all his might to prevent the beat of the engine taking up the rhythm of one of the old Wilderham cricket songs. That too he gave up eventually, and let his imagination wander at large over those happy school days, when all was merry, when every friend was a brick, and every exertion a sport, when the future beckoned him forward with coaxing hand. What grand times they were! Should he ever forget the last cricket match of the summer term, when he bowled three men in one over, and made the hardest catch on record in the Wilderham Close? He and Blandford—

Ah, Blandford! His mind swerved on the points here, and branched off into the recollection of that ill-starred dinner at the Shades, and the unhealthy bloated face of the cad Pillans. How he would have liked to knock the idiot down, just as he had knocked Durfy down that night when young Gedge—

Ah, another point here and another swerve. Would Horace be sure and keep his eye on the young 'un, and was there any chance of getting him down to Liverpool?

Once more a swerve, and this time into a straight reach of meditation for miles and miles ahead. He thought of everything. He pictured his own little office and living-room. He drew a mental portrait of the housekeeper, and the cups and saucers he would use at his well-earned meals. He made up his mind the board-room would be furnished in green leather, and that the Bishop of S— would be a jolly sort of fellow and fond of his joke. He even imagined what the directors would say among themselves respecting himself after he had been introduced and made his first impression. At any rate they should not say he lacked in interest for their affairs, and when he wrote home—

Ah! this was the last of all the points, and his thoughts after that ran on the same lines till the train plunged into the smoke and gloom of the great city which was henceforth to extend to him its tender mercies.

If Reginald had reckoned on a deputation of directors of the Select Agency Corporation to meet their new secretary at the station, he was destined to be disappointed. There were plenty of people there, but none concerning themselves with him as he dragged his carpet-bag from under the seat and set foot on the platform.

The bag was very heavy, and Shy Street, so he was told, was ten-minutes' walk from the station. It did occur to him that most secretaries of companies would take a cab under such circumstances and charge it to "general expenses." But he did not care to spend either the Corporation's money or his own for so luxurious a purpose, and therefore gripped his bag manfully and wrestled with it out into the street.

The ten-minutes grew to considerably more than twenty before they both found themselves in Shy Street. A long, old-fashioned, dismal street it was, with some shops in the middle, and small offices at either end. No imposing-looking edifice, chaste in architecture and luxurious in proportions, stood with open doors to receive its future lord. Reginald and his bag stumbled up a side staircase to the first floor over a chemist's shop, where a door with the name "Medlock" loomed before him, and told him he had come to his journey's end.

Waiting a moment to wipe the perspiration from his face, he turned the handle and found himself in a large, bare, carpetless room, with a table and a few chairs in the middle of it, a clock over the chimneypiece, a few directories piled up in one corner, and a bundle of circulars and wrappers in another; and a little back room screened off from the general observation with the word "private" on the door. Such was the impression formed in Reginald's mind by a single glance round his new quarters.

In the flutter of his first entrance, however, he entirely overlooked one important piece of furniture—namely, a small boy with long lank hair and pale blotched face, who was sitting on a low stool near the window, greedily devouring the contents of a pink-covered periodical. This young gentleman, on becoming aware of the presence of a stranger, crumpled his paper hurriedly into his pocket and rose to his feet.

"What do yer want?" he demanded.

"Is Mr Medlock here?" asked Reginald.

"No fear," replied the boy.

"Has he left any message?"

"Don't know who you are. What's yer name?"

"I'm Mr Cruden, the new secretary."

"Oh, you're 'im, are yer? Yes, you've got to address them there envellups, and 'e'll be up in the morning."

This was depressing. Reginald's castles in the air were beginning to tumble about his ears in rapid succession. The bare room he could excuse, on the ground that the Corporation was only just beginning its operations. Doubtless the carpet was on order, and was to be delivered soon. He could even afford not to afflict himself much about this vulgar, irreverent little boy, who was probably put in, as they put in a little watch-dog, to see to the place until he and his staff of assistants rendered his further presence unnecessary. But it did chill him to find that after his long journey, and his farewell to his own home, no one should think it worth while to be here to meet him and install him with common friendliness into his new quarters. However, Mr Medlock was a man of business, and was possibly prevented by circumstances over which he had no control from being present to receive him.

"Where's the housekeeper?" demanded he, putting down his bag and relieving himself of his overcoat.

"'Ousekeeper! Oh yus," said the boy, with a snigger; "no 'ousekeepers 'ere."

"Where are my rooms, then?" asked Reginald, beginning to think it a pity the Corporation had brought him down all that way before they were ready for him.

"Ain't this room big enough for yer?" said the boy; "ain't no more 'sep' your bedroom—no droring-rooms in this shop."

"Show me the bedroom," said Reginald.

The boy shuffled to the door and up another flight of stairs, at the head of which he opened the door of a very small room, about the size of one of the Wilderham studies, with just room to squeeze round a low iron bedstead without scraping the wall.

"There you are—clean and haired and no error. I've slep' in it myself."

Reginald motioned him from the room, and then sitting down on the bed, looked round him.

He could not understand it. Any common butcher's boy would be better put up. A little box of a bedroom like this, with no better testimonial to its cleanliness and airiness than could be derived from the fact that the dirty little watch-dog downstairs had occupied it! And in place of a parlour that bare gaunt room below in which to sit of an evening and take his meals and enjoy himself. Why ever had the Corporation not had the ordinary decency to have his permanent accommodation ready for him before he arrived?

He washed himself as well as he could without soap and towel, and returned to the first floor, where he found the boy back on his old stool, and once more absorbed in his paper.

The reader looked up as Reginald entered.

"Say, what's yer name," said he, "ever read *Tim Tigerskin?*"

"No, I've not," replied Reginald, staring at his questioner, and wondering whether he was as erratic in his intellect as he was mealy in his countenance.

"'Tain't a bad 'un, but 'tain't 'arf as prime as *The Pirate's Bride*. The bloke there pisons two on 'em with prussic acid, and wouldn't ever 'ave got nabbed if he 'adn't took some hisself by mistake, the flat!"

Reginald could hardly help smiling at this appetising *résumé*.

"I want something to eat," he said. "Is there any place near here where I can get it?"

"Trum's, but 'is sosseges is off at three o'clock. Better try Cupper's— he's a good 'un for bloaters; *I* deals with 'im."

Reginald felt neither the spirit nor the inclination to make a personal examination into the merits of the rival caterers.

"You'd better go and get me something," he said to the boy; "coffee and fish or cold meat will do."

"No fear; I ain't a-goin' for nothing," replied the boy. "I'll do your errands for a tanner a week and your leavings, but not no less."

"You shall have it," said Reginald. Whereupon the boy undertook the commission and departed.

The meal was a dismal one. The herrings were badly over-smoked and the coffee was like mud, and the boy's conversation, which filled in a running accompaniment, was not conducive to digestion.

"I'd 'most a mind to try some prussic in that corfee," said that bloodthirsty young gentleman, "if I'd a known where the chemist downstairs keeps his'n. Then they'd 'a said you'd poisoned yourself 'cos you was blue coming to this 'ere 'ole. I'd 'a been put in the box at the inquige, and I'd 'a said Yes, you was blue, and I thought there was a screw loose the minit I see yer, and I'd seen yer empty a paper of powder in your corfee while you thort nobody wasn't a-looking. And the jury'd say it was tempory 'sanity and sooiside, and say they considers I was a honest young feller, and vote me a bob out of the poor-box. There you are. What do you think of that?"

"I suppose that's what the man in *The Pirate's Bride* ought to have done," said Reginald, with a faint smile.

"To be sure he ought. Why, it's enough to disgust any one with the flat, when he goes and takes the prussic hisself. Of course he'd get found out."

"Well, it's just as well you've not put any in my coffee," said Reginald. "It's none too nice as it is. And I'd advise you, young fellow, to burn all those precious story-books of yours, if that's the sort of stuff they put into your head."

The boy stared at him in horrified amazement.

"Burn 'em! Oh, Walker!"

"What's your name?" demanded Reginald.

"Why, Love," replied the boy, in a tone as if to say you had only to look at him to know his name.

"Well then, young Love, clear these things away and come and make a start with these envelopes."

"No fear. I ain't got to do no envellups. You're got to do 'em."

"I say you've got to do them too," said Reginald, sternly; "and if you don't choose to do what you're told I can't keep you here."

The boy looked up in astonishment.

"You ain't my governor," said he.

"I am, though," said Reginald, "and you'd better make up your mind to it. If you choose to do as you're told we shall get on all right, but I'll not keep you here if you don't."

His tone and manner effectually overawed the mutinous youngster. He could not have spoken like that unless he possessed sufficient authority to back it up, and as it did not suit the convenience of Mr Love just then to receive the "sack" from any one, he capitulated with the honours of war, put his *Tim Tigerskin* into his pocket, and placed himself at his new "governor's" disposal.

The evening's work consisted in addressing some two hundred or three hundred envelopes to persons whose names Mr Medlock had ticked in a directory, and enclosing prospectuses therein. It was not very entertaining work; still, as it was his first introduction to the operations of the Corporation, it had its attractions for the new secretary. A very fair division of labour was mutually agreed upon by the two workers before starting. Reginald was to copy out the addresses, and Master Love, whose appetite was always good, was to fold and insert the circulars and "lick up" the envelopes.

This being decided, the work went on briskly and quietly. Reginald had leisure to notice one or two little points as he went on, which, though trivial in themselves, still interested him. He observed for one thing that the largest proportion of the names marked in the directory were either ladies or clergymen, and most of them residing in the south of England. Very few of them appeared to reside in any large town, but to prefer rural retreats "far from the madding crowd," where doubtless a letter, even on the business of the Corporation, would be a welcome diversion to the monotony of existence. As to the clergy, doubtless their names had been suggested by the good Bishop of S—, who would be in a position to introduce a considerable connection to his fellow-directors. Reginald also noticed that only one name had been marked in each village, it doubtless being assumed that every one in these places being on intimate terms with his neighbour, it was unnecessary to waste stamps and paper in making the Corporation known to two people where one would answer the same purpose.

He was curious enough to read one of the circulars, and he was on the whole pleased with its contents. It was as follows:—

"Select Agency Corporation, Shy Street, Liverpool.—Reverend Sir," (for the ladies there were other circulars headed "Dear Madam"), "The approach of winter, with all the hardships that bitter season entails on those whom Providence has not blessed with sufficient means, induces us to call your attention to an unusual opportunity for providing yourself and those dear to you with a most desirable comfort at a merely nominal outlay. Having acquired an enormous bankrupt stock of *winter clothing* of most excellent material, and suitable for all measures, we wish, in testimony to our respect for the profession of which you are an honoured representative, to acquaint you *privately* with the fact before disposing of the stock in the open market. For £3 we can supply you with a complete clerical suit of the best make, including overcoat and gloves, etcetera, etcetera, the whole comprising an outfit which would be cheap at £10. In *your* case we should have no objection to meet you by taking £2 with your order and the balance *any time within six months.* Should you be disposed to show this to any of your friends, we may say we shall be pleased to appoint you our agent, and to allow you ten per cent, on all sales effected by you, which you are at liberty to deduct from the amount you remit to us with the orders. We subjoin full list of winter clothing for gentlemen, ladies, and children. Money orders to be made payable to Cruden Reginald, Esquire, Secretary, 13, Shy Street, Liverpool."

"Hullo!" said Reginald, looking up excitedly, "don't fold up any more of those, boy. They've made a mistake in my name and called me Cruden Reginald instead of Reginald Cruden. It will have to be altered."

"Oh, ah. There's on'y a couple of billions on 'em printed; that won't take no time at all," said Master Love, beginning to think longingly of *Tim Tigerskin.*

"It won't do to send them out like that," said Reginald.

"Oh yes, it will. Bless you, what's the odds if you call me Tommy Love or Love Tommy? I knows who you mean. And the governor, 'e is awful partickler about these here being done to-night. And we sent off millions on 'em last week. My eye, wasn't it a treat lickin' up the envellups!"

"Do you mean to say a lot of the circulars have been sent already?"

"'Undreds of grillions on 'em," replied the boy.

Of course it was no use after that delaying these; so Reginald finished off his task, not a little vexed at the mistake, and determined to have it put right without delay.

It was this cause of irritation, most likely, which prevented his dwelling too critically on the substance of the circular so affectionately dedicated to the poor country clergy. Beyond vaguely wondering where the Corporation kept their "bankrupt" stock of clothing, and how by the unaided light of nature they were to decide whether their applicants were stout or lean, or tall or short, he dismissed the matter from his mind for the time being, and made as short work as possible of the remainder of the task.

Then he wrote a short line home, announcing his arrival in as cheerful words as he could muster, and walked out to post it. The pavements were thronged with a crowd of jostling men and women, returning home from the day's work; but among them all the boy felt more lonely than had he been the sole inhabitant of Liverpool. Nobody knew him, nobody looked at him, nobody cared two straws about him. So he dropped his letter dismally into the box, and turned back to Shy Street, where at least there was one human being who knew his name and heeded his voice.

Master Love had made the most of his opportunities. He had lit a candle and stuck it into the mouth of an ink-bottle, and by its friendly light was already deep once more in the history of his hero.

"Say, what's yer name," said he, looking up as Reginald re-entered, "this here chap" as scuttled a ship, and drowned twenty on 'em. 'E was a cute 'un, and no error. He rigs hisself up as a carpenter, and takes a tile off the ship's bottom just as the storm was a-coming on; and in corse she flounders and all 'ands."

"And what became of him?" asked Reginald.

"Oh, in corse he stows hisself away in the boat with a lifebelt, and gets washed ashore; and he kills a tiger for 'is breakfast, and—"

"It's a pity you waste your time over bosh like that," said Reginald, not interested to hear the conclusion of the heroic Tim's adventures; "if you're fond of reading, why don't you get something better?"

"No fear—I like jam; don't you make no error, governor."

With which philosophical albeit enigmatical conclusion he buried his face once more in his hands, and immersed himself in the literary "jam" before him.

Reginald half envied him as he himself sat listless and unoccupied during that gloomy evening. He did his best to acquaint himself, by the aid of papers and circulars scattered about the room, with the work that lay before him. He made a careful tour of the premises, with a view to possible alterations and improvements. He settled in his own mind where the directors' table should stand, and in which corner of the private room he should establish his own desk. He went to the length of designing a seal for the Corporation, and in scribbling, for his own amusement, the imaginary minutes of an imaginary meeting of the directors. How would this do?

"A meeting of directors of the Select Agency Corporation"—by the way, was it "Limited"? He didn't very clearly understand what that meant. Still, most companies had the word after their name, and he made a note to inquire of Mr Medlock whether it applied to them—"was held on October 31st at the company's offices. Present, the Bishop of S— in the chair, Messrs Medlock, Blank, M.P., So-and-so, etcetera. The secretary, Mr

Cruden, having been introduced, took his seat and thanked the directors for their confidence. It was reported that the receipts for the last month had been (well, say) £1,000, including £50 deposited against shares by the new secretary, and the expenses £750. Mr Medlock reported the acquisition of a large bankrupt stock of clothing, which it was proposed to offer privately to a number of clergymen and others as per a list furnished by the right reverend the chairman. The following cheques were drawn:—Rent for offices for a month, £5; printing and postage, £25; secretary's salary for one month, £12 10 shillings; ditto, interest on the £50 deposit, 4 shillings 2 pence; office-boy (one month), £2; Mr Medlock for bankrupt stock of clothing, £150; etcetera, etcetera. The secretary suggested various improvements in the offices and fittings, and was requested to take any necessary steps. After sundry other routine business the Board adjourned."

This literary experiment concluded, Reginald, who after the fatigues and excitement of the day felt ready for sleep, decided to adjourn too.

"Do you stay here all night?" said he to Love.

"Me? You and me sleeps upstairs."

"I'm afraid there's no room up there for two persons," said Reginald; "you had better go home to-night, Love, and be here at nine in the morning."

"Go on—as if I 'ad lodgin's in the town. If you don't want me I know one as do. Me and the chemist's boy ain't too big for the attick."

"Very well," said Reginald, "you had better go up to bed now, it's late."

"Don't you think you're having a lark with me," said the boy; "'tain't eleven, and I ain't done this here Tigerskin yet. There's a lump of reading in it, I can tell you. When he'd killed them tigers he rigged hisself up in their skins, and—"

"Yes, yes," said Reginald. "I'm not going to let you stay up all night reading that rot. Cut up to bed now, do you hear?"

Strange to say, the boy obeyed. There was something about Reginald which reduced him to obedience, though much against his will. So he shambled off with his book under his arm, secretly congratulating himself that the bed in the attic was close to the window, so that he would be able to get a jolly long read in the morning.

After he had gone, Reginald followed his example, and retired to his own very spare bed, where he forgot all his cares in a night of sound refreshing sleep.

Chapter Fourteen
The Select Agency Corporation loses its Office-Boy

Mr Medlock duly appeared next morning. He greeted the new secretary with much friendliness, hoped he had a good journey and left them all well at home, and so on. He further hoped Reginald would find his new quarters comfortable. Most unfortunately they had missed securing the lease of a very fine suite of offices in Lord Street, and had to put up with these for the present. Reginald must see everything was comfortable; and as of course he would be pretty closely tied to the place (for the directors would not like the offices left in charge of a mere office-boy), he must make it as much of a home as possible.

As to money, salaries were always paid quarterly, and on Christmas Day Reginald would receive his first instalment. Meanwhile, as there were sure to be a few expenses, Reginald would receive five pounds on account (a princely allowance, equal to about thirteen shillings a week for the eight weeks between now and Christmas!)

The directors, Mr Medlock said, placed implicit confidence in the new secretary. He was authorised to open all letters that came. Any money they might contain he was strictly to account for and pay into the bank daily to Mr Medlock's account. He needn't send receipts, Mr Medlock would see to that. Any orders that came he was to take copies of, and then forward them to Mr John Smith, Weaver's Hotel, London, "to be called for," for execution. He would have to answer the questions of any who called to make inquiries, without of course disclosing any business secrets. In fact, as the aim of the Corporation was to supply their supporters with goods at the lowest possible price, they naturally met with a good deal of jealousy from tradesmen and persons of that sort, so that Reginald must be most guarded in all he said. If it became known how their business was carried on, others would be sure to attempt an imitation; and the whole scheme would fail.

"You know, Mr Reginald," said he—

"Excuse me," interrupted Reginald, "I'm afraid you're mistaken about my name. You've printed it Cruden Reginald, it should be Reginald Cruden."

"Dear me, how extraordinarily unfortunate!" said Mr Medlock; "I quite understood that was your name. And the unlucky part of it is, we have got all the circulars printed, and many of them circulated. I have also given your name as Mr Reginald to the directors, and advertised it, so that I don't see what can be done, except to keep it as it is. After all, it is a common thing, and it would put us to the greatest inconvenience to alter it now. Dear me, when I saw you in London I called you Mr Reginald, didn't I?"

"No, sir; you called me Mr Cruden."

"I must have supposed it was your Christian name, then."

"Perhaps it doesn't matter much," said Reginald; "and I don't wish to put the directors to any trouble."

"To be sure I knew you would not. Well, I was saying, Reginald (that's right, whatever way you take it!) the directors look upon you as a gentleman of character and education, and are satisfied to allow you to use your discretion and good sense in conducting their business. You have their names, which you can show to any one. They are greatly scattered, so that our Board meetings will be rare. Meanwhile they will be glad to hear how you are getting on, and will, I know, appreciate and recognise your services. By the way, I believe I mentioned (but really my memory is so bad) that we should ask you to qualify to the extent of £50 in the shares of the company?"

"Oh yes, I have the cheque here," said Reginald, taking it out of his pocket.

"That's right. And of course you will give yourself a receipt for it in the company's name. Curious, isn't it?"

With which pleasantry Mr Medlock departed, promising to look in frequently, and meanwhile to send in a fresh directory marked, and some new circulars for him to get on with.

Reginald, not quite sure whether it was all as good as he expected, set to work without delay to put into practice the various instructions he had received.

Mr Medlock's invitation to him to see everything was comfortable could hardly be fully realised on 13 shillings a week. That must wait for Christmas, and meanwhile he must make the best of what he had.

He set Love to work folding and enclosing the new circulars (this time calling attention to some extremely cheap globes and blackboards for ladies' and infants' schools), while he drew himself up a programme of his daily duties, in accordance with his impression of the directors' wishes. The result of this was that he came to the conclusion he should have his hands very full indeed—a possibility he by no means objected to.

But it was not clear to him how he was to get much outdoor exercise or recreation, or how he was to go to church on Sundays, or even to the bank on weekdays, if the office was never to be left. On this point he consulted Mr Medlock when he called in later in the day, and arranged that for two hours on Sunday, and an hour every evening, besides the necessary walk to the bank, he might lock up the office and take his walks abroad. Whereat he felt grateful and a little relieved.

It was not till about four days after his arrival that the first crop of circulars sown among the clergy yielded their firstfruits. On that day it was a harvest with a vengeance. At least 150 letters arrived. Most of them contained the two pounds and an order for the suit. In some cases most elaborate measurements accompanied the order. Some asked for High Church waistcoats, others for Low; some wished for wideawake hats, others for broad-brimmed clericals. Some sent extra money for a school-boy's suit as well, and some contained instructions for a complete family outfit. All were very eager about the matter, and one or two begged that the parcel might be sent marked "private."

Reginald had a busy day from morning till nearly midnight, entering and paying in the cash and forwarding the orders to Mr John Smith. He organised a beautiful tabular account, in which were entered the name and address of each correspondent, the date of their letters, the goods they ordered, and the amount they enclosed, and before the day was over the list had grown to a startling extent.

The next day brought a similar number of applications and remittances as to the globes and blackboards, and of course some more also about the clerical suits. And so, from day to day, the post showered letters in at the door, and the secretary of the Select Agency Corporation was one of the hardest worked men in Liverpool.

Master Love meanwhile had very little time for his "penny dreadfuls," and complained bitterly of his hardships. And indeed he looked so pale and unhealthy that Reginald began to fear the constant "licking" was undermining his constitution, and ordered him to use a sponge instead of his tongue. But on this point Love's loyalty made a stand. Nothing would induce him to use the artificial expedient. He deliberately made away with the sponge, and after a battle royal was allowed his own way, and continued to lick till his tongue literally clave to the roof of his mouth.

By the end of a fortnight the first rush of work was over, and Reginald and his henchman had time to draw breath. Mr Medlock had gone to London, presumably to superintend the dispatch of the various articles ordered.

It was about this time that Reginald had written home to Horace complaining of the dulness of his life, and begging him to repay Blandford the 6 shillings 6 pence, which had been weighing like lead on his mind ever since he left town, and which he now despaired of ever being able to spare out of the slender pittance on which he was doomed to subsist till Christmas. Happily that festive season was only a few weeks away now, and then how delighted he should be to send home a round half of his income, and convince himself he was after all a main prop to that dear distant little household.

Had he been gifted with ears sharp enough to catch a conversation that took place at the Bodega in London one evening about the same time, the Christmas spirit within him might have experienced a considerable chill.

The company consisted of Mr Medlock, Mr Shanklin, and Mr Durfy. The latter was present by sufferance, not because he was wanted or invited, but because he felt inclined for a good supper, and was sharp enough to know that neither of his employers could afford to fall out with him just then.

"Well, how goes it?" said Mr Shanklin. "You've had a run lately, and no mistake."

"Yes, I flatter myself we've done pretty well. One hundred pounds a day for ten days makes how much, Durfy?"

"A thousand," said Durfy.

"Humph!" said Mr Shanklin. "Time to think of our Christmas holidays."

"Wait a bit. We've not done yet. You say your two young mashers are still in tow, Alf?"

"Yes; green as duckweed. But they're nearly played out, I guess. One of them has a little bill for fifty pounds coming due in a fortnight, and t'other— well, he wagered me a hundred pounds on a horse that never ran for the Leger, and he's got one or two trifles besides down in my books."

"Yes, I got you that tip about the Leger," said Durfy, beginning to think himself neglected in this dialogue of self-congratulation.

"Yes; you managed to do it this time without botching it, for a wonder!" said Mr Shanklin.

"Yes; and I hope you'll manage to give me the ten-pound note you promised me for it, Mr S.," replied Durfy, with a snarl. "You seem to have forgotten that, and my commission too for finding you your new secretary."

"Yes. By the way," said Mr Medlock, "he deserves something for that; it's the best stroke of business we've done for a long time. It's worth three weeks to us to have him there to answer questions and choke off the inquisitive. He's got his busy time coming on, I fancy. Bless you, Durfy, the fellow was born for us! He swallows anything. I've allowed him thirteen shillings a week till Christmas, and he says, 'Thank you.' He's had his name turned inside out, and I do believe he thinks it an improvement! He sticks in the place all day with that young cockney gaol-bird you picked us up too, Durfy, and never growls."

"Does he help himself to any of the money?"

"Not a brass farthing! I do believe he buys his own postage-stamps when he writes home to his mamma!"

This last announcement was too comical to be received gravely.

"Ha, ha! he ought to be exhibited!" said Shanklin.

"He ought to be starved!" said Durfy viciously. "He knocked me down once, and I wouldn't have told you of him if I didn't owe him a grudge—the puppy!"

"Oh, well, I daresay you'll be gratified some day or other," said Medlock.

"I tell you one thing," said Durfy; "you'd better put a stopper on his writing home too often; I believe he's put his precious brother up to watch me. Why, the other night, when I was waiting for the postman to get hold of that letter you wanted, I'm blessed if he didn't turn up and rout me out—he and a young chum of his brother's that used to be in the swim with me. I don't think they saw me, luckily; but it was a shave, and of course I missed the letter."

"Yes, you did; there was no mistake about that!" said Mr Shanklin viciously. "When did you ever not miss it?"

"How can I help it, when it's your own secretary is dogging me?"

"Bless you! think of him dogging any one, the innocent! Anyhow, we can cut off his letters home for a bit, so as to give you no excuse next time."

"And what's the next job to be, then?" asked Durfy.

"The most particular of all," replied the sporting man. "I want a letter with the Boldham postmark, or perhaps a telegram, that will be delivered to-morrow night by the last post. There's a fifty pounds turns on it, and I must have it before the morning papers are out. Never mind what it is; you must get it somehow, and you'll get a fiver for it. As soon as that's done, Medlock, and the young dandies' bills have come due, we can order a cab. Your secretary at Liverpool will hold out long enough for us to get to the moon before we're wanted."

"You're right there!" said Mr Medlock, laughing. "I'll go down and look him up to-morrow, and clear up, and then I fancy he'll manage the rest himself; and we can clear out. Ha, ha! capital sherry, this brand. Have some more, Durfy."

Mr Medlock kept his promise and cheered Reginald in his loneliness by a friendly visit.

"I've been away longer than I expected, and I must say the way you have managed matters in my absence does you the greatest credit, Reginald. I shall feel perfectly comfortable in future when I am absent."

A flush of pleasure rose to Reginald's cheeks, such as would have moved to pity any heart less cold-blooded than Mr Medlock's.

"No one has called, I suppose?"

"No, sir. There's been a letter, though, from the Rev. T. Mulberry, of Woolford-in-the-Meadow, to ask why the suit he ordered has not yet been delivered."

Mr Medlock smiled.

"These good men are so impatient," said he; "they imagine their order is the only one we have to think of. What would they think of the four hundred and odd suits we have on order, eh, Mr Reginald?"

"I suppose I had better write and say the orders will be taken in rotation, and that his will be forwarded in a few days."

"Better say a few weeks. You've no notion of the difficulty we have in trying to meet every one's wishes. Say before Christmas—and the same with the globes and other things. The time and trouble taken in packing the things really cuts into the profits terribly."

"Could we do any of it down here?" said Reginald. "Love and I have often nothing to do."

It was well the speaker did not notice the fiendish grimace with which the young gentleman referred to accepted the statement.

"You're very good," said Mr Medlock; "but I shouldn't think of it. We want you for head work. There are plenty to be hired in London to do the hand work. By the way, I will take up the register of orders and cash you have been keeping, to check with the letters in town. You won't want it for a few days."

Reginald felt sorry to part with a work in which he felt such pride as this beautifully kept register. However, he had made it for the use of the Corporation, and it was not his to withhold.

After clearing up cautiously all round, with the result that Reginald had very little besides pen, ink, and paper left him, Mr Medlock said good morning.

"I may have to run up to town for a few days," he said, "but I shall see you again very soon, I hope. Meanwhile, make yourself comfortable. The directors are very favourably impressed with you already, and I hope at Christmas they may meet and tell you so in person. Boy, make a parcel of these books and papers and bring them for me to my hotel."

Love obeyed surlily. He was only waiting for Mr Medlock's departure to dive into the mystery of *Trumpery Toadstool, or Murdered for a Lark*, in which he had that morning invested. He made a clumsy parcel of the books, and then shambled forth in a somewhat homicidal spirit in Mr Medlock's wake down the street.

At the corner that gentleman halted till he came up.

"Well, young fellow, picked any pockets lately?"

The boy scowled at him inquisitively.

"All right," said Mr Medlock. "I never said you had. I'm not going to take you to the police-station, I'm going to give you half a crown."

This put a new aspect on the situation. Love brightened up as he watched Mr Medlock's hand dive into his pocket.

"What should you do with a half-crown if you had it?"

"Do? I know, and no error. I'd get the *Noogate Calendar*, that's what I'd do."

"You can read, then?"

"Ray-ther; oh no, not me."

"Can you read writing?"

"In corse."

"Do you always go to the post with the letters?"

"In corse."

"Do you ever see any addressed to Mrs Cruden or Mr Cruden in London?"

"'Bout once a week. That there sekketery always gives 'em to me separate, and says I'm to be sure and post 'em."

"Well, I say they're not to be posted," said Mr Medlock. "Here's half a crown; and listen: next time you get any to post put them on one side; and every one you can show me you shall have sixpence for. Mind what you're at, or he'll flay you alive if he catches you. Off you go, there's a good boy."

And Love pocketed his half-crown greedily, and with a knowing wink at his employer sped back to the office.

That afternoon Reginald wrote a short polite note to the Rev. T. Mulberry, explaining to him the reason for any apparent delay in the execution of his order, and promising that he should duly receive it before Christmas. This was the only letter for the post that day, and Love had no opportunity of earning a further sixpence.

He had an opportunity of spending his half-crown, however, and when he returned from the post he was radiant in face and stouter under the waistcoat by the thickness of the coveted volume of the *Newgate Calendar* series.

With the impetuosity characteristic of his age, he plunged into its contents the moment he found himself free of work, and by the time Reginald returned from his short evening stroll he was master of several of its stories. *Tim Tigerskin* and *The Pirate's Bride* were nothing to it. They all performed their incredible exploits on the other side of the world, but these heroes were beings of flesh and blood like himself, and, for all he knew, he might have seen them and talked to them, and have known some of the very spots in London which they frequented. He felt a personal interest in their achievements.

"Say, governor," said he as soon as Reginald entered, "do you know Southwark Road?"

"In London? Yes," said Reginald.

"This 'ere chap, Bright, was a light porter to a cove as kep' a grocer's shop there, and one night when he was asleep in the arm-cheer he puts a sack on 'is 'ead and chokes 'im. The old cove he struggles a bit, but—"

"Shut up!" said Reginald angrily. "I've told you quite often enough. Give me that book."

At the words and the tones in which they were uttered Love suddenly turned into a small fiend. He struggled, he kicked, he cursed, he howled to keep his treasure. Reginald was inexorable, and of course it was only a matter of time until the book was in his hands. A glance at its contents satisfied him.

"Look here," said he, holding the book behind his back and parrying all the boy's frantic efforts to recover it, "don't make a fool of yourself, youngster."

"Give it to me! Give me my book, you—"

And the boy broke into a volley of oaths and flung himself once more tooth-and-nail on Reginald. Already Reginald saw he had made a mistake. He had done about the most unwise thing he possibly could have done. But it was too late to undo it. The only thing, apparently, was to go through with it now. So he flung the book into the fire, and, catching the boy by the arm, told him if he did not stop swearing and struggling at once he would make him.

The boy did not stop, and Reginald did make him.

It was a poor sort of victory, and no one knew it better than Reginald. If the boy was awed into silence, he was no nearer listening to reason—nay, further than ever. He slunk sulkily into a corner, glowering at his oppressor and deaf to every word he uttered. In vain Reginald expostulated, coaxed, reasoned, even apologised. The boy met it all with a sullen scowl. Reginald offered to pay him for the book, to buy him another, to read aloud to him, to give him an extra hour a day—it was all no use; the injury was too deep to wash out so easily; and finally he had to give it up and trust that time might do what arguments and threats had failed to effect.

But in this he was disappointed; for next morning when nine o'clock arrived, no Love was there, nor as the day wore on did he put in an appearance. When at last evening came, and still no signs of him, Reginald began to discover that the sole result of his well-meant interference had been to drive his only companion from him, and doom himself henceforth to the miseries of solitary confinement.

For days he scarcely spoke a word. The silence of that office was unearthly. He opened the window, winter as it was, to let in the sound of cabs and footsteps for company. He missed even the familiar rustle of the "penny dreadfuls" as the boy turned their pages. He wished anybody, even his direst foe, might turn up to save him from dying of loneliness.

Chapter Fifteen
A Letter from Horace

"Dear Reg," (so ran a letter from Horace which Reginald received a day or two after Master Love's desertion), "I'm afraid you are having rather a slow time up there, which is more than can be said for us here. There's been no end of a row at the *Rocket*, which you may like to hear about, especially as two of the chief persons concerned were your friend Durfy and your affectionate brother.

"Granville, the sub-editor, came into the office where Booms and Waterford and I were working on Friday morning, and said, in his usual mild way,—

"'I should like to know who generally clears the post-box in the morning?'

"'I do,' said Booms. You know the way he groans when he speaks.

"'The reason I want to know is, because I have an idea one or two letters lately have either been looked at or tampered with before the editor or I see them.'

"'I suppose I'm to be given in charge?' said Booms. 'I didn't do it; but when once a man's suspected, what's the use of saying anything?'

"Even Granville couldn't help grinning at this.

"'Nonsense, Booms. I'm glad to say I know you three fellows well enough by this time to feel sure it wasn't one of you. I shouldn't have spoken to you about it if I had.'

"Booms seemed quite disappointed he wasn't to be made a martyr of after all.

"'You think I know all about it?' he said.

"'No, I don't; and if you'll just listen without running away with ridiculous notions, Booms,' said Granville, warming up a bit, 'I'll explain myself. Two letters during the last fortnight have been undoubtedly opened before I saw them. They both arrived between eight o'clock in the evening and nine next morning, and they both came from sporting correspondents of ours in the country, and contained information of a private nature intended for our paper the next day. In one case it was about a horse race, and in the other about an important football match. The letters were not tampered with for the purpose of giving information to any other papers, because we were still the only paper who gave the news, so the probability is some one who wanted to bet on the event has tried to get hold of the news beforehand.'

"'I never made a bet in my life,' said Booms.

"We couldn't help laughing at this, for the stories he tells us of his terrific sporting exploits when he goes out of an evening in his high collar would make you think he was the loudest betting man in London.

"Granville laughed too.

"'Better not begin,' he said, and then blushed very red, as it occurred to him he had made an unintentional pun. But we looked quite grave, and did not give any sign of having seen it, and that put him on his feet again.

"'It's not a comfortable thing to happen,' said he, 'and what I want to propose is that one or two of you should stay late for a night or two and see if you can find out how it occurs. There are one or two events coming off during the next few days about which we expect special communications, so that very likely whoever it is may try again. You must be very careful, and I shall have to leave you to use your discretion, for I'm so busy with the new Literary Supplement that I cannot stay myself.'

"Well, when he'd gone we had a consultation, and of course it ended in Waterford and me determining to sit up. Poor Booms's heart would break if he couldn't go 'on the mash' as usual; and though he tried to seem very much hurt that he was not to stay, we could see he was greatly relieved. Waterford and I were rather glad, as it happened, for we'd some work on hand it just suited us to get a quiet evening for.

"So I wrote a note to Miss Crisp. Don't get excited, old man; she's a very nice girl, but she's another's. (By the way, Jemima asks after you every time I meet her, which is once a week now; she's invited herself into our shorthand class.) And after helping to rig old Booms up to the ninety-nines, which wasn't easy work, for his 'dicky' kept twisting round to the side of his neck, and we had to pin it in three places before it would keep steady, I gave him the note and asked him would he ever be so kind as to take it round for me, as it was to ask Miss Crisp if she would go and keep my mother company during my absence.

"After that I thought we should never get rid of him. He insisted on overhauling every article of his toilet. At least four more pins were added to fix the restless dicky in its place on his manly breast. We polished up his eye-glasses with wash-leather till the pewter nearly all rubbed off; we helped him roll his flannel shirt-sleeves up to the elbows for fear—horrible idea!—they should chance to peep out from below his cuffs; we devoted an anxious two minutes to the poising of his hat at the right angle, and then passed him affectionately from one to the other to see he was all right. After which he went off, holding my letter carefully in his scented handkerchief and saying—dear gay deceiver!—that he envied us spending a cosy evening in that snug office by the fire!

"The work Waterford and I have on hand is—tell it not in Gath, old man, and don't scorn a fellow off the face of the earth—to try to write something that will get into the Literary Supplement. This supplement is a new idea of the editor's, and makes a sort of weekly magazine. He writes a lot of it himself, and we chip a lot of stuff for him out of other papers. The idea of having a shot at it occurred to us both independently, in a funny and rather humiliating way. It seems Waterford, without saying a word to me or anybody, had sat down and composed some lines on the 'Swallow'— appropriate topic for this season of the year. I at the same time, without saying a word to Waterford or anybody except mother, had sat down and, with awful groanings and wrestlings of mind, evolved a lucubration in prose on 'Ancient and Modern Athletic Sports.' Of course I crammed a lot of it up out of encyclopaedias and that sort of thing. It was the driest rot you ever read, and I knew it was doomed before I sent it in. But as it was written I thought I might try. So, as of course I couldn't send it in under my own name, I asked Miss Crisp if I might send it under hers. The obliging little lady laughed and said, 'Yes,' but she didn't tell me at the same time that Waterford had come to her with his 'Swallow' and asked the very same thing. A rare laugh she must have had at our expense! Well, I sent mine in and Waterford sent in his.

"We were both very abstracted for the next few days, but little guessed our perturbation arose from the same cause. Then came the fatal Wednesday—the 'd.w.t.' day as we call it—for Granville always saves up his rejected addresses for us to 'decline with thanks' for Wednesdays. There was a good batch of them this day, so Waterford and I took half each. I took a hurried skim through mine, but no 'Ancient and Modern Athletic Sports' were there. I concluded therefore Waterford had it. Granville writes in the corner of each 'd.w.t.,' or 'd.w.t. note,' which means 'declined with thanks' pure and simple, or 'declined with thanks' and a short polite note to be written at the same time stating that the sub-editor, while recognising some merit in the contribution, regretted it was not suitable for the Supplement. I polished off my pure and simple first, and then began to tackle the notes.

About the fourth I came to considerably astonished me. It was a couple of mild sonnets on the 'Swallow,' with the name M.E. Crisp attached!

"'Hullo,' I said to Waterford, tossing the paper over to him, 'here's Miss Crisp writing some verses. I should have thought she could write better stuff than that, shouldn't you?'

"Waterford, very red in the face, snatched up the paper and glanced at it.

"'Do you think they're so bad?' said he.

"'Frightful twaddle,' said I; 'fancy any one saying—'"

"The drowsy year from winter's sleep ye wake,
Yet two of ye do not a summer make."

"'Well,' said he, grinning, 'you'd better tell her straight off it's bosh, and then she's not likely to make a fool of herself again. Hullo, though, I say,' he exclaimed, picking up a paper in front of him, every smudge and blot of which I knew only too well, 'why, she's at it again. What's this?

"'"Ancient and Mod—" Why, it's in your writing; did you copy it out for her?'

"'I wrote that out, yes,' said I, feeling it my turn to colour up and look sheepish.

"Waterford glanced rapidly through the first few lines, and then said,—

"'Well, all I can say is, it's a pity she didn't stick to poetry. I'm sure the line about waking the drowsy year is a jolly sight better than this awful rot.'

"'Though we are not told so in so many words, we may reasonably conclude that athletic sports were not unpractised by Cain and Abel prior to the death of the latter!

"'As if they could have done it after!'

"'I never said they could,' I said, feeling very much taken down.

"'Oh—it was you composed it as well as wrote it, was it?' said he laughing. 'Ho, ho! that's the best joke I ever heard. Poor little Crisp, what a shame to get her to father—or mother a thing like this; ha, ha! "prior to the death of the latter"—that's something like a play of language! My eye, what a game she's been having with us!'

"'Us! then you're the idiot who wrote about the Swallows!' said I.

"'Suppose I am,' said he, blushing all over, 'suppose I am.'

"'Well, all I can say is, I'm precious glad the little Crisp isn't guilty of it. "Two of ye do not a summer make," indeed!'

"'Well, they don't,' said he.

"'I know they don't,' said I, half dead with laughing, 'but you needn't go and tell everybody.'

"'I'm sure it's just as interesting as "Cain and Abel"—'

"'There now, we don't want to hear any more about them,' said I, 'but I think we ought to send them both back to Miss Crisp, to give her her laugh against us too.'

"We did so; and I needn't tell you she lets us have it whenever we get within twenty yards of her.

"Here's a long digression, but it may amuse you; and you said you wanted something to read.

"Well, Waterford and I recovered in a few days from our first reverse, and decided to have another shot; and so we were rather glad of the quiet evening at the office to make our new attempts. We half thought of writing a piece between us, but decided we'd better go on our own hooks after all, as our styles were not yet broken in to one another. We agreed we had better this time both write on subjects we knew something about; Waterford accordingly selected 'A Day in a Sub-Sub-Editor's Life' as a topic he really could claim to be familiar with; while I pitched upon 'Early Rising,' a branch of science in which I flatter myself, old man, *you* are not competent to tell me whether I excel or not. Half the battle was done when we had fixed on our subjects; so as soon as every one was gone we poked up the fire and made ourselves snug, and settled down to work.

"We plodded on steadily till we heard the half-past nine letters dropped into the box. Then it occurred to us we had better turn down the lights and give our office as deserted a look as we could. It was rather slow work sitting in the dark for a couple of hours, not speaking a word or daring to move a toe. The fire got low, but we dared not make it up; and of course we both had awful desires to sneeze and cough—you always do at such times—and half killed ourselves in our efforts to smother them. We could hear the cabs and omnibuses in Fleet Street keeping up a regular roar; but no footsteps came near us, except once when a telegraph boy (as we guessed by his shrill whistling and his smart step) came and dropped a telegram into the box. I assure you the click the flap of the letter-box made that moment, although I knew what it was and why it was, made my heart beat like a steam-engine.

"It was beginning to get rather slow when twelve came and still nothing to disturb us. We might have been forging ahead with our writing all this time if we had only known.

"Presently Waterford whispered,—

"'They won't try to-night now.'

"Just as he spoke we heard a creak on the stairs outside. We had heard lots of creaks already, but somehow this one startled us both. I instinctively picked up the ruler from the table, and Waterford took my arm and motioned me close to the wall beside him. Another creak came presently and then another. Evidently some one was coming down the stairs cautiously, and in the dark too, for we saw no glimmer of a light through the partly-opened door. We were behind it, so that if it opened we should be quite hidden unless the fellow groped round it.

"Down he came slowly, and there was no mistake now about its being a human being and not a ghost, for we heard him clearing his throat very quietly and snuffling as he reached the bottom step. I can tell you it was rather exciting, even for a fellow of my dull nerves.

"Waterford nudged me to creep a little nearer the gas, ready to turn it up at a moment's notice, while he kept at the door, to prevent our man getting out after he was once in.

"Presently the door opened very quietly. He did not fling it wide open, luckily, or he was bound to spot us behind it; but he opened it just enough to squeeze in, and then, feeling his way round by the wall, made straight for the letter-box. Although it was dark he seemed to know his way pretty well, and in a few seconds we heard him stop and fumble with a key in the lock. In a second or two he had opened it, and then, crouching down, began cautiously to rub a match on the floor. The light was too dim to see anything but the crouching figure of a man bending over the box and examining the addresses of one or two of the letters in it. His match went out before he had found what he wanted.

"It was hard work to keep from giving him a little unexpected light, for my fingers itched to turn up the gas. However, it was evidently better to wait a little longer and see what he really was up to before we were down on him.

"He lit another match, and this time seemed to find what he wanted, for we saw him put one letter in his pocket and drop all the others back into the box, blowing out his match as he did so.

"Now was our time. I felt a nudge from Waterford and turned the gas full on, while he quietly closed the door and turned the key.

"I felt quite sorry for the poor scared beggar as he knelt there and turned his white face to the light, unable to move or speak or do anything. You'll have guessed who it was.

"'So, Mr Durfy,' said Waterford, leaning up against the door and folding his arms, 'it's you, is it?'

"The culprit glared at him and then at me, and rose to his feet with a forced laugh.

"'It looks like it,' he said.

"'So it does,' said Waterford, taking the key out of the door and putting it in his pocket; 'very like it. And it looks very much as if he would have to make himself comfortable here till Mr Granville comes!'

"'What do you mean?' exclaimed the fellow. 'I've as much right to be here as you have, for the matter of that, at this hour.'

"'Very *well*, then,' said Waterford, as cool as a cucumber, 'we'll all three stay here. Eh, Cruden?'

"'I'm game,' said I.

"He evidently didn't like the turn things were taking, and changed his tack.

"'Come, don't play the fool!' he said coaxingly, 'The fact is, I expected a letter from a friend, and as it was very important I came to get it. It's all right.'

"'You may think so,' said Waterford; 'you may think it's all right to come here on tiptoe at midnight with a false key, and steal, but other people may differ from you, that's all! Besides, you're telling a lie; the letter you've got in your pocket doesn't belong to you!'

"It was rather a rash challenge, but we could see by the way his face fell it was a good shot.

"He uttered an oath, and advanced threateningly towards the door.

"'Sit down,' said Waterford, 'unless you want to be tied up. There are two of us here, and we're not going to stand any nonsense, I can tell you!'

"'You've no right—'

"'Sit down, and shut up!' repeated Waterford.

"'I tell you if you—'

"'Cruden, you'll find some cord in one of those drawers. If you don't shut up, and sit down, Durfy, we shall make you.'

"He caved in after that, and I was rather glad we hadn't to go to extremes.

"'Hadn't we better get the letter?' whispered I.

"'No; he'd better fork it out to Granville,' said Waterford.

"He was wrong for once, as you shall hear.

"Durfy slunk off and sat down on a chair in the far corner of the room, swearing to himself, but not venturing to raise his voice above a growl.

"It was now about half-past twelve, and we had the lively prospect of waiting at least eight hours before Granville turned up.

"'Don't you bother to stay,' said Waterford. 'I can look after him.'

"But I scouted the idea, and said nothing would induce me to go.

"'Very well, then,' said he; 'we may as well get on with our writing.'

"So we pulled our chairs up to the table, with a full-view of Durfy in the corner, and tried to continue our lucubrations.

"But when you are sitting up at dead of night, with a prisoner in the corner of the room cursing and gnashing his teeth at you, it is not easy to grow eloquent either on the subject of 'A Day in a Sub-sub-Editor's Life,' or 'Early Rising.' And so we found. We gave it up presently, and made up the fire and chatted together in a whisper.

"Once or twice Durfy broke the silence.

"'I'm hungry,' growled he, about two o'clock.

"'So are we,' said Waterford.

"'Well, go and get something. I'm not going to be starved, I tell you. I'll make you smart for it, both of you.'

"'You've been told to shut up,' said Waterford, rising to his feet with a glance towards the drawer where the cord was kept.

"Durfy was quiet after that for an hour or so. Then I suppose he must have overheard me saying something to Waterford about you, for he broke out with a vicious laugh, —

"'Reginald! Yes, he'll thank you for this. I'll make it so hot for him—'

"'Look here,' said Waterford, 'this is the last time you're going to be cautioned, Durfy. If you open your mouth once more you'll be gagged; mind that. I mean what I say.'

"This was quite enough for Durfy. He made no further attempt to speak, but curled himself up on the floor and turned his face to the wall, and disposed himself to all appearances to sleep. Whether he succeeded or not I can't say. But towards morning he glowered round at us. Then he took out some tobacco and commenced chewing it, and finally turned his back on us again and continued dozing and chewing alternately till the eight o'clock bell rang and aroused us.

"Half an hour later Granville arrived, and a glance at our group was quite sufficient to acquaint him with the state of affairs.

"'So this is the man,' said he, pointing to Durfy.

"'Yes, sir. We caught him in the act of taking a letter out of the box at midnight. In fact, he's got it in his pocket this moment.'

"Durfy gave a fiendish grin, and said,— "'That's a lie. I've no letter in my pocket!'

"And he proceeded to turn his pockets one after the other inside out.

"'All I know is we both saw him take a letter out of the box and put it in his pocket,' said Waterford.

"'Yes,' snarled Durfy, 'and I told you it was a private letter of my own.'

"'Whatever the letter is, you took it out of the box, and you had better show it quietly,' said Granville; 'it will save you trouble.'

"'I tell you I have no letter,' replied Durfy again.

"'Very well, then, Cruden, perhaps you will kindly fetch a policeman.'

"I started to go, but Durfy broke out, this time in tones of sincere terror,—

"'Don't do that, don't ruin me! I did take it, but—'

"'Give it to me then.'

"'I can't. I've eaten it!'

"Wasn't this a thunderbolt! How were we to prove whose the letter was? Wild thoughts of a stomach-pump, or soap and warm water, did flash through my mind, but what was the use? The fellow had done us after all, and we had to admit it.

"No one stopped him as he went to the door, half scowling, half grinning.

"'Good morning, gentlemen!' said he. 'I hope you'll get a better night's rest to-morrow. I promise not to disturb you,' (here followed a few oaths). 'But I'll pay you out, some of you—Crudens, Reginalds, sneaks, prigs—all of you!'

"With which neat peroration he took his leave, and the *Rocket* has not seen him since.

"Here's a long screed! I must pull up now.

"Mother's not very well, she's fretting, I'm afraid, and her eyes trouble her. I can't say we shall be sorry when Christmas comes, for try all we can, we're in debt at one or two of the shops. I know you'll hate to hear it, but it's simply unavoidable on our present means. I wish I could come down and see you; but for one thing, I can't afford it, and for another, I can't leave mother. Mrs Shuckleford is really very kind, though she's not a congenial spirit.

"Young Gedge and I see plenty of one another: he's joined our shorthand class, and is going in for a little steady work all round. He owes you a lot for befriending him at the time you did, and he's not forgotten it. I promised to send you his love next time I wrote. Harker will be in town next week, which will be jolly. I've never seen Bland since I called to pay the 6 shillings 6 pence. I fancy he's got into rather a fast lot, and is making a fool of himself, which is a pity.

"You tell us very little about your Corporation; I hope it is going on all right. I wish to goodness you were back in town. I never was in love with the concern, as you know, and at the risk of putting you in a rage, I can't help saying it's a pity we couldn't all have stayed together just now. Forgive this growl, old man.

"Your affectionate brother,—

"Horace.

"Wednesday, 'd.w.t.' day. To our surprise and trepidation, neither the 'Day in a Sub-Sub-editor's Life' nor 'Early Rising' were among the papers given out to-day to be 'declined with thanks.' Granville may have put them into the fire as not even worth returning, or he may actually—*O mirabile dictu*—be going to put us into print?"

Chapter Sixteen
Visitors at Number 13, Shy Street

The concluding sentences of Horace's long letter, particularly those which referred to his mother's poor health and the straitened circumstances of the little household, were sufficiently unwelcome to eclipse in Reginald's mind the other exciting news the letter had contained. They brought on a fit of the blues which lasted more than one day.

For now that he had neither companion nor occupation (for the business of the Select Agency Corporation had fallen off completely) there was nothing to prevent his indulgence in low spirits.

He began to chafe at his imprisonment, and still more at his helplessness even were he at liberty to do anything. Christmas was still a fortnight off, and till then what could he do on thirteen shillings a week? He might cut down his commissariat certainly, to, say, a shilling a day, and send home the rest. But then, what about coals and postage-stamps and other incidental expenses, which had to be met in Mr Medlock's absence out of his own pocket? The weather was very cold—he could hardly do without coals, and he was bound in the interests of the Corporation to keep stamps enough in the place to cover the necessary correspondence.

When all was said, two shillings seemed to be the utmost he could save out of his weekly pittance, and this he sent home by the very next post, with a long, would-be cheerful, but really dismal letter, stoutly denying that he was either miserable or disappointed with his new work, and anticipating with pleasure the possibility of being able to run up at Christmas and bring with him the welcome funds which would clear the family of debt and give it a good start for the New Year.

When he had finished his letter home he wrote to Mr Medlock, very respectfully suggesting that as he had been working pretty hard and for the last few days single-handed, Mr Medlock might not object to advance him at any rate part of the salary due in a fortnight, as he was rather in need of money. And he ventured to ask, as Christmas Day fell on a Thursday, and no business was likely to be done between that day and the following Monday, might he take the *two* or three days' holiday, undertaking, of course, to be back at his post on the Monday morning? He enclosed a few post-office orders which had come to hand since he last wrote, and hoped he should soon have the pleasure of seeing Mr Medlock—"or anybody," he added to himself as he closed the letter and looked wearily round the gaunt, empty room.

Now, if Reginald had been a believer in fairies he would hardly have started as much as he did when, almost as the words escaped his lips, the door opened, and a female marched into the room.

A little prim female it was, with stiff curls down on her forehead and a very sharp nose and very thin lips and fidgety fingers that seemed not to know whether to cling to one another for support or fly at the countenance of somebody else.

This formidable visitor spared Reginald the trouble of inquiring to what fortunate circumstance he was indebted for the honour of so unlooked-for a visit.

"Now, sir!" said she, panting a little, after her ascent of the stairs, but very emphatic, all the same.

The observation was not one which left much scope for argument, and Reginald did not exactly know what to reply. At last, however, he summoned up resolution enough to say politely,—

"Now, madam, can I be of any service?"

Inoffensive as the observation was, it had the effect of greatly irritating the lady.

"None of your sauce, young gentleman," said she, putting down her bag and umbrella, and folding her arms defiantly. "I've not come here to take any of your impertinence."

Reginald's impertinence! He had never been rude to a lady in all his life except once, and the penance he had paid for that sin had been bitter enough, as the reader can testify.

"You needn't pretend not to know what I've come here for," continued the lady, taking a hasty glance round the room, as if mentally calculating from what door or window her victim would be most likely to attempt to escape.

"Perhaps she's Love's mother!" gasped Reginald, to himself.—"Oh, but what a Venus!"

This classical reflection he prudently kept to himself, and waited for his visitor to explain her errand further.

"You know who I am," she said, walking up to him.

"No, indeed," said Reginald, hardly liking to retreat, but not quite comfortable to be standing still. "Unless—unless your name is Love."

"Love!" screamed the outraged "Venus."

"I'll Love you, young gentleman, before I've done with you. Love, indeed, you impudent sauce-box, you!"

"I beg your pardon," began Reginald.

"Love, indeed! I'd like to scratch you, so I would!" cried the lady, with a gesture so ominously like suiting the action to the word, that Reginald fairly deserted his post and retreated two full paces.

This was getting critical. Either the lady was mad, or she had mistaken Reginald for some one else. In either case he felt utterly powerless to deal with the difficulty. So like a prudent man he decided to hold his tongue and let the lady explain herself.

"Love, indeed!" said she, for the third time. "You saucy jackanapes, you. No, sir, my name's Wrigley!"

She evidently supposed this announcement would fall like a thunderbolt on the head of her victim, and it disconcerted her not a little when he merely raised his eyebrows and inclined his head politely.

"Now do you know what I'm come about?" said she.

"No," replied he.

"Yes you do. You needn't think to deceive me, sir. It won't do, I can tell you."

"I *really* don't know," said poor Reginald. "Who are you?"

"I'm the lady who ordered the globe and blackboard, and sent two pounds along with the order to you, Mr Cruden Reginald. There! *Now* perhaps you know what I've come for!"

If she had expected Reginald to fly out of the window, or seek refuge up the chimney, at this announcement, the composure with which he received the overpowering disclosure must have considerably astonished her.

"Eh?" she said. "Eh? Do you know me now?"

"I have no doubt you are right," said he. "We had more than a hundred orders for the globes and boards, and expect they will be delivered this week or next."

"Oh! then you have been imposing on more than me?" said the lady, who till this moment had imagined she had been the only correspondent of the Corporation on the subject.

"We've been imposing on no one," said Reginald warmly. "You have no right to say that, Mrs Wrigley."

His honest indignation startled the good lady.

"Then why don't you send the things?" she demanded, in a milder tone.

"There are a great many orders to attend to, and they have to be taken in order as we receive them. Probably yours came a good deal later than others."

"No, it didn't. I wrote by return of post, and put an extra stamp on too. You must have got mine one of the very first."

"In that case you will be one of the first to receive your globe and board."

"I know that, young man," said she. "I'm going to take them with me now!"

"I'm afraid you can't do that," said Reginald. "They are being sent off from London."

The lady, who had somewhat moderated her wrath in the presence of the secretary's unruffled politeness, fired up as fiercely as ever at this.

"There! I *knew* it was a swindle! From London, indeed! Might as well say New York at once! *I'm* not going to believe your lies, you young robber! Don't expect it!"

It was a considerable tax on Reginald's temper to be addressed in language like this, even by a lady, and he could not help retorting rather hotly, "I'm glad you are only a woman, Mrs Wrigley, for I wouldn't stand being called a thief by a man, I assure you!"

"Oh, don't let that make any difference!" said she, fairly in a rage, and advancing up to him. "Knock me down and welcome! You may just as well murder a woman as rob her!"

"I can only tell you again your order is being executed in London."

"And I can tell you I don't believe a word you say, and I'll just have my two pounds back, and have done with you! Come, you can't say you never got *that*!"

"If you sent it, I certainly did," said Reginald.

"Then perhaps you'll hand it up this moment?"

"I would gladly do so if I had it, but—"

"I suppose it's gone to London too?" said she, with supernatural calmness.

"It has been paid in with all the money to the bank," said Reginald. "But if you wish it I will write to the managing director and ask him to return it by next post."

"Will you?" said she, in tones that might have frozen any one less heated than Reginald. "And you suppose I've come all the way from Dorsetshire to get that for an answer, do you? You're mistaken, sir! I don't leave this place till I get my money or my things! So now!"

"Then," said Reginald, feeling the case desperate, and pushing a chair in her direction, "perhaps you'd better sit down."

She glared round at him indignantly. But perhaps it was the sight of his haggard, troubled face, or the faint suspicion that he, after all, might be more honest than his employers, or the reflection that she could get her rights better out of the place than in it. Whatever the reason was, she changed her mind.

"You shall hear of me again, sir!" said she; "mind that! Love, indeed!" whereupon she bounced out of the office and slammed the door behind her.

Reginald sat with his eyes on the door for a full two minutes before he could sufficiently collect his wits to know where he was or what had happened.

Then a sense of indignation overpowered all his other feelings—not against Mrs Wrigley, but against Mr Medlock, for leaving him in a position where he could be, even in the remotest degree, open to so unpleasant a charge as that he had just listened to.

Why could he not be trusted with sufficient money and control over the operations of the Corporation to enable him to meet so unfounded a charge? What would the Bishop of S— or the other directors think if they heard that a lady had come all the way from Dorsetshire to tell them they were a set of swindlers and thieves? If he had had the sending off of the orders to see to, he was confident he could have got every one of them off by this time, even if he had made up every parcel with his own hands.

What, in short, was the use of being called a secretary if he was armed with no greater authority than a common junior clerk?

He opened the letter he had just written to Mr Medlock, and sat down to write another, more aggrieved in its tone and more urgent in its request that Mr Medlock would come down to Liverpool at once to arrange matters on a more satisfactory footing. It was difficult to write a letter which altogether pleased him; but at last he managed to do it, and for fear his warmth should evaporate he went out to post it, locking the office up behind him.

He took a walk before returning—the first he had taken for a week. It was a beautiful crisp December day, when, even through the murky atmosphere of Liverpool, the sun looked down joyously, and the blue sky, flecked with little fleecy clouds, seemed to challenge the smoke and steam of a thousand chimneys to touch its purity. Reginald's steps turned away from the city, through a quiet suburb towards the country. He would have to walk too far, he knew, to reach real open fields and green lanes, but there was at least a suggestion of the country here which to his weary mind was refreshing.

His walk took him past a large public school, in the playground of which an exciting football match was in active progress. Like an old war horse, Reginald gazed through the palings and snorted as the cry of battle rose in the air.

"Hack it through, sir!" "Well run!" "Collar him there!"

As he heard those old familiar cries it seemed to him as if the old life had come back to him with a sudden rush. He was no longer a poor baited secretary, but a joyous school-boy, head of his form, lord and master of half a dozen fags, and a caution and example to the whole junior school. He had chums by the score; his study was always crowded with fellows wanting him to do this or help them in that. How jolly to be popular! How jolly, when the ball came out of the scrimmage, to hear every one shout, "Let Cruden have it!" How jolly, as he snatched it up and rushed, cleaving his way to the enemy's goal, to hear that roar behind him, "Run indeed, sir!"

"Back him up!"

"Well played!" Yes, he heard them still, like music; and as he watched the shifting fortunes of this game he felt the blood course through his veins with a strange, familiar ardour.

Ah, here came the ball out of the scrimmage straight towards him! Oh, the thrill of such a moment! Who does not know it? A second more and he would have it—

Alas! poor Reginald awoke as suddenly as he had dreamed. A hideous paling stood between him and the ball. He was not in the game at all. Nothing but a lonely, friendless drudge, whom nobody wanted, nobody cared about.

With a glistening in his eyes which he would have scornfully protested was not a tear, he turned away and walked moodily back to Shy Street, caring little if it were to be the last walk he should ever take.

He was not, however, to be allowed much time for indulging his gloomy reflections on reaching his journey's end. A person was waiting outside the office, pacing up and down the pavement to keep himself warm. The stranger took a good look at Reginald as he entered and let himself in, and then followed up the stairs and presented himself.

"Is Mr Reginald at home?" inquired he blandly.

Reginald noticed that he was a middle-aged person, dressed in a sort of very shabby clerical costume, awkward in his manner, but not unintelligent in face.

"That is my name," replied he.

"Thank you. I am glad to see you, Mr Reginald. You were kind enough to send me a communication not long ago about—well, about a suit of clothes."

His evident hesitation to mention anything that would call attention to his own well-worn garb made Reginald feel quite sorry for him.

"Oh yes," said he, taking good care not to look at his visitor's toilet, "we sent a good many of the circulars to clergymen."

"Very considerate," said the visitor. "I was away from home and have only just received it."

And he took the circular out of his pocket, and seating himself on a chair began to peruse it.

Presently he looked up and said,—

"Are there any left?"

"Any of the suits? Oh yes, I expect so. We had a large number."

"Could I—can you show me one?"

"Unfortunately I haven't got them here; they are all in London."

"How unfortunate! I did so want to get one."

Then he perused the paper again.

"How soon could I have one?" he said.

"Oh very soon now; before Christmas certainly," replied Reginald.

"You are sure?"

"Oh yes. They will all be delivered before then."

"And have you had many orders?" said the clergyman.

"A great many," said Reginald.

"Hundreds, I daresay. There are many to whom it would be a boon at this season to get so cheap an outfit."

"Two hundred, I should say," said Reginald. "Would you like to leave an order with me?"

"Two hundred! Dear me! And did they all send the two pounds, as stated here, along with their order?"

"Oh yes. Some sent more," said Reginald, quite thankful to have some one to talk to, who did not regard him either as a fool or a knave.

"It must have been a very extensive bankrupt stock you acquired," said the clergyman musingly. "And were all the applicants clergymen like myself?"

"Nearly all."

"Dear me, how sad to think how many there are to whom such an opportunity is a godsend! We are sadly underpaid, many of us, Mr Reginald, and are apt to envy you gentlemen of business your comfortable means. Now you, I daresay, get as much as three or four of us poor curates get together."

"I hope not," said Reginald with a smile.

"Well, if I even had your £200 a year I should be thankful," said the poor curate.

"But I haven't that by £50," said Reginald. "Shall I put you down for a complete suit, as mentioned in the circular?"

"Yes, I'm afraid I cannot well do without it," said the other.

"And what name and address?" said Reginald.

"Well, perhaps the simplest way would be, as I am going back to London, for you to give me an order for the things to present at your depot there. It will save carriage, you know."

"Very well," said Reginald, "I will write one for you. You notice," added he, "that we ask for £2 with the order."

"Ah, yes," said the visitor, with a sigh, "that appears to be a stern necessity. Here it is, Mr Reginald."

"Thank you," said Reginald. "I will write you a receipt; and here is a note to Mr John Smith, at Weaver's Hotel, London, who has charge of the clothing. I have no doubt he will be able to suit you with just what you want."

"John Smith? I fancy I have heard his name somewhere. Is he one of your principals—a dark tall man?"

"I have never seen him," said Reginald, "but all our orders go to him for execution."

"Oh, well, thank you very much. I am sure I am much obliged to you. You seem to be single-handed here. It must be hard work for you."

"Pretty hard sometimes."

"I suppose clothing is what you chiefly supply?"

"We have also been sending out a lot of globes and blackboards to schools."

"Dear me, I should be glad to get a pair of globes for our parish school—very glad. Have you them here?"

"No, they are in London too."

"And how do you sell them? I fear they are very expensive."

"They cost £3 the set, but we only ask £2 with the order."

"That really seems moderate. I shall be strongly tempted to ask our Vicar to let me get a pair when in London. Will Mr Smith be able to show them to me?"

"Yes, he is superintending the sending off of them too."

"How crowded Weaver's Hotel must be, with so many bulky articles!" said the curate.

"Oh, you know, I don't suppose Mr Smith keeps them there; but he lives there while he's in town, that's all. Our directors generally put up at Weaver's Hotel."

"I should greatly like to see a list of the directors, if I may," said the clergyman. "There's nothing gives one so much confidence as to see honoured names on the directorate of a company like yours."

"I can give you a list if you like," said Reginald.

"I daresay you know by name the Bishop of S—, our chairman?"

"To be sure, and—dear me, what a very good list of names! Thank you, if I may take one of these, I should like to show it to my friends. Well, then, I will call on Mr Smith in London, and meanwhile I am very much obliged to you, Mr Reginald, for your courtesy. Very glad to have made your acquaintance. Good afternoon."

And he shook hands cordially with the secretary, and departed, leaving Reginald considerably soothed in spirit, as he reflected that he had really done a stroke of work for the Corporation that day on his own account.

It was well for his peace of mind that he did not know that the clergyman, on turning the corner of Shy Street, rubbed his hands merrily together, and said to himself, in tones of self-satisfaction, —

"Well, if that wasn't the neatest bit of work I've done since I came on the beat. The innocent! He'd sit up, I guess, if he knew the nice pleasant-spoken parson he's been blabbing to was Sniff of the detective office. My eye — it's all so easy, there's not much credit about the business after all. But it's pounds, shillings and pence to Sniff, and that's better!"

Chapter Seventeen
Samuel Shuckleford finds himself busy

"Jemima, my dear," said Mrs Shuckleford one day, as the little family in Number 4, Dull Street, sat round their evening meal, "I don't like the looks of Mrs Cruden. It's my opinion she don't get enough to eat."

"Really, ma, how you talk!" replied the daughter. "The butcher's boy left there this very afternoon. I saw him."

"I'm afraid, my dear, he didn't leave anything more filling than a bill. In fact, I 'eard myself that the butcher told Mrs Marks he thought Number 6 'ad gone far enough for 'im."

"Oh, ma! you don't mean to say they're in debt?" said Jemima, who, by the way, had been somewhat more pensive and addicted to sitting by herself since Reginald had gone north.

"Well, if it was only the butcher I heard it from I wouldn't take much account of it, but Parker the baker 'as 'is doubts of them; so I 'eard the Grinsons' maid tell Ford when I was in 'is shop this very day. And I'm sure you've only to look at 'Orace's coat and 'at to see they must be in debt: the poor boy looks a reg'lar scarecrow. It all comes, my dear, of Reginald's going off and leaving them. Oh, 'ow I pity them that 'as a wild son."

"Don't talk nonsense, ma," said Miss Jemima, firing up. "He's no more wild than Sam here."

"You seem to know more about Reginald than most people, my dear," said her mother significantly.

To the surprise of the mother and brother, Jemima replied to this insinuation by bursting into tears and walking out of the room.

"Did you ever see the like of that? She always takes on if any one mentions that boy's name; and she's old enough to be his aunt, too!"

"The sooner she cures herself of that craze the better," said Sam, pouring himself out some more tea. "She don't know quite so much about him as I do!"

"Why, what do you know about 'im, then?" inquired Mrs Shuckleford, in tones of curiosity.

"Never you mind; we don't talk business out of the office. All I can tell you is, he's a bad lot."

"Poor Mrs Cruden! no wonder she takes on. What an infliction a wicked son is to a mother, Sam!"

"That'll do," said the dutiful Sam. "What do you know about it? I tell you what, ma, you're thick enough with Number 6. You'd better draw off a bit."

"Oh, Sam, why so?"

"Because I give you the tip, that's all. The old lady may not be in it, but I don't fancy the connection."

"But, Sam, she's starving herself, and 'Orace is in rags."

"Send her in a rump-steak and a suit of my old togs by the housemaid," said Sam; "or else do as you like, and don't blame me if you're sorry for it."

Mrs Shuckleford knew it was no use trying to extract any more lucid information from her legal offspring, and did not try, but she made another effort to soften his heart with regard to the Widow Cruden and her son.

"After all they're gentlefolk in trouble, as we might be," said she, "and they do behave very nice at the short-'and class to Jemima."

"Gentlefolk or not," said Sam decisively, spreading a slice of toast with jam, "I tell you you'd better draw off, ma—and Jim must chuck up the class. I'm not going to have her mixing with them."

"But the child's 'eart would break, Sam, if—"

"Let it break. She cares no more about shorthand than she does about county courts. It's all part of her craze to tack herself on that lot. She's setting her cap at *him* while she's making up to his ma; any flat might see that; but she's got to jack up the whole boiling now—there. We needn't say any more about it."

And, having finished his tea, Mr Samuel Shuckleford went down to his "club" to take part in a debate on "Cruelty to Animals."

Now the worthy captain's widow, Mrs Shuckleford, had lived long enough in this world to find that human nature is a more powerful law even than parental obedience; she therefore took to heart just so much of her son's discourse as fitted with the one, and overlooked just so much as exacted the latter. In other words, she was ready to believe that Reginald Cruden was a "bad lot," but she was not able to bring herself on that account to desert her neighbour at the time of her trouble.

Accordingly that same evening, while Samuel was pleading eloquently on behalf of our dumb fellow-creatures, and Jemima, having recovered from her tears, was sitting abstractedly over a shorthand exercise in her own bedroom, Mrs Shuckleford took upon herself to pay a friendly call at Number 6.

It happened to be one of Horace's late evenings, so that Mrs Cruden was alone. She was lying wearily on the uncomfortable sofa, with her eyes shaded from the light, dividing her time between knitting and musing, the latter occupation receiving a very decided preference.

"Pray don't get up," said Mrs Shuckleford, the moment she entered. "I only looked in to see 'ow you was. You're looking bad, Mrs Cruden."

"Thank you, I am quite well," said Mrs Cruden, "only a little tired."

"And down in your spirits, too; and well you may be, poor dear," said the visitor soothingly.

"No, Mrs Shuckleford," said Mrs Cruden brightly. "Indeed, I ought not to be in bad spirits to-day. We've had quite a little family triumph to-day. Horace has had an article published in the *Rocket*, and we are so proud."

"Ah, yes; he's the steady one," said Mrs Shuckleford. "There's no rolling stone about 'Orace."

"No," said the mother warmly.

"If they was only both alike," said the visitor, approaching her subject delicately.

"Ah! but it often happens two brothers may be very different in temper and mind. It's not always a misfortune."

"Certainly not, Mrs Cruden; but when one's good and the other's wicked—"

"Oh, then, of course, it is very sad," said Mrs Cruden.

"Sad's no name for it," replied the visitor, with emotion. "Oh, Mrs Cruden, 'ow sorry I am for you."

"You are very kind. It is a sad trial to be separated from my boy, but I've not given up hopes of seeing him back soon."

Mrs Shuckleford shook her head.

"'Ow you must suffer on 'is account," said she. "If your 'eart don't break with it, it must be made of tougher stuff than mine."

"But after all, Mrs Shuckleford," said Mrs Cruden, "there are worse troubles in this life than separation."

"You're right. Oh, I'm so sorry for you."

"Why for me? I have only the lighter sorrow."

"Oh, Mrs Cruden, do you call a wicked son a light sorrow?"

"Certainly not, but my sons, thank God, are good, brave boys, both of them."

"And who told you 'e was a good, brave boy? Reggie, I mean."

"Who told me?" said Mrs Cruden, with surprise. "Who told me he was anything else?"

"Oh, Mrs Cruden! Oh, Mrs Cruden!" said Mrs Shuckleford, beginning to cry.

Mrs Cruden at last began to grow uneasy and alarmed. She sat up on the sofa, and said, in an agitated voice,—

"What *do* you mean, Mrs Shuckleford? Has anything happened? Is there any bad news about Reginald?"

"Oh, Mrs Cruden, I made sure you knew all about it."

"What is it?" cried Mrs Cruden, now thoroughly terrified and trembling all over. "Has anything happened to him? Is he—dead?" and she seized her visitor's hand as she asked the question.

"No, Mrs Cruden, not dead. Maybe it would be better for 'im if he was."

"Better if he was dead? Oh, please, have pity and tell me what you mean!" cried the poor mother, dropping back on to the sofa with a face as white as a sheet.

"Come, don't take on," said Mrs Shuckleford, greatly disconcerted to see the effect of her delicate breaking of the news. "Perhaps it's not as bad as it seems."

"Oh, what is it? what is it? I can't bear this suspense. Why don't you tell me?" and she trembled so violently and looked so deadly pale that Mrs Shuckleford began to get alarmed.

"There, there," said she soothingly; "I'll tell you another time. You're not equal to it now. I'll come in to-morrow, or the next day, when you've had a good night's rest, poor dear."

"For pity's sake tell me all now!" gasped Mrs Cruden; "unless you want to kill me."

It dawned at last on the well-meaning Mrs Shuckleford that no good was being done by prolonging her neighbour's suspense any further.

"Well, well! It's only that I'm afraid he's been doing something—well—dreadful. Oh, Mrs Cruden, how sorry I am for you!"

Mrs Cruden lay motionless, like one who had received a stab.

"What has he done?" she whispered slowly.

"I don't know, dear—really I don't," said Mrs Shuckleford, beginning to whimper at the sight of the desolation she had caused. "It was Sam, my son, told me—he wouldn't say what it was—and I 'ope you won't let 'im know it was me you 'eard it from, Mrs Cruden, for he'd be very— Mercy on us!"

Mrs Cruden had fainted.

Help was summoned, and she was carried to her bed. When Horace arrived shortly afterwards he found her still unconscious, with Mrs Shuckleford bathing her forehead, and tending her most gently.

"You had better run for a doctor, 'Orace," whispered she, as the scared boy entered the room.

"What is the matter? What has happened?" gasped he.

"Poor dear, she's broken down—she's— But go quick for the doctor, 'Orace."

Horace went as fast as his fleet feet would carry him. The doctor pronounced Mrs Cruden to be in a state of high fever, produced by nervous prostration and poor living. He advised Horace, if possible, to get a nurse to tend her while the fever lasted, especially as she would probably awake from her swoon delirious, and would for several days remain in a very critical condition.

In less than five minutes Horace was at Miss Crisp's, imploring her assistance. The warm-hearted little lady undertook the duty without a moment's hesitation, and from that night, and for a fortnight to come, hardly quitted her friend's bedside.

Mrs Shuckleford, deeming it prudent not to refer again to the unpleasant subject which had been the immediate cause of Mrs Cruden's seizure, waited till she was assured that at present she could be of no further use, and then withdrew, full of sympathy and commiseration, which she manifested in all sorts of womanly ways during her neighbour's illness. Not a day passed but she called in, morning and afternoon, to inquire after the patient, generally the bearer of some home-made delicacy, and sometimes to take her post by the sick bed while Miss Crisp snatched an hour or so of well-earned repose.

As for Horace, he could hardly be persuaded to leave the sick chamber. But the stern necessity of work, greater than ever now at this time of special emergency, compelled him to take the rest necessary for his own health and daily duties. With an effort he dragged himself to the office every morning, and like an arrow he returned from it every evening, and often paid a flying visit at midday. His good-natured companions voluntarily relieved him of all late work, and, indeed, every one who had in the least degree come into contact with the gentle patient seemed to vie in showing sympathy and offering help.

Young Gedge was amongst the most eager of the inquirers at the house. He squandered shillings in flowers and grapes, and sometimes even ran the risk of disgrace at the *Rocket* by lingering outside the house during a doctor's visit, in order to hear the latest bulletin before he went back to work.

In his mind, as well as in Horace's, a faint hope had lurked that somehow Reginald might contrive to run up to London for a day or two at least, to cheer the house of watching. Mrs Cruden, in her delirium, often moaned her absent son's name, and called for him, and they believed if only he were to come, her restless troubled mind might cease its wanderings and find rest.

But Reginald neither came nor wrote.

Since Horace, on the first day of her illness, had written, telling him all, no one had heard a word from him.

At last, when after a week Horace wrote again, saying,—

"Come to us, if you love us," and still no letter or message came back, a new cloud of anxiety fell over the house.

Reginald must be ill, or away from Liverpool, or something must have happened to him, or assuredly, they said, he would have been at his mother's side at the first breath of danger.

Mrs Shuckleford only, as day passed day, and the prodigal never returned, shook her head and said to herself, it was a blessing no one knew the reason, not even the poor delirious sufferer herself. Poor people! they had trouble enough on them not to need any more just now! so she kept her own counsel, even from Jemima.

This was the more easy to do because she knew nothing either of Reginald or his doings beyond what her son had hinted, and as Samuel was at present in the country on business, she had no opportunity of prosecuting her inquiries on the subject.

Sam, in fact, whether he liked it or not, happened just now to hold the fortunes of the family of Cruden pretty much in his own hands.

A few days before the conversation with his mother already reported, he had been sitting in his room at the office, his partner and the head clerk both being absent on County Court business.

Samuel felt all the dignity of a commander-in-chief, and was therefore not at all displeased when the office-boy had come and knocked at his door, and said that a lady of the name of Wrigley had called, and wished to see him.

"Show the lady in," said Sam grandly, "and put a chair."

Mrs Wrigley was accordingly ushered in, the dust of travel still on her, for she had come direct from Liverpool by the night train, determined to put her wrongs in the hands of the law. Mr Crawley, Samuel's principal, had been legal adviser to the late Mr Wrigley; it was only natural, therefore, that the widow, not liking to entrust her secret to the pettifogging practitioner of her own village, should make use of a two hours' break in her journey to seek his aid.

"Your master's not in, young man?" said she, as she took the proffered seat. "That's a pity."

"I'm sure he'll be very sorry," said Sam; "but if it's anything I can do—"

"If you can save poor defenceless women from being plundered, and punish those that plunder them—then you can."

Here was a slice of luck for Samuel! The first bit of practice on his own account that had ever fallen in his way. If he did not make a good thing out of it his initials were not S.S.!

He drew his chair confidentially beside that of the injured Mrs Wrigley, and drank in the story of her woes with an interest that quite won her heart. At first he failed to recognise either the name of the delinquent Corporation or its secretary, but when presently his client produced one of the identical circulars sent out, with the name Cruden Reginald at the foot, his professional instincts told him he had discovered a "real job, and no mistake."

He made Mrs Wrigley go back and begin her story over again (a task she was extremely ready to perform), and took copious notes during the recital. He impounded the document, envelope and all, cross-examined and brow-beat his own witness—in fact, did all a rising young lawyer ought to do, and concluded in judicial tones, "Very good, Mrs Wrigley; I think we can do something for you. I think we know something of the parties. Leave it to us, madam; we will put you right."

"I hope you will," said the lady. "You see, as I've been all the way up to Liverpool and back, I think I ought to be put right."

"Most certainly you ought, and you shall be."

"And to think of his brazen-faced impudence in calling me 'Love,' young man. There's a profligate for you!"

Samuel was knowing enough to see that it would greatly please the outraged lady if he took a special note of this disclosure, which he accordingly did, and then rising, once more assured his client of his determination to put her right, and bade her a very good morning.

"Well, if that ain't a go," said he to himself, as he returned to his desk. "I never did have much faith in the chap, but I didn't fancy he was that sort. Cruden Reginald, eh? Nice boy you are. Never mind! I'm dead on you this time. Nuisance it is that ma's gone and mixed herself up with that lot. Can't be helped, though; business is business; and such a bit of practice too. Cruden Reginald! But you don't get round Sam Shuckleford when he's once round your way, my beauty."

To the legal mind of Sam this transposition of Reginald's name was in itself as good as a verdict and sentence against him. Any one else but himself might have been taken in by it, but you needed to get up very early in the morning to take in a cute one like S.S.!

He said nothing about the affair to his principal when he returned, preferring to "nurse" it as a little bit of business of his own, which he would manage by himself for once in a way.

And that very evening fortune threw into his way a most unexpected and invaluable auxiliary.

He was down at his "club," smoking his usual evening pipe over the *Rocket*, when a man he had once or twice seen before in the place came up and said,—

"After you with that paper."

"All serene," said Sam; "I'll be done with it in about an hour."

"You don't take long," said the other.

"Considering I'm on the committee," said Sam, with ruffled dignity, "I've a right to keep it just as long as I please. Are you a member here?"

"No, but I'm introduced."

"What's your name?"

"Durfy."

"Oh, you're the man who was in the *Rocket*. I heard of you from a friend of mine. By the way," and here his manner became quite civil, as a brilliant idea occurred to him, "look here, it was only my chaff about keeping the paper; you can have it. I'll look at it afterwards."

"All right, thanks," said Durfy, who felt no excuse for not being civil too.

"By the way," said Sam, as he was going off with the paper, "there was a fellow at your office, what was his name, now—Crowder, Crundell? Some name of that sort—I forget."

"Cruden you mean, perhaps," said Durfy, with a scowl.

"Ah, yes—Cruden. Is he still with you? What sort of chap is he?"

Durfy described him in terms far more forcible than affectionate, and added, "No, he's not there now; oh no. I kicked him out long ago. But I've not done with him yet, my boy."

Sam felt jubilant. Was ever luck like his? Here was a man who evidently knew Reginald's real character, and could, doubtless, if properly handled, put him on the scent, and, as he metaphorically put it to himself, "give him a clean leg up over the job."

So he called for refreshments for two, and then entered on a friendly discourse with Durfy on things in general, and offered to make him a member of the club; then bringing the conversation round to Reginald, he hinted gently that *he* too had his eye on that young gentleman, and was at the present moment engaged in bowling him out.

Whereupon Durfy, after a slight hesitation, and stipulating that his name should not be mentioned in the matter, gave Sam what information he considered would be useful to him, suppressing, of course, all mention of the real promoters of the Select Agency Corporation, and giving the secretary credit for all the ingenuity and cunning displayed in its operations.

The two new friends spent a most agreeable evening, Sam flattering himself he was squeezing Durfy beautifully into the service of his "big job," and Durfy flattering himself that this bumptious young pettifogger was the very person to get hold of to help him pay off all his old scores with Reginald Cruden.

Chapter Eighteen
Poverty and Love both come in at the Door

We left Reginald in a somewhat comfortable frame of mind after his interview with the pleasant clergyman and the stroke of business he had transacted on behalf of the Corporation. It had been refreshing to him to converse in terms of peace with any fellow-mortal; and the ready satisfaction of this visitor with the method of business adopted by the Company went far to dispel the uneasy impressions which Mrs Wrigley's visit had left earlier in the day.

After all, he felt that he was yet on probation. When Christmas came, and he was able to discuss matters personally with the directors, he had no doubt his position would be improved. He flattered himself they might think he was useful enough to be worth while keeping; and in that case of course he would have a right to ask to be put on rather more comfortable a footing than he possessed at present, and to be entrusted with a certain amount of control over the business of the Corporation. He would also be able mildly to suggest that it would be more convenient to him to receive his salary monthly than quarterly, so as to enable him not only to live respectably himself, as became their secretary, but also to give regular help to his mother at home. As it was, with a beggarly thirteen shillings a week to live on, he was little better than a common office-boy, he would have said to himself, but at that particular moment the door opened, and the very individual whom his thoughts connected with the words appeared before him.

It was the very last apparition Reginald could have looked for. He had given up all idea of seeing the young desperado any more.

Though he could not exactly say, "Poverty had come in at the door and Love had flown out of the window"—for the young gentleman had departed by the door—he yet had made up his mind that Cupid had taken to himself wings and flown away, with no intention of ever returning to the scene of his late struggle.

But a glance at the starved, emaciated figure before him explained very simply the mystery of this strange apparition. The boy's hands and lips were blue with cold, and his cheek-bones seemed almost to protrude through his pallid, grimy cheeks. He looked, in fact, what he was, the picture of misery, and he had no need of any other eloquence to open the heart of his late "governor."

"Say, what's yer name," he said, in a hollow imitation of his old voice, "beg yer pardon, gov'nor—won't do it no more if yer overlook it this time."

"Come in out of the cold and warm yourself by the fire," said Reginald, poking it up to a blaze.

The boy obeyed, half timidly. He seemed to be not quite sure whether Reginald was luring him in to his own destruction. But at any rate the sight of the fire roused him to heroism, and, reckless of all consequences, he walked in.

"Don't do nothink to me this time, gov'nor," whimpered he, as he got within arm's length; "let us off, do you hear? this time."

"Poor boy," said Reginald kindly, putting a stool for him close beside the fire; "I'm not going to do anything but warm you. Sit down, and don't be afraid."

The boy dropped almost exhausted on the stool, and gazed in a sort of rapture into the fire. Then, looking up at Reginald, he said,—

"Beg your pardon, gov'nor,—ain't got a crust of bread you don't want, 'ave yer?"

The hint was quite enough to send Reginald flying to his little "larder."

The boy devoured the bread set before him with a fierceness that looked as if he had scarcely touched food since he had gone away. He made clear decks of all Reginald had in the place; and then, slipping off the stool, curled himself up on the floor before the fire like a dog, and dropped off into a heavy sleep. Reginald took the opportunity to make a hurried excursion to the nearest provision shop to lay in what store his little means would allow. He might have spared himself the trouble of locking the door behind him, though, for on his return the boy had never stirred.

The little sleeper lay there all night, until, in fact, the coals could hold out no longer, and the fire went out. Then Reginald woke him and carried him off to his own bed, where he dropped off into another long sleep which lasted till midday. After partaking of the meal his benefactor had ready for him on waking, he seemed more like himself, and disposed to make himself useful.

"Ain't got no envellups to lick, then?" said he, looking round the deserted room.

"No, there's nothing to do here just now," said Reginald.

The boy looked a little disappointed, but said, presently,—

"Want any errands fetched, gov'nor?"

"No, not now. I've got all I want in for the present."

"Like yer winders cleaned?"

"Not much use with this frost on them," said Reginald.

Thwarted thus on every hand, the boy asked no more questions, but took upon himself to go round the office and dust it as well as he could with the ragged tail of his coat. It was evidently his way of saying, "Thank you," and he seemed more easy in his mind when it was done.

He stopped once in the middle of his task as he caught Reginald's eyes fixed half curiously, half pityingly upon him.

"Say—gov'nor, I ain't going to read no more books; do ye hear?"

There was something quite pathetic in the tones in which this declaration of renunciation was made. It was evidently a supreme effort of repentance, and Reginald felt almost uncomfortable as he heard it.

"That there *Noogate Calendar* made a rare flare-up, didn't it, gov'nor?" continued Love, looking wistfully towards the grate, if perchance any stray leaves should have escaped the conflagration.

"Not such a flare-up as you did," said Reginald, laughing. "Never mind, we'll try and get something nicer to read."

"No fear! Never no more. I ain't a-goin' to read nothink again, I tell yer," said the boy, quite warmly.

And for fear of wavering in his resolution he went round the room once more, rubbing up the cheap furniture till it shone, and ending with polishing up the very hearth that had served as the sacrificial altar to his beloved *Newgate Calendar* only a few days before. There was little or no more work to be done during the day. A few letters had come by the morning's post, angrily complaining of the delay in delivering the promised goods. To these Reginald had replied in the usual form, leaving to Love the privilege of "licking them up." He also wrote to Mr Medlock, enclosing the two pounds the pleasant clergyman had left the day before, and once more urging that gentleman to come down to Liverpool.

He went out, happily unconscious of the fact that a detective dogged every step he took, to post these letters himself, and at the same time to lay in a day's provisions for two. It was with something like a qualm that he saw his last half-sovereign broken over this purchase. With nine shillings left in his pocket, and twelve days yet to Christmas, it was as clear as daylight that things were rapidly approaching a crisis. It was almost a relief to feel it.

On his way back to the office he passed a secondhand book-stall. He had lingered in front of it many times before now, turning over the leaves of this and that odd volume, and picking up the scraps of amusement and information which are always to be found in such an occupation. To-day, however, he overhauled the contents of the trays with rather more curiosity than usual; not because he expected to find a pearl of great price among the dust and dog's ears of the "threepenny" tray. Reginald was the last person in the world to consider himself a child of fortune in that respect.

No! he had Master Love on his mind, and the memory of that blazing *Newgate Calendar* on his conscience, and, even at the cost of a further reduction of his vanishing income, he determined not to return provided with food for Love's body only, but also for Love's mind.

Accordingly he selected two very shabby and tattered volumes from the "threepenny" tray—one a fragment of *Robinson Crusoe*, the other Part One of the *Pilgrim's Progress*, and with these in his pocket and the eatables in his hands, he returned to his charge as proud as a general who has just relieved a starving garrison.

After the frugal supper the books were triumphantly produced, but Master Love, still mindful of his recent tribulations, regarded them shyly at first, as another possible bait to his own undoing; but presently curiosity, and the sight of a wonderful picture of Giant Despair, overcame his scruples, and he held out his hand eagerly.

It was amusing to watch the critical look on his face as he took a preliminary glance through the pages of the two books. Reginald was half sorry he had not produced them one at a time; but it being too late now to recall either, he awaited with no little excitement the decision of the young connoisseur upon them. Apparently Love found considerable traces of what he would call "jam" in both. The picture of Crusoe coming upon the footprint in the sand, and that of the great battle between Christian and Apollyon, seemed to gather into themselves the final claims of the two rivals, and for a few moments victory trembled in the balance. At last he shut up *Robinson Crusoe* and stuffed it in his pocket.

"Say, what's yer name," said he, looking up and laying his finger on the battle scene; "which of them two does for t'other?"

"The one in the armour," said Reginald.

"Thought so—t'other one's a flat to fight with that there long flagpole. Soon as 'e's chucked it away 'e's a dead 'un. Say, what did they do with 'is dead body? No use a 'idin' of it. If I was 'im I'd a cut 'is throat, and left the razor in 'is 'and, and they'd a brought it in soosanside. Bless you, coroners' juries is reg'lar flats at findin' out them sort of things."

"Suppose you read what it says," said Reginald, hardly able to restrain a laugh; "if you like you can read it aloud; I'd like to hear it again myself."

The boy agreed, and that evening the two queerly assorted friends sat side by side in the dim candle-light, going over the wonderful story of the Pilgrim. Reginald judiciously steered the course through the most thrilling parts of the narrative, carefully avoiding whatever might have seemed to the boy dull or digressive.

Love stopped in his reading frequently to discuss the merits of the story and deliver himself of his opinion as to what he would have done under similar circumstances. He would have made short work with the lions chained by the roadside; he would have taken a bull's-eye lantern through the dark valley; and as for the river at the end, he couldn't understand anybody coming to grief there. Why, at Victoria Park last Whit Monday he had swum three-quarters of a mile himself!

In vain Reginald pointed out that Christian had his armour on. The young critic would not allow this as an excuse, and brought up cases of gentlemen of his acquaintance who had swum incredible distances in their clothes and boots.

But the story that delighted him most was that of the man who hacked his way into the palace. This was an adventure after his own heart. He read it over and over again, and was unsparing in his admiration of the hero, whom he compared for prowess with "Will Warspite the Pirate," and "Dick Turpin," and even his late favourite "Tim Tigerskin." His interest in him was indeed so great that he allowed Reginald in a few simple words to say what it meant, and to explain how we could all, if we went the right way about it, do as great things as he did.

"Why you, youngster, when you made up your mind you wouldn't read any more of those bad books, you knocked over one of your enemies."

"Did I, though? how far in did I get?"

"You got over the doorstep, anyhow; but you've got plenty more to knock over before you get right into the place. So have I."

"My eye, gov'nor," cried the boy, his grimy face lighting up with an excited flush, "we'll let 'em 'ave it!"

They read and discussed and argued far into the night; and when at last Reginald gave the order to go to bed there were no two friends more devoted than the Secretary of the Select Agency Corporation and his office-boy.

Love's sleep that night was like the sleep of a pugilistic terrier, who in his dreams encounters and overcomes even deep-mouthed mastiffs and colossal Saint Bernards. He sniffed and snorted defiance as he lay, and his brow was damp with the sweat of battle, and his lips curled with the smile of victory. As soon as he awoke his hand sought the pocket where the wonderful book lay; and even as he tidied up the office and prepared the gov'nor's breakfast, he was engaged in mortal inward combats.

"Say, gov'nor," cried he, with jubilant face, as Reginald entered, "I've done for another of 'em. Topped him clean over."

"Another of whom?" said Reginald.

"Them pals a-waitin' in the 'all," said he; "you know, in that there pallis."

"Oh! in the Beautiful Palace we were reading about," said Reginald. "Who have you done for this time?"

"That there Medlock," said the boy.

"Medlock! What *are* you talking about?" said Reginald, in blank amazement.

"Oh, I've give him a wonner," said the boy, beaming. "He says to me, 'Collar all the letters your gov'nor writes 'ome,' he says, 'and I'll give you a tanner for every one you shows me.'"

"Love, you're talking rubbish!" said Reginald indignantly.

"Are I? don't you make no mistake," said the boy confidently; "I knows what he says; and that there letter you wrote home last night and leaves on the table, 'That's a tanner to me,' says I to myself when I sees it this morning. 'A lie,' says I, recollecting of that chap in the story-book. So I lets it be; and my eye, ain't that a topper for somebody—oh no!"

Reginald stared at the boy, half stupefied. The room whirled round him; and with a sudden rush the hopes of his life seemed to go from under him. It was not for some time that he could find words to say, hoarsely,—

"Love, is this the truth, or a lie you are telling me?"

"Lie—don't you make no error, gov'nor—I ain't on that lay, I can tell you. I'm goin' right into that there pallis, and there's two on 'em topped a'ready."

"You mean to say Mr Medlock told you to steal my letters and give them to him?"

"Yes, and a tanner apiece on 'em, too. But don't you be afraid, he don't get none out of me, not if I swings for it."

"You can go out for a run, Love," said Reginald. "Come back in an hour. I want to be alone."

"You aren't a-giving me the sack?" asked the boy with falling countenance.

"No, no."

"And you ain't a-goin' to commit soosanside while I'm gone, are yer?" he inquired, with a suspicious glance at Reginald's blanched face.

"No. Be quick and go."

"'Cos if you do, they do say as a charcoal fire—"

"Will you go?" said Reginald, almost angrily, and the boy vanished.

I need not describe to the reader all that passed through the poor fellow's mind as he paced up and down the bare office that morning. The floodgates had suddenly been opened upon him, and he felt himself overwhelmed in a deluge of doubt and shame and horror.

It was long before he could collect his thoughts sufficiently to see anything clearly. Why Mr Medlock should take the trouble to prevent his home letters reaching their destination was incomprehensible, and indeed it weighed little with him beside the fact that the man who had given him his situation, and on whom he was actually depending for his living, was the same who could bribe his office-boy to steal his letters. If he were capable of such a meanness, was he to be trusted in anything else? How was Reginald to know whether the money he had regularly remitted to him was properly accounted for, or whether the orders were being conscientiously executed?

Then it occurred to him the whole business of the Corporation had been done in his—Reginald's—name, that all the circulars had been signed by him, and that all the money had come addressed to him. Then there was that awkward mistake about his name, which, accidental or intentional, was Mr Medlock's doing. And beyond all that was the fact that Mr Medlock had taken away the only record Reginald possessed of the names of those who had replied to the circulars and sent money.

He found himself confronted with a mountain of responsibility, of which he had never before dreamed, and for the clearing of which he was entirely dependent on the good faith of a man who had, not a week ago, played him one of the meanest tricks imaginable.

What was he to make of it—what else could he make of it except that he was a miserable dupe, with ruin staring him in the face?

His one grain of comfort was in the names of some of the directors. Unless that list were fictitious, they would not be likely to allow a concern with which they were identified to collapse in discredit. Was it genuine or not?

His doubts on this question were very speedily resolved by a letter which arrived that very afternoon.

It was dated London, and ran as follows:—

"Cruden Reginald, Esquire.

"Sir,—The attention of the Bishop of S— having been called to the unauthorised, and, as it would appear, fraudulent use of his name in connection with a company styled the Select Agency Corporation, of which you are secretary, I am instructed, before his lordship enters on legal proceedings, to request you to furnish me with your authority for using his lordship's name in the manner stated. Awaiting your reply by return, I am, sir, yours, etcetera,—

"A. Turner, Secretary."

This was a finishing stroke to the disillusion. In all his troubles and perplexities the good Bishop of S— had been a rock to lean on for the poor secretary.

But now even that prop was snatched away, and he was left alone in the ruins of his own hopes.

He could see it all at last. As he went back over the whole history of his connection with the Corporation he was able to recognise how at every step he had been duped and fooled; how his very honesty had been turned to account; how his intelligence had been the one thing disliked and discouraged.

And what was to become of him now?

Anything but desert the sinking ship—that question never cost Reginald two thoughts. He would right himself if he could. He would protest his innocence of all fraud or connivance at fraud. He would even do what he could to bring the real offenders to justice; but as long as the Corporation had a creditor left he would be there to face him and suffer the consequence of his own folly and stupidity.

Young Love got little sympathy that day in his reading. Indeed, he could not but notice that something unusual had happened to the "gov'nor," and that being so, not even the adventures of Christian or the unexplored marvels of Robinson Crusoe could satisfy him. He polished up the furniture half a dozen times, and watched Reginald's eye like a dog, ready to catch the first sign of a want or a question. Presently he could stand it no longer, and said,—"Say, gov'nor, what's up? 'taint nothing along of me, are it?"

"No, my boy," said Reginald. "Is it along of that there Medlock?" Reginald nodded.

It was well for Mr Medlock that he was not in the room at that moment.

"I'll top 'im, see if I don't," muttered the boy; "I owes 'im one for carting me down 'ere, and I owes 'im four or five now; and you'll see if I don't go for 'im, gov'nor."

"You'd better go back to your home," said Reginald, with a kindly tremor in his voice; "I'm afraid you'll get into trouble by staying with me."

It was fine to see the flash of scorn in the boy's face as he said,—

"Oh yus, me go 'ome and leave yer! Walker—I stays 'ere."

"Very well, then," said Reginald, with a sigh. "We may as well go on with the book. Suppose you read me about Giant Despair."

Chapter Nineteen
The Shades lose several good Customers

It would be unfair to Samuel Shuckleford to say that he had no compunction whatever in deciding upon a course of action which he knew would involve the ruin of Reginald Cruden.

He did not like it at all. It was a nuisance; it was a complication likely to hamper him. He wished his mother and sister would be less gushing in the friendships they made. What right had they to interfere with his business prospects by tacking themselves on to the family of a man who was afterwards to turn out a swindler?

Yes, it was a nuisance; but for all that it must not be allowed to interfere with the course that lay before the rising lawyer. Business is business after all, and if Cruden is a swindler, whose fault is it if Cruden's mother breaks her heart? Not S.S.'s, at any rate. But S.S.'s fault it would be if he made a mess of this "big job"! That was a reproach no one should lay at his door.

Samuel may not have been quite the Solomon he was wont to estimate himself. Still, to do him justice once more, he displayed no little ability in tracing out the different frauds of the Select Agency Corporation and establishing Reginald's guilt conclusively in his own mind.

It all fitted in like a curious puzzle. His sudden mysterious departure from London—his change of name—the selection of Liverpool as headquarters—the distribution of the circulars among unsuspecting schoolmistresses in the south of England—the demand for money to be enclosed with the order—and the fiction of the dispatch of the goods from London. What else could it point to but a deliberate, deeply-laid scheme of fraud? The further Samuel went, the clearer it all appeared, and the less compunction he felt for running to earth such a scoundrel.

But he was going to do nothing in a hurry. S.S. was not the man to dish himself by showing his cards till he was sure he had them all in his hand. Possibly Cruden was not alone in the swindle. He might have accomplices. Even his mother and brother—who can answer for the duplicity of human nature?—might know more of his operations than they professed to know. He might have confederates among his old companions at the *Rocket*, or even among his old school acquaintances. Yes; there was plenty to go into before Samuel put down his foot, and who knew better how to go into it than S.S.?

So he kept his own counsel, and, except for cautioning his mother and sister to "draw off" from the undesirable connection, and intimidating the maid-of-all-work at Number 6, Dull Street, by most horrible threats of the penalties of the law, to detain and give to him every letter bearing the Liverpool postmark which should from that time forward come to the house, no matter to whom addressed—for in his zeal it was easy to forget that by such a proceeding he was sailing uncommonly close to the wind himself—showed no sign of taking any immediate step either in this or any other matter.

Had he been aware that one Sniff, of the Liverpool detective police, had some days ago arrived, by a series of independent and far more artistic investigations, at as much knowledge as he himself possessed of the doings of the Corporation, Samuel would probably have been content to make the most of the cards he held before the chance of using them at all had slipped by.

It is doubtful, however, whether in any case he would have succeeded in forestalling the wary Mr Sniff. That gentleman had discovered in a few hours what it had taken Samuel days of patient grubbing to unearth. And his discoveries would have decidedly astonished the self-complacent little practitioner. He would have been astonished, for instance, to hear that the Liverpool post-office had received instructions from the Home Office to hand over every letter addressed to Cruden Reginald, 13, Shy Street, to the police. He would also have been astonished if he had known that a detective in plain clothes dined every evening at the Shades, near to the table occupied by Mr Durfy and his friends; that the hall-porter of Weaver's Hotel was a representative of the police in disguise, and that representatives of the police had called on business at the *Rocket* office, had brushed up against Blandford at street-corners, and had even taken the trouble to follow him— Samuel Shuckleford—here and there in his evening's perambulations.

Yes, small job as it was in Mr Sniff's estimation, he knew the way to go about it, and had a very good notion what was the right scent to go on and what the wrong.

The one thing that did put him out at first was Reginald's absolutely truthful replies to all the pleasant clergyman's questions. This really did bother Mr Sniff. For when a swindler is face to face with his victim the very last thing you expect of him is straightforward honesty. So when Reginald had talked about Weaver's Hotel and Mr John Smith, and had mentioned the number of orders that had arrived, and the account of money that had accompanied them, and had even confided the amount of his own salary, Mr Sniff had closed one of his mental eyes and said to himself, "Yes; we know all about that."

But when it turned out that, so far from such statements being fabrications to delude him, they were simply true — when the letter Reginald had written to Mr Medlock that very evening lay in his hands and corroborated all he had said — when he himself followed the poor fellow an hour or two later on his errand of mercy, and stood beside him as he spent that precious sixpence over *Robinson Crusoe* and the *Pilgrim's Progress*, Mr Sniff did feel for a moment disconcerted.

But, unusual as it was, he made the bold venture of jumping to the conviction of Reginald's innocence; and that theory once started, everything went beautifully.

On the evening following Mrs Cruden's sudden illness, Mr Durfy strolled down in rather a disconsolate frame of mind towards the Shades.

Since his expulsion from the *Rocket* office things had not been going pleasantly with him. For a day or two he had deemed it expedient to keep in retirement, and when at last he did venture forth, in the vague hope of picking up some employment worthy of his talents, he took care to keep clear of the haunts of his former confederates, whom, after his last failure, he rather dreaded meeting.

It had been during this period that he had made the acquaintance of Shuckleford, and the prospect of revenge which that intimacy opened to him was a welcome diversion to the monotony of his existence.

But prospects of revenge do not fill empty stomachs, and Durfy at the end of a week began to discover that there might be an end even to the private resources of the late overseer of an evening newspaper and the part proprietor of an Agency Corporation. He was, in fact, getting hard up, and therefore, putting his pride in his empty pocket, he strolled down moodily to the Shades, determined at any rate to have a supper at somebody else's expense.

He had not reckoned without his host, for after about half an hour's impatient kicking of his heels outside, Mr Medlock and Mr Shanklin appeared on the scene, arm in arm.

They appeared by no means elated at seeing him, but that mattered very little to the hungry Durfy, who followed them into the supper-room and took his seat at the table beside them. If he had been possessed of any sensitiveness, it might have been wounded by the utter indifference, after the first signs of displeasure, they paid to his presence. They continued their conversation as though no third party had been near, and except that Mr Medlock nodded when the waiter said "For three?" seemed to see as little of him as Hamlet's mother did of the Ghost.

However, for the time being that nod of Mr Medlock's was all Durfy particularly coveted. He was hungry. Time enough to stand on his dignity when the knife and fork had done their work.

"Yes," said Mr Shanklin, "time's up to-day. I've told him where to find us. If he doesn't, you must go your trip by yourself; I can safely stay and screw my man up."

"Think he will turn up?"

"Can't say. He seems to be flush enough of money still."

"Well, he can't say you've not helped him to get rid of it."

"I've done my best," said Mr Shanklin, laughing.

"I shall be glad of a holiday. It's as hard work sponging one fool as it is fleecing a couple of hundred sheep, eh?"

"Well, the wool came off very easily, I must say. I reckon there'll be a clean £500 to divide on the Liverpool business alone."

"Nice occupation that'll be on the Boulogne steamer to-morrow," said Mr Shanklin. "Dear me, I hope it won't be rough, I'm such a bad sailor!"

"Then, of course," said Mr Medlock, "there'll be your little takings to add to that. Your working expenses can't have been much."

Mr Shanklin laughed again.

"No. I've done without circulars and a salaried secretary. By the way, do you fancy any one smells anything wrong up in the North yet?"

"Bless you, no. The fellow's pretty near starving, and yet he sent me up a stray £2 he received the other day. It's as good as a play to read the letters he sends me up about getting the orders executed in strict rotation, as entered in a beautiful register he kept, and which I borrowed, my boy. Ha! ha! He wants me to run down to Liverpool, he says, as he's not quite satisfied with his position there. Ho! ho! And he'd like a little money on account, as he's had to buy stamps and coals and all that sort of thing out of his own thirteen shillings a week. It's enough to make one die of laughing, isn't it?"

"It is funny," said Mr Shanklin. "But you're quite right to be on the safe side and start to-morrow. You did everything in his name, I suppose—took the office, ordered the printing, and all that sort of thing?"

"Oh yes, I took care of that. My name or yours was never mentioned, except mine on the dummy list of directors. That won't hurt."

"Well, the Corporation's had a short life and a merry one; and your precious secretary's likely to have a merry Christmas after it all—unless you'd like to go down and spend it with him, Durfy," added Mr Shanklin, taking notice for the first time of the presence of their visitor.

Durfy replied by a scowl.

"I shall be far enough away by then," said he.

"Why, where are you going?"

"I'm going with you, to be sure," said he, doggedly.

Messrs Medlock and Shanklin greeted this announcement with a laugh of genuine amusement.

"I'm glad you told us," said Mr Shanklin. "We should have forgotten to take a ticket for you."

"You may grin," said Durfy. "I'm going, for all that."

"You're a bigger fool even than you look," said Mr Medlock, "to think so. You can consider yourself lucky to get a supper out of us this last night."

"You forget I can make it precious awkward for you if I like," growled Durfy.

"Awkward! *You've* a right to be a judge of what's awkward after the neat way you've managed things," sneered Shanklin. "It takes you all your time to make things awkward for yourself, let alone troubling about us."

Durfy always hated when Mr Shanklin alluded to his blunders, and he scowled all the more viciously now because he felt that, after all, he could do little against his two patrons which would not recoil with twofold violence on his own head. No, he had better confine his reprisals to the Crudens by Mr Shuckleford's assistance, and meanwhile make what he could out of these ungrateful sharpers.

"If you don't want me with you," said he, "you'll have to make it worth my while to stay away, that's all. You'd think it a fine joke if you found yourself in the police-station instead of the railway-station to-morrow morning, wouldn't you?"

And Mr Durfy's face actually relaxed into a smile at this flash of pleasantry.

"You'd find it past a joke if you found yourself neck-and-crop in the gutter in two minutes," said Mr Shanklin, in a rage, "as you will do if you don't take care."

"I'll take care for fifty pounds," said Durfy. "It's precious little share I've had out of the business, and if you want me mum, that's what will do it. There, I could tell you a thing or two already; you don't know—"

"Tush! Durfy, you're a born ass! Come round to my hotel to-morrow at eight, and I'll see what I can do for you," said Mr Medlock.

Durfy knew how to value such promises, and did not look by any means jubilant at the prospect held out. However, at this moment Blandford and Pillans entered the supper-room, and his hosts had something better to think about than him.

He was hustled from his place to make room for the new guests, and surlily retired to a neighbouring table, where, if he could not hear all that was said, he could at least see all that went on.

"Hullo!" said Shanklin gaily, "here's a nice time to turn up, dear boys. Medlock and I have nearly done supper."

"Couldn't help. We've been to the theatre, haven't we, Pillans?" said Blandford, who appeared already to be rather the worse for drink.

"I have. You've been in the bar most of the time," said Pillans.

"Ha! ha! I was told Bland was studying for the Bar. I do like application," said Mr Medlock.

Blandford seemed to regard this as a compliment, and sitting down at the table, told the waiter to bring a bottle of champagne and some more glasses.

"Well," he said, with a simper, "what I say I'll do, I'll do. I said I'd turn up here and pay you that bill, Shanklin, and I have turned up, haven't I?"

"Upon my honour, I'd almost forgotten that bill," said Mr Shanklin, who had thought of little else for the last week. "It's not inconvenient, I hope?"

Blandford laughed stupidly.

"Sorry if a trifle like that was inconvenient," said he, with all the languor of a millionaire. "Forget what it was about. Some take in, I'll swear. Never mind, a debt's a debt, and here goes. How much is it?"

"Fifty," said Mr Shanklin.

Blandford produced a pocket-book with a flourish, and took from it a handful of notes that made Durfy's eyes, as he sat at the distant table, gleam. The half-tipsy spendthrift was almost too muddled to count them correctly, but finally he succeeded in extracting five ten-pound notes from the bundle, which he tossed to Shanklin.

"Thanks, very much," said that gentleman, putting them in his pocket. "I find I've left your bill at home, but I'll send it round to you in the morning."

"Oh, all serene!" said Blandford, putting his pocketbook back into his pocket. "Have another bottle of cham—do—just to celebrate—settling—old scores. Hullo, where are you, Pillans?"

Pillans had gone off to play billiards with Mr Medlock, so Blandford and Mr Shanklin attacked the bottle themselves. When it was done, the former rose unsteadily, and, bidding his friend good-night, said he would go home, as he'd got a headache. Which was about as true an observation as man ever uttered.

"Good-night—old—feller," said he; "see you to-morrow."

And he staggered out of the place, assisted to the door by Mr Shanklin, who, after an affectionate farewell, sauntered to the billiard-room, where Mr Medlock had already won a five-pound note from the ingenuous Mr Pillans.

"Your friend's in good spirits to-night," said Mr Shanklin. "Capital fellow is Bland."

"So he is," said Pillans.

"Capital fellow, with plenty of capital, eh?" said Mr Medlock; "your shoot, Pillans, and I don't mind going a sov. with you on the cannon."

Of course Pillans lost his sovereign, as he did several others before the game was over. Then, feeling he had had enough enjoyment for one evening, he said good-bye and followed his friend home.

But some one else had already followed his friend home.

Durfy, in whose bosom the glimpse of that well-lined pocket-book had roused unusual interest, found himself ready to go home a very few moments after Blandford had quitted the Shades. It may have been only coincidence, or it may have been idle curiosity to see if the tipsy lad could find his way home without an accident, or it may have been a laudable determination that, no one should take advantage of his helpless condition to deprive him of that comfortable pocket-book. Whatever it was, Durfy followed the reeling figure along the pavement as it threaded its way westward from the Shades.

Blandford may have had reason enough left to tell him that it would be better for his headache to walk in the night air than to take a cab, and Mr Durfy highly approved of the decision. He was able without difficulty or obtrusiveness to follow his man at a few yards' distance, and even give proof of his solicitude by an occasional steadying hand on his arm.

Presently the wanderer turned out of the crowded thoroughfare up a by-street, where he had the pavement more to himself. Indeed, except for a few stragglers hurrying home from theatres or concerts, he encountered no one; and as he penetrated farther beyond the region of public houses and tobacco-shops into the serener realms of offices and chambers, and beyond that into the solitude of a West-end square, not a footstep save his own and that of his escort broke the midnight silence.

Durfy's heart beat fast, for he had a heart to beat on occasions like this. A hundred chances on which he had never calculated suddenly presented themselves. What if some one might be peering out into the night from one of the black windows of those silent houses? Suppose some motionless policeman under the shadow of a wall were near enough to see and hear! Suppose the cool night air had already done its work and sobered the wayfarer enough to render him obstinate or even dangerous! He seemed to walk more steadily. If anything was to be done, every moment was of consequence. And the risk?

The vision of that pocket-book and the crisp white notes flashed across Durfy's memory by way of answer.

Yes, to Durfy, the outcast, the dupe, the baffled adventurer, the risk was worth running.

He quickened his step and opened the blade of the penknife in his pocket as he did so. Not that he meant to use it, but in case—

Faugh! the fellow was staggering as helplessly as ever! He never even heeded the pursuing steps, but reeled on, muttering to himself, now close to the palings, now on the kerb, his hat back on his head and the cigar between his lips not even alight.

Durfy crept silently behind, and with a sudden dash locked one arm tightly round his victim's neck, while with the other he made a swift dive at the pocket where lay the coveted treasure.

It was all so quickly done that before Blandford could exclaim or even gasp the pocket-book was in the thief's hands. Then as the arm round his neck was relaxed, he faced round, terribly sobered, and made a wild spring at his assailant.

"Thief!" he shouted, making the quiet square ring and ring again with the echo of that word.

His hand was upon Durfy's collar, so fiercely that nothing but a hand-to-hand struggle could release its grip; unless—

Durfy's hand dropped to his pocket. There was a flash and a scream, and next moment Blandford was clinging, groaning, to the railings of the square, while Durfy's footsteps died away in the gloomy mazes of a network of back streets.

When Pillans got home to his lodgings that night he found his comrade in bed with a severe wound in the shoulder, unable to give any account of himself but that he had been first garotted, then robbed, and finally stabbed, on his way home from the Shades.

Mr Durfy did not present himself at Mr Medlock's hotel at the appointed hour next morning.

Nor, although it was a fine calm day, and their luggage was all packed up and labelled, did Mr Medlock and his friend Mr Shanklin succeed in making their promised trip across the Channel. A deputation of police awaited them on the Victoria platform, and completely disconcerted their arrangements by taking them in a cab to the nearest police-station on a charge of fraud and conspiracy.

Chapter Twenty
Samuel Shuckleford finds
Virtue its own Reward

It was just as well for Horace's peace of mind, during his time of anxious watching, that two short paragraphs in the morning papers of the following day escaped his observation.

"At — police-court yesterday, two men named Medlock and Shanklin were brought before the magistrate on various charges of fraud connected with sham companies in different parts of the country. After some formal evidence they were remanded for a week, bail being refused."

"A youth named Reginald was yesterday charged at Liverpool with conspiracy to defraud by means of fictitious circulars addressed in the name of a trading company. He was remanded for three days without bail, pending inquiries."

It so happened that it fell to Booms's lot to cut the latter paragraph out. And as he was barely aware of the existence of Cruden's brother, and in no case would have recognised him by his assumed name, the news, even if he read it, could have conveyed no intelligence to his mind.

Horace certainly did not read it. Even when he had nothing better to do, he always regarded newspapers as a discipline not to be meddled with out of office hours. And just now, with his mother lying in a critical condition, and with no news day after day of Reginald, he had more serious food for reflection than the idle gossip of a newspaper.

The only other person in London whom the news could have interested was Samuel Shuckleford. But as he was that morning riding blithely in the train to Liverpool, reading the *Law Times,* and flattering himself he would soon make the public "sit up" to a recognition of his astuteness, he saw nothing of them.

He found himself on the Liverpool platform just where, scarcely three months ago, Reginald had found himself that dreary afternoon of his arrival. But, unlike Reginald, it cost the young ornament of the law not a moment's hesitation as to whether he should take a cab or not to his destination. If only the cabman knew whom he had the honour to carry, how he would touch up his horse!

"Shy Street. Put me down at the corner," said Samuel, swinging himself into the hansom.

So this was Liverpool. He had never been there before, and consequently it was not to be wondered at that the crowds jostling by on the pavement, without so much as a glance in his direction, neither knew him nor had heard of him. He could forgive them, and smiled to think how different it would be in a few days, when all the world would point at him as he drove back to the station, and say, —

"There goes Shuckleford, the clever lawyer, who first exposed the Select Agency Corporation, don't you know?"

Don't you know? What a question to ask respecting S.S.!

At the corner of Shy Street he alighted, and sauntered gently down the street, keeping a sharp look-out on both sides of him, without appearing to regard anything but the pavement.

Humph! The odd numbers were on the left side, so S.S. would walk on the right, and get a good survey of Number 13 from a modest distance.

What, thought he, would the precious Cruden Reginald (ha! ha!) think if he knew who was walking down the other side of the road?

Ah! he was getting near it now. Here was 17, a baker's; 15, a greengrocer's; and 13—eh? a chemist's? Ah, yes, he noticed that the first floors of all the shops were let for offices, and the first floor of the chemist's shop was the place he wanted.

He could see through the grimy window the top rail of a chair-back and the corner of a table, on which stood an inkpot and a tattered directory. No occupant of the room was visible; doubtless he found it prudent to keep away from the window; or he might possibly have seen the figure of S.S. advancing down the street.

Samuel crossed over. No name was on the chemist's side-door, but it stood ajar, and he pushed it open and peered up the gloomy staircase. There was a name on the door at the top, so he crept stealthily up the stairs to decipher the word "Medlock" in dim characters on the plate.

"Medlock!" Ho! ho! He was getting warm now. Not only was his man going about with his own name turned inside out, but he had the effrontery to stick up the name of one of his own directors on his door!

Samuel knew Mr Medlock—whom didn't he know? He had been introduced to him by Durfy, and had supped with him once at the Shades. A nice, pleasant-spoken gentleman, who had made some very complimentary little speeches about Samuel in Samuel's own hearing. This was the man whose name Cruden had borrowed for his door-plate, in the hope of further mystifying the public as to his own personality!

Ah! ah! He might mystify the public, but there was one whose initials were S.S. whom it would need a cleverer cheat than Cruden Reginald, Esquire, to mystify!

He listened for a moment at the door, and, hearing no sound, made bold to enter. Had Reginald been in, he was prepared to represent that, being on a chance visit to Liverpool, he had been unable to pass the door of an old neighbour without giving him a friendly call.

But he was not put to this shift, for the room was empty. "Gone out to his dinner, I suppose," said Sam to himself. "Well, I'll take a good look round while I am here."

Which he proceeded to do, much to his own satisfaction, but very little to his information, for scarcely a torn-up envelope was to be found to reward the spy for his trouble. The only thing that did attract his attention as likely to be remotely useful was a fragment of a pink paper with the letters "gerskin" on it—a relic Love would have recognised as part of the cover of an old favourite, but which to the inquiring mind of the lawyer appeared to be a document worth impounding in the interests of justice.

As nobody appeared after the lapse of half an hour, Samuel considered his time was being wasted, and therefore withdrew. He looked into the chemist's shop as he went down, but the chemist was not at home; so he strolled into the greengrocer's next door, and bought an orange, which he proceeded to consume, making himself meanwhile cunningly agreeable to the lady who presided over the establishment.

"Fine Christmas weather," said he, looking up in the middle of a prolonged suck.

"Yes," said the lady.

"Plenty of customers?"

She shrugged her shoulders. Sam might interpret that as he liked.

"I suppose you supply the Corporation next door?" said Sam, digging his countenance once more into the orange.

"Eh?" said the lady.

"The—what's-his-name?—Mr Reginald—I suppose he deals with you?"

"He did, if you want to know."

"I thought so—a friend of mine, you know."

"Oh, is he?" said the lady, finding words at last, and bridling up in a way that astonished her cross-examiner; "then the sooner you go and walk off after him the better!"

"Oh, very well," said Sam. "He's not at home just now, though."

"Oh, ain't he?" said the woman, "that's funny!"

"Why, what do you mean?"

"Oh, nothing—what should I? If you're a friend of his, you'd better take yourself off! That's what I mean."

"All right; no offence, old lady. Perhaps he's come in by this time."

The lady laughed disagreeably. The Corporation had bought coals of her three months ago.

Samuel returned to the office, but it was as deserted as ever. He therefore resolved to try what his blandishments could do with the chemist's boy downstairs in the way of obtaining information.

That young gentleman, as the reader will remember, had been a bosom friend of Love in his day, and was animated to some extent by the spirit of his comrade.

"Hullo, my man!" said Sam, walking into the shop. "Governor's out, then?"

"Yus."

"Got any lollipops in those bottles?"

"Yus."

"Any brandy-balls?"

"No."

"Any acid-drops?"

"Yus."

"I'll take a penn'orth, then. I suppose you don't know when the gentleman upstairs will be back?"

The boy stopped short in his occupation and stared at Sam.

"What gentleman?" he asked.

"Mr Medlock, is it? or Reginald, or some name like that?"

"Oh yus, I do!" said the boy, with a grin.

"When?"

"Six months all but a day. That's what I reckon."

"Six months! Has he gone away, then?"

"Oh no—he was took off."

"Took off—you don't mean to say he's dead?"

"Oh, ain't you a rum 'un! As if you didn't know he's been beaked."

"Beaked! what's that?"

The boy looked disgusted at the fellow's obtuseness.

"'Ad up in the p'lice-court, of course. What else could I mean?"

Samuel jumped off his stool as if he had been electrified.

"What do you say?" said he, gaping wildly at the boy.

"Go on; if you're deaf, it's no use talkin' to you. He's been up in the p'lice-court," said he, raising his voice to a shout. "Yesterday—there you are—and there's your drops, and you ain't give me the penny for them."

Samuel threw down the penny, and, too excited to take up the drops, dashed out into the street.

What! yesterday—while he was lounging about town, fancying he had the game all to himself. Was ever luck like his?

He rushed to a shop and bought a morning paper. There, sure enough, was a short notice of yesterday's proceedings, and you might have knocked S.S. down with a feather as he read it.

"Anyhow," said he to himself, crumpling up the paper in sheer vexation, "they won't be able to do without me, I'll take care of that. I can tell them all about it—but catch me doing it now, the snobs, unless they're civil."

With which valiant determination he swung himself into another cab, and ordered the man to drive to the head police-station.

The inspector was not in, but his second-in-command was, and to him, much against his will, Samuel had to explain his business.

"Well, what do you know about the prisoner?" asked the official.

"Oh, plenty. You'd better subpoena me for the next examination," said Sam.

The sub-inspector smiled.

"You're like all the rest of them," he said, "think you know all about it. Come, let's hear what you've got to say, young fellow; there's plenty of work to be done here, I can tell you, without dawdling our time."

"Thank you," said Sam, "I'd sooner tell the magistrate."

"Go and tell the magistrate then!" shouted the official, "and don't stay blocking up the room here."

This was not what Samuel expected. There was little chance of the magistrate being more impressed with his importance than a sub-inspector. So he felt the only thing for it was to bring himself to the unpleasant task of showing his cards after all.

"The fact is—" he began.

"If you're going to say what you know about the case, I'll listen to you," said the sub-inspector, interrupting him, "if not, go and talk in the street."

"I am going to say what I know," said the crestfallen Sam.

"Very well. It's a pity you couldn't do it at first," said the official, getting up and standing with his back turned, warming his hands at the fire.

Under these depressing circumstances Samuel began his story, showing his weakest cards first, and saving up his trumps as long as he could. The sub-inspector listened to him impassively, rubbing his hands, and warming first one toe and then the other in the fender.

At length it was all finished, and he turned round.

"That's all you know?"

"Yes—at present—I expect to discover more, though, in a day or two."

"Just write your name and address on one of those envelopes," said the sub-inspector, pointing to a stationery case on his table.

Sam obeyed, and handed the address to the official.

"Very well," said the latter, folding the paper up without looking at it, and putting it into his waistcoat pocket, "if we want you, we'll fetch you."

"I suppose I had better put my statement down in writing?" said Samuel, making a last effort at pomposity.

"Can if you like," said the sub-inspector, yawning, "when you've nothing else to do."

And he ended the conference by calling to a constable outside to tell 190 C he might come in.

Grievously crestfallen, Samuel withdrew, bemoaning the hour when he first heard the name of Cruden, and was fool enough to dirty his hands with a "big job." What else was he to expect when once these official snobs took a thing up? Of course they would put every obstacle and humiliation in the way of an outsider that jealousy could suggest. He had very little doubt that this sub-inspector, the moment his back was turned, would sit down and make notes of his information, and then take all the credit of it to himself. Never mind, they were bound to want him when the trial came on, and wouldn't he just show up their tricks! Oh no! S.S. wasn't going to be flouted and snubbed for nothing, he could tell them, and so they'd discover.

It was no use staying in Liverpool, that was clear. The Liverpool police should have the pleasure of fetching him all the way from London when they wanted him; and possibly, with Durfy's aid, he might succeed in getting hold of another trump-card meanwhile to turn up when they least expected it.

The journey south next day was less blithe and less occupied with the *Law Times* than the journey north had been. But as he got farther away from inhospitable Liverpool his spirits revived, and before London was reached he was once more in imagination "the clever lawyer, Shuckleford, don't you know, who gave the Liverpool police a slap in the face over that Agency Corporation business, don't you know."

Two "don't you knows" this time!

On reaching home, any natural joy he might be expected to feel on being restored to the bosom of his family was damped by the discovery that his mother was that very moment in next door relieving guard with Miss Crisp at the bedside of Mrs Cruden.

"What business has she to do it when I told her not?" demanded Sam wrathfully of his sister.

"She's not bound to obey you," said Jemima; "she's your mother."

"She is. And a nice respectable mother, too, to go mixing with a lot of low, swindling jail-birds! It's sickening!"

"You've no right to talk like that, Sam," said Jemima, flushing up; "they're as honest as you are—more so, perhaps. There!"

"Go it; say on," said Samuel. "All I can tell you is, if you don't both of you turn the Cruden lot up, I'll go and live in lodgings by myself."

"Why should we turn them or anybody up for you, I should like to know?" said Jemima, with a toss of her head. "What have they done to you?"

"You're an idiot," said Sam, "or you wouldn't talk bosh. Your dear Reginald—"

"Well, what about him?" said Jemima, her trembling lip betraying the inward flutter with which she heard the name.

"How would you like to know your precious Reginald was this moment in prison?"

"What!" shrieked Jemima, with a clutch at her brother's arm.

He was glad to see there was some one he could make "sit up," and replied, with brutal directness,—

"Yes—in prison, I tell you; charged with swindling and theft ever since he set foot in Liverpool. There, if that's not reason enough for turning them up, I give you up. You can tell mother so, and say I'm down at the club, and she'd better leave supper up for me; do you hear?"

Jemima did not hear. She sat rocking herself in her chair, and sobbing as if her heart would break. Vulgar young person as she was, she had a heart, and, quite apart from everything else, the thought of the calamity which had befallen the fatherless family was in itself enough to move her deep pity; but when to that was added her own strange but constant affection for Reginald himself, despite all his aversion to her, it was a blow that fell heavily upon her.

She would not believe Reginald was guilty of the odious crimes Sam had so glibly catalogued; but guilty or not guilty, he was in prison, and it is only due to the honest, warm-hearted Jemima to say that she wished a hundred times that wretched evening that she could be in his place.

But could nothing be done? She knew it was no use trying to extract any more particulars from Samuel. As it was, she guessed only too truly that he would be raging with himself for telling her so much. Her mother could do nothing. She would probably fly with the news to Mrs Cruden's bedside, and possibly kill her outright.

Horace! She might tell him, but she was afraid. The news would fall on him like a thunderbolt, and she dreaded being the person to inflict the blow.

Yet he ought to knew, even if it doubled his misery and ended in no good to Reginald. Suppose she wrote to him.

At that moment a knock came at the door, followed by the entrance of Booms in all the gorgeousness of his evening costume. He frequently dropped in like this, especially since Mrs Cruden's illness, to hear how she was, and to inquire after Miss Crisp; and this was his errand this evening.

"No better, I suppose?" said he, dolefully, sitting down very slowly by reason of the tightness of his garments.

"Yes, the doctor says she's better; a little, a very little," said Jemima.

"And *she*, of course she's quite knocked up?" said he, with a groan.

"No. Miss Crisp's taking a nap, that's all; and mother's keeping watch next door."

Booms sat very uncomfortably, not knowing what fresh topic to discourse on. But an inspiration seized him presently.

"Oh, I see you're crying," he said. "You're in trouble, too."

"So I am," said Jemima.

"Something I've done, I suppose?" said Booms.

"No, it isn't. It's about—about the Crudens."

"Oh, of course. What about them?"

"Well, isn't it bad enough they have this dreadful trouble?" said Jemima; "but it isn't half the trouble they really are in."

"You know I can't understand what you mean when you talk like that," said Booms.

"Will you promise, if I tell you, to keep it a secret?"

"Oh, of course. I hate secrets, but go on."

"Oh, Mr Booms, Mr Reginald is in prison at Liverpool, on a charge—a false charge, I'm certain—of fraud. Isn't it dreadful? And Mr Horace ought to know of it. Could you break it to him?"

"How can I keep it a secret and break it to him?" said Mr Booms, in a pained tone. "Oh yes, I'll try, if you like."

"Oh, thank you. Do it very gently, and be sure not to let my mother, or his, or anybody else hear of it, won't you?"

"I'll try. Of course every one will put all the blame on me if it does spread."

"No, I won't. Do it first thing to-morrow, won't you, Mr Booms?"

"Oh yes"; and then, as if determined to be in time for the interview, he added, "I'd better go now."

And he departed very like a man walking to the gallows.

Shuckleford returned at midnight, and found the supper waiting for him, but, to his relief, neither of the ladies.

He wrote the following short note before he partook of his evening meal:—

"Dear D.,—Come round first thing in the morning. The police have dished us for once, but we'll be quits with them if we put our heads together. Be sure and come. Yours, S. S."

After having posted this eloquent epistle with his own hand at the pillar-box he returned to his supper, and then went, somewhat dejected, to bed.

Chapter Twenty One
Reginald finds himself "Dismissed with a Caution"

There is a famous saying of a famous modern poet which runs—

"Sudden the worst turns the best to the brave."

And so it was with Reginald Cruden when finally the whole bitter truth of his position broke in upon his mind. If the first sudden shock drove him into the dungeon of Giant Despair, a night's quiet reflection, and the consciousness of innocence within, helped him to shake off the fetters, and emerge bravely and serenely from the crisis.

He knew he had nothing to be proud of—nothing to excuse his own folly and shortsightedness—nothing to flatter his self-esteem; but no one could accuse him of dishonour, or point the finger of shame in his way. So he rose next morning armed for the worst.

What that would be he could not say, but whatever it was he would face it, confident in his own integrity and the might of right to clear him.

He endeavoured, in a few words, to explain the position of affairs to Love, who was characteristically quick at grasping it, and suggesting a remedy.

"That there Medlock's got to be served, and no error!" he said. "I'll murder 'im!"

"Nonsense!" said Reginald; "you can't make things right by doing wrong yourself. And you know you wouldn't do such a thing."

"Do I know? Tell you I would, gov'nor! I'd serve him just like that there 'Pollyon in the book. Or else I'd put rat p'ison in his beer, and—my! wouldn't it be a game to see the tet'nus a-comin' on 'im, and—"

"Be quiet," said Reginald; "I won't allow you to talk like that. It's as bad as the *Tim Tigerskin* days, Love, and we've both done with them."

"You're right there!" said the boy, pulling his *Pilgrim's Progress* from his pocket. "My! don't I wish I had the feller to myself in the Slough o'

Despond! Wouldn't I 'old 'is 'ead under! Oh no, not me! None o' yer Mr
'Elpses to give 'im a leg out, if I knows it!"

"Perhaps he'll get punished enough without us," said Reginald. "It
wouldn't do us any good to see him suffering."

"Wouldn't it, though? Would me, I can tell yer!" said the uncompromising
Love.

It was evidently hopeless to attempt to divert his young champion's
mind into channels of mercy. Reginald therefore, for lack of anything else
to do, suggested to him to go on with the reading aloud, a command the
boy obeyed with alacrity, starting of his own accord at the beginning of the
book. So the two sat there, and followed their pilgrim through the perils
and triumphs of his way, each acknowledging in his heart the spell of the
wonderful story, and feeling himself a braver man for every step he took
along with the valiant Christian.

The morning went by and noon had come, and still the boy read on,
until heavy footsteps on the stairs below startled them both, and sent a
quick flush into Reginald's cheeks.

It needed no divination to guess what it meant, and it was almost with
a sigh of relief that he saw the door open and a policeman enter.

He rose to his feet and drew himself up as the man approached.

"Is your name Cruden Reginald?" said the officer.

"No; it's Reginald Cruden."

"You call yourself Cruden Reginald?"

"I have done so; yes."

"Then I must trouble you to come along with me, young gentleman."

"Very well," said Reginald, quietly. "What am I charged with?"

"Conspiracy to defraud, that's what's on the warrant. Are you ready
now?"

"Yes, quite ready. Where are you going to take me?"

"Well, we shall have to look in at the station on our way, and then go
on to the police-court. Won't take long. Bound to remand you, you know,
for a week or something like that, and then you'll get committed, and the
assizes are on directly after the new year, so three weeks from now will see
it all over."

The man talked in a pleasant, civil way, in a tone as if he quite supposed
Reginald might be pleased to hear the programme arranged on his behalf.

"We'd better go," said Reginald, moving towards the door.

His face was very white and determined. But there was a tell-tale quiver in his tightly-pressed lips which told that he needed all his courage to help him through the ordeal before him. Till this moment the thought of having to walk through Liverpool in custody had not entered into his calculations, and he recoiled from it with a shiver.

"I needn't trouble you with these," said the policeman, taking a pair of handcuffs from his pocket; "not yet, anyhow."

"Oh no. I'll come quite quietly."

"All right. I've my mate below. You can walk between. Hulloa!"

This last exclamation was addressed to Master Love, who, having witnessed thus much of the interview in a state of stupefied bewilderment, now recovered his presence of mind sufficiently to make a furious dash at the burly policeman.

"Do you hear? Let him be; let my governor go. He ain't done nothink to you or nobody. It's me, I tell yer. I've murdered dozens, do you 'ear? and robbed the till, and set the Manshing 'Ouse o' fire, do you 'ear? You let 'im go. It's me done it!"

And he accompanied the protest with such a furious kick at the policeman's leg that that functionary grew very red in the face, and making a grab at the offender, seized him by the collar.

"Don't hurt him, please," said Reginald. "He doesn't mean any harm."

"Tell you it's me," cried the boy, trembling in the grasp of the law, "me and that there Medlock. My gov'nor ain't done it."

"Hush, be quiet, Love," said Reginald. "It'll do no good to make a noise. It can't be helped. Good-bye."

The boy fairly broke down, and began to blubber piteously.

Reginald, unmanned enough as it was, had not the heart to wait longer, and walked hurriedly to the door, followed by the policeman. This movement once more raised the faithful Love to a final effort.

"Let 'im go, do you 'ear?" shouted he, rushing down the stairs after them. "I'll do for yer if you don't. Oh, guv'nor, take me too, can't yer?"

But Reginald could only steel his heart for once, and feign not to hear the appeal.

The other policeman was waiting outside, and between his two custodians he walked, sick at heart, and faltering in courage, longing only to get out of the reach of the curious, critical eyes that turned on him from every side, and beyond the sound of that pitiful whimper of the faithful little friend as it followed him step by step to the very door of the police-station.

At the station Mr Sniff awaited the party with a pleasant smile of welcome.

"That's right," said he to Reginald, encouragingly; "much better to come quietly, looks better. Look here, young fellow," he added, rather more confidentially, "the first question you'll be asked is whether you're guilty or not. Take my advice, and make a clean breast of it."

"I shall say not guilty, which will be the truth."

Mr Sniff, as the reader has been told, had already come to the same conclusion. Still, it being the rule of his profession always to assume a man to be guilty till he can prove himself innocent, he felt it was no business of his to assist the magistrate in coming to the decision by stating what he *thought*. All he had to do was to state what he *knew*, and meanwhile, if the prisoner choose to simplify matters by pleading guilty, well, why shouldn't he?

"Please yourself about that. Have you made your entries, Jones? The van will be here directly. See you later on," added he, nodding to Reginald.

Reginald waited there for the van like a man in a dream. People came in and out, spoke, laughed, looked about them, even mentioned his name. But they all seemed part of some curious pageant, of which he himself formed not the least unreal portion. His mind wandered off on a hundred little insignificant topics. Snatches of the *Pilgrim's Progress* came into his mind, half-forgotten airs of music crossed his memory, the vision of young Gedge as he last saw him fleeted before his eyes. He tried in vain to collect his thoughts, but they were hopelessly astray, leaving him for the time barely conscious, and wholly uninterested in what was taking place around him.

The van came at last, a vehicle he had often eyed curiously as it rumbled past him in the streets. Little had he ever dreamed of riding one day inside it.

The usual knot of loungers waited at the door of the police-court to see the van disgorge its freight. Sometimes they had been rewarded for their patience by the glimpse of a real murderer, or wife-kicker, or burglar, and sometimes they had had their bit of fun over a "tough customer," who, if he must travel at her Majesty's expense, was determined to travel all the way, and insisted on being carried by the arms and legs across the pavement into the tribunal of justice. There was no such fun to be got out of Reginald as he stepped hurriedly from the van, and with downcast eyes entered by the prisoners' door into the court-house.

A case was already in progress, and he had to wait in a dimly-lit underground lobby for his summons. The constable who had arrested him was still beside him, and other groups, mostly of police, filled up the place. But he heeded none, longing—oh! how intensely—to hear his name called and to know the worst.

Presently there was a bustle near the door, and he knew the case upstairs was at an end.

"Six months," some one said.

Some one else whistled softly.

"Whew—old Fogey's in one of his tantrums, then. He'd have only got three at Dark Street."

Then some one called the name "Reginald," and the policeman near him said "Coming." Then, turning to the prisoner, he said,—

"Fogey's on the bench to-day, and he's particular. Look alive."

Reginald found himself being hurried to the door through a lane of officials and others towards the stairs.

"Your turn next, Grinder," he heard some one say as he passed. "Ten-minutes will do this case."

To Reginald the stairs seemed interminable. There was a hum of voices above, and a shuffling of feet as of people taking a momentary relaxation in the interval of some performance. Then a loud voice cried, "Silence—order in the court, sit down, gentlemen," and there fell an unearthly stillness on the place.

"To the right," said the policeman, coming beside him, and taking his arm as if to direct him.

He was conscious of a score of curious faces turned on him, of some one on the bench folding up a newspaper and adjusting his glasses, of a man at a table throwing aside a quill pen and taking another, of a click of a latch closing behind him, of a row of spikes in front of him. Then he found himself alone.

What followed he scarcely could tell. He was vaguely aware of some one with Mr Sniff's voice making a statement in which his (Reginald's) own name occurred, another voice from the bench breaking in every now and then, and yet another voice from the table talking too, accompanied by the squeaking of a pen across paper. Then the constable who had arrested him said something, and after the constable some one else.

Then followed a dialogue in undertone between the bench and the table, and once more Mr Sniff's voice, and at last the voice from the bench, a gruff, unsympathetic voice, said,—

"Now, sir, what have you got to say for yourself?"

The question roused him. It was intended for him, and he awoke to the consciousness that, after all, he had some interest in what was going on.

He raised his head and said,—

"I'm not guilty."

"You reserve your defence, then?"

"Tell him yes," said the policeman.

"Yes, sir."

"Very well, then. I shall remand you for three days. Bring him up again on Friday."

And the magistrate took up his newspaper, the clerk at the table laying down his pen; the bustle and shuffling of feet filled the room, and in another moment Reginald was down the staircase, and the voice he had heard before called,—

"Remand three days. Now then, Grinder, up you go—"

In all his conjectures as to what might befall him, the possibility of being actually sent to prison had never entered Reginald's head. That he would be suspected, arrested, taken to the police-station, and finally brought before a magistrate, he had foreseen. That was bad enough, but he had steeled his resolution to the pitch of going through with it, sure that the clearing of his character would follow any inquiry into the case.

But to be lodged for three days as a common felon in a police cell was a fate he had not once realised, and which, when its full meaning broke upon him, crushed the spirit out of him.

He made no resistance, no protest, no complaint as they hustled him back into the van, and from the van to the cell which was to be his dreary lodging for those three days. He felt degraded, dishonoured, disgraced, and as he sat hour after hour brooding over his lot, his mind, already overwrought, lost its courage and let go its hope.

Suppose he really had done something to be ashamed of? Suppose he had all along had his vague suspicions of the honesty of the Corporation, and yet had continued to serve them? Suppose, with the best of intentions, he had shut his eyes wilfully to what he might and must have seen? Suppose, in fact, his negligence had been criminal? How was he ever to hold up his head again and face the world like an honest man, and say he had defrauded no man?

And then there came up in terrible array that long list of customers to the Corporation whom he had lured and enticed by promises he had never taken the trouble to inquire into to part with their money. And the burden of their loss lay like an incubus on his spirit, till he actually persuaded himself he was guilty.

I need not sadden the reader with dwelling on the misery of those three days. Any one almost could have endured them better than Reginald. He began a letter to Horace, but he tore it up when half-written. He drew up a statement of his own defence, but when fact after fact appeared in array on the paper it seemed more like an indictment than a defence, and he tore it up too.

At length the weary suspense was over, and once more he found himself in the outer air, stepping with almost familiar tread across the pavement into the van, and taking his place among the waiters in the dim lobby at the foot of the police-court stairs.

When at last he stood once more in the dock none of his former bewilderment remained to befriend him. It was all too real this time. When some one spoke of the "prisoner" he knew it meant himself, and when they spoke of fraud he knew they referred to something he had done. Oh, that he could see it all in a dream once more, and wake up to find himself on the other side!

"Now, Mr Sniff, you've got something to say?" said the magistrate.

"Yes, your worship," replied Mr Sniff, not moving to the witness-box, but speaking from his seat. "We don't propose to continue this case."

"What? It's a clear case, isn't it?" said the magistrate, with the air of a man who is being trifled with.

"No, your worship. There's not evidence enough to ask you to send the prisoner to trial."

"Then I'd better sentence him myself."

"I think not, your worship. Our evidence only went to show that the prisoner was in the employment of the men who started the company. But we have no evidence that he was aware that the concern was fraudulent, and as he does not appear to have appropriated any of the money, we advise dismissing the case. The real offenders are in custody, and have practically admitted their guilt."

The magistrate looked very ill-tempered and offended. He did not like being told what he was told, especially by the police, and he had a righteous horror of cases being withdrawn from his authority.

He held a snappish consultation with his clerk, which by no means tended to pacify him, for that functionary whispered his opinion that as the case had been withdrawn there was nothing for it but for his worship to dismiss the case.

Somebody, at any rate, should smart for his injured feelings, and as he did not know law enough to abuse Mr Sniff, and had not pretext sufficient to abuse his clerk, he gathered himself for a castigation of the prisoner, which should not only serve as a caution to that youth for his future guidance, but should also relieve his own magisterial mind.

"Now, prisoner," began he, setting his spectacles and leaning forward in his seat, "you've heard what the officer has said. You may consider yourself fortunate—very fortunate—there is not enough evidence to convict you. Don't flatter yourself that a breakdown in the prosecution clears your character. In the eyes of the law you may be clear, but morally, let me tell you, you are far from being so. It's affectation to tell me you could live for three months the centre of a system of fraud and yet have your hands clean. You must make good your account between your own conscience and the hundreds of helpless, unfortunate poor men and women you have been the means of depriving of their hard-earned money. You have already been kept in prison for three days. Let me hope that will be a warning to you not to meddle in future with fraud, if you wish to pass as an honest man. If you touch pitch, sir, you must expect to be denied. Return to paths of honesty, young man, and seek to recover the character you have forfeited, and bear in mind the warning you have had, if you wish to avoid a more serious stain in the future. The case is dismissed."

With which elegant peroration the magistrate, much relieved in his own mind, took up his newspaper, and Reginald was hurried once more down those steep stairs a free man.

"Slice of luck for you, young shaver!" said the friendly policeman, slipping off the handcuffs.

"Regular one of Sniff's little games!" said another standing near; "he always lets his little fish go when he's landed his big ones! To my mind it's a risky business. Never mind."

"You can go when you like now," said the policeman to Reginald; "and whenever we come across a shilling for a drink we'll drink your health, my lad."

Reginald saw the hint, and handed the policeman one of his last shillings. Then, buttoning his coat against the cold winter wind, he walked out, a free man, into the street.

Chapter Twenty Two
The Darkest Hour before the Dawn

If the worshipful magistrate flattered himself that the reprimand he had addressed to Reginald that afternoon would move his hearer to self-abasement or penitence, he had sadly miscalculated the power of his own language.

Every word of that "caution" had entered like iron into the boy's soul, and had roused in him every evil passion of which his nature was capable. A single word of sympathy or kindly advice might have won him heart and soul. But those stinging, brutal sentences goaded him almost to madness, and left him desperate.

What was the use of honesty, of principle, of conscientiousness, if they were all with one accord to rise against him and degrade him?

What was the use of trying to be better than others when the result was an infamy which, had he been a little more greedy or a little less upright, he might have avoided?

What was the use of conscious innocence and unstained honour, when they could not save him from a sense of shame of which no convicted felon could know the bitterness?

It would go out to all the world that Reginald Cruden, the suspected swindler, had been "let off" for lack of evidence after three days' imprisonment. The victims of the Corporation would read it, and regret the failure of justice to overtake the man who had robbed them. His father's old county friends would read it, and shake their heads over poor Cruden's prodigal. The Wilderham fellows would read it, and set him down as one more who had gone to the bad. Young Gedge would read it, and scorn him for a hypocrite and a humbug. Durfy would read it, and chuckle. His mother and Horace would read it. Yes, and what would they think? Nothing he could say would convince them or anybody. They might forgive him, but—

The thought made his blood boil within him. He would take forgiveness from no man or woman. If they chose to believe him guilty, let them; but let them keep their forgiveness to themselves. Rather let them give the dog a bad name and hang him. He did not care! Would that they could!

Such was the rush of thought that passed through his mind as he stood that bleak winter afternoon in the street, a free man.

Free! he laughed at the word, and envied the burglar with his six months. What spirit of malignity had hindered Mr Sniff from letting him lose himself in a felon's cell rather than turn him out "free" into a world every creature of which was an enemy?

Are you disgusted with him, reader? With his poor spirit, his weak purpose, his blind folly? Do you say that you, in his shoes, would have done better? that you would never have lost courage? that you would have held up your head still, and braved the storm? Alas, alas, that the Reginalds are so many and the heroes of your sort so few!

Alas for the sensitive natures whom injustice can crush and make cowards of! You are not sensitive, thank God, and you do not know what crushing is. Pray that you never may; but till you have felt it deal leniently with poor Reginald, as he goes recklessly out into the winter gloom without a friend — not even himself.

It mattered little to him where he went or what became of him. It made no odds how and when he should spend his last shilling. He was hungry now. Since early that morning nothing had passed his lips. Why not spend it now and have done with it?

So he turned into a coffee-shop, and ordered coffee and a plate of beef.

"My last meal," said he to himself, with a bitter smile.

His appetite failed him when the food appeared, but he ate and drank out of sheer bravado. His enemies—Durfy, and the magistrate, and the victims of the Corporation—would rejoice to see him turn with a shudder from his food. He would devour it to spite them.

"How much?" said he, when it was done.

"Ninepence, please," said the rosy-cheeked girl who waited.

Reginald tossed her the shilling.

"Keep the change for yourself," said he, and walked out of the shop.

He was free now with a vengeance! He might do what he liked, go where he liked, starve where he liked.

He wandered up and down the streets that winter evening recklessly indifferent to what became of him. The shops were gaily lighted and adorned with Christmas decorations. Boys and girls, men and women, thronged them, eager in their purchases and radiant in the prospect of the coming festival. There went a grave father, parading the pavement with a football under his arm for the boy at home; and here a lad, with his mother's arm in his, stood halted before an array of fur cloaks, and bade her choose the best among them. Bright-eyed school-girls brushed past him with their brothers, smiling and talking in holiday glee; and here a trio of school-chums, arm-in-arm, bore down upon him, laughing over some last-term joke. He watched them all.

Times were when his heart would warm and soften within him at the memories sights like these inspired; but they were nothing to him now; or if they were anything, they were part of a universal conspiracy to mock him. Let them mock him; what cared he?

The night drew on. One by one the gay lights in the shops went out, and the shutters hid the crowded windows. One by one the passengers dispersed, some to besiege the railway-stations, some to invade the trams, others to walk in cheery parties by the frosty roads; all to go home.

Even the weary shopmen and shop-girls, released from the day's labours, hurried past him homeward, and the sleepy cabman whipped up his horse for his last fare before going home, and the tramps and beggars vanished down their alleys, and sought every man his home.

Home! The word had no meaning to-night for Reginald as he watched the streets empty, and found himself a solitary wayfarer in the deserted thoroughfares.

The hum of traffic ceased. One by one the bedroom lights went out, the clocks chimed midnight clearly in the frosty air, and still he wandered on.

He passed a newspaper-office, where the thunder of machinery and the glare of the case-room reminded him of his own bitter apprenticeship at the *Rocket*. They might find him a job here if he applied. Faugh! who would take a gaol-bird, a "let-off" swindler, into their employ?

He strolled down to the docks. The great river lay asleep. The docks were, deserted; the dockyards silent. Only here and there a darting light, or the distant throb of an engine, broke the slumber of the scene.

A man came up to him as he stood on the jetty.

"Now then, sheer off; do you hear?" he said. "What do you want here?"

"Mayn't I watch the river?" said Reginald.

"Not here. We've had enough of your sort watching the river. Off you go," and he laid his hand on the boy's collar and marched him off the pier.

Of course! Who had not had enough of his sort? Who would not suspect him wherever he went? Cain went about with a mark on his forehead for every one to know him by. In what respect was he better off, when men seemed to know by instinct and in the dark that he was a character to mistrust and suspect?

The hours wore on. Even the printing-office when he passed it again was going to rest. The compositors one by one were flitting home, and the engine was dropping asleep. He stood and watched the men come out, and wondered if any of them were like himself—whether among them was a young Gedge or a Durfy?

Then he wandered off back into the heart of the town. A wretched outcast woman, with a child in her arms, stood at the street corner and accosted him.

"Do, kind gentleman, give me a penny. The child's starving, and we're so cold and hungry."

"I'd give you one if I had one," said Reginald; "but I'm as poor as you are."

The woman sighed, and drew her rags round the infant.

Reginald watched her for a moment, and then, taking off his overcoat, said,—

"You'd better put this round you."

And he dropped it at her feet, and hurried away before she could pick up the gift, or bless the giver.

He gave himself no credit for the deed, and he wanted none. What did he care about a coat? he who had been frozen to the heart already. Would a coat revive his good name, or cover the disgrace of that magisterial caution?

The clocks struck four, and the long winter night grew bleaker and darker. It was eleven hours since he had taken that last defiant meal, and Nature began slowly to assert her own with the poor outcast. He was faint and tired out, and the breeze cut him through. Still the rebel spirit within him denied that he was in distress. No food or rest or shelter for him! All he craved was leave to lose himself and forget his own name.

Is it any use bidding him, as we bade him once before, turn round and face the evil genius that is pursuing him? or is there nothing for him now but to run? He has run all night, but he is no farther ahead than when he stood at the police-court door. On the contrary, it is running him down fast, and as he staggers forward into the darkest hour of that cruel night, it treads on his heels and begins to drag him back.

Is there no home? no voice of a friend? no helping hand to save him from that worst of all enemies—his evil self?

It was nearly five o'clock when, without knowing how he got there, he found himself on the familiar ground of Shy Street. In the dim lamplight he scarcely recognised it at first, but when he did it seemed like a final stroke of irony to bring him there, at such a time, in such a mood. What else could it be meant for but to remind him there was no escape, no hope of losing himself, no chance of forgetting?

That gaunt, empty window of Number 13, with the reflected glare of the lamp opposite upon it, seemed to leer down on him like a mocking ghost, claiming him as its own. What was the use of keeping up the struggle any longer? After all, was there not one way of escape?

What was it crouching at the door of Number 13, half hidden in the shade? A dog? a woman? a child?

He stood still a moment, with beating heart, straining his eyes through the gloom. Then he crossed. As he did so the figure sprang to its feet and rushed to meet him.

"I knowed it, gov'nor; I knowed you was a-comin'," cried a familiar boy's voice. "It's all right now. It's all right, gov'nor!"

Never did sweeter music fall on mortal ears than these broken, breathless words on the spirit of Reginald. It was the voice he had been waiting for to save him in his extremity—the voice of love to remind him he was not forsaken; the voice of trust to remind him some one believed in him still; the voice of hope to remind him all was not lost yet. It called him back to himself; it thawed the chill at his heart, and sent new life into his soul. It was like a key to liberate him from the dungeon of Giant Despair.

"Why, Love, is that you, my boy?" he cried, seizing the lad's hand.

"It is so, gov'nor," whimpered the boy, trembling with excitement, and clinging to his protector's hand. "I knowed you was a-comin', but I was a'most feared I wouldn't see you too."

"What made you think I would come?" said Reginald, looking down with tears in his eyes on the poor wizened upturned face.

"I knowed you was a-comin'," repeated the boy, as if he could not say it too often; "and I waited and waited, and there you are. It's all right, gov'nor."

"It *is* all right, old fellow," said Reginald. "You don't know what you've saved me from."

"Go on," said the boy, recovering his composure in the great content of his discovery. "I ain't saved you from nothink. Leastways unless you was a-goin' to commit soosanside. If you was, you was a flat to come this way. That there railway-cutting's where I'd go, and then at the inkwidge they don't know if you did it a-purpose or was topped over by the train, and they gives you the benefit of the doubt, and says, 'Found dead.'"

"We won't talk about it," said Reginald, smiling, the first smile that had crossed his lips for a week. "Do you know, young 'un, I'm hungry; are you?"

"Got any browns?" said Love.

"Not a farthing."

"More ain't I, but I'll—" He paused, and a shade of doubt crossed his face as he went on. "Say, gov'nor, think they'd give us a brown for this 'ere *Robinson*?"

And he pulled out his *Robinson Crusoe* bravely and held it up.

"I'm afraid not. It only cost threepence."

Another inward debate took place; then drawing out his beloved *Pilgrim's Progress*, he put the two books together, and said,—

"Suppose they'd give us one for them two?"

"Don't let's part with them if we can help," said Reginald. "Suppose we try to earn something?"

The boy said nothing, but trudged on beside his protector till they emerged from Shy Street and stood in one of the broad empty main streets of the city.

Here Reginald, worn out with hunger and fatigue, and borne up no longer by the energy of desperation, sank half fainting into a doorstep.

"I'm—so tired," he said; "let's rest a bit. I'll be all right—in a minute."

Love looked at him anxiously for a moment, and then saying, "Stay you there, gov'nor, till I come back," started off to run.

How long Reginald remained half-unconscious where the boy left him he could not exactly tell; but when he came to himself an early streak of dawn was lighting the sky, and Love was kneeling beside him.

"It's all right, gov'nor," said he, holding up a can of hot coffee and a slice of bread in his hands. "Chuck these here inside yer; do you 'ear?"

Reginald put his lips eagerly to the can. It was nearly sixteen hours since he had touched food. He drained it half empty; then stopping suddenly, he said,—

"Have you had any yourself?"

"Me? In corse! Do you suppose I ain't 'ad a pull at it?"

"You haven't," said Reginald, eyeing him sharply, and detecting the well-meant fraud in his looks. "Unless you take what's left there, I'll throw it all into the road."

In vain Love protested, vowed he loathed coffee, that it made him sick, that he preferred prussic acid; Reginald was inexorable, and the boy was obliged to submit. In like manner, no wile or device could save him from having to share the slice of bread; nor, when he did put it to his lips, could any grimace or protest hide the almost ravenous eagerness with which at last he devoured it.

"Now you wait till I take back the can," said Love. "I'll not be a minute," and he darted off, leaving Reginald strengthened in mind and body by the frugal repast.

It was not till the boy returned that he noticed he wore no coat.

"What have you done with it?" he demanded sternly.

"Me? What are you talking about?" said the boy, looking guiltily uneasy.

"Don't deceive me!" said Reginald. "Where's your coat?"

"What do I want with coats? Do you—"

"Have you sold it for our breakfast?"

"Go on! Do you think—"

"Have you?" repeated Reginald, this time almost angrily.

"Maybe I 'ave," said the boy; "ain't I got a right to?"

"No, you haven't; and you'll have to wear mine now."

And he proceeded to take it off, when the boy said,—

"All right. If you take that off, gov'nor, I slides—I mean it—so I do."

There was a look of such wild determination in his pinched face that Reginald gave up the struggle for the present.

"We'll share it between us, at any rate," said he. "Whatever induced you to do such a foolish thing, Love?"

"Bless you, I ain't got no sense," replied the boy cheerily.

Day broke at last, and Liverpool once more became alive with bustle and traffic. No one noticed the two shivering boys as they wended their way through the streets, trying here and there, but in vain, for work, and wondering where and when they should find their next meal. But for Reginald that walk, faint and footsore as he was, was a pleasure-trip compared with the night's wanderings.

Towards afternoon Love had the rare good fortune to see a gentleman drop a purse on the pavement. There was no chance of appropriating it, had he been so minded, which, to do him justice, he was not, for the purse fell in a most public manner in the sight of several onlookers. But Love was the first to reach it and hand it back to its owner.

Now Love's old story-books had told him that honesty of this sort is a very paying sort of business; and though he hardly expected the wonderful consequences to follow his own act which always befall the superfluously honest boys in the "penny dreadfuls," he was yet low-souled enough to linger sufficiently long in the neighbourhood of the owner of the purse to give him an opportunity of proving the truth of the story-book moral.

Nor was he disappointed; for the good gentleman, happening to have no less than fifty pounds in gold and notes stored up in this particular purse, was magnanimous enough to award Love a shilling for his lucky piece of honesty, a result which made that young gentleman's countenance glow with a grin of the profoundest satisfaction.

"My eye, gov'nor," said he, returning radiant with his treasure to Reginald, and thrusting it into his hand; "'ere, lay 'old. 'Ere's a slice o' luck. Somethink like that there daily bread you was a-tellin' me of t'other day. No fear, I ain't forgot it. Now, I say sassages. What do you say?"

Reginald said "sausages" too; and the two friends, armed with their magic shilling, marched boldly into a cosy coffee-shop where there was a blazing fire and a snug corner, and called for sausages for two. And they never enjoyed such a meal in all their lives. How they did make those sausages last! And what life and comfort they got out of that fire, and what rest out of those cane-bottomed chairs!

At the end of it all they had fourpence left, which, after serious consultation, it was decided to expend in a bed for the night.

"If we can get a good sleep," said Reginald, "and pull ourselves together, we're bound to get a job of some sort to-morrow. Do you know any lodging-house?"

"Me? don't I? That there time you jacked me up I was a night in a place down by the river. It ain't a dainty place, gov'nor, but it's on'y twopence a piece or threepence a couple on us, and that'll leave a brown for the morning."

"All right. Let's go there soon, and get a long night."

Love led the way through several low streets beside the wharves until he came to a court in which stood a tumble-down tenement with the legend "Lodgings" scrawled on a board above the door. Here they entered, and Love in a few words bargained with the sour landlady for a night's lodging. She protested at first at their coming so early, but finally yielded, on condition they would make the threepence into fourpence. They had nothing for it but to yield.

"Up you go, then," said the woman, pointing to a rickety ladder which served the house for a staircase. "There's one there already. Never mind him; you take the next."

Reginald turned almost sick as he entered the big, stifling, filthy loft which was to serve him for a night's lodging. About a dozen beds were ranged along the walls on either side, one of which, that in the far corner of the room, was, as the woman had said, occupied. The atmosphere of the place was awful already. What would it be when a dozen or possibly two dozen persons slept there?

Reginald's first impulse was to retreat and rather spend another night in the streets than in such a place. But his weary limbs and aching bones forbade it. He must stay where he was now.

Already Love was curled up and asleep on the bed next to that where the other lodger lay; and Reginald, stifling every feeling but his weariness, flung himself by his side and soon forgot both place and surroundings in a heavy sleep.

Heavy but fitful. He had scarcely lain an hour when he found himself suddenly wide awake. Love still lay breathing heavily beside him. The other lodger turned restlessly from side to side, muttering to himself, and sometimes moaning like a person in pain. It must have been these latter sounds which awoke Reginald. He lay for some minutes listening and watching in the dim candle-light the restless tossing of the bed-clothes.

Presently the sick man—for it was evident sickness was the cause of his uneasiness—lifted himself on his elbow with a groan, and said,—

"For God's sake—help me!"

In a moment Reginald had sprung to his feet, and was beside the sufferer.

"Are you ill," he said. "What is the matter?"

But the man, instead of replying, groaned and fell heavily back on the bed. And as the dim light of the candle fell upon his upturned face, Reginald, with a cry of horror, recognised the features of Mr Durfy, already released by death from the agonies of smallpox.

Chapter Twenty Three
Lost And Found

Booms was not exactly the sort of man to be elated by the mission which Miss Shuckleford had thrust upon him. He passed a restless night in turning the matter over in his mind and wondering how he could break the news gently to his friend.

For he was fond of Horace, and in his saturnine way felt deeply for him in his trouble. And on this account he wished Jemima had chosen any other confidant to discharge the unpleasant task.

He hung about outside Mrs Cruden's house for an hour early that morning, in the hope of being able to entrap Miss Crisp and get her to take the duty off his hands. But Miss Crisp had been sitting up all night with the patient and did not appear.

He knocked at the door and asked the servant-girl how Mrs Cruden was. She was a little better, but very weak and not able to speak to anybody.

"Any news from Liverpool?" inquired Booms. This had become a daily question among those who inquired at Number 6, Dull Street.

"No, no news," said the girl, with a guilty blush. She knew the reason why. Reginald's last letter, written just before his arrest, was at that moment in her pocket.

"Has Mr Horace started to the office?"

"No; he's a-going to wait and see the doctor, and he says I was to ask you to tell the gentleman so."

"Can I see him?"

"No; he's asleep just now," said the girl.

So Booms had to go down alone to the *Rocket*, as far as ever from getting the burden of Jemima's secret off his mind.

He had a good mind to pass it on to Waterford, and might have done so, had not that young gentleman been engaged all the morning on special duty, which kept him in Mr Granville's room.

Booms grew more and more dispirited and nervous. Every footstep that came to the door made him tremble, for fear it should be the signal for the unhappy disclosure. He tried hard to persuade himself it would be kinder after all to say nothing about it. What good could it do now?

Booms, as the reader knows, had not a very large mind. But what there was of it was honest, and it told him, try how he would, there was no getting out of a promise. So he busied himself with concocting imaginary phrases and letters, by way of experiment as to the neatest way of breaking his bad news.

Still he dreaded his friend's arrival more and more; and when at last a brisk footstep halted at the door, he started and turned pale like a guilty thing, and wished Jemima at the bottom of the sea!

But the footstep was not Horace's. Whoever the arrival was, he tapped at the door before entering, and then, without waiting for a reply, walked in.

It was a youth of about seventeen or eighteen, with a bright honest face and cheery smile.

"Is Horace Cruden here?" he inquired eagerly.

"Oh no," said Booms, in his most doleful accents.

"Isn't this where he works?"

"It is indeed."

"Well, then, is anything wrong? Is he ill?"

"No. *He* is not ill," said Booms, emphasising the pronoun.

"Is Reginald ill, then, or their mother?"

A ray of hope crossed Booms's mind. This stranger was evidently a friend of the family. He called the boys by their Christian names, and knew their mother. Would he take charge of the dismal secret?

"His mother is ill," said he. "Do you know them?"

"Rather. I was Horace's chum at Wilderham, you know, and used to spend my holidays regularly at Garden Vale. Is she very ill?"

"Very," said Booms; "and the worst of it is, Reginald is not at home."

"Where is he. Horrors told me he had gone to the country."

Booms *would* tell him. For the visitor called his friend Horrors, a pet name none but his own family were ever known to use.

"They don't know where he is. But I do," said Booms, with a tragic gesture.

"Where? where? What's wrong, I say? Tell me, there's a good fellow."

"He's in prison," said Booms, throwing himself back in his chair, and panting with the effort the disclosure had cost him.

"In prison! and Horace doesn't know it! What *do* you mean? Tell me all you know."

Booms did tell him, and very little it was. All he knew was from Jemima's secondhand report, and the magnitude of the news had quite prevented him from inquiring as to particulars.

"When did you hear this?" said Harker; for the reader will have guessed by this time that the visitor was no other than Horace's old Wilderham ally.

"Yesterday."

"And he doesn't know yet?"

"How could I tell him? Of course I'm to get all the blame. I expected it."

"Who's blaming you?" said Harker, whom the news had suddenly brought on terms of familiarity with his friend's friend. "When will he be here?"

"Very soon, I suppose."

"And then you'll tell him?"

"You will, please," said Booms, quite eagerly for him.

"Somebody must, poor fellow!" said Harker. "We don't know what we may be losing by the delay."

"Of course it's my fault for not waking him up in the middle of the night and telling him," said Booms dismally.

"Is there anything about it in the papers?" said Harker, taking up a *Times*.

"I've seen nothing."

"You say it was a day or two ago. Have you got the *Times* for the last few days?"

"Yes; it's there."

Harker hastily turned over the file, and eagerly searched the police and country intelligence. In a minute or two he looked up and said,—

"Had Cruden senior changed his name?"

"How *do* I know?" said Booms, with a bewildered look.

"I mean, had he dropped his surname? Look here."

And he showed Booms the paragraph which appeared in the London papers the morning after Reginald's arrest.

"That looks very much as if it was meant for Cruden," said Harker—"all except the name. If it is, that was Tuesday he was remanded, and to-day is the day he is to be brought up again. Oh, why didn't we know this before?"

"Yes. I knew I was to blame. I knew it all along," said Booms, taking every expression of regret as a personal castigation.

"It will be all over before any one can do a thing," said Harker, getting up and pacing the room in his agitation. "Why *doesn't* Horace come?"

As if in answer to the appeal, Horace at that moment opened the door.

"Why, Harker, old man!" he exclaimed with delight in his face and voice as he sprang towards his friend.

"Horrors, my poor dear boy," said Harker, "don't be glad to see me. I've bad news, and there's no time to break it gently. It's about Reginald. He's in trouble—in prison. I'll come with you to Liverpool this morning; there is a train in twenty minutes."

Horace said nothing. He turned deadly pale and gazed for a moment half scared, half appealing, at his friend. Booms remembered something he had to do in another room, and went to the door.

"Do you mind getting a hansom?" said Harker.

The words roused Horace from his stupor.

"Mother," he gasped, "she's ill."

"We shall be home again to-night most likely," said Harker.

"I must tell Granville," said Horace.

"Your chief. Well, be quick, the cab will be here directly."

Horace went to the inner room and in a minute returned, his face still white but with a burning spot on either cheek.

"All right?" inquired Harker.

Horace nodded, and followed him to the door.

In a quarter of an hour they were at Euston in the booking office.

"I have no money," said Horace.

"I have, plenty for us both. Go and get some papers, especially Liverpool ones, at the book-stall while I get the tickets."

It was a long memorable journey. The papers were soon exhausted. They contained little or no additional news respecting the obscure suspect in Liverpool, and beyond that they had no interest for either traveller.

"We shall get down at three," said Harker; "there's a chance of being in time."

"In time for what? what can we do?"

"Try and get another remand, if only for a couple of days. I can't believe it of Reg. There must be some mistake."

"Of course there must," said Horace, with a touch of scorn in his voice, "but how are we to prove it?"

"It's no use trying just now. All we can do is to get a remand."

The train seemed to drag forward with cruel slowness, and the precious moments sped by with no less cruel haste. It was five minutes past three when they found themselves on the platform of Liverpool station.

"It's touch and go if we're in time, old boy," said Harker, as they took their seats in a hansom and ordered the man to drive hard for the police-court; "but you mustn't give up hope even if we're late. We'll pull poor old Reg through somehow."

His cheery words and the brotherly grip on his arm were like life and hope to Horace.

"Oh, yes," he replied. "What would I have done if you hadn't turned up like an angel of help, Harker, old man?"

As they neared the police-court the cabman pulled up to allow a police van to turn in the road. The two friends shuddered. It was like an evil omen to daunt them.

Was *he* in that van—so near them, yet so hopelessly beyond their reach?

"For goodness' sake drive on!" shouted Harker to the cabman.

It seemed ages before the lumbering obstruction had completed its revolution and drawn to one side sufficiently to allow them to pass.

In another minute the cab dashed to the door of the court.

It was open, and the knot of idlers on the pavement showed them that some case of interest was at that moment going on.

They made their way to the policeman who stood on duty.

"Court's full—stand back, please. Can't go in," said that official.

"What case is it?"

"Stand back, please—can't go in," repeated the stolid functionary.

"Please tell us—"

"Stand back there!" once more shouted the sentinel, growing rather more peremptory.

It was clearly no use mincing matters. At this very moment Reginald might be standing defenceless within, with his last chance of liberty slipping from under his feet.

Harker drew a shilling from his pocket and slipped it into the hand of the law.

"Tell us the name of the case, there's a good fellow," said he coaxingly.

"Bilcher—wife murder. Stand back, please—court's full."

Bilcher! Wife murder! It was for this the crowd had gathered, it was for the result of this that that knot of idlers were waiting so patiently outside.

Bilcher was the hero of this day's gathering. Who was likely to care a rush about such a lesser light as a secretary charged with a commonplace fraud.

"Has the case of Cruden come on yet?" asked Horace anxiously.

The policeman answered him with a vacant stare.

"No," said Harker, "the name would be Reginald, you know. I say," added he to the policeman, "when does Reginald's case come on?"

"Stand back there—Reginald—he was the last but one before this— don't crowd, please."

"We're too late, then. What was—what did he get?"

Now the policeman considered he had answered quite enough for his shilling. If he went on, people would think he was an easy fish to catch. So he affected deafness, and looking straight past his eager questioners again repeated his stentorian request to the public generally.

"Oh, pray tell us what he got," said Harker, in tones of genuine entreaty; "this is his brother, and we've only just heard of it."

The policeman for a moment turned a curious eye on Horace, as if to convince himself of the truth of the story. Then, apparently satisfied, and weary of the whole business, he said,—

"Let off. *Will you* keep back, please? Stand back. Court's full."

Let off. Horace's heart gave a bound of triumph as he heard the words. Of course he was! Who could even suspect him of such a thing as fraud?

Unjustly accused he might be, but Reg's character was proof against that any day.

Harker shared his friend's feelings of relief and thankfulness at the good news, but his face was still not without anxiety.

"We had better try to find him," said he.

"Oh, of course. He'll probably be back at Shy Street."

But no one was at Shy Street. The dingy office was deserted and locked, and a little street urchin on the doorstep glowered at them as they peered up the staircase and read the name on the plate.

"Had we better ask in the shop? they may know," said Horace.

But the chemist looked black when Reginald's name was mentioned, and hoped he should never see him again. He'd got into trouble and loss enough with him as it was—a hypocritical young—

"Look here," said Horace, "you're speaking of my brother, and you'd better be careful. He's no more a hypocrite than you. He's an honest man, and he's been acquitted of the charge brought against him."

"I didn't know you were his brother," said the chemist, rather sheepishly, "but for all that I don't want to see him again, and I don't expect I shall either. He won't come near here in a hurry, unless I'm mistaken."

"The fellow's right, I'm afraid," said Harker, as they left the shop. "He's had enough of this place, from what you tell me. It strikes me the best thing is to go and inquire at the police-station. They may know something there."

To the police-station accordingly they went, and chanced to light on one no less important than Mr Sniff himself.

"We are interested in Reginald Cruden, who was before the magistrate to-day," said Harker. "In fact, this is his brother, and I am an old schoolfellow. We hear the charge against him was dismissed, and we should be much obliged if you could tell us where to find him."

Mr Sniff regarded the two boys with interest, and not without a slight trace of uneasiness. He had never really suspected Reginald, but it had appeared necessary to arrest him on suspicion, not only to satisfy the victims of the Corporation, but on the off chance of his knowing rather more than he seemed to know about the doings of that virtuous association. It had been a relief to Mr Sniff to find his first impressions as to the lad's innocence confirmed, and to be able to withdraw the charge against him. But the manner in which the magistrate had dismissed the case had roused even his phlegmatic mind to indignation, and had set his conscience troubling him a little as to his own conduct of the affair. This was why he now felt and looked not quite happy in the presence of Reginald's brother and friend.

"Afraid I can't tell you," said he. "He left the court as soon as the case was over, and of course we've no more to do with him."

"He is not back at his old office," said Horace, "and I don't know of any other place in Liverpool he would be likely to go to."

"It struck me, from the looks of him," said Mr Sniff, quite despising himself for being so unprofessionally communicative—"it struck me he didn't very much care where he went. Very down in the mouth he was."

"Why, but he was acquitted; his character was cleared. Whatever should he be down in the mouth about?" said Horace.

Mr Sniff smiled pityingly.

"He was let off with a caution," he said; "that's rather a different thing from having your character cleared, especially when our friend Fogey's on the bench. I was sorry for the lad, so I was."

This was a great deal to come from the lips of a cast-iron individual like Mr Sniff, and it explained the state of the case forcibly enough to his two hearers. Horace knew his brother's nature well enough to imagine the effect upon him of such a reprimand, and his spirits sank within him.

"Who can tell us now where we are to look for him?" said he to Harker. "Anything like injustice drives him desperate. He may have gone off, as the detective says, not caring where. And then Liverpool is a fearfully big place."

"We won't give it up till we have found him," said Harker; "and if you can't stay, old man, I will."

"I can't go," said Horace, with a groan. "Poor Reg!"

"Well, let us call round at the post-office and see if Waterford has remembered to telegraph about your mother."

They went to the post-office and found a telegram from Miss Crisp: "Good day. Better, decidedly. Knows you are in Liverpool, but nothing more. Any news? Do not telegraph unless all right."

"It's pretty evident," said Horace, handing the message to his friend, "we can't telegraph to-day. I'll write to Waterford and get him to tell the others. But what is the next thing to be done?"

"We can only be patient," said Harker. "We are bound to come across him or hear of him in time."

"He's not likely to have gone home?" suggested Horace.

"How could he with no money?"

"Or to try to get on an American ship? We might try that."

"Oh yes, we shall have to try all that sort of thing."

"Well, let's begin at once," said Horace impatiently, "every minute may be of consequence."

But for a week they sought in vain—among the busy streets by day and in the empty courts by night, among the shipping, in the railway-stations, in the workhouses, at the printing-offices.

Mr Sniff did them more than one friendly turn, and armed them with the talisman of his name to get them admittance where no other key would pass them. They inquired at public-houses, coffee-houses, lodging-houses, but all in vain. No one had seen a youth answering their description, or if they had it was only for a moment, and he had passed from their sight and memory.

False scents there were in plenty—some which seemed to lead up hopefully to the very last, and then end in nothing, others too vague even to attempt to follow.

Once they heard that the body of a youth had been found floating in the Mersey—and with terrible forebodings they rushed to the place and demanded to see it. But he was not there. The dead upturned face they looked on was not his, and they turned away, feeling more than ever discouraged in their quest.

At length at the end of a week a man who kept an early coffee-stall in one of the main streets told them that a week ago a ragged little urchin had come to him with a pitiful tale about a gentleman who was starving, and had begged for a can of coffee and a slice of bread to take to him, offering in proof of his good faith his own coat as payment. It was a bitterly cold morning, and the man trusted him. He had never seen the gentleman, but the boy brought back the empty can in a few minutes. The coffee man had kept the jacket, as it was about the size of a little chap of his own. But he had noticed the boy before parting with it take two ragged little books out of its pockets and transfer them to the bosom of his shirt. That was all he remembered, and the gentleman might take it for what it was worth.

It was worth something, for it pointed to the possibility of Reginald not being alone in his wanderings. And putting one thing and another together they somehow connected this little urchin with the boy they saw crouching on the doorstep of Number 13, Shy Street the day of their arrival, and with the office-boy whom Mr Sniff described as having been Reginald's companion during his last days at the office.

They would neither of them believe Reginald was not still in Liverpool, and cheered by the very feeble light of this discovery they resumed their search with unabated vigour and even greater thoroughness.

Happily the news from home continued favourable, and, equally important, the officials at the *Rocket* made no demur to Horace's prolonged stay. As for Harker, his hopefulness and pocket-money vied with one another in sustaining the seekers and keeping alive within them the certainty of a reward, sooner or later, for their patience.

Ten days had passed, and no fresh clue. Once or twice they had heard of the pale young gentleman and the little boy, but always vaguely, as a fleeting vision which had been seen about a fortnight ago.

On this day they called in while passing to see Mr Sniff, and were met by that gentleman with a smile which told them he had some news of consequence to impart.

"I heard to-day," said he, "that a patient—a young man—was removed very ill from a low lodging-house near the river—to the smallpox hospital yesterday. His name is supposed to be Cruden (a common name in this country), but he was too ill to give any account of himself. It may be worth your while following it up."

In less than half an hour they were at the hospital, and Horace was kneeling at the bedside of his long-lost brother.

Chapter Twenty Four
Love fights his Way into the beautiful Palace

Reginald recollected little of what happened on that terrible night when he found himself suddenly face to face with his dead enemy.

He had a vague impression of calling the landlady and of seeing the body carried from the pestiferous room. But whether he helped to carry it himself or not he could not remember.

When he next was conscious of anything the sun was struggling through the rafters over his head, as he lay in the bed beside Love, who slept still, heavily but uneasily.

The other lodgers had all risen and left the place; and when with a shudder he glanced towards the corner where the sick man last night had died, that bed was empty too.

He rose silently, without disturbing his companion, and made his way unsteadily down the ladder in search of the woman.

She met him with a scowl. She had found two five-pound notes in the dead man's pocket, and consequently wanted to hear no more about him.

"Took to the mortuary, of course," said she, in answer to Reginald's question. "Where else do you expect?"

"Can you tell me his name, or anything about him? I knew him once."

She looked blacker than ever at this. It seemed to her guilty conscience like a covert claim to the dead man's belongings, and she bridled up accordingly.

"I know nothing about him—no more than I know about you."

"Don't you know his name?" said Reginald.

"No. Do I know *your* name? No! And I don't want to!"

"Don't be angry," he said. "No one means any harm to you. How long has he been here?"

"I don't know. A week. And he was bad when he came. He never caught it here."

"Did any doctor see him?"

"Doctor! no," snarled the woman. "Isn't it bad enough to have a man bring smallpox into a place without calling in doctors, to give the place a bad name and take a body's living from them? I suppose you'll go and give me a character now. I wish I'd never took you in. I hated the sight of you from the first."

She spoke so bitterly, and at the same time so anxiously, that Reginald felt half sorry for her.

"I'll do you no harm," said he, gently. "Goodness knows I've done harm enough in my time."

The last words, though muttered to himself, did not escape the quick ear of the woman, and they pleased her. She was used to strange characters in her place, seeking a night's shelter before escaping to America, or while hiding from justice. It was neither her habit nor her business to answer questions. All she asked was to be let alone and paid for her lodgings. She knew Reginald had her in a sense at his mercy, for he knew the disease the man had died of, and a word from him out of doors would bring her own pestiferous house about her ears and ruin her.

But when he muttered those words to himself she concluded he was a criminal of some sort in hiding, and criminals in hiding, as she knew, were not the people to go and report the sanitary arrangements of their lodgings to the police.

So she mollified towards him somewhat, and told him she would look after her affairs if he looked after his, and as he had not had a good night last night, well, if no one else wanted the bed to-night he could have it at half-price; and after that she hoped she would have done with him.

Reginald returned to the foul garret, and found Love still asleep, but tossing restlessly, and muttering to himself the while.

He sat down beside him and waited till he opened his eyes.

At first the boy looked round in a bewildered way as though he were hardly yet awake, but presently his eyes fell on Reginald and his face lit up.

"Gov'nor," he said, with a smile, sitting up.

"Well, old boy," said Reginald, "what a long sleep you've had. Are you rested?"

"I 'ave 'ad sich dreams, gov'nor, and—my, ain't it cold!" And he shivered.

Reginald Cruden | 223

The room was stifling. Scarcely a breath of fresh air penetrated through its battered roof, still less through the tiny unopened window at the other end.

"We'll get some breakfast to make you warm," said Reginald. "This horrible place is enough to make any one feel sick."

The boy got slowly out of bed.

"We 'ave got to earn some browns," he said, "afore we can get any breakfast."

He shivered still, and sat down on the edge of the bed for a moment. Then he gathered himself together with an effort and walked to the ladder. Reginald's heart sank within him. The boy was not well. His face was flushed, his walk was uncertain, and his teeth chattered incessantly. It might be only the foul atmosphere of the room, or it might be something worse. And as he thought of it he too shivered, but not on account of the cold.

They descended the ladder, and for a little while the boy seemed revived by the fresh morning air. Reginald insisted on his taking their one coat, and the boy seemed to lack the energy to contest the matter. For an hour they wandered about the wharves, till at last Love stopped short and said,—

"Gov'nor, I don't want no breakfast. I'll just go back and—"

The sentence ended in a whimper, and but for Reginald's arm round him he would have fallen.

Reginald knew now that his worst fears were realised. Love was ill, and it was only too easy to surmise what his illness was, especially when he called to mind the boy's statement that he had been taking shelter in the infected lodging-house ten days ago, during his temporary exile from Shy Street.

He helped him back tenderly to the place—for other shelter they had none—and laid him in his bed. The boy protested that he was only tired, that his back and legs ached, and would soon be well. Reginald, inexperienced as he was, knew better, or rather worse.

He had a battle royal, as he expected, with the landlady on the subject of his little patient. At first she would listen to nothing, and threatened to turn both out by force. But Reginald, with an eloquence which only extremities can inspire, reasoned with her, coaxed her, flattered her, bribed her with promises, and finally got far enough on the right side of her to obtain leave for the boy to occupy Durfy's bed until some other lodger should want it. But she must have a shilling down, or off they must go.

It was a desperate alternative,—to quit his little charge in his distress, or to see him turned out to die in the street. Reginald, however, had little difficulty in making his choice.

"Are you comfortable?" said he to the boy, leaning over him and soothing the coarse pillow.

"Yes, gov'nor—all right—that there ache will be gone soon, and see if I don't pick up some browns afore evening."

"Do you think you can get on if I leave you a bit? I think I know where I can earn a little, and I'll be back before night, never fear."

"Maybe you'll find me up and about when you comes," said the boy; "mayhap the old gal would give me a job sweeping or somethink."

"You must not think of it," said Reginald, almost sternly. "Mind, I trust you to be quiet till I come. How I wish I had some food!"

With heavy heart he departed, appealing to the woman, for pity's sake, not to let harm come to the boy in his absence.

Where should he go? what should he do? Half a crown would make him feel the richest man in Liverpool, and yet how hard, how cruelly hard, it is to find a half-crown when you most want it!

He forgot all his pride, all his sensitiveness, all his own weariness—everything but the sick boy, and left no stone unturned to procure even a copper. He even begged, when nothing else succeeded.

Nobody seemed to want anything done. There were scores of hungry applicants at the riverside and dozens outside the printing-office. There were no horses that wanted holding, no boxes or bags that wanted carrying, no messages or errands that wanted running. No shop or factory window that he saw had a notice of "Boys Wanted" posted in it; no junior clerk was advertised for in any paper he caught sight of; not even a scavenger boy was wanted to clean the road.

At last he was giving it up in despair, and coming to the conclusion he might just as well hasten back to his little charge and share his fate with him, when he caught sight of a stout elderly lady standing in a state of flurry and trepidation on the kerb of one of the most crowded crossings in the city.

With the instinct of desperation he rushed towards her, and, lifting his hat, said,—

"Can I help you across, ma'am?"

Reginald Cruden | 225

The lady started to hear words so polite and in so well-bred a tone, coming from a boy of Reginald's poor appearance, for he was still without his coat.

But she jumped at his offer, and allowed him to pilot her and her parcels over the dangerous crossing.

"It may be worth twopence to me," said Reginald to himself as he landed her safe on the other side.

How circumstances change us! At another time Reginald would have flushed crimson at the bare idea of being paid for an act of politeness. Now his heart beat high with hope as he saw the lady's hand feel for her pocket.

"You're a very civil young man," said she, "and—dear me, how ill you look."

"I'm not ill," said Reginald, with a boldness he himself marvelled at, "but a little boy I love is—very ill—and I have no money to get him either food or lodging. I know you'll think I'm an impostor, ma'am, but could you, for pity's sake, give me a shilling? I couldn't pay you back, but I'd bless you always."

"Dear, dear!" said the lady, "it's very sad—just at Christmas-time, too. Poor little fellow! Here's something for him. I think you look honest, young man; I hope you are, and trust in God."

And to Reginald's unbounded delight she slipped two half-crowns into his hand and walked away.

He could only say, "God bless you for it." It seemed like an angel's gift in his hour of direst need, and with a heart full of comfort he hastened back to the lodgings, calling on his way at a cookshop and spending sixpence of his treasure on some bread and meat for his patient.

He was horror-struck to notice the change even a few hours had wrought on the sufferer. There was no mistaking his ailment now. Though not delirious, he was in a high state of fever, and apparently of pain, for he tossed incessantly and moaned to himself.

The sight of Reginald revived him.

"I knowed you was comin'," said he; "but I don't want nothing to eat, gov'nor. On'y some water; I do want some water."

Reginald flew to get it, and the boy swallowed it with avidity. Then, somewhat revived, he lay back and said, "I 'ave got 'em, then?"

"Yes, I'm afraid it's smallpox," said Reginald; "but you'll soon be better."

"Maybe I will, maybe I won't. Say, gov'nor, you don't ought to stop here; you'll be cotchin' 'em too!"

"No fear of that," said Reginald, "I've been vaccinated. Besides, who'd look after you?"

"My! you're a good 'un to me!" said the boy. "Think of that there Medlock—"

"Don't let's think of anything so unpleasant," said Reginald, seeing that even this short talk had excited his patient unduly. "Let me see if I can make the bed more comfortable, and then, if you like, I can read to you. How would you like that?"

The boy beamed his gratitude, and Reginald, after doing his best to smooth the wretched bed and make him comfortable, produced the *Pilgrim's Progress* and settled down to read.

"That there *Robinson* ain't a bad 'un," said Love, before the reading began; "I read 'im while I was a-waitin' for you. But 'e ain't so good as the Christian. Read about that there pallis ag'in, gov'nor."

And Reginald read it—more than once.

The evening closed in, the room grew dark, and he shut the book. The boy was already asleep, tossing and moaning to himself, sometimes seeming to wake for a moment, but dropping off again before he could tell what he wanted or what was wrong with him.

Once or twice Reginald moistened his parched mouth with water, but as the evening wore on the boy became so much worse that he felt, at all hazards, he must seek help.

"I *must* bring a doctor to see him," said he to the landlady; "he's so ill."

"You'll bring no doctor—unless you want to see the boy chucked out in the road!" said she. "The idea! just when my lodgers will be coming home to bed too!"

"It's only eight o'clock; no one will come till ten. There'll be plenty of time."

"What's the use? You know as well as I do the child won't last above a day or two in his state. What's the use of making a disturbance for nothing?" said the woman.

"He won't die—he shall not die!" said Reginald, feeling in his heart how foolish the words were. "At any rate, I must fetch a doctor. I might have fetched one without saying a word to you, but I promised I wouldn't, and now I want you to let me off the promise."

The woman fretted and fumed, and wished ill to the day when she had ever seen either Reginald or Love. He bore her vituperation patiently, as it was his only chance of getting his way.

Presently she said, "If you're bent on it, go to Mr Pilch, round the corner; he's the only doctor I'll let come in my house. You can have him or nobody, that's flat!"

In two minutes Reginald was battering wildly at Mr Pilch's door. That gentleman—a small dealer in herbs, who eked out his livelihood by occasional unauthorised medical practice—happened to be in, and offered, for two shillings, to come and see the sick boy. Reginald tossed down the coin with eager thankfulness, and almost dragged him to the bedside of his little charge.

Mr Pilch may have known very little of medicine, but he knew enough to make him shake his head as he saw the boy.

"Regular bad case that. Smallpox and half a dozen things on the top of it. I can't do anything."

"Can you give me no medicine for him, or tell me what food he ought to take or what? Surely there's a *chance* of his getting better?"

Mr Pilch laughed quietly.

"About as much chance of his pulling through that as of jumping over the moon. The kindest thing you can do is to let him die as soon as he can. He may last a day or two. If you want to feed him, give him anything he will take, and that won't be much, you'll find. It's a bad case, young fellow, and it won't do you any good to stop too near him. No use my coming again. Good-night."

And the brusque but not unkindly little quack trotted away, leaving Reginald in the dark without a gleam of hope to comfort him.

"Gov'nor," said the weak little voice from the bed, "that there doctor says I are a-goin' to die, don't he?"

"He says you're very ill, old boy, but let's hope you'll soon be better."

"Me—no fear. On'y I wish it would come soon. I'm afeared of gettin' frightened."

And the voice trembled away into a little sob.

They lay there side by side that long restless night. The other lodgers, rough degraded men and women, crowded into the room, but no one heeded the little bed in the dark corner, where the big boy lay with his arm round the little uneasy sufferer. There was little sleep either for patient or nurse. Every few minutes the boy begged for water, which Reginald held to his lips, and when after a time the thirst ceased and only the pain remained, nothing soothed and tranquillised him so much as the repetition time after time of his favourite stories from the wonderful book, which, happily, Reginald now knew almost by heart.

So the night passed. Before daylight the lodgers one by one rose and left the place, and when about half-past seven light struggled once more in between the rafters these two were alone.

The boy seemed a little revived, and sipped some milk which Reginald had darted out to procure.

But the pain and the fever returned twofold as the day wore on, and even to Reginald's unpractised eye it was evident the boy's release was not far distant.

"Gov'nor," said the boy once, with his mind apparently wandering back over old days, "what's the meaning of 'Jesus Christ's sake, Amen,' what comes at the end of that there prayer you taught me at the office—is He the same one that's in the *Pilgrim* book?"

"Yes, old boy; would you like to hear about Him?"

"I would so," said the boy, eagerly.

And that afternoon, as the shadows darkened and the fleeting ray of the sun crossed the floor of their room, Love lay and heard the old, old story told in simple broken words. He had heard of it before, but till now he had never heeded it. Yet it seemed to him more wonderful even than *Robinson Crusoe* or the *Pilgrim's Progress*. Now and then he broke in with some comment or criticism, or even one of his old familiar tirades against the enemies of his new hero. The room grew darker, and still Reginald went on. When at last the light had all gone, the boy's hand stole outside the blanket and sought that of his protector, and held it till the story came to an end.

Then he seemed to drop into a fitful sleep, and Reginald, with the hand still on his, sat motionless, listening to the hard breathing, and living over in thought the days since Heaven in mercy joined his life to that of his little friend.

How long he sat thus he knew not. He heard the voices and tread of the other lodgers in the room; he heard the harsh groan of the bolt on the outer door downstairs; and he saw the candle die down in its socket. But he never moved or let go the boy's hand.

Presently—about one or two in the morning, he thought—the hard breathing ceased, and a turn of the head on the pillow told him the sleeper was awake.

"Gov'nor, you there?" whispered the boy.

"Yes, old fellow."

"It's dark; I'm most afeared."

Reginald lay on the bed beside him, and put an arm round him.

The boy became more easy after this, and seemed to settle himself once more to sleep. But the breathing was shorter and more laboured, and the little brow that rested against the watcher's cheek grew cold and damp.

For half an hour more the feeble flame of life flickered on, every breath seeming to Reginald as he lay there motionless, scarcely daring to breathe himself, like the last.

Then the boy seemed suddenly to rouse himself and lifted his head.

"Gov'nor—that pallis!—I'm gettin' in—I hear them calling—come there too, gov'nor!"

And the head sank back on the pillow, and Reginald, as he turned his lips to the forehead, knew that the little valiant soul had fought his way into the beautiful palace at last, and was already hearing the music of those voices within as they welcomed him to his hero's reward.

Chapter Twenty Five
There is no Place like Home

It is strange how often our fortunes and misfortunes, which we are so apt to suppose depend on our own successes or failures, turn out to have fallen into hands we least expected, and to have been depending on trains of circumstances utterly beyond our range of imagination.

Who, for instance, would have guessed that a meeting of half a dozen business men in a first-floor room of a New York office could have any bearing on the fate of the Cruden family? Or that an accident to Major Lambert's horse while clearing a fence at one of the —shire hunts should also affect their prospects in life?

But so it was.

While Reginald, tenderly nursed by his old school friend, was slowly recovering from his illness in Liverpool, and while Mrs Cruden and Horace, in their shabby London lodging, were breaking into their last hundred pounds, and wondering how, even with the boy's improved wages and promise of literary success, they should be able to keep a comfortable home for their scattered but shortly to be reunited family—at this very time a few of the leading creditors of the Wishwash and Longstop Railway assembled in the old office of that bankrupt undertaking, and decided to accept an offer from the Grand Roundabout Railway to buy up their undertaking at half-price, and add its few hundred miles of line to their own few thousand.

A very important decision this for the little Dull Street family. For among the English creditors of this same Wishwash and Longstop Railway Mr Cruden had been one of the most considerable—so considerable that the shares he held in it had amounted to about half his fortune.

And when the division of the proceeds of the sale of the railway came to be divided it turned out that Mr Cruden's administrators, heirs, and assigns were entitled to about a third of the value of that gentleman's shares, or in other words, something like a sixth of their old property, which little windfall, after a good deal of wandering about and search for an owner, came finally under the notice of Mr Richmond's successors, who in turn passed it over to Mrs Cruden with a very neat little note of congratulation on the good fortune which had made her and her sons the joint proprietors of a snug little income of from £300 to £400 a year.

Of course the sagacious reader will remark on this that it is only natural that towards the end of my story something of this sort should happen, in order to finish up with the remark that "they lived happily ever after." And his opinion of me will, I fear, be considerably lowered when he finds that instead of Reginald dying in the smallpox hospital, and Mrs Cruden and Horace ending their days in the workhouse, things looked up a little for them towards the finish, and promised a rather more comfortable future than one had been led to expect.

It is sad, of course, to lose any one's good esteem, but as things really did look up for the Crudens — as Reginald really did recover, as Mrs Cruden and Horace really did not go to the workhouse, and as the Grand Roundabout Railway really was spirited enough to buy up the Wishwash and Longstop Railway at half-price, I cannot help saying so, whatever the consequences may be.

But several weeks before Mr Richmond's successors announced this windfall to their clients, the accident to Major Lambert's horse had resulted in comfort to the Crudens of another kind, which, if truth must be told, they expected quite as little and valued quite as much.

That worthy Nimrod, once an acquaintance and neighbour of the Garden Vale family in the days of their prosperity, was never known to miss a winter's hunting in his own county if he could possibly help it, and during the present season had actually come all the way from Malta, where his regiment was stationed, on short leave, for the sake of two or three days of his favourite sport in the old country.

Such enthusiasm was worthy of a happier fate than that which befell him. For on his first ride out his horse came to grief, as we have said, over a hedge, and left the gallant major somewhat knocked about himself, with nothing to do for half a day but to saunter disconsolately up and down the country lanes and pay afternoon calls on some of his old comrades.

Among others, he knocked at the door of an elderly dowager named Osborn, who was very sympathetic with him in his misfortunes, and did her best to comfort him with afternoon tea and gossip.

The latter lasted a good deal longer than the former. One after another the major's old friends were mentioned and discussed and talked about as only folk can be talked about over afternoon tea.

"By the way," said the caller, "I hear poor Cruden didn't leave much behind him after all. Is Mrs Cruden still at Garden Vale?"

"No, indeed," said the lady; "it's a sad story altogether. Mr Cruden left nothing behind him, and Garden Vale had to be sold, and the family went to London, so I was told, in very poor circumstances."

"Bless me!" said the honest major, "haven't you looked them up? Cruden was a good sort of a fellow, you know."

"Well, I've always intended to try and find out where they are living, but really, major, you have no idea how one's time gets filled up."

"I've a very good idea," said the major with a groan. "I have to sail in a week, and there's not much spare time between now and then, I can tell you. Still, I'd like to call and pay my respects to Mrs Cruden if I knew where she lived."

"I daresay you could find out. But I was going to say that only yesterday I saw something in the paper which will hardly make Mrs Cruden anxious to see any of her old friends at present. The eldest son, I fear, has turned out badly."

"Who? young—what was his name?—Reginald? Can't believe it. He always seemed one of the right sort. A bit of a prig perhaps, but straight enough. What has he been up to?"

"You'd better see for yourself, major," said the lady, extracting a newspaper from a heap under the dinner-waggon. "He seems to have been mixed up in a rather discreditable affair, as far as I could make out, but I didn't read the report through."

The major took the paper, and read a short report of the proceedings at the Liverpool Police-Court.

"You didn't read it through, you say," observed he, when he had finished; "you saw he was let off?"

"Yes, but I'm afraid—well, it's very sad for them all."

"Of course it is," blurted out the soldier, "especially when none of their old friends seem to care anything about them. Excuse me, Mrs Osborn," added he, seeing that the lady coloured. "I wasn't meaning you, but myself. Cruden was on old comrade, who did me more than one good turn. I must certainly take a day in town on my way back and find them out. As for the boy, I don't believe he's got it in him to be a blackleg."

The major was as good as his word. He sacrificed a day of his loved pastime to look for his old friend's widow in London.

After a good deal of hunting he discovered her address, and presented himself, with not a little wonderment at the shabbiness of her quarters, at Dull Street.

Barely convalescent, and still in the agony of suspense as to Reginald's fate, Mrs Cruden was able to see no one. But the major was not thus to be baulked of his friendly intentions. Before he left the house he wrote a letter, which in due time lay in the widow's hands and brought tears to her eyes.

"Dear Mrs Cruden,—I am on my way back to Malta, and sorry not to see you. We all have our troubles, but you seem to have had more than your share; and what I should have liked would be to see whether there was anything an old friend of your husband could do to serve you. I trust you will not resent the liberty I take when I say I have instructed my agent, whose address is enclosed, to put himself at your disposal in any emergency when you may need either advice or any other sort of aid. He is a good fellow, and understands any service you may require (and emergencies often do arise) is to be rendered on my account. As to your eldest son, about whom I read a paragraph in the papers the other day, nothing will make me believe he is anything but his honest father's honest son. My brother-in-law, whom you will remember, is likely shortly to have an opportunity of introducing a young fellow into an East India house in the City. I may mention this because, should you think well to tell Reginald of it, I believe there would not be much difficulty in his getting the post. But you will hear about this from my brother-in-law, whom I have asked to write to you. I don't expect to get leave again, for eighteen months; but I hope then to find you all well.

"Believe me, dear Mrs Cruden,—

"Yours truly,—

"Thomas Lambert."

This simple warm-hearted letter came to Mrs Cruden as the first gleam of better things on the troubled waters of her life. Things were just then at their worst. Reginald lost, Horace away in search of him, herself slowly recovering from a sad illness into a still more sad life, with little prospect either of happiness or competency, nothing to look forward to but a renewal of the old struggles, possibly single-handed. At such a time Major Lambert's letter came to revive her drooping spirits and remind her of a Providence that never sleeps less than when we are ready to consider ourselves forgotten.

All she could do was to write a grateful reply back, and then await news from Horace, trusting meanwhile it would not be necessary to draw on the major's offered help. A few days later Horace was home again, jubilant at having found his brother, but anxious both as to his immediate recovery and the state of mind in which restored health would find him.

"He told me lots about the past, mother," said he. "No one can conceive what a terrible three months he has had since he left us, or how heroically he has borne it. He doesn't think so himself, and is awfully depressed about his trial and the way in which the magistrate spoke to him—the brute!"

"Poor boy! he is the very last to bear that sort of thing well."

"He's got a sort of idea he's a branded man, and is to be dragged down all his life by it. Perhaps when he hears that an old friend like Major Lambert believes in him, he may pick up. You know, mother, I believe his heart is in the grave where that little office-boy of his lies, and that he would have been thankful if—well, perhaps not so bad as that—but just at present he can't speak or even think of the boy without breaking down."

"According to the letter from Major Lambert's brother-in-law, the post that is offered him is one he will like, I think," said Mrs Cruden. "I do hope he will take it. To have nothing to do would be the worst thing that could happen to him."

"To say nothing of the necessity of it for you, mother," said Horace; "for there's to be no more copying out manuscripts, mind, even if we all go to the workhouse."

Mrs Cruden sighed. She knew her son was right, but the wolf was at the door, and she shrank from becoming a useless burden on her boys' shoulders.

"I wonder, Horace," said she, presently, "whether we could possibly find less expensive quarters than these. They are—"

"Hullo, there's the postman!" said Horace, who had been looking from the window; "ten to one there's a line from Harker."

And he flew down the stairs, just in time to see the servant-girl take a letter from the box and put it in her pocket.

"None for us?" said he.

The girl, who till this moment was not aware of his presence, turned round and coloured very violently, but said nothing.

"Show me the letter you put into your pocket just now," said Horace, who had had experience before now in predicaments of this kind.

The girl made no reply, but tried to go back to the kitchen. Horace, however, stopped her.

"Be quick!" said he. "You've a letter for me in your pocket, and if I don't have it before I count twenty I'll give you in charge;" and he proceeded to count.

Before he had reached ten the girl broke out into tears, and took from her pocket not only the letter in question, but three or four others.

"There you are; that's all of them. I've done with it!" sobbed she.

Horace glanced over them in bewilderment. One was in Reginald's writing, written three weeks ago; two were from himself to his mother, written last week, and the last was from Harker, written yesterday.

"Why," exclaimed he, too much taken aback almost to find words, "what does it mean? How do you come—"

"Oh, I'll tell you," said the girl; "I don't care what they do to me. I'd sooner be sent to prison than go on at it. He told me to do it, and threatened me all sorts of things if I didn't. Oh dear! oh dear!"

"Who told you?"

"Why, Mr Shuckleford. He said Mr Reginald was a convict, or something, and if I didn't mind every letter that came to the house from Liverpool I'd get sent to prison too for abetting him. I'm sure I don't want to abet no one, and I can't help if they do lock me up."

"You mean to say Mr Shuckleford told you to do this?" said—or rather roared—Horace.

"Yes, he did; and he had them all before that one," said the girl, pointing to the letter from Reginald. "But he's never been for these, and I didn't dare not to keep them for him. Please, sir, look over it this time."

Horace was too agitated to heed her tears or entreaties. He rushed from the house with the letters in his hand, and made straight for the Shucklefords' door. But, with his hand on the bell, he hesitated. Mrs Shuckleford and her daughter had been good to his mother; he could not relieve his mind to Samuel in their presence. So he resolved to postpone that pleasure till he could find the young lawyer alone, and meanwhile hurried back to his mother and rejoiced her heart with the good news of Reginald contained in Harker's letter.

How and when Horace and Shuckleford settled accounts no one exactly knew, but one evening, about a week afterwards, the latter came home looking very scared and uncomfortable, and announced that he was getting tired of London, the air of which did not agree with his constitution. He intended to close with an offer he had received some time ago from a firm in the country to act as their clerk; and although the sacrifice was considerable, still the country air and change of scene he felt would do him good.

So he went, much lamented by his mother and sister and club. But of all his acquaintances there was only one who knew the exact reason why, just at that particular time, the country air promised to be so beneficial for his constitution.

Three weeks passed, and then one afternoon a cab rolled slowly up to the door of Number 6, Dull Street. Horace was away at the office, and Mrs Cruden herself was out taking a walk.

So the two young men who alighted from the cab found themselves monarchs of all they surveyed, and proceeded upstairs to the parlour with no one to ask what their business was.

"Now, old man," said the sturdier of the two, "I won't stay. I've brought you safe home, and you needn't pretend you'll be sorry to see my back."

"I won't pretend," said the other, with a smile on his pale face, "but if you're not back very soon, in an hour or two, I shall be very very sorry."

"Never fear, I'll be back."

And he went.

The pale youth sat down, and looked with a strange mixture of sadness and eagerness round the little room. He had seen it before, and yet he seemed hardly to recognise it. He got up and glanced at a few envelopes lying on the mantel-piece. He took into his hands a piece of knitting that lay on one of the chairs and examined it. He turned over the leaves of a stray book, and read the name on the title-page. It all seemed so strange—yet so familiar. Then he crept silently to the half-open door of a little bedroom and peeped in, and his heart beat strangely as he recognised a photograph on the dressing-table, and by its side a letter written in his own handwriting. From this room he turned to another still smaller and more roughly furnished. A walking-stick stood in the corner that he knew well, and there was a cap on the peg behind the door, the sight of which sent a thrill through him.

Yet he felt he dared touch nothing—that he scarcely dare let his foot be heard as he paced across the room, or venture even to stir the little fire that was dying out in the grate.

The slight flush which the excitement of his first arrival had called up faded from his cheeks as the minutes wore on.

Presently his ears caught a light footfall on the pavement outside, and his heart almost stood still as it halted and the bell rang below.

It was one of those occasions when a man may live a lifetime in a minute. With a mighty rush his thoughts flew back to the last time he had heard that step. What goodness, what hope, what love did it not bring back to his life! He had taken it all for granted, and thought so little of it; but now, after months of loveless, cheerless drudgery and disappointment, that light step fell with a music which flooded his whole soul.

He sat almost spell-bound as the street-door closed and the steps ascended the stairs. The room seemed to swim round him, and to his broken nerves it seemed for a moment as though he dreaded rather than longed for what was coming. But as the door opened the spell broke and all the mists vanished; he was his own self once more—nothing but the long-lost boy springing to the arms of the long-lost mother.

"Mother!"

"My boy!"

That was all they said. And in those few words Reginald Cruden's life entered on a new era.

When Horace half an hour later came flying on to the scene they still sat there hand in hand, trying to realise it all, but not succeeding. Horace, however, helped them back to speech, and far into the night they talked. About ten o'clock Harker looked in for a moment, and after them young Gedge, unable to wait till the morning. But they stayed only a moment, and scarcely interrupted the little family reunion.

What those three talked about it would be hard for me to say. What they did not talk about in the past, the present, and the future would be almost easier to set down. And when at last Mrs Cruden rose, and in her old familiar tones said, —

"It's time to go to bed, boys," the boys obeyed, as in the days long ago, and came up to her and kissed her, and then went off like children, and slept, like those who never knew what care was, all the happy night.

Chapter Twenty Six
Turning over Leaves, new and old

A very few words more, reader, and my story is done.

The trial of Medlock and Shanklin took place in due time, and among the witnesses the most important, but the most reluctant, was Reginald Cruden. It was like a hateful return to the old life to find himself face to face with those men, and to have to tell over again the story of their knavery and his own folly. But he went through with it like a man.

The prisoners, who were far more at their ease than the witness, troubled him with no awkward cross-examination, and when presently the jury retired, he retired too, having neither the curiosity nor the vindictiveness to remain and hear their sentence.

On his way out a familiar voice accosted him.

"Cruden, old man, will you shake hands? I've been a cad to you, but I'm sorry for it now."

It was Blandford, looking weak and pale, with one arm still in a sling.

Reginald took his proffered hand eagerly and wrung it.

"I've been bitten over this affair, as you know," continued Blandford, "and I've paid up for my folly. I wish I could come out of it all with as easy a conscience as you do, that's all! Among them all I've lost a good deal more than money; but if you and Horrors will take me back in your set there'll be a chance for me yet. I'm going to University College, you know, so I shall be staying in town. Harker and I will probably be lodging together, and it won't be my fault if it's far away from your quarters."

And arm in arm the old schoolfellows walked, with their backs on the dark past and their faces turned hopefully to the future.

Had Reginald remained to hear the end of the trial, he would have found himself the object of a demonstration he little counted on.

The jury having returned with their expected verdict, and sentence having been passed on the prisoners, the counsel for the prosecution got up and asked his lordship for leave to make one observation. He spoke in the name of the various victims of the sham Corporation when he stated that his clients desired to express their conviction that the former secretary of the Corporation, whose evidence that day had mainly contributed to the exposure of the fraud, was himself entirely clear of any imputation in connection with the conspiracy.

"I should not mention this, my lord," said the counsel, "had not a certain magistrate, in another place, at an earlier stage of this inquiry, used language—in my humble opinion harsh and unwarranted—calculated to cast a slur on that gentleman's character, if not to interfere seriously with his future prospects. I merely wish to say, my lord, that my clients, and those of us who have gone fully into the case, and may be expected to know as much about it even as a north-country magistrate, are fully convinced that Mr Cruden comes out of this case with an unsullied character, and we feel it our duty publicly to state our opinion to that effect."

The counsel sat down amid signs of approval from the Court, not unmixed with amusement at the expense of the north-country magistrate, and the judge, calling for order, replied, "I make no objection whatever to the statement which has just fallen from the lips of the learned counsel, and as it commends itself entirely to my own judgment in the matter, I am glad to inform Mr Cruden, if he be still in court, that he will quit it to-day clear of the slightest imputation on his character unbecoming an upright but unfortunate gentleman."

Reginald was not in court, but he read every word of it next day with grateful and overflowing heart.

Three months have passed. The winter has given way to spring, and Number 3, Dull Street is empty. Jemima Shuckleford still nurses her sorrow in secret, and it will be a year or two yet before the happy man is to turn up who shall reconcile her to life, and disestablish the image of Reginald Cruden from her soft heart. Meanwhile she and her mother are constant visitors at the little house in Highbury where the Crudens now live, and as often as they go they find a welcome. Samuel writes home from the country that he is doing great things, and expects to become Lord Chancellor in a few years. Meanwhile he too contemplates matrimony with a widow and four children, who will probably leave him among them very little leisure for another experiment in the amateur detective business.

The Shuckleford ladies were invited, but unfortunately were unable to go, to a little quiet house-warming given by the Crudens on the occasion of their taking possession of the new house.

But though they could not go, Miss Crisp could, and, as a matter of course, Mr Booms, in all the magnificence of last year's spring costume. And Waterford came too, and young Gedge, as did also the faithful Harker, and—with some little trepidation—the now sobered Blandford.

The company had quite enough to talk about without having to fall back on shouting proverbs or musical chairs. Indeed, there were several little excitements in the wind which came out one by one, and made the evening a sort of epoch in the lives of most of those present.

For instance, young Gedge was there no longer as a common compositor. He had lately been made, youth as he was, overseer in the room of Durfy; and the dignity of his new office filled him with sobriety and good-humour.

"It's no fault of mine," said he, when Mrs Cruden congratulated him on his promotion. "If Cruden hadn't stood by me that time he first came to the *Rocket*, I should have gone clean to the dogs. I mean it. I was going full tilt that way."

"But I went off and left you after all," said Reginald.

"I know you did; and I was sorry at the time you hadn't left that cab-horse to finish his business the evening you picked me up. But Horace here and Mrs Cruden—"

"Picked you up again," said Waterford. "Regular fellow for being picked up, you are. All comes of your habit of picking up types. One of nature's revenges—and the last to pick you up is the *Rocket*. What an appetite she's got, to be sure!"

"I should think so from the way she swallows your and Horace's lucubrations every week," says Gedge, laughing. "Why, I actually know a fellow who knows a fellow who laughed at one of your jokes."

"Come, none of your chaff," said Horace, looking not at all displeased. "You never laughed at a joke, I know, because you never see one."

"No more I do. That's what I complain of," replied the incorrigible young overseer.

"Never mind, we shall have our revenge when he has to put our joint novel in print," said Waterford. "Ah, I thought you'd sit up there, my boy. Never mind, you'll know about it some day. The first chapter is half done already."

"Jolly work that must be," says Harker. "More fun than higher mathematics and Locke on the Understanding, eh, Bland?"

"Perhaps they would be glad to change places with us before they are through with it, though," observes Blandford.

"Never knew such a beggar for grinding as Bland is turning out," says Harker. "He takes the shine out of me; and I'm certain he'll knock me into a cocked hat at the matric.."

"You forget I've lost time to make up," replies Blandford, gravely; "and I'm not going to be content if I don't take honours."

"Don't knock yourself up, that's all," says Reginald, "especially now cricket's beginning. We ought to turn out a good eleven with four old Wilderhams to give it a backbone, eh?"

And at the signal the four chums somehow get together in a corner, and the talk flies off to the old schooldays, and the battles and triumphs of the famous Wilderham Close.

Meanwhile Booms and Miss Crisp whisper very confidentially together in another corner. What they talk about no one can guess. It may be collars, or it may be four-roomed cottages, or it may be only the weather. Whatever it is, Booms's doleful face relaxes presently into a solemn smile, and Miss Crisp goes over and sits by Mrs Cruden, who puts her arm round the blushing girl and kisses her in a very motherly way on the forehead. It is a curious piece of business altogether, and it is just as well the four young men are too engrossed in football and cricket to notice it, and that Gedge and Waterford find their whole attention occupied by the contents of the little bookcase in the corner to have eyes for anything else.

"Jolly lot of books you've got," says Waterford, when presently the little groups break up and the big circle forms again. "I always think they are such nice furniture in a room, don't you, Mrs Cruden?"

"Yes, I do," says Mrs Cruden; "especially when they are all old friends."

"Some of these seem older friends than others," says Waterford, pointing to a corner where several unbound tattered works break the ranks of green-cloth gilt-lettered volumes. "Look at this weatherbeaten little fellow, for instance, a bit of a *Pilgrim's Progress*. That must be a very poor relation; surely you don't count him in?"

"Don't I," says Reginald, taking the book in his hands, and speaking in a tone which makes every one look up at him. "This little book is worth more to me than all the rest put together."

And as he bends his head over the precious little relic, and turns its well-thumbed pages one by one, he forgets where he is, or who is looking on. And a tear steals into his eyes as his mind flies far away to a little green grave in the north country over which the soft breezes of spring play lovingly, and seem to whisper in a voice he knows and loves to remember—"Come there too, guv'nor."